D0594456

THE Palest Ink

Also by Kay Bratt

Silent Tears; A Journey of Hope in a Chinese Orphanage

Chasing China; A Daughter's Quest for Truth

Mei Li and the Wise Laoshi

The Bridge

A Thread Unbroken

Train to Nowhere

Eyes Like Mine

The Palest Ink

TALES OF THE SCAVENGER'S DAUGHTERS

The Scavenger's Daughters

Tangled Vines

Bitter Winds

Red Skies

THE Palest Ink

KAY BRATT

LAKE UNION
PUBLISHING

Published by Lake Union Publishing, Seattle
www.apub.com

Amazon, the Amazon logo, and Lake Union Publishing are trademarks of Amazon.com, Inc., or its affiliates.

ISBN-13: 9781503949447 (hardcover)
ISBN-10: 1503949443 (hardcover)
ISBN-13: 9781503946163 (paperback)
ISBN-10: 1503946169 (paperback)

Cover design by: Mumtaz Mustafa

Printed in the United States of America

First edition

To Ben

"Music in the soul can be heard by the universe."

—Lao Tzu

What if all your life you lived with the belief that you were special, then suddenly someone or something came and took it from you?

Like a figure in the shrouded mist of your imagination, your normal is yanked out from under you and in its place comes a new reality of fear, confusion, and oppression. When the terror and ravaging subsides, could you return to being the same person you were? I think not. More concisely, I know not. For just such a wrong was done to me, leaving me forever changed.

Now, it's time to tell the story.

Not just any story, but my story, written down because as an ancient Chinese proverb says, the palest ink is better than the best memory.

PART ONE

The Calm Before

Chapter One

Shanghai
January, 1966

Benfu supposed most men who knew they were about to meet the woman they'd take as their wife would most likely hurry along, but he'd never been like others—and to prove it, his gait slowed to that of a tortoise.

A lame tortoise.

Possibly even a lame *and* blind tortoise.

So yes, he was aware that he was a bit nervous about the impending meeting.

Juan Hui. Her name practically rolled off his tongue if he allowed himself to utter it when he was alone. Together, the two characters meant beautiful, graceful, and kind. Benfu had heard her name mentioned many times growing up, but she'd always seemed like a fairy-tale creature from his imagination. Someone he'd never really meet. As a boy, his mother had dangled the name in front of him, teasing that his beloved had been chosen and was being groomed for him, but Benfu never paid much attention. For the most part, thoughts of girls, lucky dates, and marriage had never taken residence in his mind. But now—at only sixteen—his childhood was falling away behind him because the day had come. Juan Hui would no longer be only a name in his imagination; today she'd truly stand before him, and he'd hear the voice that would one day be in his life forever and be given a face to finally match the name in his head.

And by late afternoon, she'd officially be his betrothed.

Perhaps he would like her. Maybe he'd even play her a song on his violin. Then he quickly rejected the thought, remembering that he was being forced into spending the rest of his life with someone not of his choosing.

Benfu imagined a quiet, obedient girl with long, dark hair hiding her face like a curtain, waiting for him to stand before her in the meticulous parlor his petite mother ruled with an iron fist. She might even be frightened, and would likely sit holding a steaming cup of their best tea—the Green Snail Spring tea from Taihu Lake—and maybe even demurely sip from his cup, the porcelain one with the delicate gold rim that had been his since birth. They'd be expected to make small talk as the mothers hovered, encouraging them to begin the courting process.

He'd look like a fool.

Benfu paused at the corner and waited for a lull in the traffic of bicycles, rickshaws, and the handful of cars that had found their way onto the narrow roads snaking through the French concession of Shanghai. His thoughts swirled back and forth between the mysterious girl who awaited him at home, and the indignant teacher he'd left behind at his high school only minutes before. Some might think the upcoming afternoon event should be cause for excitement, but Benfu wasn't thrilled.

His mother had been ecstatic that the matchmaker had reported from the fortune teller that the eight characters from both Benfu's and the girl's birthdates had been perfectly aligned. Yet something still told Benfu that familial duty or not, marrying a stranger would not be easy.

He didn't know much about Juan Hui, only that she came from three generations of scholars with a family line that had begun in

Nanjing and not Shanghai like his. They wouldn't marry right away, but today would start the complicated and lengthy courtship with ongoing negotiations between their families for the marriage. A gift list would also be passed to his father today, a symbolic gesture that meant the proposal had been accepted by her parents.

Amid the nervous butterflies in his stomach over the upcoming meeting, he still felt the sting of shame from the verbal beating his teacher had just given him. His crime? Though he thought he'd phrased it respectfully, he'd dared to question the man's whitewashed version of the current condition of their country. Benfu had only wanted to point out that Chairman Mao's last campaign, one Mao labeled *the Great Leap Forward,* had actually been a giant move backward for China. Though information was closely guarded and only siphoned out to the people in tiny increments, hushed stories were that, because of Mao's obsession to beat the world's output of steel, the people in the rural areas of China had experienced a horrible famine from which they were still trying to recover.

Benfu's quiet but heartfelt speech had earned him total silence from his classmates—from all but Pony Boy, his best friend since they were in split pants. Pony Boy had given a nod of reassurance but had held his tongue. At least Benfu hadn't felt completely alone as he'd voiced his thoughts on the subject. That didn't mean that Pony Boy agreed with him, though. The truth was, they held total opposite views on the affairs of the country, and all the new directives being sent out by Chairman Mao. Pony Boy was a staunch supporter of Mao, while Benfu wasn't. But they didn't let that hurt their friendship—at least not thus far. Just in the last year, they'd had many discussions and Benfu appreciated having someone to talk to about it, someone who would listen before firing back against him, someone to intelligently debate the pros and cons of a country led by a man such as Mao Zedong.

Lately though, Benfu had found himself feeling more passionate about politics, while Pony Boy preferred to talk about taking pictures or seeing movies. For Benfu, it wasn't that easy to put it all aside. Mao's supposed Great Leap Forward had all but ended a few years before, but Benfu still had bad dreams in which the stories that circulated entered his mind and tormented him through the nights.

Dreams haunted him. Flashes of peasant parents mixing up huge pots of their own family's blood to feed their dying children, visions of people eating dogs and cats—even insects and bark from the trees— anything to fill the empty ache in their starving stomachs. One story told among his classmates was of people in northwest China who'd abandoned their children along the roads, placing them in holes dug in the soft soil to keep them cool as their fate hinged on passing travelers discovering and taking pity on them, to either feed them or better yet, take them to their own homes and care for them. Benfu could hardly imagine the horrors that had gone on around China as people fought to survive the hardest years of their lives. It seemed to him that the government would learn from their mistakes. He couldn't understand why information was kept so secret, nor did he comprehend the officials' constant rewriting of history just to save face.

His teacher had asked him to stay behind and, after his classmates had left the room one by one, Laoshi warned him that though Mao had been reprimanded and had lost ground because of his Great Leap Forward, he was now steadily regaining control of the party, and more importantly, was winning over the people. Benfu had read the caution in Laoshi's eyes and in the tone of his voice—basically a silent admonishment that he was treading a dangerous path when daring to criticize Mao publicly.

Benfu crossed the street and made a slight detour toward the park. He thought he felt a drop of rain on his head. He stuck out his tongue, then wished that he'd held that same tongue and had refrained from commenting in his classroom. It was, after all, what his father had been advising him to do since the day he'd begun to question the current events of their country. Now his teacher would make him pay dearly for his outburst, probably for the rest of the school year. And just when he thought his day couldn't possibly get any worse, in only an hour—or however long it took him to procrastinate in his usually short walk home—he'd enter his family home and shed his school uniform, then don a heavy, traditional dragon-embroidered robe and meet the girl he would marry.

He wasn't ready for this.

Turning the corner, he stood aside to let an elderly woman pass with her frazzled old broom. He saw that she was a street sweeper, someone that most people treated as invisible. Benfu gave her a small smile and was rewarded with a nod of approval. It was simple—she could be somebody's grandmother, and that meant she deserved some respect, no matter what station she'd sunk to in life.

Mother wouldn't feel the same. She constantly drilled into Benfu's head that he was from a higher station in life than most, a class many tried their entire lives to reach. He'd come from a long line of esteemed scholars, she'd remind him as she demanded he quote a line of poetry until he got it perfect. No, they were not as prestigious as royalty, but in her opinion they were next in line because if it weren't for scholars, the royals wouldn't have been educated enough to rule China.

Sometimes Benfu felt that Mother's beliefs about their social status made their life lonelier than it had to be. It wasn't that they didn't socialize—Benfu had some memories of being surrounded by friends and family—but now that he was older, he could see that each person had been carefully selected before any sort of coziness was allowed. His one true friend was the only one who'd fallen into his path and had not been chosen according to his family origins or connections. And he was the only one that Benfu's mother was strongly opposed to.

He stopped at the gate of the park and leaned over it, taking a deep breath to calm his nerves. Responsibility—that was all his life was. He tried to stifle a random thought before it took over his mood even more, but the words still swam in his brain—*would he ever taste the essence of freedom?*

He felt someone at his side and turned to look. An old man, much older than his own father, had moved in to stand close to Benfu as he picked at the shell of an egg. The man, dressed in a faded blue tunic and a pair of baggy trousers, held his shoulders erect and his head high. Benfu noted the man still wore his hair slicked back in the outdated style of one long braid falling down his back. His beard was white, pulled into a neat bundle and tied with a small piece of leather.

An aroma of rich earth mixed with the scent of the egg made its way to Benfu and he moved over a bit, giving the man more room. The man also stepped over, closing again the gap between them.

Benfu saw his mother's face in his mind, reminding him that he wasn't supposed to cavort with people of the streets. "Do you live around here?" he asked the man, choosing to disregard the constraints of propriety. At first difficult, once the words were out, Benfu felt fine, but he still found himself looking around to be sure his mother hadn't somehow appeared to witness his slip of obedience.

"You are quiet by nature, but you were born in the year of the tiger, am I correct?" The old man, most likely a simple scavenger, stared at Benfu as he calmly picked at the egg, neatly peeling the shell and putting the pieces in his pocket.

"How did you know?" Benfu asked, intrigued by the man's accurate assumption.

The man looked up from the egg, meeting Benfu's eyes with his intense stare. Benfu felt his breath stop when he realized he was looking at someone with one eye dark as the night, and the other white as snow. "I can see it in the way you hold yourself. You were standing there struggling with some internal thought, and your expression was fierce. Quietly fierce—but still fierce."

Benfu felt a tingle run up his arms. The man was right. He had been struggling—battling with his own sense of right and wrong, and the feelings of oppression that were more evident every day.

"True," Benfu said softly. "Today hasn't been such a good day, and I feel it's only going to get worse in the next few hours."

The man nodded solemnly. "Maybe. But remember, tigers are notorious for their courage and will stand up for what is right, despite the consequences to their own well-being." He nodded his head to the other side of the street where a group of students gathered, some shooting curious glances their way. "Lao Tzu tells us that if we care about what others think, we will always be their prisoner."

The message hit home. Benfu recognized a few of the boys and knew he'd probably be ridiculed for speaking to the scavenger—the next day at school would be full of taunts and insults. But he didn't care. Anything that gave him reason to delay arriving home was worth the consequences.

As the minutes ticked by, the man gifted Benfu with a few short stories, most of which were laced with Taoist advice disguised as poetry and proverbs. When he stopped speaking for a moment, he ate the rest of the hard-boiled egg, then wiped his mouth with a yellowed handkerchief from his pocket. "I'd better move along now, but if you'll allow, I'd like to leave you with some words of wisdom and a request."

He waited, as if giving Benfu the choice to walk away.

Benfu noticed that the sun was beginning to set and realized that more time had passed than he'd realized. But still, he felt frozen in place, as though the man held the key to a secret that Benfu wanted to hear and shouldn't miss. When the man finally spoke again, Benfu listened closely.

"You should remember this: all of us see much turmoil in our lifetimes, but we must stand strong in our convictions. If we keep our resolve, even our enemies will respect our courage."

Benfu listened, taking in the advice. It sounded logical. He'd always been told that since he was a tiger born at night, his life would be stormy and full of danger, yet so far it had been full of strict rules, lessons of etiquette and tradition, and basically, utter boredom. Other than the time he spent with his violin, he felt no sense of control or choice in his life. His parents—especially his mother—had made sure of that, orchestrating his every move since the day he'd been born.

While others his age had traveled and seen much of China, at sixteen, the most excitement he'd experienced was finally mastering a western piece of music on his violin, bringing a parlor full of his parents' colleagues to their feet in a standing ovation. It had been a memorable moment; when he allowed himself, he could truly get lost in his music. And though he'd wished for more instances of excitement, something nagged at him, telling him his life until now was simply the calm before the storm—a respite for harder days to come.

How that could be, he didn't know. He lived a comfortable existence in one of the better neighborhoods in Shanghai and he wanted for nothing. His parents both worked for the university and they spoiled him needlessly in their efforts to soften the blow of being an only child. He had his own room, an esteemed musical tutor, and could come and go as he pleased, as long as he stayed on the strict schedule his mother set up for him.

Yet something was amiss.

The country was in a state of unrest, and it infuriated him that his parents quietly accepted the scattered national directives like terrified sheep going to slaughter. Yet he had questions about it all. Questions that could never be asked, so most likely wouldn't be answered. To them, all that mattered was that their family name continue, as respectfully as possible. Benfu found it exasperating they couldn't see what he saw, feel what he felt—that the country was headed for yet another disaster.

He had no say, because he wasn't considered an adult yet. But if one good thing came of the day, it would be that his status would change in the next hour when he officially became betrothed. He would then be considered an adult and in the next year would hopefully attend one of the most prestigious music schools in China.

Beside him the man stiffened and looked out at the street. Coming along the walkway was a trio of blue-uniformed men. The man in the lead, possibly the one in charge, was tall and skinny like a lamppost, a dark scowl upon his face. The two that followed were short and somewhat pudgy, and they hurried to match the pace of the one in front.

"I need you to do something for me," the man next to Benfu said quietly.

"Me?" Benfu asked. He wasn't sure what he could do for the old man; he didn't have any money on him at all.

The trio paused to cross the street, the tall one keeping his eyes on the old man. It appeared the threesome heading their way and it wasn't going to be a social call. Benfu stepped back, ready to walk away, but felt the old man grab his arm like a vise, holding him in place.

"First, I must ask, are you an honorable and trustworthy man?" he said. "This I need to know."

A man? After today maybe, *yes*. Benfu nodded and a lull in the traffic opened the path for the uniformed men. They stepped into the street, coming closer. Benfu couldn't tell if they were police, security, or what, but he could tell by the looks on their faces and their purposeful strides that they were determined.

The old man turned and his eyes once again bore into Benfu, frantically searching.

"*Dui*, I have honor," Benfu said, "but I need to go. Now."

The man reached under his jacket and pulled out a wrinkled brown envelope. With his back to the approaching men, he kept it hidden as he pushed it into Benfu's pocket.

"I give you this and ask you not to open it. It is not money, and its only value is to me personally. Keep it safe, and return here each week at this day and time until I am able to come and retrieve it from you. Can you do this?"

Benfu nodded. What else could he do? He just wanted to leave. And what could be more valuable than money?

"What is your name?"

"Benfu. Zheng Benfu."

The man stared into his eyes, and Benfu felt as if he were hesitating on his decision, that he might at any second snatch the envelope back and run. But in the next second, he pushed Benfu away and turned his back, facing the men making a direct line straight to him.

"Teng Bao, you're wanted in Beijing for questioning," the tall one said, pulling a baton from a sheath in the back of his belt.

Stunned, Benfu stepped back and watched as the old scavenger man dropped to his knees and covered his head. The officer held the baton high, ready to bring it down on the old man. The other two officers moved around the man until he was blocked on three sides.

"*Qing wen,*" Benfu yelled out. "Excuse me. What has he done that you would treat him with such force?"

The tall officer paused, turning to look at Benfu as he still held the baton in the air. "Who are you? Are you related to this man? You know this traitor?"

Benfu looked down at the scavenger, and saw the old man shake his head ever so slightly. Benfu could feel his knees trembling. "No sir, I do not know him, but he appears ready to go with you peaceably. No need for such force."

The two shorter officers sneered, even as the one in charge lowered the stick. He looked around, and Benfu could see that he was taking into account that a crowd had gathered. The people stood watching curiously, waiting for the next move. Benfu realized he was holding his breath, and he let it out slowly. Violence on the streets was nothing new, but Benfu had never been so close to it before. His heart pounded as if he were running a race.

The officer tucked his baton back into his belt and jerked the old man's arm, yanking him to his feet. He then gave him a shove and the scavenger plunged forward, into the chests of the two other officers, who straightened him and then each took an arm.

The tall officer raised his eyes to look at Benfu, his anger evident as he pointed a knobby finger. "It doesn't do for bystanders to get involved in police business." The officer looked Benfu up and down, from his shiny black shoes up to his collared and ironed school shirt. When he spoke, his voice was low and threatening. "I have a feeling you accidentally landed here, unknowing that you were cavorting with criminals. So I'll tell you what—I'm going to give you a pass. Run along home and we'll pretend this never happened. But never question authority again, *shào nián.*"

Benfu didn't answer and didn't move. He didn't know the old man, didn't know if he was really a scavenger or just a beggar. What he knew in his gut was that the man wasn't a criminal. But what could he do about it? He looked at him and once again, they locked eyes silently. Then the man gave one solemn nod, as if telling Benfu he knew what he must do.

Benfu nodded back. He'd keep his envelope safe, and he would return it to him. He'd show the man that he did indeed have honesty and honor in his blood.

If he ever saw him again.

The tall officer beckoned to the others to follow, and he led the way as the other two practically dragged the old man down the street. Benfu watched them go for a moment, then turned back toward his way home.

He remembered that despite the old man's sudden misfortune, his own future awaited him, so he picked up the pace. It wouldn't do to be so late that his mother might shame him in front of his future bride. He might not wish to be engaged, or to be a part of such ancient traditions, but he did have his pride and knew it would be important for him to not lose face in front of his future family. He put his hand in his pocket, feeling the corner of the envelope from the old man.

A secret.

He didn't know what it was, but it felt good that someone felt they could trust him—even if that trust came from a desperate stranger.

As Benfu approached the house—or the villa, as Mother called it—he tried to see it through a stranger's eyes. Perhaps even through Juan Hui's eyes. What had she thought as she approached his front stoop? Was she captivated by the finely manicured front yard, or possibly teased by the gurgle of the fountain cascade feeding into the koi pond? Intrigued by the water dotted with colorful glimpses of the imported fish his mother was so proud of? Would she be happy living there, even building their family there? Though one of the nicer villas on the street, could it be too simple to be the center of a world for someone expected to birth a long line of Zheng males? So many questions, Benfu felt dizzy with anticipation and perhaps a bit of dread. He supposed the answers depended on what sort of home she herself came from.

His house was more than worthy, mainly because it was swathed in history. In his neighborhood, set among the tall London Plane trees that lined the streets, there were a variety of styles of architecture. Tucked in behind the modern houses built for the influx of French citizens who immigrated to Shanghai long ago, remained many traditional Chinese houses—like his—facing south for good *feng shui* and built around the customary courtyards. Benfu's family owned one of the oldest, located just beyond the famous streets that now boasted the newer, fancy houses, restaurants, and shops.

His schoolmates thought he was lucky because the cinema was within walking distance of his home. In that detail, Benfu agreed, as at least disappearing into the cinema allowed him a reprieve from his strict everyday life filled with endless lessons and lectures of duty. His favorite film, seen with Pony Boy over two years ago, was still *Visitors on the Icy Mountain*, a spy thriller set during the Korean War in the mountains of China's western border region. Benfu still remembered the silent awe of the crowd in the theater as they watched the drama unfold between

the Kuomintang and the Communist Party. Benfu had sat mesmerized, enjoying the details of a life bravely lived in a hostile setting while
others around him buzzed about the political implications of the story.

He stopped at the gate and opened it, took a deep breath, then
slipped through.

"Benfu *shào nián*, you're late," Old Butler muttered, pausing from
his efforts to pull gangly weeds from the flower bed. "You were expected
over two hours ago."

"*Dui bu qi*, Old Butler," Benfu apologized and realized it didn't
bother him for Old Butler to call him lad, though it had when the
policeman had used the term. He thought of the old man at the park.
"I met someone and we talked about life. And courage."

He didn't mention the envelope, but his mind raced as he considered where to hide it.

Old Butler slowly stood and wiped his gloved hands against each
other, dislodging a cloud of dust. He looked around, then lowered his
voice as he leaned in to Benfu. "You think too much, lad. I see it in
your eyes, that never-ending tendency to question everything around
you. Sometimes—you cannot control fate. You must just hold on and
hope that it leads you in the way that you want to go. Sit right here for
a minute, let me tell you about something."

Benfu squatted down on the ground and Old Butler did the same.
"You ever hear of the Four Pests Campaign?"

He nodded. They'd talked about it in school when studying the
concept of agriculture in relation to economy.

Old Butler looked into the tree, pointing at a bird that perched
on a small limb. "They're back now. You were just a small boy when it
happened so I know you can't possibly remember. People in Shanghai
and other cities didn't understand how devastating it was when orders
came down from all the top officials for everyone to rid China of the
four pests—rats, flies, mosquitos, and sparrows."

"Devastating?"

"*Dui*, devastating," Old Butler said. "I had family in the country and I was there at one point during the height of the campaign. There wasn't a problem with ridding households and farms of the rats, or even the flies and mosquitos. But the birds—that was a problem. And at first the people agreed that the sparrows must go, as they were thieving around the farms, stealing the grain seeds, resulting in a loss of some of the crop."

Benfu knew the end of the story, but he let Old Butler tell it anyway.

"I'm not an expert on farming, but I know a few things."

That was an understatement, Benfu thought. Old Butler seemed to know something about everything. The old man was one of the smartest men he'd ever known.

Old Butler continued. "I knew that when you take away the sparrows, you are messing with the laws of nature. For you see, sparrows were created for a reason and they serve a purpose."

"To keep the locust population down," Benfu said, unable to stop himself.

"That's right, Benfu. Yet when the countryside declared war on the sparrows and began killing them, shredding their nests, smashing their eggs, and scaring them so badly they dropped straight out of the skies to their deaths, I just kept my mouth shut."

Benfu knew from his studies that the peasants had beaten drums and banged together pots and pans or anything they could to keep the birds from landing, until the scared creatures dropped from the sky in exhaustion, falling to their deaths. "Why didn't you say anything?"

Old Butler sighed. "Because in this instance, the wheels were set in motion and I had no way to stop what fate had decreed. But my gut instincts were right—in the next season, the locust counts skyrocketed and they ruined the crops. If the sparrows had still been there, they'd have eaten a huge part of that locust population; without the birds on their side, the farmers had desperately tried to save their crops with little success. Many families suffered through starvation because of the orders from those above them—those who didn't understand farming. My family barely made it through and it grieved me to see them suffer as they did."

"How did they get the sparrows back?"

"One at a time," Old Butler said. "It took years of patience. And like the Sparrow Campaign was for me, this next phase of your life is somewhat out of your hands. Now come, we must hurry before your mother has both of us striped for your delay. I've laid out your robe and slippers. Go wash up. Your fiancé awaits you."

Benfu was surprised at the small lecture from Old Butler. The man didn't normally speak out of turn. His unusual behavior told Benfu that the old man sympathized with his plight, so he nodded obediently, though his stomach felt as though it held a heavy rock.

Cook popped her head around the corner and held a hand up.

"If anyone has any extra time, I'd appreciate some help getting these last bundles of flowers separated, cut, and placed around the house," she said, then disappeared again. Her request wasn't for him. Cook and Old Butler had long ago learned to work as a team, each helping out when the other was overwhelmed.

Old Butler waved Benfu along.

Benfu paused, feeling his breath catch in his throat. When Old Butler noticed no one walking behind him, he turned back, his expression showing his impatience.

"I can't do this," Benfu whispered.

Old Butler sighed, then returned and put out his hand, letting it settle on Benfu's shoulder. "There comes a time when we all have to take those first steps to becoming a man," he said softly. "No one's asking you to marry her today, lad. Just meet her. Who knows what the future will bring?"

Benfu nodded and Old Butler led the way around to the back of the house, his finger to his lips to beckon complete silence so the guests wouldn't peek out the window and see Benfu in his simple school clothes, looking like the boy he felt inside and not the man he'd be presented as. This time Benfu followed, ready to get it over with so that he could eventually retreat alone to his own quarters and find solace by pouring his unrest out through the bow on his violin.

But first, he'd continue to be a good Chinese son and wouldn't dare to disrespect his parents' wishes. That was the way of China, after all. He belonged to a country filled with customs, superstitions, and familial obligations. There was nothing else to do but follow along. Benfu tried to conjure up the last photo he'd seen of the girl and in his nervousness, could not imagine her face. More than looks, though, he wanted her to be kind and a good partner in life—but to be honest, he just hoped she didn't look like the backside of a bullfrog at midnight's light.

Chapter Two

There is absolutely no chance she'd look like he'd imagined all these years, Benfu thought as he walked slowly past the elaborate paintings of his somber-faced ancestors, drawing closer to the parlor. He felt ridiculous and had argued with Old Butler that the heavy robe was too small for his larger-than-average frame. Old Butler had insisted it fit correctly, and after smoothing his hair down with oil, had literally pushed him out of the room and down the hall before disappearing like a phantom into a dimly lit side room. Benfu paused and took a huge breath, trying to calm his nerves. Now was the moment, and there was no backing out of it. He'd finally see the girl his mother found worthy to be her future daughter-in-law. He wondered what she would wear. Would she be dressed in the now-popular drab-colored tunic and pants that most women were wearing in public? Or for the occasion would she be dressed formally, like him, and feeling just as out of place, as though they were playing parts in a stage opera?

He took a few more steps and realized that the sudden intake of air made him see stars, so he paused just outside the room. From his peripheral view, Benfu saw Juan Hui was seated strategically in one of the two hand-carved rosewood palace chairs that Benfu's mother was so proud to have had shipped in from Hong Kong. He could also tell that her attention was turned to his mother's beloved tank of goldfish, her eyes most likely following the brightly colored fish as they gracefully glided around.

Benfu entered the room. He avoided looking at his mother because he knew she'd be impatient with his tardiness. Instead he focused on the empty chair that sat opposite Juan Hui. He studied the familiar carving of a deer standing under a peach blossom tree, the scene on the chair that he'd seen a million times before and had even traced with his own chubby toddler fingers. His eyes followed the graceful curved arms and lingered down the legs to the paw-like forms that grasped the floor.

Finally, with nothing else to save him, he glanced at Juan Hui. Then he looked away before he could even completely grasp what she looked like. Standing on either side of her, his mother and hers watched him silently, waiting for his response at seeing his future wife for the first time. Benfu looked around, trying to find his father. He wished fervently that Ba would come into the room and give him some moral support in this world of feminine charades that he knew nothing about.

"Say something, Benfu," his mother said, her voice sounding foreign at her obvious attempt to soften her usually brisk tone.

Benfu felt heat flood his neck and face. Why wasn't he prepared for this moment? They'd talked about it for years, but if they'd ever coached him, he'd be damned if he could remember what it was he was supposed to do or say. He stole another glance at Juan Hui. Her gaze remained on the floor; clearly she'd listened more raptly to lessons on how to act on the day she met her fiancé.

It all began to come back to him. The first moments were indeed to be orchestrated carefully. At dinner the night before, he'd been reminded about the goose and that his father would enter and present it to Juan Hui's mother as a symbol of their son's promise. The family was supposed to keep the goose alive and set it in a family pond to thrive on its own.

He should say hello. Yes, that was the first thing she'd told him to do. *"Ni hao Xiao Ju—uh—"* Benfu said, finally looking full on at her, stumbling when it came to saying her name and then giving up. At his greeting, she looked up and met his eyes, something that would've never been allowed a few decades before, and she smiled demurely. And he was right, she didn't look as he'd imagined all these years.

She was pretty. Not beautiful—but still easily in the category of women who could brag about their looks. She also struck him as somewhat mysterious. He studied her as he waited for a response. She looked small—almost diminutive in the chair that looked huge around her. She'd also dressed traditionally, donning a long modest gown of midnight-blue, a colorful peacock embroidered over her breast with its multicolored feathers entangling her sleeve like a rainbow of flowers. Her hair was the glossiest black he'd ever seen, but wasn't allowed to hang loose. Instead it was woven into a tight braid that fell over her shoulder, so long that the tip of it hung in her lap. She appeared older than the fifteen years she was supposed to be but it could've been because of the beauty mark above her mouth. It was quite large and Benfu wondered if it was real or painted on for dramatic affect. That led his eyes to her lips and as he watched, they parted gently, showing a tiny line of exquisitely perfect teeth. For a moment—

Baba interrupted the line of thought as he finally entered the room. Dressed in his best meeting clothes with his own hair slicked down and parted to the side, Ba looked almost as nervous as Benfu felt. With one hand he wiped away beads of sweat from his upper lip. Under his arm he held a white goose and he walked softly and quietly, so as not to disturb the animal. Tradition also said that if the goose stayed quiet during the transaction, it meant the groom had a good, calm personality. Otherwise, it would mean that Benfu held a quick and inhospitable temper. Benfu remembered that, for weeks, his mother had bemoaned finding the perfect goose, until just the night before when she'd declared victory and promised the bird had been found. A goose of just the right weight with a flawless coat of feathers, she'd boasted, then claimed it also held the personality she'd searched for. She'd acted as though she was searching for his wife, not the goose to be given to the girl who would become his wife.

Benfu felt the first warning of unwelcome humor enter his head and squashed it down. He breathed deeply, waiting for the next step. The scene was supposed to be stoic and symbolic, but to Benfu it felt so contrived as to border on ridiculous. Before he could stop himself, he blurted out the most inappropriate thing anyone in his position could think of.

"You couldn't find a fatter goose?"

His mother gasped, then covered her mouth with her hands. Juan Hui's mother followed suit, covering all but her eyes in her reaction to his inexcusable blunder. His father's face paled as he stood speechless, holding a suddenly struggling goose. But Juan Hui—she had gained the first ounce of respect from him. Instead of sharing the shocked outbursts of the women around her, she looked straight into his eyes and burst out laughing.

Juan Hui was serious again, her expression passive after she was prompted by her mother to stop the unsuitable laughter. The symbolic gesture of showing off the goose was finished, but would probably never be forgotten. Thankfully, Juan Hui's mother had still agreed to accept it, but the animal would be leaving their home in disgrace, having lost all nobility in its moment of panic. It had resisted the path of peace with one final gesture of bravery, flapping so violently that it escaped captivity for a few chaotic moments. While everyone else had fled to the corners of the room for safety, Old Butler had run in and thrown a tablecloth over the bird, then taken it out of the room, supposedly to return it to its wooden crate in the courtyard. Benfu hoped it would find a measure of quiet in its new home on Juan Hui's family pond, being fattened even more to prepare it for the wedding feast. Then he wondered, would the goose even live that long? A date wasn't set yet, but surely the wedding would wait until after his education was finished? And how long did geese live, after all?

He pushed the silly thought away and focused again on Juan Hui. Once propriety and calmness had been re-established, the mothers had thankfully left them alone—though with strict instructions not to move from their assigned chairs. Benfu studied the girl, trying to determine her mood, but found it impossible to read her suddenly guarded expression. He found himself tongue-tied, and searched his mind frantically for something to say. He felt the heat climb up his neck and into his face, then beads of sweat on his upper lip betrayed him by showing up.

"What are your interests?" she finally asked, breaking the awkward silence and looking at him expectantly.

Benfu gave a sigh of relief, then considered what to tell her. His mother would expect him to impress Juan Hui, not regale her with the true essence of who he was and who he hoped to be one day. He'd be expected to nurture her confidence that she would be marrying well. He decided to stagger the truth.

"I enjoy poetry and history."

She nodded and for a moment, Benfu hoped that perhaps they would find something in common. He waited for her to agree that poetry and history were important.

"What poets do you read?" she asked, her voice laced with boredom.

Benfu read them all but only in the last few years had he truly begun to enjoy the words and the stories of love, loss, and loyalty that most of them entailed. As a young boy, he'd simply been a memorizing machine, doing what was required of him in his studies and his many responsibilities as the future head of the household. His mother told him constantly how he was being groomed to fill his father's shoes one day; a task Benfu didn't think would ever be possible. His father was the pillar of their existence and, though Mother tried to rule the roost, it was Ba who held the majority of Benfu's respect and affection, for he was a man of strength who only needed a few words to calm the sometimes-restless soul of his only son. His father was respected, held in high esteem at the university where he worked as well as in their neighborhood. It wasn't that he did much or was seen often; it was in his quiet character of truth and justice—*that* was what people were drawn to. Benfu knew he'd never measure up to the man his father was. Just like now—he'd talk about subjects that were general and expected, never getting to the gist of what the other was made of. Niceties—that's all they'd perform.

"My favorite is Li Shang-Yin," he hesitated for a brief second, then added, "as well as the works of Shi Zhi."

Juan Hui raised an eyebrow. Not quite an impressed gesture but at least showing a bit of interest, as well it should. The latter poet was not from days of old like others Benfu was forced to study, but instead was a modern writer, one that so far had declined to use his gift of prose to exalt Mao.

"Do you read poetry?" he asked, though he knew all young ladies were taught the most famous passages of verse as they were being groomed for marriage.

She shrugged. "It was required at my boarding school, but I didn't enjoy it. I find most poets to be morose and depressing."

He didn't know how to respond to her critique of poetry without starting a debate, so he focused on the other part of her answer. "You went to boarding school?"

She nodded. "For two years when I was ten and eleven. My parents didn't have time to tend to me and my brother as they were busy transcribing journals for technical experts working with Russia. So we were sent away for a time."

Her voice trembled, telling Benfu that the years she spent away from home weren't happy ones. The tidbit about Russia intrigued him, and he supposed she was also learning how to speak Russian, since only it and English were offered as mandatory second language classes.

Boarding school was a subject that fascinated him. He couldn't ever imagine being sent away from his home.

"What was that like?"

She looked up and over Benfu's shoulder. When she saw the hall was empty behind him, she stared back down at her tiny feet encased in silk slippers of the deepest reds. "Three words. Lonesome. Cold. Hungry."

She tried to disguise it but he heard the pain in her voice and it warned him not to ask more. He'd heard the stories of boarding school students climbing trees to shake the flowers out, using them to make tea or soup for their empty stomachs. He'd also heard of children freezing as they tried to sleep, covering themselves with every piece of clothing they owned in their attempts to stay warm in the frigid government buildings that weren't heated even in the dead of winter. Even when he wondered how much truth there was to the stories, his stomach clenched at the thought of such hardship. But now, hearing her tell of her experiences, it told him that it wasn't just exaggerations passed from province to province—there was truth in her three words.

"Have you read anything written by Chairman Mao?" she asked, taking Benfu by surprise.

He nodded, but kept his expression and voice neutral. "I have."

She lit up, her boredom disappearing in a sudden burst of enthusiasm. "My high school was chosen to be visited by the Chinese People's Liberation Army. More than a dozen came and read us pieces of Chairman Mao's works. It was quite an honor."

Benfu felt his pulse race. It was talks about Mao that got him into the most trouble and he'd need to be cautious not to lose his tongue.

"I agree—what an honor that must have been," he said carefully. His teacher would've dropped from a stroke if Mao had deigned to step foot in his classroom. Benfu quite honestly wasn't yet won over by the man, but he knew what was good for him and what could cause his parents to lose face, so he'd pretend right along with everyone else that Mao was China's savior, regardless of how many mistakes he'd already made.

She leaned toward him.

"I have his book of quotations and I've memorized at least a third of it."

He smiled weakly. The little red book was comprised of supposedly inspiring statements from Mao's speeches, and pieces of his writings. His teacher had a copy and read aloud from it almost daily. But Benfu didn't have one of his own and quite honestly, didn't care to.

The silence grew between them again while Juan Hui picked at her nails. Finally, she looked up expectantly. "Your mother claims you're an accomplished violinist and that you'll play for me. Enough talk. I'm ready to judge your skills for myself."

Despite her tone, Benfu sighed with relief. His violin would bridge the awkward air between them, his music could take the place of the stilted conversation. His violin was *his* savior.

Three hours later Juan Hui was gone and Benfu watched, amused, as his mother puttered around the room, needlessly plumping pillows and straightening the silk scrolls on the walls.

Benfu's mother picked an invisible piece of lint from the back of the chair his father sat on. She hesitated before Ba, then moved on without touching him. It was unsettling how they avoided affection. But there must be some love between them—or how would he have been born? A part of him longed to see some proof of their bond, some bit of warmth between the two who had created his life. How was he supposed to even know how to interact with a woman when the only example he had seemed so wrong?

"Well, I'd say all went well, Feiyan," Ba said to Mother and rattled the paper in his hand. "Now can we have some peace in this house? For at least a week or two? You've had everyone in an uproar for so long. Now that we've met the girl, we all deserve a holiday."

Benfu hoped the subject of the goose didn't come up.

Mother turned to him and threw her hands in the air, an exasperated gesture she did so often that they no longer took much notice of it. "Zheng Ju, you know she's not at all like the photos they've sent to me. She's at least two hands shorter than I'd expected. And did you see that mole? What were they thinking? They plumped it up and powdered her face so that she looked more like a concubine being presented to an emperor than an elegant and worthy young woman chosen to be our daughter-in-law!"

Benfu caught Ba's eye and shrugged. He'd thought the mole was striking and made Juan Hui look more mature than her fifteen years, but nothing like a concubine—whatever that meant. She'd been polite, and she at least acted a bit interested in his music, so that was a plus. And with all the talk about their birth numbers corresponding and how lucky that everything was in line to be a good match, did her looks really matter that much? Not that he wanted to marry an ugly woman, but he considered Juan Hui pretty enough. He wondered if his mother had caught on to the feisty side of Juan Hui that she'd worked to hide.

Ba held the paper up for Mother to take. "At least with this we know they've accepted the proposal. Have you read this list of items they want us to have ready for the bridal gifts? You'd think they have royalty in their bloodline."

Mother snatched the gift list from Ba's hands and went to the settee. She studied the paper as if it were her first time seeing it, though Benfu knew she'd already read over it at least a dozen times before handing it over to his Ba.

"*Aiya*—she's even asked for a red porcelain chamber pot! What nerve. What does she think, that she's got a backside made of precious gemstones?" Mother said.

Benfu and his Ba both burst out laughing. A chamber pot was not an unusual item for a new bride to ask for, but a red one—that did seem a bit ridiculous. Benfu wondered if Juan Hui had anything to do with the list, or if it was all made up by her mother. The answer to who actually wanted the fancy pot meant only to relieve Juan Hui during the cold nights would tell a lot about his future bride. Was she really so delicate? She'd seemed tougher than that.

"What kind of crazy activities are you dreaming up for the summer months, Feiyan? I heard the girl's mother say Juan Hui would be staying in Shanghai, so I assume we'll be entertaining a lot more."

"Dui," Mother said. "She'll be staying with her aunt so that she and Benfu can get to know each other better. Now let me finish reading what's on this horribly long list." She used her finger as she read, tracing the list of items her soon-to-be daughter-in-law required to seal the deal. Benfu was bored but maybe a bit amused as Mother read out the other items. Along with requests for an antique bedroom ensemble and carved screens for the foyer, the list was riddled with other smaller things like bedding made of the finest Suzhou silk, and new tailored clothes for any sort of social event that could be thought up—the theatre, a family wedding, a formal dinner. Benfu wondered how he would afford to do so much socializing and entertaining once they were married, and when—if ever—he'd have time for his music.

When she finished, she looked up. "Benfu, as you can see, your bride will have expensive tastes. You'll have to study harder to get the highest entrance scores to attend the best university. Your future depends on it, son."

Benfu didn't answer. He looked at his father, who now appeared engrossed in a book pulled from the shelf beside him. Benfu hesitated. Now could be a good time to talk to her about his dream of being a musician instead of a professor.

"We will make sure that you reach levels of esteem that even your father hasn't been able to attain," Mother said.

Ba's head jolted upright as if pulled by a string. "Feiyan, what are you trying to say?"

Benfu watched the silent sparring. He knew it came from his mother's unspoken reproach that his father had failed to get the promotion that would have had them living part time in Hong Kong—a dream his mother had of retiring from the university to be the mistress of two houses and play the part of a well-traveled family. When his father's colleague had been offered the position, Mother had retreated to her room for days, silently pouting that now she'd never see Hong Kong. Not much had been said after that, but obviously, she hadn't forgotten it.

Benfu saw the look of disappointment and shame on his father's face and felt sorry for him. And he knew that now was not a time to bring up his desire to forfeit a career as a scholar. But soon he would get the nerve to tell her that he wanted to be his own man, and choose his own future. He'd marry the girl his mother wanted him to marry—but he would find a way to spend his days surrounded by music, on that he would not compromise. He'd tell her that, too.

Soon.

Chapter Three

Benfu laid the bow against the violin, allowing it to rest for a moment before attempting once more to work through the complicated rendition of *The Butterfly Lovers Concerto*. He felt out of breath, as if the music he'd made had drained his energy. As he hesitated, he knew the opposite was true—though it was exhausting to perform, the music satisfied him, filling that empty place in his soul that came from a lifetime of feeling out of place. He was getting better every day at the violin, giving him a reason to believe that perhaps he had one small thing that made him special, one attribute other than being the coveted son from a long line of scholars. The music was his alone—a gift not earned, but generously given to him by the gods that be, a separate blessing from the moderate wealth and intelligence his parents claimed to have handed down.

And Benfu knew that if he worked hard—harder than he'd ever worked in his life—he had more than a slight chance of being accepted into the Shanghai Conservatory of Music. His father and his tutor knew of his secret plan to apply, but they had yet to break it to his mother. Obviously she felt that being a musician should take second chair to being a scholar. He thought of Juan Hui and was glad that their visits were staged months apart. Since the day he'd met her, they'd had only one more encounter, and it had been almost as awkward as the first. It was going to take him a while to get used to the idea that one day they'd be married. Instead of coming to visit more often, Juan Hui's mother had taken to sending frequent letters, some stuffed with new photographs of her daughter. Benfu had put one in his money pouch, carrying it with him, but only because he was expected to, not yet because he felt any affection for her. But as his father had advised him, that would come in time. For now, he had the solace of his violin.

He took a deep breath, closed his eyes, and released the bow.

The door burst open.

His mother stomped in and began pacing the floor, wringing her hands as she moved, stopping to mumble something new and jumbled every few seconds. Benfu stopped playing and smothered a sigh of frustration at her intrusion. It would do no good to remind her that she'd promised not to bother him.

"Once she is done shining the windows, Ming Lei is putting together tea for this afternoon. I expect you to be dressed up a bit nicer and ready for instruction," she said, her voice more nervous-sounding than usual. Even in her distress, she looked perfectly put together, not a hair out of place or a wrinkle on any piece of her clothing. Yet despite her meticulous exterior, Benfu knew total chaos reigned inside her.

"What were you playing?" she demanded as she turned and headed toward the far wall.

"Nothing," Benfu answered. "Just practicing."

He didn't want to let his mother know he was taking on such a challenging piece as *The Butterfly Lovers Concerto*. As of yet, no one had heard him play it because it still wasn't perfect. And if he ever succeeded in conquering it, his violin teacher would be the first to hear it, anyway. His mother—more than likely she wouldn't approve.

"Well, have you told anyone you've seen it?" She turned to Benfu again, her eyes steely and crazed, her hands on her hips.

"Seen what?"

She stopped long enough to roll her eyes at his impudence. "You know what, Benfu. The opera play—*Hai Rui Dismissed from Office.*"

Benfu nodded. "*Dui*, everyone in my class knows I've seen it, just as many of them have. We discussed it, Mother. As a class assignment."

"*Aiya*, we shouldn't have seen it. We shouldn't have seen it."

She resumed her pacing, now adding a shake of the head as she moved back and forth across the room. Benfu wished she'd picked another room to conduct her interrogation. The cozy library had always been his favorite place in the house—a sanctuary of peace and quiet when he most needed it, a place to read or play his violin in private.

Besides his father's prized collection of miniature jade-carved animals, Benfu loved the woodsy aroma of the hundreds of books lining the floor-to-ceiling mahogany shelves, and the rows of antique scrolls of poems and letters slid into their cubby holes in the wall to keep them pristine. There were many days he'd grabbed a book at random just to have it in his grasp when he sunk contentedly into his father's reading chair, the only piece of furniture in the house that provided padding for comfort and strayed from the clean, hard lines of the usual traditional pieces. When Benfu was just a child, the library was where he knew he'd always find Ba and be welcomed into his strong arms, a safe haven from his mother's constant pestering.

"What time will Ba be home?" he asked. He tried to keep his voice even, not wanting to push his mother over the edge. He focused on the shelf behind her, staring at his favorite jade piece, a carved water buffalo.

She stopped pacing and turned around. "Concentrate, Benfu. This is important. We should've never gone to see that play."

"Mother, Chairman Mao praised the play. I saw his compliments in the *China Daily* newspaper with my own eyes."

His mother shook her head. "That was before."

"Before what?"

She threw her hands up in the air. "Before all this chaos! Mark my words, Benfu, things are getting senseless and Mao is going to retract his praise and everyone who has any connection to the play will end up in trouble."

"Seeing it in the theatre is a connection?" He tried to keep his voice respectful, but he was truly confused. "There were hundreds of people there, all seeing the same thing."

His mother locked eyes with him. "Don't you understand? The play was written about an honest official from the Ming days. The man jeopardized his position by sympathizing with the people. He was so brash he carried a list of complaints to the Emperor, then criticized those in power until he was dismissed from office. Now there are rumors that the emperor in the play represents Mao and the official is Peng Dehuai, fighting for the rights of the people. If these rumors make it all the way up the ladder to Mao, he'll be incensed!"

"Surely, Mother, he isn't that distrustful or that arrogant. To be compared to an emperor? That's ridiculous," Benfu said, though internally he had no doubt that Mao was indeed that pompous. And that paranoid. Some of his new overly oppressive directives made it appear that the leader thought he was losing control of his people. And he did have it out for Peng Dehuai, the official who'd recently publicly criticized Mao's Great Leap Forward.

"That Peng Dehuai is too brave for his own good." Mother stopped to stare out the window, a look of concentration replacing the fearful one she'd worn only seconds before. She pointed her finger at Benfu. "And you—I want you to forget you ever saw that play. Never speak of it again, for your own safety. For the protection of this family."

Benfu nodded agreeably to appease her, but in truth, he respected Dehuai for not being afraid to speak his own opinion, an action that was getting harder and more dangerous to do in China.

With the nod of agreement from him, Mother fled the room, most likely intent on finding the next thing to set off her skewed sense of sensibility and paranoia. Benfu hoped that his Ba would arrive home soon to be the deflector of the next bout of drama that was sure to come.

He picked up his bow, closed his eyes, and began again.

Hours later, Ba held the newspaper close to his face, releasing occasional frustrated sighs. He'd been at it for close to half an hour and Benfu was surprised at his deviation from his usual after-dinner routine. By now on most evenings he would have retired to his chair in the courtyard to smoke his pipe and watch the fish. But dinner was an hour gone by, the delicious dumplings now holding residence in all of their bellies, making Benfu sleepy, yet still Ba remained in the parlor focused on the newspaper he'd brought home.

Across from him, Mother sat in her chair with her feet propped on her footstool, reading a thick book with the characters making up the title *The Water Margin* elaborately painted across the cover. Benfu knew it to be a novel about a group of outlaws banding together to fight against foreign invaders. A classic, and a story he himself had enjoyed years before.

Benfu held his notebook full of poetry and secret pages filled with snippets of compositions he was working on. He didn't dare to open it to anything but the poetry, though. His mother was like a hawk, never missing a chance to take him to task.

"Mother, don't forget tomorrow after lunch I'm going over to Pony Boy's house."

She sniffed in disdain. "You have lessons, Benfu. You don't need to go running around Shanghai with that peasant boy, wasting a valuable Saturday. Now that you're engaged, you have responsibilities."

"He's not a peasant, Mother. I've told you before, his father is a postman and his mother works in a factory. They're Shanghainese, just like us. So they can't be peasants," Benfu said, keeping his voice patient but firm.

Mother snorted. "Ask him to trace his lineage. I'll just bet he doesn't have to go far back to realize his family came here from the country."

"Let him go, Feiyan. Benfu will get his lessons done before he leaves—as he always does. He's not a married man yet, just engaged. Let him enjoy himself for a few more years. And Pony Boy is a fine young man," Ba said, never taking his nose out of the paper. His voice trailed off until the last words were spoken too low for Mother to hear. "Even if he does seem to never stop talking."

Benfu felt grateful his father was there, and that he'd taken the rare liberty of standing up to Mother. But even if he hadn't, Benfu would've snuck away. His friendship with Pony Boy was one that Benfu stubbornly held on to. It was simple. While others judged him based on his name and family line, Pony Boy didn't care about any of that—their difference in family background just didn't matter to him. They could spend hours together, talking and laughing. Or if it wasn't a day for that, they didn't have to fill the air with meaningless conversation; they were just that comfortable. Benfu would never give up a friendship like that.

A shuffle of feet alerted him that Cook was returning from the kitchen and he stood to open the door, holding it as she came through carrying the tray of fragrant tea. She set it on the table, lit the candle in the warming tray, and then turned to leave the room.

"Bring me my cozy slippers, Ming Lei," Mother said, barely giving Cook time to finish one task before ordering her to another.

"*Xie xie*, Cook," Benfu said as the door swung shut behind her. "Ba, are you going to share what is so interesting?" he asked, then knelt in front of the table and poured the steaming tea into the ceramic cups. He took two and set them at the small tables beside each of his parents. His mother gave him a smile and murmured something about a good Chinese son. Benfu waited for his father to answer.

"The American president Johnson announced a pause in bombing," Ba finally said.

"What does that mean?"

Mother answered before Ba could. "It means he's a fool. Those Vietnamese are taking advantage of the pause in fighting and instead of considering the offer of reconciliation, they're buying time to send more troops and supplies into the South. But who can blame them? Everyone knows the Americans are liars and charlatans."

"I don't know about that, but I do know it looks like they're going to make the same mistake as the French," Ba said. "They're sending their men into those thick jungles, knowing each one will only come out in a body bag, or worse, be left there to rot until they're one with the rich soil."

Benfu listened carefully as his parents discussed what was happening in Vietnam. He'd always been intrigued by Americans, especially since the news had slipped into China that the foreign devils had sent in over three thousand of their finest fighters to defend the American air base in Da Nang. His imagination raged out of control with visions of fighter jets, big-nosed foreigners, and the brave Vietnamese taking them on. World news didn't find its way into China often, or at least not to the people, but that military action was something that couldn't help but be spread far and wide by those with access to news of current events. And from there, it slowly leaked until a few local newspapers printed small announcements about it. The consensus was that even Chairman Mao was covertly involved, advising and supporting the North Vietnamese in their fight against the Americans.

Ba brought the paper down and set it on the table beside him. "Enough about that—it's just propaganda and it doesn't affect our country. More importantly, Chairman Mao has launched a new campaign."

"What's this one aimed toward?" Benfu asked. It felt like every day lately there were new directives and campaigns being created and passed down to the people.

"Public health. He's publicly criticized the Ministry of Health because he thinks that the urban health-care system is unfair to those in the countryside."

"So what does he want to do? Bring the peasants to the cities and treat them one by one, by doctors with proper training?" Mother lowered her book as she spoke. "Who'll pay for that? Surely not the peasants, they can barely buy rice to feed their families."

Cook made another silent entry and set a tray of fruit on the side table before backing out of the room, her face impassive.

Ba shook his head. "No, he's trying to reform medical education. He says there are too many hurdles and exams to overcome and the people outside the cities need doctors now, not after ten or more years of study."

"I agree with him on that," Benfu said. "Doctors spend too much time studying diseases and treatments that most peasants have probably never heard of."

Ba nodded. "Basically that's what Mao is saying. He's ordering that new students of medicine with only a few months or a year or so of study should be prepared to go out to the countryside to treat the masses."

Benfu was surprised, but finally he was hearing something about Chairman Mao that he could respect and agree with, and knew that the majority of China's people would, too.

His father snorted contemptuously. "He also says there is too much focus on reading and studying and that the average man worries too much about how much he has read. He says doctors are made through practice—not education."

While his mother quietly shut her book and slid it back into the bookcase, Benfu considered what his father said. Surely more of both were needed—more study as well as an increase in practice?

His father continued, "Next thing you know, there'll be uneducated villagers running around the countryside calling themselves doctors and using trial and error—or some homemade remedies—to stop sickness and disease. If they aren't allowed to read and learn, I wonder what sort of medical care they'll be able to offer?"

Mother's eyebrows rose up to high arches. Benfu knew she wouldn't approve of the new approach of minimizing studying. But he also knew she wouldn't openly criticize Mao, no matter what he said that countered her long-held beliefs.

"Well, look at all those young men and women who've been sent to the countryside to work beside the peasants. They come from good families, too. Yet they are out there using their hands to seed and harvest, working with pigs, and basically letting their brains waste away. I think Mao has some marvelous ideas for this country, but I don't think the *Haifeng* way is one of them."

"Feiyan, doing farm work can help the youth mature faster. Working hard with their hands can make them realize that when they do return to their cities, they'd better take the opportunity to figure out how they want to add value to our country. And you never know, some of them may decide that farming is for them after all."

His mother looked doubtful. She talked on about the youth wasting their opportunities and Benfu listened intently. The *Haifeng* Movement—basically youths focusing on patriotic self-sacrifice to work with the common people—was a fascinating directive that fizzled out decades ago but was now being revived. What was then a program to send peasant youth back to their parents' homelands, or the villages their ancestors came from before settling in Shanghai, had now evolved into youth from all backgrounds joining forces in the countryside to help boost the country's economic position. Benfu thought that, for much of the country, the focus was no longer on education meant to strengthen the future of China; instead he believed citizens had grown more interested in earning recognition through symbolic gestures of loyalty to the country.

Ba stood and stretched. "This is too much. I'm going out to smoke. Benfu, would you like to join me?"

Mother gasped.

Benfu laughed at his mother's expression. "Relax, Mother. He's only asking me to come outside with him, not to smoke."

Ba slapped him on the back as they left the room. "You're right about that, son. You decide to take up smoking and if all of Shanghai's medical staff are too busy, you'll need one of those barefoot doctors yourself. Then who knows what kind of treatment they'll give you. Better to stay away from my bad habits and keep your health intact."

Behind them Mother clicked her tongue in irritation. She didn't like for them to talk negatively about Chairman Mao. Even if no one outside the family was listening, her paranoia made her believe that the walls could or would talk.

Benfu sighed. She could be a tyrant, but she was still his mother and despite her sometimes senselessness, she meant well. As he slipped out the door, he turned back and smiled, his attempt to reassure her that the sky was not falling.

Chapter Four

Pony Boy was so thrilled it was Saturday and he was free from school that his mood bordered on festive. School did not agree with him and vice versa. He hated classes and every Friday afternoon was reason for a silent celebration in his head. Better yet, there was only one more week until the glorious summer break would begin. That meant he only had to keep up his good behavior for a while longer. But he could do it—it was almost over! He'd woken with the urge to be loud and happy, even to declare his countdown to the end of the school term, but he couldn't.

Not yet.

He peeked around the corner, checking to make sure his baby sister was still sleeping. Mei laid on her pallet in the living room, curled up with her knees to her chest, her tiny thumb all but invisible as she sucked it in her sleep. He slipped in and pulled the thin quilt over her shoulders, then backed away and returned to the bedroom. Bending down, he dragged his box out from under the bed, used his key to pop the lock, then slowly lifted the lid to keep it from creaking.

He brushed the lock of hair out of his eyes so he could see better. His mother had told him just the night before that she needed to give him a trim, but Pony Boy liked the longer style and the girls looked at him more often since he'd strayed from the clean-cut look typical of his classmates. It had taken a long time, but he thought he'd finally grown into the large teeth and long face that had prompted his childhood nickname—a name that had stuck and he no longer minded.

From the box he pulled out his most prized possession and cradled it in his hands, then pushed it down into his satchel. He checked to make sure it was protected on all sides by a few pairs of socks, before zipping the bag and tossing it over his shoulder. The camera meant everything to him. He'd heard of its existence from a boy in his photography club at school, who had seen it when the boy had accompanied his family on a weekend excursion to the small town of Wuxi. Once Pony Boy knew of it, he had to have it, but it had taken a year of collecting empty aluminum cans and doing odd jobs for whoever would hire him. He'd not only emptied overflowing night pots for the elderly who were too feeble to carry them to the canal themselves, but he'd carried off trash, whitewashed courtyard walls, and even laundered clothing and sheets, hanging his head as he worked like a girl to drape it to dry.

Even after all his work, he'd still had to grudgingly accept a loan from Benfu for the remainder of what he needed. He'd traveled by train to Wuxi to find the small shop that the others had talked about, but only he had mustered up the initiative to actually find it. The shopkeeper had been a worthy adversary when it came to the negotiating process, but Pony Boy had worn him down until he'd finally walked away the proud owner of a secondhand Japanese 120 Minolta.

Once he had the camera, he'd gone back to the simpler jobs of collecting newspapers and tin cans to recycle. Before and after school, he scavenged the neighborhood as well as surrounding streets to pick up anything of value. If his mother could work her fingers raw, the least he could do was scavenge for trash to be turned into coins and added to the family account.

Pony Boy left the small room and skirted out the back door, then sat on the fallen tree trunk in their courtyard, his and Benfu's meeting place. He thought of the afternoon they'd argued about the loan. He was too proud to accept charity, but Benfu had insisted it wasn't charity—that Pony Boy's eye for art was a sure investment for him to contribute to the purchase of the camera. Finally Pony Boy had accepted, but only after they'd made a pact that if he ever became famous for his photos, he'd give Benfu credit for giving him his start.

He tried to tell himself it wasn't a big deal. Benfu came from a semi-wealthy family. Or at least much richer than his own, evident by the treasure-filled house they kept and the hired help that tended it. He looked at his own yard filled with dirt and overgrown weeds, and thought of the pristine flowers, shrubs, and grasses that Benfu's butler maintained. Pony Boy had never known the luxury of a cook or a butler—in his family they all pitched together to manage the house. Even his brother Lixin, born three years after him, had become a better cook than their own mother. He'd had a lot of time to perfect his technique, too, because he was no longer in school. Though he was younger than Pony Boy, Lixin had only attended the required state-covered five years and now, until their father deemed him old enough to get a job, he filled an important role in caring for their baby sister and preparing meals.

He looked at his watch. Benfu was late.

At sixteen, Pony Boy should've been a year ahead of Benfu, but he'd been held back by the teachers who'd claimed he needed to study harder. Their move sure hadn't helped his worry about making something of himself, either. Combined with the knowledge that his penmanship and ability to read were the worst in the class, he'd lost a lot of confidence in the past year. Benfu had assured him that he'd always be there to help him get through, but Benfu just didn't understand.

Pony Boy's father held a respectable job, though it didn't pay much. He was a mail carrier, the position handed down to him from the government and gratefully accepted by his father when he was fresh out of high school. His father didn't move in the same circles as Benfu's father, but he was still respected around town. He was a man whom others trusted, and many came to him when they were down on their luck. Pony Boy's mother was much quieter and reserved, but a perfect partner to her expressive husband. She sewed for a living, putting in long hours to piece together coats for a large factory. Even with both salaries and the small bit of extra funds that Pony Boy contributed from his odd jobs, it was hard to get ahead. But they never lacked for shelter, warmth, and at least one good meal a day.

And that was enough.

It had to be.

"*Ni hao.*"

Pony Boy saw Benfu coming around the side of the house, his hand raised in a greeting.

"*Ni hao* yourself, betrothed old man. What took you so long?" Pony Boy asked. "And why are you wearing that fancy jacket on this warm day?"

Benfu looked at his watch. "What? I'm only ten minutes late. Mother insisted I finish my homework before she'd let me leave."

Pony Boy laughed. "I haven't even begun mine. It's only Saturday morning. We have all weekend. Regardless of what your parents say, you're still young! And free! Enjoy it!"

"Tell that to her," Benfu grumbled. "She almost staged a revolt to keep me from coming here. She insisted a bitter wind was coming in from the north. Then she said it was a storm watch. I was lucky to get away and would've agreed to wear a fur coat to get out of there."

Pony Boy groaned. "She must have heard about how my latest prank got out of hand."

He'd hoped Benfu's mother wouldn't have caught wind of the joke he'd played on their teacher. It was only supposed to be harmless fun. Who would've thought when the man had sat too long on the glue-coated chair that getting up would've ripped his pants and left his underwear visible for all to see?

"No, not that I've heard. If she knows, she hasn't mentioned it to me. Oh, and Cook says hello. She sent us some snacks." Benfu patted the satchel that hung around his shoulder.

Pony Boy smiled. Cook was his silent ally in Benfu's house, even though Benfu's mother didn't approve of him—or his family. Many times he'd walked out of the room where Benfu's mother was making him feel smaller and less significant than an ant, into the kitchen where Cook treated him like a long-lost family member.

He heard a cry and jumped up from the log. "It's Mei. *Aiya*, she's awakened. We'll have to try to get her back to sleep before Lixin gets home, or we won't be able to go anywhere."

Pony Boy led the way and Benfu followed him into the house. They went through the kitchen and found Mei sitting up on her bamboo pallet, clutching her blanket in her tight fist. He bit his lip to keep from laughing at her hair as he crossed the room. When he got close enough, she held her chubby arms up and he lifted her and held her against him, shushing her before her small cry became a bellow.

"Hold her for a minute, will you? I need both hands to make her bottle." He wished his brother was home to help, but since he wasn't, he crossed the room and pushed his sister into Benfu's unwilling arms.

Benfu's expression bordered between horror and shock, making Pony Boy laugh as he headed toward the kitchen. He needed to get a pot of water on to boil so he could warm up some goat's milk. "Just talk to her. And hold her head—that's what Mama always told me when I first started helping with her."

Benfu looked stricken at the advice.

"Why? Will it fall off?" Benfu asked as one hand slid up around the little girl's neck, giving Pony Boy another reason to laugh.

"No, Benfu, it won't fall off. She's a human, not a doll." He looked back to get another glimpse of Benfu awkwardly jostling Mei around.

Just as he pulled the water pot from its hook, Lixin emerged from the doorway. "I'll do it, I'll do it. Just move. I need to boil enough water to use for the corn after I make Mei's bottle," he said, dropping the two bags he held onto the countertop.

"You sure? I was going to try to get her back to sleep."

Lixin nodded his head as he began to start the fire in the belly of the old stove. "Just go take her from Benfu and entertain her while I get the bottle ready. Then you can leave, like I know you're itching to do."

Pony Boy grinned. "Are you making Egg Flower and Corn Soup?"

Lixin gave a short nod.

Pony Boy left the room feeling even more cheerful knowing he'd spend the day anticipating a taste of his favorite soup—and no one, not even their grandmother who was responsible for passing the recipe down to Lixin, could make it better than his brother. With just a few ears of corn, chicken stock saved from their last meal, scallions, eggs, and coriander for seasoning, he made it an inexpensive but tasty dinner they had often.

Just not often enough.

Pony Boy returned to the living room, amused to see Mei captivated as she twisted the tassels from Benfu's fancy weekend jacket, with at least four strings of different colors wrapped around her fingers of one hand.

"I think we'd better go," Benfu said. "I might be meeting someone at the park and I don't want to be late."

"Just as soon as Lixin gets the bottle ready. But who are we meeting?"

Benfu shrugged. "It's a long story. I'll tell you on the way."

"Fine. But this better be good. And don't think you're getting out of spilling how it went with your famous bride-to-be. I want to hear everything." He noticed his remark brought color rushing to Benfu's face.

He hoped Benfu's meeting would be a fast one. Pony Boy already had their day laid out. He planned to use up the entire roll of film he'd saved to buy. The park was a great place to start, but Benfu was in for a surprise, too. Today Pony Boy wanted to leave the park behind and explore some little-known backstreets of Shanghai, capturing the essence of real Chinese life—not the posed photos that so many created on their weekend outings.

It was going to be a good day.

Benfu leaned over the gate, searching the rolling manicured landscape of people for the white-haired man. Even with the delay of dealing with Pony Boy's sister, they'd finally made it to the park, but amidst the throngs of visitors scattered across the park, the man was nowhere to be seen. Benfu could only surmise that the officials who'd taken him into custody had not yet released him. He wasn't sure why, but it made him feel sorry for the man, and the light envelope suddenly felt heavy inside the pocket of his jacket.

"Tell me again who you're looking for?"

"Again? I didn't tell you the first time," Benfu said.

"I know, so start talking." Pony Boy spit a seed high into the air, watching it arch and then fall to the ground.

Benfu looked around, knowing it was a moment of paranoia such as his mother frequently had, but he had to be sure no one was listening. He scooted a step closer to Pony Boy, then pulled the brown envelope from his pocket.

"I stopped by here yesterday, too. I'm looking for the man who gave me this." He held the envelope up for Pony Boy to see.

Pony Boy snatched it out of his hand and brought it closer to his face.

"Don't!" Benfu said, startled. Then, before he could even get the words out, Pony Boy had torn the end from the envelope. Benfu grabbed it back and held it to his chest. "What did you do that for? He asked me to keep it sealed and come back here once a week until he returned."

Pony Boy shrugged. "Sorry. You held it out there. I thought you wanted me to open it. It's done now. Want to see what's in it?"

Benfu felt sick to his stomach. The man had trusted him and now he'd let him down. Even if he didn't look, the man would never believe he hadn't. There was no way to put the envelope back together to hide the evidence of intrusion. They might as well look.

He turned the envelope over and shook out the contents.

From the sharp intake of breath, Benfu could tell that Pony Boy was surprised when a pile of what first appeared to be papers fluttered into his hands. Looking closer, he saw they were waxy pouches containing small strips of film, each with a scrap of paper attached. On each paper was scribbled the name of a location and a date.

"What is it?"

"Negatives. They'll be photographs after they're processed," Pony Boy answered, then took one from Benfu's hands and held it up to the sky.

Benfu held up a different one and could make out the silhouette of what appeared to be a man, his fist held high in the air—perhaps for emphasis—as he stood on a platform in the middle of what appeared to be hundreds or even thousands of people. He turned to Pony Boy.

"Mine appears to be someone making a speech. What's yours?"

Pony Boy's face looked pinched. He finally looked at Benfu.

"This negative shows a man being shamed." Pony Boy pointed at the negative, where the most evident detail was a banner with painted pale characters that read, '*Struggle Against the Enemies Rally.*' Under the banner a figure of a man stood with his head bowed and a plaque hung around his neck, his arms tied behind him. His audience sat on homemade bleachers made of planks of boards lined up before him.

"It's a struggle session," Benfu said.

Pony Boy nodded.

From what Benfu had learned, struggle sessions were a directive issued by Chairman Mao in which the people turned on one another, targeting someone within their circle to point a finger at and humiliate. Usually the event required standing them in front of their neighbors, family, and peers as everyone took turns declaring grievances against them. The chosen recipient was labeled one of four bad elements—in other words, someone who wasn't loyal to the party. Sometimes the sessions went on for hours, even if the accused collapsed from exhaustion. Afterward, they were usually stripped of all their material wealth and condemned to a life of hard labor, or in political cases, even to prison. However, Benfu had never seen a photograph of a session being conducted.

"Let me see the last one." Pony Boy held out his hand and Benfu gave it to him. He put the negative up where both of them could examine it.

They were quiet as each of them tried to figure out what they were seeing. It was difficult to make much out, but from what they could see, it was a photo of a group of people huddled around a raging bonfire, on their knees with others standing over them. Some of the standing figures carried weapons and were striking those beneath them. A sign hung from what appeared to be an outside temple wall and Benfu struggled to read the tiny writing. "It says something about smashing old China, purging poisonous weeds," he said.

"Probably rich peasants."

"I don't think so." He quickly told Pony Boy about meeting the man, and how the officials had surrounded him and made a scene before taking him away.

Pony Boy shook his head. "Then these are probably not only counterrevolutionaries, but must be important people, or why would your mysterious friend ask you to hide the negatives?"

Benfu tucked them back into the envelope. "He didn't ask me to hide them—he just said keep them until he returned."

Pony Boy snorted his doubt. "Yeah, right after he slipped them to you, he was taken into custody. What does that tell you, Benfu? That he's an upstanding and respected citizen?"

He had a point, Benfu thought. Then a thought took his breath for a moment. What if even having the negatives in his possession was a criminal act? If he got caught, it would humiliate his parents, sully the family name. Suddenly the envelope felt hot to the touch and he maneuvered it back into his pocket, wishing to hide it from any prying eyes.

"*Aiya*, that wasn't what I was expecting," Benfu said. He felt nervous, imagining the terrified face of his mother should she find out the predicament he'd gotten himself into. He considered throwing the negatives in the nearest bin. Then he pictured the man again, standing beside him and taking the time to impart words of wisdom when he knew somehow that Benfu was feeling low. Then he saw the man on his knees, cringing beneath the official's baton.

Benfu couldn't let him down. He'd hold on to the envelope—at least for a few more weeks.

"What did the guy look like?" Pony Boy asked.

Benfu described him as best as he could remember. While he talked, he noticed Pony Boy's expression change and a faraway look in his eyes. "Is something wrong?"

"No—nothing's wrong. It's just that I wish I could take photographs that actually mean something," Pony Boy said wistfully. "I'm sick of the pasty faces of our schoolmates and the happy family shots I find here. I want something real, Benfu. Something like this." He pointed at the pocket that Benfu had slipped the envelope into. "I have an idea."

That made Benfu even more nervous. Pony Boy was always coming up with ideas that could get them into trouble.

"Let's try to find the temple that's in the negative. We can see the damage for ourselves and I'll take my own photos."

He looked so hopeful that Benfu could barely find the words to shoot down his idea.

"Pony Boy, we don't even know where it's at. Plus, I'm supposed to be home by dinner."

Pony Boy stepped back and lifted his chin. "I think I know where it is and I have a question for you. Comrade Zheng Benfu, aren't you almost sixteen years old?"

Benfu nodded, amused at Pony Boy's formal tone.

"And Zheng Benfu, aren't you officially betrothed?"

He nodded again.

Pony Boy pointed at Benfu. "And last question, comrade. Don't you think it's time you began acting like the man they expect you to be?"

He looked closely at Pony Boy, realizing he was being given a challenge. But the ironic part was that he also craved some excitement—some break from the monotony of the incredibly long and arduous school year.

As long as it wasn't illegal.

He put his hand in his pocket and remembered he'd just gotten his weekly allowance. It would be enough for a taxi if needed. Freedom—his coins could buy a few hours of freedom.

He smiled at Pony Boy.

"Fine. But I have to be back by dark."

He'd be in trouble for missing dinner, but if he didn't show up by dark, his mother would have all of Shanghai turned upside down looking for him. Benfu wanted freedom—but didn't care to experience the wrath of his worried mother.

Pony Boy let out a holler of glee. "Let's get going then, comrade! Our first adventure of the summer. Or—the almost summer. How about that?"

They headed toward the street when they heard someone yell behind them.

"Pony Boy!"

They turned and saw Lixin running toward them, waving his hands in the air.

"What is it?" Pony Boy asked. "And where's Mei Mei? You left her alone?"

"She's with the neighbor. You have to come home right away."

Benfu had never seen Pony Boy's brother look so frightened.

Pony Boy grabbed his brother's shirt and his face darkened. "You tell me right now what's going on. Is Mei hurt?"

Lixin wriggled out of Pony Boy's grasp.

"No, it's Baba. One of the other carriers came by and said he was taken to the People's Hospital. They think he had a heart attack. I left Mei with Widow Xu and came to find you first. Let's go, if we run we can make it in half an hour." He turned and began jogging in the direction of the hospital. Pony Boy followed.

"Wait!" Benfu called out. He felt helpless, but there was at least one thing he could do.

"I'll catch up to you later, Benfu. We need to go now!"

"Hold on a second. You can use my allowance for cab fare. It'll get you to the hospital faster." Just then a taxi was going by and Benfu whistled and held his hand up. The car stopped and Benfu opened the door.

Pony Boy grabbed his brother's shirt again and yanked him back. They both ran for the car.

"*Xie xie*, comrade." Pony Boy clapped Benfu on the shoulder as he climbed in behind his brother. Already Benfu could see his face was drained of all color.

Benfu threw the bills onto Pony Boy's lap, then the door slammed shut and the car took off. He hoped for Pony Boy—and the whole family's sake—that their father would make it.

Now he felt guilty for wishing for a little adventure. His and Pony Boy's longing for excitement had attracted more than they'd bargained for. Benfu began the walk home, his head low and his thoughts morbid.

Chapter Five

Pony Boy watched the blur of activity during the changing of staff and felt his eyelids droop. He was exhausted. They'd been at the hospital all night, and thus far, the doctors would only say that his father was holding on. The heart attack had been a big one—and unexpected. It had hit him just as he was delivering his last few pieces of mail, luckily at a *hutong* that was only a few blocks from the hospital. Widow Chou, the woman who'd come out to meet him for her letters, had found him slumped over her gate. Then she'd rallied a few neighbors and thrown him into the bucket of a pedicab, urging the driver to pedal him as fast as possible to the nearest hospital.

His father's colleague and route partner had been flagged down by the woman and given the mailbag that had been dropped during the commotion. He was the one who'd come to tell Lixin what had happened.

Then the story became spotty.

All Pony Boy knew was that at the front doors of the hospital, his baba had been given the breath of life and a good pumping on the chest to get his heart going. As soon as they'd found a pulse, they'd rushed him in to surgery.

Pony Boy was having difficulty breathing as he thought about it. Unfortunately, over the last twelve hours, the scene had played out in his head like a never-ending film reel, over and over in different ways, the *what ifs* sneaking in to torment him. What if his father was permanently disabled? What if he lost his job? What if they had to move out of their house? Thankfully his tornado of thoughts was interrupted.

"How is your mother taking this?" Benfu asked. The calm in the storm, he'd arrived early that morning and so far had refused to go home.

"She's pretty torn up," Pony Boy answered, pulling in his feet for a nurse to pass by. They sat on the floor, leaning against the wall in the hallway outside the packed waiting room. His brother lay curled beside him, his legs tucked to his chest and his head resting on his wadded jacket.

His mother was in there, probably holding Baba's hand and whispering to him to be strong and fight to make it. Pony Boy took a deep breath to keep a sob from erupting. He needed to get his mind off the dark outcome he'd concocted in his head.

"Are there any more poppy seed buns left in there?" Pony Boy asked, pointing to the satchel at Benfu's feet.

"No, you ate the last one," Benfu answered. "Didn't even save one for me."

"That was kind of Cook," Pony Boy said. Benfu had told him that Cook sent her well wishes as she packed another bag of food. The treats were appreciated, as Pony Boy and his brother had not had dinner the night before.

They'd sat in the waiting room all night, packed in with hundreds of other people. He was exhausted and his long legs ached to be stretched. Benfu showing up at first light had been a welcome diversion. After hours of silence, he was glad to have someone to talk to.

"So tell me," Pony Boy said, "Does Juan Hui have tiny feet?"

Benfu shrugged. "How would I know? I didn't look at her feet."

"Come on, Benfu. You know your mother wouldn't set you up with a girl who has big feet. I'll just bet she secured a guarantee that Juan Hui was beautiful *and had small feet* before she ever promised a proposal. Tell me again what she looks like."

"She's small—fairly short."

"How small?" Pony Boy asked. He held a hand in the air. "This tall?"

"Taller than that, you melon head," Benfu said. "She probably comes up to my chin."

Pony Boy couldn't imagine Benfu with a petite girl. He'd always been bigger than the others in his class—not fat, just taller and thicker. A strong boy, their teacher had called him once.

"I have a photo."

Pony Boy sat up straighter. "You have a photo and you haven't shown it to me? Hurry up, you fool."

Benfu struggled to lean over and pull his money pouch from his pocket. Slowly, he slipped her photo free and handed it to Pony Boy.

A low whistle erupted from Pony Boy as he stared at the picture. "Sorry, but *aiya*, she is tiny. And you didn't tell me she was this pretty!"

Benfu tucked it back in the pouch. "She may be tiny, but she has a big personality."

"In what way?"

Benfu hesitated before answering. "I don't know if I can explain it, but it felt like she was silently challenging everything I said. She has some fire in her, I think."

"Well, what did you say to her?"

"I don't know. We talked about poetry and music. She told me she was in a boarding school for a couple years," Benfu said. "She's all about Chairman Mao."

Pony Boy smiled. Benfu looked like he wanted to take the words back. He probably thought it would start a debate, but the last thing he needed was to get into it with his best friend about Chairman Mao and the direction of the country. Pony Boy just wanted simple talk—anything to fill the time before he found out whether his father would live or die. "As well she should be," he said. "All I'll say is Chairman Mao is doing great things for this country."

Pony Boy was about to get Benfu back to the good stuff—the fact that he was a fool for having agreed to marry someone. Pony Boy planned to never get reeled in by the female persuasion. He'd live his life unencumbered and free, unattached and unsoiled by romantic love. Just as he was about to start that conversation, he was saved by the sudden presence of his mother standing over them like a silent ghost.

He scrambled to his feet, trying to decipher the look on her face. She was somber. And so pale. She even looked as if she would drop to the floor at any moment. Pony Boy felt a stabbing pain in his own heart and he took a step forward, his arms open to envelop the small woman who for the first time he had ever seen, looked vulnerable and devastated.

She didn't speak.

The noise and faces around him faded as she walked into his embrace and he folded his arms around her.

Chapter Six

Benfu and Juan Hui were in the courtyard, awkwardly facing one another as they perched on the chairs that Old Butler had set up for them. It was only their third meeting and they were supposed to have been chaperoned at the cinema, but at the last minute his mother had decided against the outing. Juan Hui's mother had bustled into their house and passed on the gossip that Chairman Mao's wife, Jiang Qing, was reconsidering her previous endorsement of the film they were supposed to see. As Mao's new cultural advisor, it seemed to Benfu that she was unfairly accusing most of the well-known artists and especially prominent playwright Tian Han of being counterrevolutionary.

Benfu argued the change of plans with his mother, but she'd taken him aside and added that it was probably a good thing they weren't going. She didn't want to flash their wealth and give the wrong impression to Juan Hui's mother.

He wasn't thrilled with her decision, as not only was he looking forward to seeing what the opera looked like adapted to film on the big screen, but in the theatre they wouldn't have been forced to make much conversation. Now he was racking his brain, trying to come up with clever things to say.

He had nothing.

Remembering the goose, he thanked the gods for sending him a thought to initiate conversation. "How's the goose?"

Juan Hui shrugged. "Getting fatter. My mother is obsessed with keeping that thing alive and well."

So much for conversation, Benfu thought as the silence settled around them again. He'd believed mention of the goose might remind her of their amusing first meeting and give them something to laugh about. Or if not that, at least start her talking about the wedding they'd have one day. Didn't girls love to talk about weddings? *Obviously not this one.*

He peeked at her again and saw she was concentrating on a nest cradled high in the limbs above them, watching a mother bird hop from branch to branch to get to her chicks.

They were relatively alone, other than the occasional coming and going of his mother to check on them, and Cook who kept showing up like a quiet ghost to refill their iced milk and fruit platter.

"I've seen a photo of the *Rent Collection Courtyard*," she said.

"What are you talking about?"

"It's a series of statues sculpted by the group from the Sichuan Academy of Fine Arts. They're going to be famous now—especially since they've found a way to depict one of the issues that Chairman Mao is so passionate about."

"And that is?" Benfu hadn't heard anything about a sculpture gaining attention, and he'd discovered that Juan Hui had a knack for making him feel unworldly. He hoped it would go away before they were married.

The smile that lit her face made him forgive her tone instantly. She clapped her hands together. "It's the most incredible thing, Benfu. It's over a hundred life-size sculptures of peasants buckling under the heavy loads of their crops and money as they carry it to their greedy landlords."

"Why is every landlord suddenly considered greedy?" Benfu asked, not to be sarcastic but because he really didn't understand. There had always been landowners and those who leased the land and houses. *What was so terrible about it all of a sudden?*

"Because their renters are usually treated unfairly, I suppose. But anyway, the sculptures were set up in the courtyard of a fancy mansion. It once belonged to a landlord who had it all taken from him."

He didn't reply. It was senseless to consider every single landowner greedy. That would be like saying every single peasant was illiterate. But based on the background of her precious Chairman Mao, they knew that not to be true. Mao had been born in the country and became a voracious reader! But to argue the point about the landlords would be fruitless. He sighed, wishing he were somewhere exploring around town with Pony Boy.

"What do you think about Jiang Qing?" Juan Hui asked, breaking his concentration.

"Jiang Qing, Chairman Mao's wife?"

"*Aiya*, yes—who did you think I was talking about? I've heard she was born into a poor family and when she refused to be married off to a rich man, was sent away. She attended opera school when she was a young woman—which is why she is so interested in the theatre now."

Benfu considered his answer before speaking. Could he be honest? Probably not. "That's ironic about her background, considering how she's treating those in the arts now. But back to your question, I think that she wants to feel as important as her husband, so he gave her this project and now she's taking it too far."

Juan Hui shot him a scathing look. "That sounds chauvinistic to me. Do you think a woman is incapable of doing a fair job on any given endeavor?"

"No—ah—" He stumbled over his words, "that's not what I meant. I just think that the cultural arts were already in good shape. Now every artist, actor, and director is being picked apart, their backgrounds studied and their commitment to China questioned. It doesn't seem fair."

She shrugged. "Maybe you think that because you're an artsy type yourself. Did you know the rumor is that even the most well-known musicians are being scrutinized to see where their loyalties lie?"

"Can we talk about something else?" he asked. When it came to talking about current events, Juan Hui got a bit too animated for his taste. She was a pretty girl, and she had manners, but it still felt that underneath her composure she was itching for a fight. He needed to keep her on safe subjects. But his suggestion brought on another period of uncomfortable silence.

Finally she looked up, an idea lighting her face. "Are you excited about summer break?" she said, waving a folding fan at her face. It was hot for May—so hot that it felt like July. Already Benfu had just about used up the thin handkerchief that Old Butler had tucked into his pocket, mopping his face dry while Juan Hui tried to fan hers to death. With each wave of her fan, he caught a glimpse of the winding peach blossoms painted along the edge of the fan and the whiff of the sandalwood it was made with reached his nose.

He shrugged.

"I suppose."

Juan Hui began telling him of her summer travel plans—a few days up north to visit relatives, then several in the south to be spent at a friend's home on the coast, a special treat to celebrate her upcoming last year of high school.

"Do you swim?" he asked, genuinely curious. He wasn't much of a swimmer himself, but swimming had gained a lot of popularity recently.

She nodded. "Of course I swim. Chairman Mao says it is the best of sports—a show of man's courage to take on one of nature's beasts."

"Water is a beast?"

She gave him an impatient look. "Sometimes it can be, if you're swimming in places like he does. The Yangtze is deep and has a vicious current. Yet Chairman Mao swims it frequently."

Benfu still thought she sounded too fond of Mao, but at least today, without the formal dress, she looked normal. She wasn't wearing the recently popular drab clothing that many were, but instead was dressed casually in a long skirt and white blouse. Her feet—which were indeed tiny, he'd have to remember to tell Pony Boy—were encased in soft slippers. Not silk this time, but some sort of canvas with a white peony drawn on them. The biggest difference he saw was her face, for without the thick powder and rouge, Benfu could now clearly see that the mole was real.

She caught him staring and cleared her throat. When he looked up at her eyes, she was smiling. "Want to go down to the Huangpu River and catch the breeze coming in off the water?"

Go to the river? "I don't think your mother would approve. Or mine, for that matter." Then he realized how ridiculous she must think him— he was old enough not to have to ask his mother for everything. She must have read his mind.

"I want my future husband to be brave and to make decisions for himself," she said.

He paused, considering what could become of her reputation for going off alone with him. But she stood there with her hands on her hips, a silent challenge to his manhood. If he backed down, he'd surely lose face.

He stood. "I'm game if you are."

She jumped from her seat and clapped her hands together. "I'm always up for adventure, that's one thing you'll get to know about me. So let's get out of here."

He looked again at the house, and when he didn't see any nosy faces peeking out the window or door, he stood and led the way out of the courtyard.

They passed a line of tall buildings and Benfu pointed at one of them. "I've heard that Yao Wenyuan lives in an apartment up there."

"Yao Wenyuan, the literary critic?" Juan Hui's eyes were round with amazement.

"*Dui*, the one who has the sharp tongue in the papers."

"Ooh, I wonder if it's swanky. He's very famous—mostly because of his father's success as a writer and translator. He's with the group called the Proletarian Writers for Purity, but I've heard that he's working with Jiang Qing now," Juan Hui said.

"Working with her how?" Benfu asked. He wasn't surprised. Chairman Mao's wife was becoming such a household name, and so outrageous in her actions, that everyone was always spreading news of what she was up to and whom she was conspiring with. But he was curious about how Juan Hui got her information. He figured her parents must have connections and she picked up tidbits of news from them.

"I'm not completely sure," Juan Hui said. "You're so lucky, Benfu. Shanghai is amazing. It's so—*so alive*, I think is how I would describe it. I can't wait to live here."

She began twirling slowly in a circle, taking in all the buildings around her and examining everything from the shop windows to the people on the street. To Benfu she looked completely captivated by what he'd come to take for granted—Shanghai life. He was also pleased to figure out that getting Juan Hui away from her mother and the chains of propriety had revealed another side to her personality. *She was actually fun to be with.*

For the first time since their betrothal meeting, he considered that she might not be a bad partner in life. He couldn't say he was in love with her—but he could now say he liked her a lot more than he had thought.

He glanced over at her. Her attention was on the building that he'd pointed out as Yao Wenyuan's residence, giving him a chance to take a good look at her. She was pretty. She was lively. And definitely intelligent.

He supposed he could do worse.

"Juan Hui?"

She turned to him, the trace of laughter still on her upturned lips. "Yes?"

"Do you want to go find an iced milk?"

She smiled widely. "*Hao de*, an iced milk would hit the spot."

Chapter Seven

Benfu sat at the wooden table and watched Cook removing the gills and eyes of each crab before she dropped it into the huge dishpan of water. He couldn't bear to spend another moment in the presence of his mother. He'd heard enough about his lapse in judgment regarding wandering off with Juan Hui and the damage that could've been done to her reputation. He'd agreed his action was careless, yet how many times could one woman give the same lecture again and again? Since weeks had passed without further comment from Juan Hui's parents, Benfu felt it was time to stop harping about it. He'd finally left Mother sputtering, and slammed out of the library. He'd found himself wandering the rooms of the house in search of what, he didn't know, until he'd ended up in the kitchen.

Cook had barely given a small greeting, but she hadn't turned him away. He was grateful. Though she was little comfort in her unease to speak freely these days, she was at least someone he knew shared his sympathy for Pony Boy's predicament.

A selfish thought, but his summer was ruined. Not just by his actions with Juan Hui, either. For months he'd dreamed of the break from his studies, but when it finally came, without Pony Boy to putter around with, it meant nothing. He'd spent the last few weeks either alone or working with his violin teacher. After a lot of arguing, he'd won and gotten his language lessons canceled until the next school term. He just couldn't concentrate on anything, especially tackling the English language. He'd even gone to Pony Boy and asked if he could help him with his jobs, but his offer was determinedly declined.

Benfu felt useless.

"Did you see your nephew?" he asked Cook. He'd heard his parents saying that some of Cook's family had come to Shanghai for a few days to visit. His mother had only agreed to one afternoon off, but Benfu knew that Cook had a nephew that she'd never seen and fretted about.

She nodded. "He's walking now so I'm glad I got to meet him before he starts school." Her hands moving nimbly as she worked. The quiet settled between them with a comforting ease that at once felt familiar.

"Tell me a story." The words slipped out of his mouth before he could even block them. Her stories long ago used to entertain him for hours. She was a bottomless well of firsthand accounts of things he'd not been around to see—or was too young to remember. It had to have been at least a year since they'd talked alone together and he realized how much he missed hearing her tales.

With the last crab in the dishpan now, Cook left them to soak and returned to the counter. For being so short and stocky, she moved fast as she picked up the bundle of spring onions and chopped them into small pieces. She looked up at Benfu a few times, giving him tightly pursed lips, a sure sign of her impatience, before returning to her task. He noticed that she still liked to wear her pink lipstick, the only adornment on her otherwise clean face.

"What kind of story?" she asked quietly, giving him a quick look before returning her gaze to her work.

He shrugged. All he could think about was the hardship that Pony Boy and his family were facing. *Maybe even financial ruin. What if they lost their house?*

Cook picked up the oil and carefully added a few more drops to the pan. Oil was one of the few things still rationed, and he knew she was mindful to only use as much as absolutely necessary for each meal. She even reused the oil until she couldn't any longer.

"Tell me about when your family was surviving the famine," he said. He'd heard some of the stories before, especially the one when her family finally sent her to Shanghai and she'd landed the job as the cook and nanny in his household. But he never tired of hearing about a life so different from his own.

She looked toward the door again, then began to speak softly. "I arrived in Shanghai just when the pear blossoms began blooming in the spring of 1949, a year before you made your victorious entrance into an upside-down world."

"Upside down?" Benfu asked.

She nodded. "Yes, upside down because it was about that time that Chairman Mao was officially inaugurated as China's most supreme leader. Suddenly a country that had spent years entrenched in Nationalist ways was taken over by Communist rules. No one really understood what that would mean for the people; we only hoped that it would bring a better future."

She worked quickly until the onions were all chopped and she set them aside. She paused to dip a rag under the spigot, then wiped the counter in slow, methodical strokes. "I didn't understand politics back then, either." She grinned at him, silently acknowledging their inside joke that she rarely knew what was happening in the world. "All I knew was that I was my family's only hope to end their suffering. For you see, in my village, there were no more rations. The livestock was gone. Every last pig was roasted. My family—along with everyone else in the village—was painfully malnourished."

Benfu looked at the crabs bobbing in the dishpan across the small room and felt the heat rush up his neck and into his cheeks. She saw where his eyes wandered and clucked her tongue. "That's right, Benfu.

No delicious recipes were made in our home, not unless you count boiled soups of wild herbs, or sometimes just tree leaves when herbs were not to be found. As for grain, it was only a treat to those who had valuables to trade for it, and as you know, there's not much to be called valuable in my past."

He studied her as she paused.

"First my mother tried to marry me off, but there was no man who'd take me with absolutely no dowry. So we took inventory of what I had to offer and realized that other than what used to be good looks," she smiled shyly, "I was the best cook in the village."

Benfu could believe that with no trouble. Cook was the envy of all his mother's friends, her skills proven at every dinner party, emphasized when one or another tried to woo her away with promises of a better salary, nicer living accommodations. But Benfu knew that Cook had another asset in addition to cooking.

She was loyal. And her story was mesmerizing.

"I walked for six days in the pouring rain, only stopping to sleep when I occasionally found a safe hole to climb into—a grove of trees, sometimes an empty shed. Once I even climbed onto a roof of an abandoned building when I was desperate. I came penniless with only a few bartered buns my mother poked into my bag to keep me from starving on the trip. Bartered with what, I never knew, but I owed it to my mother and the rest of my family to make it to Shanghai. And I did."

She looked at Benfu and he waited, eager to hear more. She'd told him more this time than she ever had.

"I came to this very street and knocked on every door, being turned away each time when they saw my soiled and wrinkled clothes. I felt so out of place. Most of the bigger houses were taken by the French families and they wanted only to hire pristine and well-spoken house help. Benfu, I couldn't even speak Shanghainese!"

That was news to Benfu. She sure spoke it fluently now. He couldn't imagine her ever speaking anything else.

"But just when I was about to give up, I spotted this house tucked in behind the bigger homes, the swaying leaves of the big willow tree making it look like a shady oasis in my storm of despair. Before I came through the courtyard, I went through the back alley and checked it out. There I saw Old Butler against the back of the house, perched on a stool with a bucket of acorns at his feet. But he wasn't awake. His chin was practically lying on his chest, he was so far gone with sleep. He wasn't much older than me, but he looked kind and that gave me the courage I needed to knock one more time."

She smiled and looked into the distance, as though seeing her young self as she had been that day. "Before I returned to the front door, I knelt in the alley and said a prayer. It was my last hope, this house. I had no food left and no prospects. With all I'd been through to get to Shanghai, I felt I was on the verge of failing my family."

Benfu was captivated. He couldn't deny he was shocked that his mother had hired someone so obviously destitute, and from the country. He wanted to hear more of how it had come about.

"I took my time coming back around and by the time I laid my knuckles against the rich mahogany door of this grand home, Old Butler had woken and moved inside. He answered the door and when I saw his face, before he could open his mouth, I burst out sobbing." She laughed once. "He looked around and pulled me inside—scared me, he did! Because I didn't yet have an ear for his dialect, I didn't understand at first what he was doing. Then I realized he was giving me a chance to clean up before presenting me to your mother. He even ran down the street and asked a girl he knew in another house for a clean smock. He came rushing back and I changed into it before my interview."

"How did you manage to get her to even give you a chance?" Benfu knew how obstinate his mother could be and could just see her turning Cook away based on her first impression.

"I didn't know until much later when I began to understand what everyone was saying, but Old Butler told her I was his cousin from a faraway province. There was already a cook here, but not a very good one. Old Butler had heard talk between your parents that they'd soon try to have a child, so he knew they'd need a nanny. He told her I had experience helping with the babies in my family, and he got me this job. Your mother gave it to me based solely on his recommendation, and later when I proved I was the better cook, I took over both jobs—nanny and the head of the kitchen. Then after you became grown, I took up the housekeeping. And your mother has always run a tight ship."

A snapshot of memories burst through Benfu's head. Cook rescuing him when he climbed the trees too high, and her soothing him from dreams that frightened him awake. He remembered something else, something he'd forgotten for years. Cook used to forgo sleeping in the room set aside for her and instead lay on a pallet beside his bed, always there when he needed something—a drink of water, another blanket, just a voice in the dark. He knew these things, yet now he felt shame that he'd never considered how she'd come to be his nanny and cook—that she'd left her family behind to care for his. How hard it must have been for her to walk into a house governed by someone as strong and strict as his mother.

"But was she kind to you at first?" Benfu had to ask.

For a moment Cook said nothing.

"That's enough talk, Benfu. You're breaking my concentration," she finally said, then went quiet.

They sat that way for a while, him watching her as she began to move faster, keeping her eyes on her busy hands and the next task.

Benfu sighed. With the story done, he felt the cloud of boredom settling back around his shoulders. He was also in an irritable mood because he'd once again gone to the park without finding the white-haired man. The envelope was safely hidden again, but just possessing it made Benfu nervous and he wished the man would show up to claim it.

"Do you ever go to the park, Cook?"

"Your mother expects dinner promptly at seven," she said as she smashed the ginger with the side of her cleaver, then added it to the hot wok of oil.

"Then let me help," Benfu said, holding his hands out in a plea for her to accept his assistance.

She gave him another discouraging look, then as the steam rose around her chubby face, she added the scallions to the wok. "You know you aren't allowed to do any kitchen work, m'lord," she teased, but beneath the humor in her voice, they both knew she was serious.

Benfu inhaled the spicy aroma, a scent that would always remind him of home and his baba. Crabs with ginger and scallions were his father's favorite meal, and were served at least weekly in their household. A luxury to be sure—one that today of all days made Benfu feel ashamed.

He ignored Cook's refusal and rose, walked around to the counter and quickly plucked each crab out of the dishpan and tossed it into the now-fiery-hot wok. When the last one was in, Cook added the rice wine and put the cover on, then went to beat the eggs that would be added as the last step before serving. She had so many years of practice that all the other side items were ready and waiting, covered to be kept warm as the last course was prepared. There was a time, long ago, that she let him help in the kitchen often. She would stand him on a chair and give him a spoon and bowl, set him to some small task as he made more work for her with his messes.

"Enough about me. You might as well tell me what has your lip hanging so low," Cook said, then set the bowl of beaten eggs aside.

Benfu returned to his stool and sat down. He heaved a heavy sigh but inside he was relieved he had her to talk to—someone he didn't have to follow formalities or etiquette with.

He waved his arm toward the pot of crabs. "Here we are eating like royalty while Pony Boy's family is struggling to just pay their rent and have rice to eat. Every night we have enough food to feed three families. It's embarrassing."

She gave him a sympathetic look. "But it's not your fault. These supplies come from your parents' purse, not your own."

Benfu sure felt like it was his fault. The guilt of his pampered lifestyle was burdening him more every day. In the weeks since Pony Boy's father had survived the heart attack, he'd only seen his friend a few times, but when he had, he'd begged him to take his weekly allowance to use toward the family bills. Pony Boy stubbornly refused, even though he was clearly exhausted from working so many hours to keep them afloat. Benfu felt like telling him to stuff his damned pride and accept help.

"You know, there are ways to help that they can't turn away," Cook said softly, her eyes on the door behind him.

That piqued Benfu's attention. "What ways?"

She nodded toward the wok. "If there just happened to be too many crabs cooked for one family to possibly eat before spoiling, and if they just happened to end up on Pony Boy's doorstep after dark, who's to say that they won't be taken in and enjoyed as a mysterious gift?"

Benfu felt a smile coming on.

Cook continued. "And if there just happened to be one extra bushel of corn sitting in the supply closet that ends up missing, I know one cook who would just happen to look the other way when making out the shopping list for the next day."

Her words finally sunk in.

He jumped from his stool and crossed the room quickly. Since the day he'd left her arms to go to school, he'd barely touched her, but this time, he grabbed her cheeks with both hands and pulled her face toward him, kissing her forehead with a squishy smack. When he let go, he laughed loudly at her shocked expression.

"Cook, you shouldn't be in a kitchen. You're much too smart. Maybe you should be running this country."

She backed away and swatted him with the towel that was around her neck. "Oh you. Get out of my kitchen before I have your hide."

Benfu could tell she liked the attention, as the bright spots in her cheeks spread until her entire face was blushing crimson.

"I'll be here an hour after dinner is served." He winked at her and made his way to the dining room, a satisfied smile on his face.

Two hours later, Benfu took the back streets to Pony Boy's house, carrying the huge basket of food that Cook had put together. It had taken him longer than usual to get out of the house, as his mother insisted on their routine in the library and he'd sat through her commentary about how Mao was improving China's relations with other countries. He'd been so bored he'd almost fallen asleep.

As he moved around couples out for their evening strolls, mothers with their babies, and the elderly shuffling around to take in the summer air, his muscles strained with the weight of the crab and ears of corn tucked into the bamboo basket. It also didn't help that Cook had added a half dozen egg custard cups before shooing him out of her kitchen, her finger to her lips to warn him not to speak. She'd promised to stay on duty later than usual to try to cover for him if Mother noticed him gone, but he had to hurry.

He finally turned the corner to Pony Boy's street and saw their house was lit up. He decided to sneak down the path to the front step and leave the basket. As he approached the house, his pulse accelerated.

He heard a door slam and behind him someone called out.

"*Ni hao,*" the woman's voice rang out. "How are you all doing over there?"

Benfu cringed. The neighbor thought he was Pony Boy. He didn't turn around, but he was aggravated because now there'd be a witness.

"I say," the voice called again, "Did you hear me?"

With only a few steps to go, the front door opened and Pony Boy peeked out.

"Benfu, what are you doing here?" he asked, then pointed to the basket. "What do you have?"

Before he could answer, the woman across the street called out her question again.

"We're doing fine," Pony Boy answered her, then opened the door wide for Benfu to come in. "Come on in before she shuffles across and fixes herself in the middle of our living room. She's the nosiest one on this street."

With no choice but to face Pony Boy's wrath at the charity he brought, Benfu entered the house.

The first thing he did was set the basket on the floor by the door. When he looked up, five curious faces stared back at him. Pony Boy's family was all gathered in the room and though it was small and sparse, Benfu felt a cozy warmth settle around him.

A bed had been set up in the middle of the room and on it Mei lay snuggling under a colorful but tattered quilt, tucked under the arm of her father.

"*Laoren.*" Benfu bowed once to show his respect. "How are you feeling?"

Pony Boy's father smiled weakly. He looked drawn and pale, and had lost a lot of weight since the last time Benfu had seen him. "I've been better. But I'm improving every day."

His wife rushed to Benfu and held her arms out for an embrace. Not sure what to do, Benfu just stood there. She stepped closer and wrapped her arms around him.

"Benfu, you've been such a good friend to Pony Boy. *Xie Xie.*"

He was speechless. He hadn't really been a good friend. What had he done? He'd tried—but honestly, Pony Boy was too proud and wouldn't let him do anything. It was so frustrating. His father was now basically an invalid, and Pony Boy wouldn't let Benfu take some of the pressure off him.

She stepped back and Benfu realized something else. His own mother had never hugged him like this woman did. He wondered why his own family didn't feel the need to show their love through touch and kind words. He'd been missing out for a long time. And he made a silent vow to himself—his own wife and children would never feel devoid of warmth. In his home, if he ever had one of his own, they'd be like Pony Boy's family.

Lixin stood and pointed at the basket. "I smell something good coming from there. Something with ginger. Scallions, too. What is it?"

"I—I—" He stumbled on the words and looked at Pony Boy, hopeful his gift would be accepted. "Cook sent you some crabs and corn."

Pony Boy sighed, then held his hand out to Benfu. "*Xie xie*, comrade. We aren't starving over here but a change from noodles or rice is much appreciated."

With a flurry, Pony Boy's mother soon had a tablecloth on their scarred wooden table, and all the food separated into five bowls.

Pony Boy grabbed his food and beckoned to Benfu to follow him, then he pushed out the door and onto the front stoop. He sat down and put the bowl on the concrete between his knees, picked up a crab and began prying it apart with his pocketknife.

"This is so kind, Benfu. But you shouldn't have. Really, we're fine." He used his sleeve to wipe at the juice that ran down his chin from the quick bite of corn.

Benfu pretended not to watch Pony Boy dig in as though he'd not eaten all day. "I know you're fine. Those were left over and were going to spoil. I thought—I mean, Cook thought—your brother and sister would like a treat."

Pony Boy had finally broken through the crab and had a mouth full of white meat, so he just nodded. They let the silence fall between them while he finished eating, then Pony Boy used the end of his shirt to wipe his face clean before he spoke.

"I'm sorry if you feel I've been pushing you away."

Benfu nodded once to acknowledge the apology. He didn't trust himself to speak. The truth was, his feelings were hurt. But men didn't admit things like that.

Pony Boy stuck his elbow in Benfu's side and laughed. "You should be with me on the route sometime. I see some crazy things out there."

"I'd like that," Benfu said, feeling a rush of hope. "I could even help you. How long are you going to cover for your father?"

Pony Boy shrugged. "I don't know. As long as it doesn't get out about his heart attack, I guess. It's a good thing he's built these friendships for so long. His route partner brings me the mailbag every morning. I deliver it and so far the managers don't know anything's amiss."

Benfu was impressed. They were pulling off quite an undercover feat with Pony Boy stepping into his father's job to keep his salary going. Since his father worked for the state, he'd probably still get part of his paycheck even though he wasn't working, but it took everything he made to keep their family afloat, so Benfu could see why they were pretending the man was still on duty. Thus far only a few of his comrades in the post office knew of his near-death experience, so hopefully the secret would keep.

"So you'll be fine?"

Pony Boy shrugged. "We're still short each month. Baba was working odd jobs in the evenings and on weekends to make ends meet. He didn't earn much but every bit was needed. But Mama said we'll get through this and when he is well, we'll pay off all of our overdue debts."

"When do you think he'll be able to go back to work?"

"I don't know. Right now he can barely make it to the outhouse. Most of the time he pees in a bottle. He can't even bathe himself." Pony Boy lowered his voice to almost a whisper. "He's like a baby."

"What about school?" Benfu was concerned. He'd thought Pony Boy would be returning to school in the fall.

"I'm done."

"What do you mean you're done? For the summer, right?"

Pony Boy slapped at a mosquito. "No, I mean done. We can't afford school, Benfu. What does it matter if I make it through one more year of high school? I can't possibly go to a university, even if by some miracle I pass the entrance exams."

Benfu couldn't imagine Pony Boy just giving up. "I'll keep helping you. I'll get you through it. We'll study for the exams together. But you have to at least try."

Pony Boy stood up, cradling his empty bowl. His voice lost all the warmth it'd held moments before. "You just don't get it, Benfu. My family is on the brink of disaster. It isn't like we're debating the cost of rice. You don't know what it's like to scrimp and try to decide what should be the most important thing to cover for the month. Food? Electricity? Heat for the winter? We have choices to make and school just can't be one of them any longer."

Benfu stood, too. "I do get it. I just don't know what to do about it. Don't be mad at me."

Pony Boy let out a long breath. "I'm not angry at you. I'm angry at the gods who decided to strike my father down and leave him sprawled on the pavement, clutching at life. I'm angry that it takes all we can do to keep a roof over our heads. I'm angry at the way class lines are drawn and the rich keep getting richer while the poor keep getting poorer. I'm just angry. Not at you—but there's got to be a change, Benfu. There has to be."

"What can we do?"

Pony Boy brought his voice back to a whisper. "It might be out of our hands, anyway. Father's comrades are hearing rumors coming down the pipeline from Beijing."

"What kind of rumors?"

"There's talk that soon the government might require one child from every family be sent away for reeducation."

"Sent where?"

"To the countryside. They say the city folk need to learn from the peasants and bring back what they've been taught," Pony Boy said. "It'll be hard labor, of that there's no doubt. If someone from our family has to go, it'll be me. I won't let them take Lixin. Thankfully, Mei is too young. But if I go, and my father still can't work, what will happen to my family? I can see how the farmers and lower class might be able to teach others about pulling together with hard work, but it's bad timing for me. With my luck, I'll be sent to Mongolia."

Benfu thought about how it would affect him for a second. He was an only child. Would he have to go? Would that mean he couldn't attend music school? He pushed the selfish thought aside. He needed to reassure Pony Boy. "Maybe it's all rumors, something set up to cause controversy among the people. You won't be going anywhere, Pony Boy."

Pony Boy opened the door, then paused. "Go home, Benfu. Please thank Cook for me and my family. Things are changing fast and there's not much more that can be done by the people. Now's his chance—only Chairman Mao can change our fate now."

He went into the house and shut the door behind him, leaving Benfu staring at the scarred wood. He waited for a moment before turning to leave.

Benfu had a feeling that everything was about to change. And Pony Boy was wrong. Chairman Mao wasn't the country's savior.

Or was he?

PART TWO

The Chaos

Chapter Eight

Benfu was as surprised as anyone when a broadcast on the radio encouraged all to report to the main square in Shanghai for what was being called "an announcement of historical magnitude to beat all announcements." He wasn't sure what that could mean, but he slipped outside and joined many from his lane as they emerged out of their homes and through the streets, into the sea of people all moving in the same direction. Others around him found comrades to walk with, talk with, and to make the interruption of their usually ordinary day more enjoyable.

Benfu walked surrounded by thousands, but felt alone.

At the People's Square, the chattering had risen to a phenomenal level. The crowd sounded like a swarm of bees inching closer and closer, and if the officials didn't give them what they wanted, they might just turn vicious. He looked around, hoping for a friendly face, but saw no one he knew in the closely packed crowd.

In the middle of the plaza was a crudely constructed stage complete with a podium, large speakers, and a life-sized portrait of Chairman Mao. Benfu studied the solemn face as it rippled in the breeze, feeling Mao's eyes upon him, always watching and waiting for someone to step out of place. To the side of the stage, a large object was covered with a huge gray tarp. Ropes were tied around it, knotted in several places to secure it from any prying fingers.

Benfu was glad for the diversion, for the long days without Pony Boy had become barely tolerable. It wasn't that he had no other friends. He did, but no one who understood him like Pony Boy—no one with whom he felt as comfortable speaking his mind and discussing the changes happening around them. Benfu knew he was just going through the motions now—his summer filled with endless days of studying for next year's courses and practicing his music. His heart wasn't in it, but still, he did it. He had to if he wanted a chance at being accepted into the music school. And Pony Boy had made him solemnly swear that he would not give up on his dream.

Finally, a man in a fine suit stepped onto the stage, followed by a dozen others who lined up behind him. He tapped at the microphone crudely, and kept tapping until the crowd settled down to a low hum, eager to hear his proclamation.

Two younger men, dressed in the simple faded blue pants and shirts that most wore these days, came into view, carrying a large scroll hooked to two poles. One of the men unhooked the sides and the other unfurled one of the largest flags that Benfu had ever seen. When the crowd saw the deep red flag, they erupted with approval and those who owned copies of Mao's book of quotations waved them in the air, creating a swirl of red within the sea of dark heads.

The suited man tapped at the microphone again and the noise of the crowd slowly died down until it resembled the same swarm of bees now at a low humming buzz. The man looked around the square, then smiled. He pointed at the flag. "This is our national flag! The red background represents the revolution and the largest star is the Communist Party. The smaller stars are the people, protected by the party.

"Today is a historic day across China," he said. "I represent the Communist Party of China Central Committee, and we have given full approval and endorsement of what I am about to tell you."

The buzzing died down, the people anxious to hear what was so important for such a show.

The man paused, then appeared to wipe a tear from his eye before he looked up and bellowed out his announcement. "Today our beloved Chairman Mao has declared the beginning of a new China!" He snapped his fingers and two of the men behind him jumped from the stage and went to the wrapped object. They used pocketknives to cut the ropes, letting the material fall to the ground to unveil a huge bronze statue of Chairman Mao.

Benfu almost held his ears at the roar of approval from the crowd.

The man took a rolled sheet of paper from his pocket and carefully unwound it. He held the paper in the air until the people quieted enough for him to speak. "I have a new directive from our leader," he began, "and in it he urges you to help him launch the Great Proletarian Cultural Revolution."

More applause, whistles, and cheers from the crowd. The man held his hand up.

"We, the people, need to take a hard line and a new leap forward toward a redder China. Together, we will purge the poisonous weeds and expose the bourgeois rightists who march on the capitalist road."

Benfu listened, but he wasn't sure whom they were referring to. *Who were the so-called bourgeois rightists? How were they going to find and expose them?*

"Today starts a new effort to fulfill our economic goals as a country," he continued, now yelling in order to be heard over the crowd. "We will revitalize our revolutionary atmosphere—together, with Chairman Mao's leadership."

He pulled a red book from his pocket and held it up. "Within the next eighteen months there will be thirty-five million copies of this inspiring book printed and passed out to every man and woman. We will study and apply Mao's thoughts and WE WILL BE A BETTER CHINA!"

He roared the last few words, and this time, Benfu did cover his ears. Around him the people erupted. Some danced in the square, others embraced, many were crying.

A chant began around him and escalated until it sounded as though everyone in the world had chimed in. *"Long live Chairman Mao! Long live Chairman Mao! Long live Chairman Mao!"*

Benfu turned and pushed his way through the crowd, looking for a way out.

He felt the sweat dripping into his eyes and his heart thumping—why wasn't he as joyful as everyone else? He was hopeful—he really was. If Chairman Mao could turn around their country, and his main goal was to support the people and bring down corrupt officials, then Benfu could—and would—alter his thinking and be supportive.

At least he would try.

As he left the square, leaflets declaring Mao's new goals rained down around him. He heard them talking about right-wingers receiving severe punishment but being given chances to reform through self-criticisms.

He wasn't sure what a self-criticism was, but something told him he'd soon be hearing more about it. For now, though, he needed to get home.

Far behind him, the sounds of the people singing the now-familiar song, "The East is Red," rang out. Benfu forced himself to mouth the words as he walked past one stranger after another, careful to show his own dedication in making China the most successful country in the world. Only one question lingered in his mind as he made his way home. If Chairman Mao was their new savior, why hadn't he been elected President and Leader Number One? There were still men who held a higher status than he. Something told Benfu that not everyone was as big a supporter of Mao Zedong as they were being led to believe.

He wondered if Pony Boy had heard the announcement. Perhaps the new directives being passed down each day would help his family. Like Mao, they were from a poorer class. Didn't that mean they were favored now?

He wondered where his parents were and if they had heard the latest news. His mother's constantly worried face came to mind.

He picked up the pace.

He needed to hurry home.

"Benfu, come on. You have to see to your mother," Cook said. She'd been waiting near the back door, watching for him to come home. Benfu could tell with one look that Mother was at it again, probably claiming Cook hadn't shined the floors enough or that their dinner wasn't being prepared fast enough. One never knew what she'd find to be upset about, but they always knew it'd be something. It was simple. His mother expected perfection.

Or—he thought suddenly—she was spouting off more of her recent paranoia and frightening Cook with predictions of doom.

"What is it?"

Cook wrung her hands. "I don't know. She's ranting about snakes and weeds, and tried to tell me that we might be under suspicion, but she won't say for what. Old Butler isn't here to help me calm her like he usually does. What is she talking about?"

Benfu realized that Cook probably didn't know what was happening. He had turned the radio off when he left, and she likely hadn't left the house all day. Old Butler was her main source of information, but he was usually gone at this time, headed to the university to bring Baba home. The look on Cook's face confirmed that she was completely in the dark about the monumental announcements going on around the city.

"Chairman Mao has released a new directive and this one is big. I'll tell you about it after I tend to her." He quickly moved through the back gate and slipped into the house.

"*Hao de*, she's in the library. Please calm her down; she's scaring me more than usual."

Benfu went to his father's study and saw that Cook was right. Mother was like a possessed woman. He found her bent over a box as she wrapped the miniature jade water buffalo that had been on display in the same place since Benfu was a baby. As she worked she mumbled to herself and he strained to hear her words.

"People in the streets—chanting, singing, even marching! It's happening, it's here now."

"Mother, what are you doing with those?" he asked, alarmed that she would move Baba's most prized possessions without him there to supervise. He looked at the cubbyholes, relieved to see that she hadn't touched the antique scrolls of poems or the books of literature.

She continued packing, her words as quick as her hands. "I'm putting these away. They're worth a lot of money and are to be passed down to you, and then your firstborn son. We don't know what is going to happen now. Shanghai is in an uproar—things are changing, just like I told you was going to happen!" She placed the wrapped buffalo in the box, then plucked a green-and-brown jade elephant from the shelf and began wrapping it. "That buffalo is from the sixteenth century and the elephant from the seventeenth. I'm not taking any chances. They'll be shipped to my aunt in Hong Kong for safekeeping."

Benfu shook his head. He wasn't even married and already she was making mention of his first son? "Mother, don't you think you're being a bit irrational? What if something happens to those on the way to Hong Kong? They could be broken, or even stolen. Baba would be devastated. Aren't they safer here with us? I'm sure it will be fine."

She shook her head. "No, they won't be safer here. This city will be turned upside down to look for hidden enemies now. The committee's representatives will go house to house if they have to."

He saw that Cook had followed him and was leaning against the wall in the hallway, waiting to see if he needed her help. He tried to wave her away.

"What do you mean, *hidden enemies?*" Benfu said, the words spoken at the square coming back to him. Didn't she know that even speaking about some invisible enemy made them both sound insane?

"Enemies—counterrevolutionaries, rightists, anyone who dares to speak against this revolution that Chairman Mao has launched." She tucked the elephant in the small box, then began on the horse that Benfu had made gallop across the bookshelves on many occasions when he was a child.

Benfu felt his old normal slipping away, one jade animal at a time, and wished for things to go back to the way they had been. He also wished for his father—a composed voice to help calm the moment of irrationality.

"Mother, where is Ba?"

She looked toward the ceiling, then rolled her eyes. "He stayed at the university to attend a high-level staff meeting. One I'm not important enough to be invited to. They're probably talking about how to handle those who try to stop the revolution."

"Mother, listen to me," he said, ignoring her suddenly bitter tone. His father's higher level of seniority was something that always made her angry. Benfu wished she'd for once just be proud of Ba and all he'd accomplished.

She turned, giving him her attention. He saw confusion and fear in her eyes.

He kept his tone confident. "No one is going to stop anything. I was at the People's Square and heard the announcement. The people are ecstatic! There was singing and dancing; they were even embracing one another. Isn't this what you wanted? You've said that Chairman Mao is the answer to China's problems. Now the country is agreeing with you. So you need to settle down."

Mother heaved a long sigh, then sat down on his father's chair. She held the half-wrapped horse in her hands, staring down at it. "You're right, son. I'm sorry. It's just that I've been hearing a lot of rumors around the university. I suppose I'm silly for believing them. I'm sure everything will be fine."

He hesitated to believe her sudden about-face, but on second look, she did appear calmer. He looked at her eyes and saw they weren't flashing as they had been before. Over her head, he nodded once to Cook, who was still hovering in the hall. At his signal that all was well again, she slipped away toward the kitchen, the relief evident in her quick shuffle back to where she felt safest.

"Silly isn't a word I'd ever use to describe you," he said. It would be more along the lines of strict, worrisome, or even meddling. But never silly. "Sit back and put your feet up. I'll ask Cook to bring you some tea."

He was rewarded with a small smile. "*Hao de*, and if you are sure we'll be fine, I'll keep Ba's collection here in Shanghai."

He went to his mother and took the horse from her, setting it down on top of the other wrapped animals. He bent in front of her and took her hands. "Please, Mother. Just try to enjoy this day. It's the beginning of a new China—that's what everyone is saying. So let's have faith in our leaders." He spoke the words he thought she wanted—and needed— to hear, but Benfu didn't really feel them. He had hope though, hope that all would be as he said and they would soon be just as joyous as those in the streets.

Chapter Nine

Pony Boy pulled the last two pieces of mail from his bag. He looked down at the name on the first envelope and turned the corner. *Wang Zi*, it read. For such an old man, he sure got a lot of mail. And whoever was sending the letters had quite the flowery way of writing their characters.

It had to be a woman.

It was amusing how Wang Zi was always waiting at the gate, eager for another letter. Pony Boy had to admit, he was a debonair old man. Always wearing freshly starched shirts, his hair kept oiled and combed to the side to cover his balding head, stylish round spectacles hanging around his neck. When he smiled, it was plain to see the man was proud to still have his teeth at his late age.

Could the letters be from an admirer? Maybe someone younger? A mistress?

He laughed. Like his father, the curiosities of what was in the correspondence between strangers now filled his thoughts as he walked house to house, *hutong* to *hutong*. By now, most of the people he brought mail to knew he was filling in for his father and were eager to help keep their secret. They thought him such a loyal and dedicated son, and maybe he was, but he couldn't help feeling like an imposter sometimes. Usually he felt that way on the days that he'd rather be hiking through the backstreets with his camera, instead of his mailbag.

He only had one more street and he'd be done for the day—or at least done delivering mail. In the weeks since he'd taken over his father's route, he'd become one of the fastest carriers. His father was improving, but it was a painstakingly slow recovery. Just the night before he'd left their courtyard for the first time, venturing out into the lane and walking several meters before needing to sit down. He was going to make it—but what his future would consist of was anyone's guess, which meant the entire family's future was in limbo.

Pony Boy missed the days when he hadn't carried so much of a burden on his shoulders. Thankfully his mother still worked, but her position in the shoe factory paid only a small part of what was needed to keep a family of five afloat. And they were doing it, but barely. Pony Boy got a sick feeling when he thought of the upcoming winter when they'd need to buy coal to stay warm. He prayed his father was fully recuperated by then.

He looked up to see Wang Zi waiting at the end of the lane, leaning on his gate, as usual. Pony Boy hurried, eager to give the man the envelope that would most likely be his highlight of the week.

When he did that, he'd then report to his new position cleaning the public toilets on one specific street. No one—especially Benfu—knew of his latest endeavor and he hoped it stayed that way. His family thought he was cleaning streets. Pony Boy would have rather had a job sweeping the many walkways and curbs, but those jobs were taken by the elderly ladies walking around with their thick bamboo brooms.

So he was left with the toilets.

He was lucky the toilets at the main People's Square even had a night shift position open. It was a putrid and thankless job, but it brought in a few more coins.

He wasn't the only one exhausted, either. Everyone in their family contributed and he thought Lixin had taken on too much. But without his brother to do the cooking, cleaning, and taking care of their father and sister, Pony Boy couldn't juggle the two jobs.

At least his mother was home in the evenings to take over some of the caretaking. She moved slowly and it was obvious that she was drained. This was their life now, but it wouldn't be that way forever. His father was improving. He'd get back to work one day. Then all could go back to the way it was.

"*Zao,*" Wang Zi called out an afternoon greeting.

Pony Boy returned it and held the letter up, waving it back and forth. That was what the man wanted to know, after all, if he had any mail.

Wang Zi smiled broadly, nodding his head up and down. He opened his gate and briskly met Pony Boy halfway.

Pony Boy handed him the letter and the man held it up, then put his spectacles on. He read the front and when he recognized the handwriting, held it to his chest. He looked back at Pony Boy, pushing the spectacles higher on his nose.

"And your father? How is he today?"

"He's good, Laoren. He took a long walk yesterday. Well—long for him," Pony Boy said, leaving out the fact that the walk had left his father completely depleted for the rest of the evening.

"Tell him we can't wait to see him back on the route," Wang Zi said, then quickly turned and headed back toward his own house, already using a small penknife to neatly slice open his envelope as he walked.

"Will do," Pony Boy called out.

He felt the rumble of his stomach before he heard it. He hadn't eaten since breakfast that morning and he sure didn't have the money to visit a street vendor before his next position. He looked down at the last envelope in his hand.

Widow Chou.

And it appeared to be a bill. He hated delivering the bills most of all. He hoped Widow Chou was not at home, or maybe napping.

He approached the house and quietly swung open the gate. It usually creaked, but the gods were looking out for him because today it didn't make a sound. He crept toward the box that hung on the porch post. With one step left to go, the front door opened and there she stood. All four foot something of her, decked out in a flowery housecoat and curlers in her gray hair. A tiny yellow bird perched on her shoulder.

"Pony Boy, you're late," she scolded. "Pao Pao is fretting for you."

He shook his head, about to argue but thought better of it. He remembered he had a bill for her. "Sorry, Widow Chou. Tomorrow I'll be on time," he said. Now that he'd been caught, he'd have to go in and see Pao Pao, and the rest of the Widow Chou's family.

Her finely feathered family.

She pointed her finger at him. "I think you were trying to be a little sneaky. I shouldn't give you what I spent all morning making for you, but I will, just because you're such a good boy. But you save some for your father and that sweet little girl, you hear me?"

Pony Boy felt his hope rising. Food? Yes! He would have something to tide him over until he could get home that night! "*Dui*, Widow Chou, whatever you say."

"Of course, whatever I say. You know, I was the one to find your father. I'll never be able to erase that vision of him slumping over my gate. I thought he was dead! Anyway, I'm glad he's not."

"Me too, Widow Chou," Pony Boy answered obediently.

"I know you need to hurry along but before I give you the treats, you come in and say hello." She turned and with one arm outstretched to give her balance, she seemed to flutter more than walk as she disappeared inside the house, her voice trailing away.

He hesitated and she called out again for him to come in and shut the door before one of her birds got out. He stepped in and shut the door behind him. His arrival was met with a sudden cacophony of greetings—whistles, chirps, and even one random but curiously human-sounding *ni hao* from the kingpin of the room, Duo Duo.

Around the room at least a dozen wicker or bamboo birdcages were sitting or hanging from chains suspended from the ceiling. The cages were beautiful, most of them mimicking in miniature the style of the traditional pagodas in and around China. Surprisingly, nothing smelled. Widow Chou kept her house, the cages, and even the birds meticulously clean. She had the time and after all, they were her whole life. Every bird was named and each day she peppered him with tidbits about their lives.

He hurried over to Pao Pao's cage and stuck his finger through, making sure to give the bird attention before Widow Chou accused him of ignoring it. It was just a lark, but with its bright yellow bib that contrasted against its brown back, Pony Boy thought it a handsome bird. She tilted her head to look at him, as if waiting for him to speak to her, then he heard the widow returning.

"No morning walk today for Pao Pao?" he asked.

"I took Mynah and Pao Pao was jealous. She might be pretty, but she's a spoiled little biddy. If she'd conquer the thirteen sounds of a lark—in order—I'd take her more often so that I could show her off, but she's got a ways to go. She's stubborn." She handed him a paper bag spotted with wet marks. It smelled delicious and Pony Boy had to fight the urge to dig into it right then and there.

"*Xie xie*, Widow Chou. You shouldn't have," he said, but was glad she did.

"Pssh. Well yes, of course I should have, so I did. Your baba has carried my mail to me every day for the last thirty years, even in snowdrifts as high as your waist and rain that would drown a Peking duck. I think I can give up some of my precious sugar to make a few sizzling caramelized apples for him and his family. There's one for each of you in there. Don't you be selfish and eat what doesn't belong to you."

"I won't, I promise. Now I'd better run." He was out the door and on the porch, hoping to get away before she remembered what he was supposed to be there for. But she caught him as he scaled the last step with a leap.

"Wait. What about my mail? Anything for me today?" She peeked out the door and looked at his satchel, her face hopeful.

Pony Boy shook his head. He'd already shoved the bill back into his mailbag. It could wait. He wasn't going to reward her kindness with a notice of taxes due. He backed out of her courtyard, his mouth already watering. He knew he wouldn't make it off her street before his apple found its way into his belly.

Two hours later, the apple was nothing but a faint memory, the juices now having soured in his mouth as the others taunted him from their safe place in the bottom of his bag. The sweet taste that had lingered briefly on his tongue had been rubbed out mostly by the more than dozen barrels of human waste he'd carried from the toilets and dumped into the waiting truck. It had been the busiest night since he'd taken the job. The People's Square was still packed with people who had lingered after the announcement of Mao's Cultural Revolution from earlier in the afternoon. It was like a circus now, people laughing and singing, exalting his name and reading from the red book.

Pony Boy knew exactly what they were up to because he'd easily heard them from where he worked a street over. When the final word was given and the papers of printed propaganda rained down, the crowd had gone almost manic with excitement, fighting for scraps of what would most likely be treasured memorabilia from an historic day. Pony Boy had grabbed one before he'd headed back to the toilets, afraid his absence would be noticed. He shouldn't have worried, though. As soon as he returned, he'd seen the lucky farmer chosen to take away the night's load was sleeping behind the wheel of his truck, parked against the curb, his unmoving body proof of his unwillingness to help Pony Boy with the dirty job to get it done quicker. Frustrated, Pony Boy felt like opening his door and setting one heaping bucket right beside the man to teach him some compassion, but he knew he'd lose his job for the slightest sign of rebellion.

He tucked his head into an emptied stall and saw his short absence had left him falling behind in the battle of the onslaught of feces. He heaved a sigh of resignation and went back to work. The lines were forming at every door and he needed to hurry. As one man came out of the next stall, he peeked in and saw that yes, he needed to do a cleanup on it, too. Why people couldn't hit the hole, he didn't know. He blocked the next patron and moved inside, quickly cleaning the mess, then carrying and dumping the bucket into the truck bed.

He headed back to the next stall. Even in his current circumstances, he couldn't help but feel a touch of excitement about Mao's proclamation. He'd only had time to read the highlights of the paper he'd picked up and couldn't wait to read it in its entirety later.

It had said Mao wanted *"a purging of those who followed the path of capitalism."* What that meant exactly, Pony Boy wasn't totally sure. He did know that Chairman Mao had always drawn a line in the sand between the rich and the poor, the educated and the illiterate, the uppers and the lowers. He'd come from an impoverished background himself. Maybe that was why he felt such a respect for the man. He'd raised himself up by his bootstraps—just like Pony Boy was doing. People like him, and Chairman Mao, didn't give in because of their meager beginnings. They just worked harder and longer than everyone else. And one day, he hoped to be able to say it was all worth it.

He used the rag tucked into his pocket to scrub a brown spot from the wall, wondering again how people did such gymnastic moves with their bowel movements. When he was finished, he went on to the next one. It wasn't so bad, the floor wasn't that dirty, but the bucket did need to be switched out. He lifted the wooden frame, pulled out the bucket and exchanged it for an empty one. Backing out of that stall, he startled when a woman yelled out.

"Dui bu qi," he apologized, turning around to see the woman he'd almost trampled.

Suddenly he stopped. It wasn't a woman, but a girl. And for the first time in his life, Pony Boy was struck speechless. She was tall, at least up to his eyebrows and that was saying a lot, as he was the tallest in his class. His gaze followed the length of her hair, as dark as midnight and shinier than drops of rain streaming down a windowpane. Almond-shaped eyes, brown as those of a baby deer, peeked out from under the straight fringe of bangs.

She stared back at him, waiting for him to say something, or move, or—or anything but stand there in the way. Finally she smiled softly, taking pity on his moment of awkwardness, and with that one small gesture he felt his heart lurch in his chest. He was sure she heard it beating, for how could she not? It rang out like a drum, chanting *she's so pretty, she's so pretty, she's so pretty . . .*

He wanted to die.

Here was the most beautiful girl he'd ever seen and he was standing there looking like an idiot, holding a wet mop and a bucket of shit.

She looked crisp and clean, like she'd never touched a turd in her life.

He almost wept with the unfairness of it all.

"It's fine," she finally said, breaking the awkward moment. "I was waiting for you to finish so I could use the cleanest one."

He still couldn't speak, but he held open the door, offering her entrance without using the usual required coin. When she stepped in, she grabbed the handle, her eyes twinkling with amusement as she closed the door.

With her finally out of his sight, Pony Boy's senses returned. He ignored the lines of others waiting for him to clean each mess. Instead, he dropped the mop, then set the bucket down on the ground. He said a quick prayer that the lazy driver wouldn't pick this minute out of all others to finally waken and want to help. He ran to the spigot, figuring he had maybe two minutes, turned it on and washed his hands. Then he cupped water and poured it over his head, pushing his hair back and using his fingers to reposition the long lock over his forehead.

He turned around, wondering what else he could do. He remembered his school shirt still wadded in his satchel, probably wrinkled from weeks of being ignored, but it was clean. Or at least cleaner than what he was wearing.

A click sounded from the other side and he knew she was about to come out, then walk out of his life forever. Then he realized something else.

Forever was a long time.

He couldn't let it happen. Grabbing his satchel from his hiding place in the tree, he almost ran to the front of the stalls, tore his dirty shirt over his head, slipped on the clean one, then took something else from the bag.

He leaned on a lamppost, attempting to appear calm and collected, though his heart was beating out of his chest. One deep breath. Two.

The door opened.

When she stepped out he was waiting, holding one of Widow Chou's caramelized apples in the palm of his shaking hand, extending it to her like a gift.

Chapter Ten

Before Benfu knew it, summer ended and school was back in session. However, it was a school term like none he'd ever known. Everything had changed. Today it felt like the hours were dragging on indefinitely as he stood in line, three away from his turn. He didn't want to reach the front, didn't want to compete against others who cared more deeply about the distance thrown than he did.

Seconds passed and he was two away.

He stepped forward.

One away.

His turn.

He sighed in frustration, then picked up the wooden hand grenade. He gave it a good toss and watched as it fell short. The instructor turned to him, the red hue already rising from his thin neck and coloring his face and ears to match. "What are you doing? That could mean death to you in one instant of nonchalant tossing, don't you understand that?"

"Yes, if this were a real situation. But we are not *really* at war," Benfu answered.

"But we *could be* any day. That is the point, Zheng. And who told you to talk back to me?"

Benfu turned his eyes to the ground, biting his tongue to keep from having more trouble heaped on his shoulders. The students around him had quieted, so he knew everyone had witnessed his humiliation. His teacher was livid but Benfu felt nothing but frustration. The man had asked a question, and he answered it.

"So pick up another and this time, make it count," the gym teacher screamed into his face.

White-painted stakes were set out at different intervals on the barren sports field behind the school—the same field that only a year before was filled with healthy, lush green grass that was a pleasure to walk or run on. But then Mao had decided grass was bourgeois and flowers were poisonous weeds to the soul, and should be removed. Coincidentally the remodel came about the same time schools across the country were ordered to begin training students in case they were invaded by foreign devils. So all the classrooms had taken turns, spending weeks of their daily physical fitness period on their knees, pulling and yanking at the grass and stubborn roots until nothing remained but the dirt on the ground and the calluses and cuts on their fingers. Now it was nothing but an ugly field used in their nationwide quest to be stronger, fitter, and more ready for the unexpected than any other nation.

Benfu stepped closer to the line and plucked another wooden chunk from the bucket. He pulled his arm back and threw the grenade as hard as he could, then stood still, watching it fly through the air. He held his breath, hoping this time, his grenade would sail the farthest of all those thrown.

It did.

He let out a sigh of relief just as he felt his instructor's heavy slap of congratulations hit his back. "You did it, Benfu! I knew you could."

Benfu remembered the first few times he'd thrown the grenade. Just like a few minutes before, he'd tried to be careful with his arm, thinking only of the repercussions of playing the violin with a sprained or torn muscle. But when the throws had fallen short, he'd been heckled by his classmates. *"You are not loyal to China!"* they'd called out, along with, *"The American imperialists must be your comrades!"*

Now that his mark was as competitive as some of the other athletes, Benfu hoped the taunting was over. School was hard enough without his peers turning on him. These days it felt less like an education and more like indoctrination. Their class periods were filled with constant self-examinations and criticisms—directives from Chairman Mao and his goal for a new China.

He looked at his watch. Two more hours and he'd be free. He was going to Pony Boy's house after school, and he couldn't wait to tell him that most of their classes had been cut in half to make time for not only the mandatory swimming, but also running, high jumping, and working on upper-body strength by using the parallel bars. It was a strange new school life and one that most of the students were thrilled with, but quietly, Benfu wished for the days when they held long debates and discussed history, even performed interesting science experiments.

The instructor's voice shook Benfu back to the present.

"Three rounds on the field, then return to your afternoon classes," he barked, then turned and began walking back to the school building.

Afternoon classes. *Aiya, more like afternoon brainwashing,* Benfu thought to himself as he took off running. Though he could've pulled ahead, he smoothly moved into the middle of the pack, just where he wanted to be. He had no urge to stand out, or to fall behind and be heckled for being slow. Blending in was a safer choice these days, especially since it felt as though he was the only one doubting the revolution.

As if on cue, the chanting began and he obediently joined in. *"Long live Chairman Mao!"* they called as they ran. *"Long live the Red Sun!"*

Together they ran and together they chanted. One body, one mind. Or at least that's what it felt like. Where was the individualism? The freedom of thought? Were they nothing but a bunch of robots?

Inwardly, he hoped that maybe he was wrong, and everyone else was right. A stronger nation was what they needed, and if Chairman

Mao could make that happen in his so-called revolution, then who was he to try to defame him or stand in his way?

Benfu made a silent oath to try harder to understand their leader. He would support him and learn all there was to know about him. When he'd absorbed all the information he could find, he would then consider that perhaps his gut instinct had been mistaken.

From now on, he would try to support Chairman Mao.

Pony Boy would be pleased.

As usual, the hours flew by while he visited with Pony Boy's family, and Benfu enjoyed every minute of the homey, comfortable setting. When it finally appeared that everyone was starting to get sleepy and settle in for the night, he stood. "I should go."

"No, don't go yet," Mrs. Wei said from the rocking chair where she held a soundly sleeping Mei in her lap, her limbs wrapped around her mother like a baby monkey.

"Stay for a little longer, Benfu," Pony Boy said.

Benfu returned to his seat. He wasn't ready to leave anyway. He'd come empty-handed this time, following orders not to bring them any more charity. It was probably a good thing, too, as news of tighter rations was coming down the grapevine and Cook had already begun inventing ways to make their supplies of oil and flour last longer. The last thing they needed was for his mother to catch them using their rationed supplies for another family.

"Are you really getting married, Benfu?" Lixin asked, breaking the silence.

Everyone in the room hushed, then Pony Boy's mother gave Lixin a scolding look. "Don't be rude, son."

Lixin's face turned scarlet. *"Dui bu qi,"* he apologized in a muffled mumble.

Benfu waved his hand in the air. Thus far he'd avoided conversation about Juan Hui to Pony Boy's family, but he knew he couldn't escape it forever. "No, it's fine, really. I don't mind his questions. I'm officially engaged, but I don't plan on marrying for a few years yet. I have to finish school."

He expected Pony Boy to say something sarcastic and was surprised to see he remained quiet, his eyes wandering to the door every few minutes as if he were expecting someone.

"Did you know that Chairman Mao got married when he was only fourteen?" Lixin said.

Pony Boy's father sat up straighter in bed. "Who told you that?"

"It's true. I told him," Mrs. Wei said, her voice soothing and slow, matching the rocking of her chair. "His parents married him off to his cousin who was several years older than he. But they never even lived together and she died when she was twenty-one."

"How did she die?" Benfu asked.

Mrs. Wei situated Mei on her lap and shrugged. "I'm not sure. But then he married the daughter of his teacher and she gave him several sons before she was executed by Kuomintang forces."

"Why was she killed?" Benfu asked, intrigued. After all they'd studied in school about Chairman Mao, details of his private affairs was something they'd never touched on.

"Because they wanted her to renounce Chairman Mao and communism and she refused. For that, she lost her head," Mama whispered as she held her hands over Mei's ears. "Then her youngest son died a year later from some sort of illness, but I think he couldn't live without his mother."

Pony Boy's father snorted. "Sounds to me like being married to Chairman Mao brought them bad luck. The man is a remarkable leader, I'll give him that, but he has a hard time keeping a wife."

"It sounds like his enemies went after his wives to punish him," Pony Boy said.

Benfu leaned back in his chair. He loved listening to them talk back and forth, each giving to the conversation and respected for their input, unlike his home where if he didn't agree with his mother she'd fly off the handle, and his father mostly kept his thoughts to himself.

"His next wife was the one who really suffered," Mrs. Wei said. "She fell in love with Mao and even accompanied him on the Long March. She was the most loyal, giving him five daughters in their nine years of marriage before she fell ill and was sent to live out her days far from home, committed to a mental hospital in Russia. After she was diagnosed as mentally ill, Mao shunned her and the story goes that she died alone, without even her daughters near to comfort her."

Mama fell quiet and stroked Mei's hair. No one said anything. It was such a sad tale for a woman they didn't even know. Benfu thought of his mother and how sometimes he felt she'd be a candidate for a sanatorium, then he pushed the thought aside. He'd never do that to her.

"But the biggest scandal was when Mao met his current wife, Jiang Qing," Mrs. Wei said, her voice hushed. "He was still married to his latest wife, but the party granted him a divorce so he could marry Jiang Qing. People say that he was mesmerized by her beauty and the fact that she was an actress. If you ask me, she hypnotized him with her reputation of being so worldly."

"So that's why she's so interested in the arts," Benfu said. "Since she's married to Mao, she's probably not allowed to act any longer, so she's found another way to stay involved."

Mrs. Wei shrugged. "Maybe so."

Benfu stood and went to the door. He hated to leave, but it was getting quite late. "I should get back home. My parents will be worried."

Pony Boy joined him and after Benfu bid everyone good-bye, they walked outside. When the door shut behind them, Pony Boy leaned in to whisper, "Benfu, I've been waiting all night to tell you something. I've met a girl."

He turned and saw Pony Boy's grin that went from ear to ear. "What girl? Where?"

"You have to meet her, Benfu. You'll not believe your eyes. I can't even see why she's talking to me." Pony Boy gushed on and on, skimming over first one detail and then another, his words racing against each other to describe their first meeting and then the flawlessness of the girl's face, hair, and, surprisingly—even her intelligence.

"How long has this been going on?" Benfu asked, surprised that Pony Boy had kept such a secret from him.

"I saw her nearly every day over the summer."

The grin that remained on Pony Boy's face made it clear that he was smitten. Benfu was worried. Pony Boy had never been interested in *just one girl*.

"Take it easy, friend. Slow down. I thought you never wanted to get serious with anyone?"

Pony Boy shrugged. "That was before."

"Before what?" Benfu asked.

Pony Boy crossed his arms and smiled again. "Before the gods sent me the perfect one."

Benfu thought of Juan Hui and wondered why he hadn't been as excited as Pony Boy when he'd met her. She was a great match. Pretty and very smart. All the same attributes that Pony Boy's girl had, but obviously something was missing because he certainly wasn't that thrilled. More than anything, he felt an enormous pressure when he was around her. Not only to her as his future wife, but she was a constant reminder that he was his parents' only hope to continue the family name.

They expected too much.

On that note, he stepped off the porch. "Gotta run but you can tell me all about her the next time—if you're still infatuated with her, that is. I suspect that this will pass before I see you again, comrade."

Pony Boy gave him a short wave good-bye, then called out, "Then you don't know me as well as you think you do, Benfu. She's the one."

He turned and disappeared back into the house and Benfu trotted to the street. He needed to hurry home, but now he'd have a faceless girl on his mind. He couldn't imagine what female had captured the rogue heart of his best friend, but she had to be something. He laughed to himself as he remembered Pony Boy's love-struck look, but Benfu was confident that this girl was only the first in what would be many future conquests.

Chapter Eleven

Pony Boy couldn't stop thinking of her.

Zu Wren.

Or just Wren, as she'd told him to drop the formality of her family name, something unusual for simple acquaintances. That said a lot to him, that maybe what he felt for her wasn't one-sided. That just possibly, fate had smiled down on him and she felt the same. He tried not to stare as she pulled the brilliant red berries from the tree and dropped them into her small bag. Every so often she paused to bite into one, closing her eyes as the juice dribbled over her lips. It was excruciating to watch, as he wanted to be the juice, but he couldn't keep his eyes off her. Even after weeks of seeing her, nothing had slowed. He was only falling faster—something he'd vowed would never happen to him.

"I can't believe they just allow you to take what you want." Wren smiled, then resumed picking. "*Yangmei* is my favorite kind of berries, but we usually get them at the market and spend too much time bargaining for a good price."

"My father has carried their mail for years and they know he's trying to recuperate. The man who owns them makes bayberry wine. But even without the wine, the berries are good for healing." He'd spent the day before racking his brain for somewhere new—and private—for them to meet on his route. He was glad the secret bayberry patch behind a row of houses was a hit, but he still worried over finding the right time to bring her home and introduce her to his parents.

Wren finished filling her small bag and then came to sit beside Pony Boy. He moved over enough to allow her to also use the stump to lean on, even though her closeness made him feel jumpy. He only had another half hour or so and he'd need to get back on the route before someone noticed he was running late. He didn't want any complaints to make it back to the post office but knowing he had to leave so soon was killing him.

"Mei calls them yum-berries," Pony Boy said, giving a little laugh. "Did you know that according to legend, the bayberry came from the death of a goddess?"

Wren wrinkled her nose at him, an expression that in the last few days he'd come to recognize as doubting. "Seriously," he said. "Her name was Mei Zhu and she was kidnapped by an evil spirit. When a courageous hunter rescued her, she fell in love with him and they married."

"That's a sweet story," Wren said.

"Not when you reach the end of it," Pony Boy said. "There's more. After they married, the demon came after her again, but this time he was so jealous that he pushed her off a cliff. As she was dying she lay in her husband's arms and he promised to never forget her."

Wren frowned.

He continued, hoping he had the story right. He loved being the center of Wren's attention. "Devastated, the husband carried her up a mountain, then buried her under an ancient but beautiful tree that bore a series of twisting branches and a gnarled old trunk."

"Then what?" Wren asked.

Pony Boy plucked a berry from the bag and held it up. "Then a few years later, the ancient tree began to bear fruit for the first time. It was a fuchsia-colored fruit such as no one had ever seen—an enticing blend of sweet and sour, just like the legend of Mei Zhu."

"It bore the bayberry to represent the sweet beginning but sour ending of her life," Wren said.

Pony Boy thrust a hand over his heart as though he'd been struck through with an arrow. "*Aiya*, you stole my thunder. I was supposed to say the last line."

She gave him an amused look.

He had an idea. "Wren, let's have a thing—when we part, instead of good-bye, we'll say meet you on the mountain."

"Meet you on the mountain?"

He nodded. "That'll be our code for whether in life or death, we'll meet again."

She laughed, and it sounded like music. Even if the legend wasn't true, he could now see how a man could become besotted with one woman. If he died at this very moment, he'd be satisfied that he'd found the most alluring woman alive. Still, the world kept turning and he had work to do. He looked at his watch. "I only have about five more minutes before I need to get back on the route."

"How long will you be delivering the mail?"

They'd talked about his dropping out of school. Thankfully, she hadn't cast judgment on him—instead she'd told him she admired his strength and commitment to his family.

"As long as it takes for my father to get back on his feet."

"I hear bitterness."

That startled him. He didn't mean to sound bitter. He was relieved that so far their plan was working and he was still getting his father's carrier pay. Of course, they were no longer getting the funds from the second job his baba had before, but Pony Boy's extra position at the toilet stalls helped.

"I'm not bitter."

She gave him a nudge with her shoulder.

"Spit it out, Pony Boy. What is it that you aren't saying?"

It was eerie how close they'd become in such a small amount of time. But from the moment she'd accepted the apple from him, they'd met nearly every afternoon. And in those stolen moments, she'd slowly gotten him to share most everything about his life.

Most everything.

"Really, I'm not bitter. I just wish—" He let his voice trail off. Why speak of things he'd dreamed of doing before that he may never be able to do in the future? He no longer just had himself to worry about. Now he had to provide for his family. He had to be a man.

"You wish what?" Her soft voice cajoled him to speak more, to give more.

All his life he'd been known as the jokester, the one who wore a smile at all times. But Wren brought out a vulnerable side of him that no one had ever seen. They'd both shared their private injustices—hers being how much it hurt her that her father had chosen to put all his attention on her little brother, taking him under his wing at the newspaper office and conveniently forgetting he had a daughter. They'd discussed the changes going on in China as if they were intellectuals, and Wren had made him see things a lot more clearly—even question Chairman Mao's intent. Of course, all of their talks were hushed and confidential. Even Benfu didn't know about his emerging change of heart.

Yes, he'd changed since meeting Wren. She'd opened his eyes to much he'd never considered.

"I wish that I still had time to take pictures."

"Why don't you?"

"Why don't I what?" He picked a berry from her bag and popped it into his mouth.

"Why don't you still take pictures?"

He stood, wiping his hands on his dark trousers. "Wren, I work two jobs and sometimes three, when I can find anything else to do to make a coin. My family is depending on me for survival. When could I possibly have time for photography?"

She stood, too, and faced him, then pointed her finger at him. "Wasn't it you who told me about the quarrel you witnessed between an elderly couple, then the moment of truce, and how moving it was?"

He nodded.

She continued. "And didn't you describe to me the day you delivered mail to a house with a courtyard filled with people welcoming their firstborn son home from the hospital? You said the father held him up for all to see, tears running down his proud face."

He stared at her, beginning to understand what she was getting at.

"You've spoken of so many interesting moments that you've witnessed on these routes, and yet you can't see that if you'd only carry your camera, you could capture these snippets . . . evidence that humanity is still present, even in these chaotic times. Sometimes, Pony Boy, I worry about you and your lack of foresight."

He was speechless.

He'd always wanted to capture real life, real people. And here it was right in front of him. Such a simple solution, so why hadn't he thought of it himself? Sure, he was forced to walk the streets and deliver mail. Then he spent hours knee-deep in human filth and waste. But no one ever said he couldn't carry his camera. No one was forcing him to push aside the one thing that gave him joy.

He looked at Wren, noticing the sly smile forming on her face.

Well, maybe one of the things that gave him joy.

He held out his arms and she easily walked into them. It was like that. They didn't hinge their actions on formality, or reputation, or what should and shouldn't be done in public. Together they reacted on impulse and followed their hearts. It had been that way since day one.

Pony Boy smothered a sigh of happiness when she laid her head on his shoulder. Sure, life was tough and probably only going to get worse in the near future.

But it wasn't over.

He had Wren.

Chapter Twelve

Benfu felt the weight of the world on his shoulders. He was late for his violin lesson and knew his mother would be livid. She just didn't understand—though she should. Music was the most important thing to him in the world, but even though his parents saw the chaos with their own eyes at the university, they ignored the madness around them and chose to stay silent to keep their own skins intact.

Several blocks from school he spotted his shiny family rickshaw parked at the corner. He'd made it clear to his father he no longer needed or wanted Old Butler to come for him, but there the man sat, waiting patiently.

Benfu jogged the rest of the way, then climbed up behind the old man and they took off.

"Xiawu hao," Old Butler muttered a greeting as he pedaled slowly. He turned his head slightly to one side, then gave it a whip and a long stream of brown tobacco juice found its way to the sidewalk beside them, barely missing two elderly women who walked arm in arm, cackling the afternoon gossip to each other.

"I'm sorry I'm late but I wasn't expecting you," Benfu said, but received nothing back. The old man had been a part of Benfu's entire childhood, yet he barely ever spoke more than pleasantries. Getting cozy with the house staff was strictly against the rules of class, but Benfu wished he could have a real relationship with the man who'd spent almost two decades waiting on him like a devoted grandfather.

"Your mother was worried for your safety."

"I'm fine. She knows that," Benfu said. He fought to keep the irritation out of his voice. When would she stop treating him like a child? Ever? He shook it off. "Is my instructor waiting?"

Old Butler shook his head. "Not today. Your session is canceled."

Canceled? That was odd. Benfu's violin lessons were never canceled. It was the one interest he had that fit with his mother's plan for cultural enlightenment and her goal to transform him into a gentleman. Playing the violin was something they agreed upon. He looked up at the sun, its position indicating it was after four o'clock. Still, if he hurried, maybe he could catch his instructor.

Benfu leaned forward. "Old Butler, how about you trade places with me and give your legs a break? You can sit back here and relax, and I'll pedal."

The old man shook his head, refusing to turn around.

Benfu tried again. "I promise I won't say anything to Mother and we can trade back again before we get to our street. They'll never know."

This was an ongoing thing between them, and Old Butler never conceded, but this time Benfu could've sworn the man hesitated. Then his gnarled brown hands tightened on the handlebars and he picked up a little speed. "No, I need to hurry to get you home today. No fooling around."

Benfu sighed.

He wished that just this once, Old Butler would've taken him up on his offer. The exercise would've helped him push away the typhoon of thoughts bombarding his head. He knew his classmates assumed him weak because of his family background. There was talk—as hushed as it was he still heard them—that because his parents were scholars and he a musician, their devotion to cultural pursuits could one day become the nails in their respective coffins.

Many like him and his parents were walking a shaky line, following and pledging allegiance to Chairman Mao, hoping no one would question their loyalty or even worse, denounce them as counterrevolutionaries.

Benfu didn't speak his thoughts aloud, as he knew he'd be called a coward or a counterrevolutionary, but the truth was he was confused. Mao had recently instructed the people to cast out the ox and snakes, those he considered class enemies, and to exalt the lower class people. The problem was, those he called ox and snakes were not only people in positions of power, but also many teachers. What that meant for Benfu's family, he didn't know yet. He'd always been proud of his parents for their vocation, and in return they'd been proud of him for his gift of music. Now they were suddenly in jeopardy of being considered enemies of the state? What sort of craziness was that?

As they turned onto his own lane, Benfu watched the people. He shook his head at what he saw. No longer did the people of Shanghai wear bright colors and tout the latest styles. Now, as far as the eye could see, the people were mimicking the peasants, dressing in the popular Mao style, which was baggy gray or blue pants and shirts. Even the women avoided skirts and dresses, their shapely bodies now cloaked by the same outfits the men wore, their hair either cut short or kept braided and pinned to their heads.

According to Chairman Mao, looking feminine was for the bourgeois and the upper class. Even Benfu's mother was no longer painting her face with blushes and lipsticks, instead leaving it naked for the first time Benfu could remember. He still got a bit of a jolt each morning when she walked into the room looking pale and unadorned. She'd packed away her jewelry and put trunk after trunk of her expensive clothing in their attic.

Old Butler slowed when their driveway came into view. With his feet barely moving, he turned his head to speak to Benfu.

"Your mother is having an episode," he said.

Another one? His mother wasn't helping their already rocky new lifestyle with her constant mood swings.

"Your father brought her home," Old Butler added, then picked up the pace again and turned into their back driveway.

Now that was different, Benfu thought and hopped off the pedicab before Old Butler could even stop. He jogged to the back door and entered the kitchen, listening to hear where his parents were.

"In the study," Cook said without looking up from where she stood chopping on a slab of pork.

Benfu passed through and made his way down the hall toward the library. As he approached, he could hear his mother's voice escalating as she babbled on about something.

"Mother? Baba?"

The room quieted immediately.

Benfu entered and found them standing there glaring at each other, both of them with hands on one of his father's scrolls. "Why are you wrestling over Baba's things?" he asked.

His baba dropped his hands immediately. "Your mother wants me to send these to my sister. We're not wrestling. We're discussing it."

Mother took the opportunity to snatch the scroll out of Baba's hands and stuff it into the huge box at her feet.

"It didn't look like you were discussing it to me," Benfu said, sinking down into his father's chair. "What's going on?"

His mother turned and put her hands on her hips. "Tell him, Ju."

"Tell me what?" Benfu said, feeling more impatient by the minute.

His baba pulled a stool closer to the chair and sat down. "There was some excitement in Beijing yesterday, and it's trickled down to most of the universities, including ours."

Benfu felt a sense of foreboding. "What excitement?"

"Someone hung a *dàzìbào* criticizing Lu Ping, the head of the Peking University," his mother practically shrieked.

"What's a *dàzìbào*?" Benfu asked. "And how does that affect us?"

His father put his head in his palms, then ran his hands through his graying hair. "It's a big character poster that picks on one person or another, accusing them of being antirevolutionary."

"Oh, that," he said, remembering the negative that he'd found in the brown envelope. "Isn't that just one of many that are going up around China? Those have been in practice for years."

His mother stabbed a finger in the air. "Not like this they haven't. This one's been authorized by Chairman Mao. He even had it published in the *People's Daily*."

Now that did make a difference. So far Benfu hadn't heard of Mao getting behind any of the big character posters. An endorsement by Mao of any specific *dàzìbào* could easily end a man's career. He could see why his mother was so shaken up.

"What did Lu Ping do to get the spotlight on him?" Benfu asked.

Baba shrugged. "I didn't read all of it, but something about his teaching methods and his refusal to alter the school curriculum to fit the expectations of Mao's new directives."

His mother grabbed another scroll from a cubbyhole and put it in the box atop the other. "Just you wait and see. Every university in China will soon be in an uproar. They can't get away with this—we're teachers! Educators! Who are these people to tell us how to teach?"

Benfu stood to leave. He was filled with pity, first for his father who was losing access to all his favorite things, and then for his mother who for so long had revered Chairman Mao.

He headed toward the door, aching for a moment alone with his thoughts. "Baba, I'm going to go out for a walk."

His baba didn't answer and for once, his mother didn't bristle at the mention of him leaving the house without her permission. She couldn't, for she was too busy stuffing his father's most prized possessions into the box at her feet.

Chapter Thirteen

Benfu should've felt it coming. He should've known that in one afternoon, his life as he knew it would change. He'd left the house clean and dry, but within a few blocks and not many more minutes, was already soaked with sweat from the humidity. *September in Shanghai wasn't usually so brutal,* he thought, using his sleeve to wipe the moisture from the top of his lip as he walked. He hurried and had reached the park in record time, only to be surprised to find Pony Boy already waiting there, with Zu Wren by his side. He'd met her the week before and yes, she was pretty, but it wasn't like she was a goddess or anything. What it was that had Pony Boy so entranced, he hadn't figured out yet.

He didn't have time to even form a greeting before Pony Boy spoke.

"Look at this," Pony Boy said, handing Benfu a piece of the *Shanghai Daily*. "Wren swiped it from her father's desk last night."

Benfu looked down at the paper. He skimmed each article until he found the one he wanted. He looked up at Wren. She was watching quietly. He wondered if her father knew she was taking pieces of his paper out of the house. Then he realized how unimportant that was in the face of what he was reading. A man was imprisoned. A man he'd met and respected.

Pony Boy tapped at the photo with his finger. "Is that him? The man you met here at the park?"

Benfu nodded. Even if he'd thought it was someone who looked eerily just like the man—down to the peculiar eyes, if that was remotely possible—the name was the same and that was too much of a coincidence. *Teng Bao.* That's what the officials had called him that day. "No wonder he never showed up at the park. He was being detained all this time. It says he's charged with counterrevolutionary actions, spreading propaganda, and perpetuating unpatriotic waves of unrest."

"Well, all that means is he sent some unapproved photos to the paper, hoping they would slip through the censorship and be published. But a Mao loyalist editor caught them and turned him in. Basically, the man is being declared a traitor to the revolution," Pony Boy said. "If anyone knows you took those negatives from him, you could also be in danger."

"You too, Pony Boy," Zu Wren added softly. "We all want to be careful, but don't the people deserve to know what's really going on? My father is too afraid to print anything that hasn't been blanched to fit the model of a perfect new China."

Benfu looked around them, suddenly paranoid that someone could be listening. They could be arrested for just discussing Mao in a negative tone. He really believed that now. Yet despite the danger, he felt something else stirring in him. "Just yesterday we heard on the radio that Mao is encouraging citizens to rise up and bombard the headquarters."

"What is that supposed to mean?" Pony Boy asked.

"It means he wants to rid the party of his rivals and enemies," Zu Wren said. "Schools are shutting down all over China today. And all those students who've sworn to support Mao and uphold his ideas? They've now been given a name."

"What name?" Benfu was almost afraid to ask. Since both his parents worked at the university, the students who'd banded together were a frequent topic of conversation in their home. His father had reassured his mother that their zeal would die down, but so far it only seemed to be gaining momentum. Benfu hoped his father was right, but from what he was hearing, the same groups were now being encouraged by Mao to denounce teachers and other authorities. That didn't sit well with Benfu. An uneasy anger that he didn't recognize welled within him.

"The Red Guards," Zu Wren said. "And Mao has made them official. They wear armbands and dress as though they're in the army. Even the girls! They're taking their new positions seriously. My father won't print anything negative about them, but he told us that he thinks someone higher up is secretly organizing them—that it isn't just a bunch of students showing their patriotism."

Benfu snorted in disgust. "Mao couldn't get the real army behind him, so he created his own, out of those who are easily manipulated—those who want to have a tiny part in shaping history. They just don't have a clue what they are being molded into."

Pony Boy tossed a rock across the small pond that lay a few feet before them and they watched it skip across the water. "Mao stated publicly yesterday that he approves of their strong revolutionary spirit. It's not his fault they're doing things they shouldn't, but now he's basically given them the go-ahead to do whatever they want."

Benfu should've already disposed of the negatives that could get him in so much trouble, but he hadn't. What had made him hold on to them so long? Suddenly, he had a thought, one that brought on an unfamiliar feeling of excitement.

He waved Pony Boy closer. "I have an idea."

"So tell us," said Zu Wren as she moved in, too, obviously miffed that Benfu would try to whisper something to Pony Boy that she couldn't hear. He looked at her over Pony Boy's bent head. She smiled slightly.

Benfu took a deep breath and then dived in. He was tired of feeling oppressed and that realization spurred him to speak now, putting to words an idea that he'd felt brewing for days but had pushed aside. This time, he embraced it. "We can make up a leaflet and with it, anonymously reveal the photos taken by Teng Bao. Then we can find a way to distribute it."

Pony Boy looked concerned. "Wren's father claims that photojournalists aren't allowed to take any negative images of denunciations or Red Guard activity. They want to twist the media into believing that everything done for the revolution is positive."

After a few weeks with a girl who held different views, it appeared Pony Boy had completely changed camps.

"I know you've been telling me for a year that Chairman Mao isn't who he portrays himself to be," Pony Boy said quietly. "I'm starting to believe that, but how do you suppose we could even pull this off? We can't very well walk into a print shop and ask for help."

Benfu looked at Pony Boy, then at Zu Wren. He raised his eyebrows.

Pony Boy grabbed his arm. "No. I know what you're thinking and Wren isn't putting herself in jeopardy by using her father's office. Think about what you're saying. I mean—think about the danger she might put herself in."

Zu Wren put her finger to her lips, hesitating before she spoke. "Wait, Pony Boy. What if instead of just a onetime leaflet, we start a regular newsletter? We'll bring the real news to the people—or at least the ones around here. It can begin small, but who knows how far and wide the messages will spread."

Benfu held his hands up. "Now wait a minute. That's not what I meant when I said we should put these negatives out there. A leaflet is one thing—but an ongoing newsletter? That's too dangerous."

Pony Boy shook his head. "He's right, it's too risky for you, Wren."

Zu Wren moved closer to them and turned her attention to Benfu. Her voice rose in excitement until Benfu put his finger to his lips to remind her to keep it down. "I know where my father keeps his keys to the office and we can get in there at night. It'll be simple to get the newsletter printed. Since Pony Boy has the mail route, he can covertly slip them into strategically chosen mailboxes around town."

Pony Boy moved a few feet away and looked out over the adjacent field where families were gathering together for a lazy afternoon. He stood still, watching them, the initial excitement he'd shown now fading to a doubtful scowl.

Zu Wren joined him and put her arm around his waist. Benfu could hear her words even though they were spoken softly. "Pony Boy, I can do this. I've worked around my father enough to know how the process works and with his loose lips, I can ferret out tips and leads that he can't publish. And you can use your photography skills to capture real history. You know we've discussed our goals to find a way to make a difference. This is something we can do. Together."

Pony Boy continued to stare for a few moments before answering. "*Aiya*, you win. I'm in. I can't be a famous musician one day like Benfu. And I'm not a scholar. I can't even join the army to defend China because I have to support my family. But this—this is one small way that I can make my mark on the world—even if no one ever knows it was me."

"*Our* mark on the world," Zu Wren added softly, then took Pony Boy's hand in hers.

Pony Boy turned to look at Benfu, his eyes questioning.

Benfu sighed, then held his hands up in resignation. "Putting Teng Bao's work out there will make me feel like I've done something to help the man, so I'll commit to one edition. After that, I'll just have to see how it goes."

Zu Wren dropped Pony Boy's hand, suddenly all business. "Teng Bao's negatives will be shocking, but what we say about them will be more important."

"You can work on the copy, Zu Wren," Benfu said. "You obviously have a way with words." His implication that she'd easily swayed Pony Boy was left unsaid.

Pony Boy didn't catch it. He shook his head and smiled at Benfu. "No, comrade. That's your job."

"Mine?" Benfu asked.

Pony Boy returned to stand beside Benfu. "You—" he patted him on the shoulder, "—are going to be our Editor-in-Chief. You've got the writing chops we need."

Benfu hesitated. He didn't know how his idea for one simple leaflet had snowballed into a renegade underground newsletter, but now he almost regretted bringing it up. "Oh no, I don't want to actually write the stories. My mother would have a nervous breakdown for sure if she found out. I can't, Pony Boy, I just can't."

Pony Boy turned to Wren. "Can you leave us for a few minutes? Take a short walk?"

She didn't look pleased at being dismissed, but she nodded, then turned and walked down the path toward a grove of trees that provided more shade.

"Benfu," Pony Boy said, "this was your idea. Wren and I can't possibly pull this off without you; it would be too much work. You say all the time that you want to make things easier for me. Now, we finally come up with something and you don't want to do it?"

Benfu felt torn. "It's not that I don't want to do it. And you know when I offered to help that I was talking about your finances. I was going to ask my father about a loan for you, but I was waiting for you to loosen your pride a little."

"I don't want your money—or your father's money. It's always been you and me working together to get ahead. I don't want to do this without you. This could be huge and I want you to be a part of it, to be on the ground floor of creation. You and I. Together."

Pony Boy's voice was pleading now and Benfu could see him as he was when he first met him, convincing him that he could let his guard down and actually be friends with someone from another class. He'd been right—Pony Boy had ended up being the best friend he'd ever had. But he also thought of his parents. Could they be held responsible if he was found out? He had to think of them, too. *Didn't he?*

"Come on, don't let me down. Don't let the people down," Pony Boy said, then looked over to where Zu Wren had settled on a bench. She waved.

"You mean don't let Zu Wren down?" Benfu asked.

Pony Boy stood motionless and quiet. Benfu's last words lay heavily between them. For the first time ever, Benfu wondered if their bond would be broken, and by a girl no less. He didn't want that. As he hesitated, Zu Wren returned and stood beside Pony Boy, her arm around his waist. She didn't speak—but she made her stand known. The expression on her face spoke volumes.

He was either in, or he was out.

Benfu's thoughts moved quickly back and forth, first discarding and then embracing the idea that he himself had born. Lately he'd found an unfamiliar feeling bubbling inside of him, a simmering anger and a longing to change the wheels of fate. Now, in this moment, he knew this was his chance to act on what he knew to be right instead of what was expected of him.

So he made a decision, one based on years of the only solid friendship he'd known and for once, embracing his own beliefs instead of following those handed down to him. He held his hand out to Pony Boy and they clasped fingers in their secret handshake, a gesture they'd concocted when just boys. "Editor-in-Chief, huh?"

Chapter Fourteen

A week later Benfu sat across the table from Pony Boy and Wren, taking notes. Now that they were all on board, they were moving forward and he had firmly pushed his fears to the back of his mind. After deciding to hold Teng Bao's negatives for a later issue after a few test runs, they were struggling to find just the right story to launch the newsletter. Already they'd discarded half a dozen ideas for either being too common or too complicated to cover. With the rumors of everything that was happening around China, they had a multitude of ideas to choose from, but picking the perfect one was proving to be difficult.

"I saw a Red Guard on the bus threaten to cut a woman's long hair," Zu Wren said. "But she cried and promised to never wear it down again."

"I'm surprised he had mercy on her, but that's not news that people don't know," Benfu said. "I'm seeing stuff like that every day on my way home from school."

This time they were lucky enough to be using Zu Wren's kitchen, as her parents were both at mandatory neighborhood meetings, another directive passed down from Mao that kept families from spending too much time together behind closed doors. He didn't know about Wren, but he was glad to get any time with Pony Boy considering the schedule he was keeping. Between delivering the mail, cleaning the street stalls, and doing most of the heavy work around his house, finding time to meet about the newsletter was getting difficult. Half the time Pony Boy was a no-show to the meetings they set up, leaving him to deal with Zu Wren and her ideas by himself. So far they'd laid out a plan, devising each step they'd take to create the newsletter, to sneak in and get copies made, and then to distribute it. Zu Wren was thorough, he gave her that. She wanted every step spelled out even before the first edition was mocked up.

He looked around her house, noting the large poster of Chairman Mao that graced most of the wall over their couch. Other than that, it was nice, though, and quite clean—a welcome change of venue for their brainstorming sessions. It was getting harder to find places to meet as they realized more and more how much trouble it could bring them.

He held his hand up for them to stop. "Wait, what are we going to call it?" he asked. "The newsletter needs a name."

Zu Wren rolled her pencil against her lips, her eyes unfocused as she thought about his question. "Hmmm. A name. I hadn't thought about that."

Pony Boy slammed his hands on the table. "You're right, Benfu. See—that's why we wanted you on the team. With Zu Wren's knowledge of how a newspaper works, and your scholarly skills, this is going to be amazing. I can't wait to get it out to the people."

"Well, first we need a name," Benfu repeated.

"What about *Under the Gun*?" Zu Wren asked, making the sign of a gun with her thumb and finger, then pretending to pull the trigger at Benfu.

"Too violent," Pony Boy said. "We're about educating the people, not inciting a riot. We'll leave that kind of stuff to Chairman Mao."

"True," Zu Wren agreed, then reached over and brushed Pony Boy's hair out of his eyes.

The gesture felt too intimate for him to be witnessing and Benfu looked away. One thing that he had noticed since getting to know Zu Wren was her easy ability to take criticism and let it bounce off her shoulders. He had a feeling that her father was quite strict, and a part of him wondered if she'd pushed the idea of a newsletter only to secretly oppose everything he stood for in his government-appointed job with the newspaper. He was also quite sure that Zu Wren's respect for her father had suffered because of his inability to write what he really wanted. Maybe since he couldn't, she felt it her duty to do it for him. Benfu didn't know for sure, but he did feel there was discord between them. As of yet, her father didn't know Pony Boy, or himself for that matter, even existed. Zu Wren said the less they knew of who she was spending time with, the better it would be if she ever got caught sneaking materials or busting into the newspaper offices. On that note, Benfu agreed.

"Benfu, you know all kinds of poetry and proverbs by heart. You think of something," Pony Boy said.

Benfu stared at the table, using his own pencil to draw invisible circles as he searched his mind. "The name should represent what we are trying to do. So in a nutshell, what's our motive?"

"What about something to do with a mirror? The Chinese say history is like a mirror; if we can see ourselves in the mirror, it gives us a way to correct ourselves," Zu Wren said.

"*Through The Looking Glass,*" Pony Boy offered, then shrugged. "Or does that sound more like a book, or a song?"

Both Zu Wren and Pony Boy nodded their heads at once and the idea was scrapped.

Benfu spoke. "I've always heard that a writer is given the chance to record history, instead of just witness it. What about *The Palest Ink*? It goes with the proverb that 'the palest ink is better than the best memory.'"

"What's that mean?" Pony Boy asked.

Zu Wren bounced on the seat, obviously excited. "It means that people's memories change over time, but if there's a written account, then it will be more accurately remembered. It's perfect, Benfu!"

Pony Boy shot her a look that told Benfu he wasn't happy with how enthusiastically she'd praised his idea. But he held it together and in true Pony Boy fashion, gave credit where credit was due. "And it also fits with our goal of recording the entire truth of the repercussions of this revolution and not just Chairman Mao's account," Pony Boy said. "I like it, too."

Benfu nodded.

It was settled and *The Palest Ink* was official. He bowed his head back over the sheet of paper, returning to his list of ideas for their first article. He felt a rush of anticipation, and perhaps even a little dread as he visualized the finished copy landing in the boxes of unsuspecting readers. Some of whom might take offence at their efforts. But even if they made enemies, he agreed with Pony Boy and Zu Wren that the people deserved to know the truth. He took a deep breath and swallowed past the fear.

He thought of Juan Hui and wondered if she would be angry if she ever found out that anything he'd written had besmirched the name of her fearless leader. But that was an easy fix—he'd just make sure she never found out.

Chapter Fifteen

A nd this street is my favorite," Pony Boy said to Wren as they turned the corner and he headed toward Widow Chou's house. He'd already told her about old man Wang and the curiosity of his frequent letters. He and Wren had walked along coming up with their own possibilities of who the letters were from, taking turns at creating stories of long-lost loves and long-distance courtship. It made his day so much more bearable and Wren appeared genuinely interested in the people on his route. Now he couldn't wait for her to meet the old woman that he'd told her so much about.

He hoped Wren liked birds. If not—it was going to make for an awkward meeting.

"Why is she your favorite?" Wren asked, then he felt her hand settle on his back.

"Just you wait and see," he said.

He was in a great mood. He'd had a perfect morning. Finally he'd tired of finding places to meet Wren on his route, and so simply talked her into joining him. He knew she was risking a lot by skipping so much school, and he was taking a chance at having people talk, but he couldn't help himself. He wanted more time with Wren. Thus far, everything had gone well and with her help, they'd cut his delivery time in half, pleasing more than one customer as they got their mail earlier than expected.

"Wait, what is that?" Pony Boy stopped and pointed. There was something going on in front of Widow Chou's house. He saw about four or five people in the green uniforms that had become so common around Shanghai. When he saw one of them wore a red armband, he felt a jolt of panic. He heard their voices raised.

"A gathering?" Wren offered.

"That's no gathering," he said, then began to run. "Hurry—it's Red Guards."

He took the last few feet to Widow Chou's courtyard so fast that mail fell out of his satchel. He wouldn't stop to pick it up. It could wait. He swung through the gate and pushed through neighbors who were watching intently.

"Stop—who are you?" The obvious leader put out a hand to stop him.

"I'm her—her—grandson," Pony Boy finally said. He couldn't see Widow Chou, but he heard her crying, just a few bodies away.

The boy moved aside. Pony Boy felt Wren's hand on his back as he stepped forward and around the two others who'd been blocking him from seeing the old woman. When the view opened, the sight before him made him sick.

Widow Chou was sprawled on her steps, clutching her flowered housecoat as a female Red Guard kicked her. The widow flinched with each kick, but didn't attempt to get up.

"Stop this—what do you think you're doing? This is an old woman you're picking on," Pony Boy yelled and reached his hand out to push the girl. Wren stopped him, giving him a warning look.

He let his hand fall, took a deep breath, and he dropped to his knees beside Widow Chou. Closer now, he could see it wasn't her gown she was clutching to her chest. He saw a flash of yellow and knew right away what she held. The sobs coming from her confirmed it.

She cradled Pao Pao, but not a single feather on the bird moved. Pony Boy had only ever seen it cheerful and full of life, and now the lifeless body almost brought him to tears.

"Oh, no. Widow Chou, I'm so sorry," he said. He knew that though he wasn't her favorite, the little bird ran a close second in her affections.

Most of the Red Guards had moved out of the courtyard and were leaving, but the one who'd kicked at Widow Chou still stood over them, her hands on her hips. Her eyes looked pulled taut at the sides and Pony Boy wondered if it was from the pin-straight braids she wore in her hair. He could see them peeking out from under her official cap. He also wondered what her own mother thought of her now—this daughter who picked on the elderly in the name of the revolution.

"Chairman Mao says that having pets is a bourgeois habit and must be relinquished. You refused, so we took action." She swept her arms out wide. "This is all your fault."

Widow Chou cried softly, the sound breaking Pony Boy's heart.

"They killed it," Wren whispered from somewhere close.

But Pony Boy couldn't see her. In his anger, he only saw the bird that had brought the old woman such joy. He looked around and saw other birds lying lifeless, spotting the courtyard like used pieces of coal. He turned back to Widow Chou.

"Pony Boy, what am I going to do now?" she cried. "And they've seen my feet. No one sees my feet. Ever. I'm so ashamed," she wailed, sounding like a little girl.

He hadn't noticed it before, but now he saw that her silk slippers had been torn from her feet and lay in shreds around the steps. Someone hadn't been content in just removing them, they'd wanted to use them as a way to intimidate. As for her feet, Widow Chou was either trying to curl them up to make them disappear, or they were just that mutilated. He looked into her eyes and saw deep dark pools of humiliation. He wiggled out of his post carrier jacket and draped it over her feet.

Then he stood, his anger making him taller than ever before.

"Who gave you the right?" he said, his words barely seething out of his gritted teeth.

"Chairman Mao," the girl said, pointing at the armband she wore.

"Pony Boy," Wren said softly, her voice warning him to not say more.

"Convenient that the color of your armband is the color of blood."

Widow Chou and Wren both gasped.

The girl pointed at them. "I should report you. We're instructed by the party to make a redder China and that's what we strive to do. This woman was not in compliance and we exposed her feet to show her neighbors who she really is—a woman from a bourgeois background."

"No, I'm not—I wasn't—I swear," Widow Chou said, her voice pleading. "My mother bound my feet and those of my sister to try to get us a better life than the poor one she could give us. But it didn't work! I was still poor!"

Some of the neighbors gasped and Pony Boy turned and told them all to leave. A few wandered back to their own homes.

"If that is the truth, then we apologize for our actions upon your troubled feet," the girl said softly, the shadow of shame crossing her face for the first time. Then she straightened again, transforming once more to the stoic soldier before she spoke louder. "But it is not loyal to the party to have pets, whether they are cats, dogs, or the flea-ridden birds you kept. For that, I won't apologize. All of us have to obey the directives handed down. What makes you so special? There is no individualism in this revolution—we are all one." The girl turned away and left the courtyard, jogging to catch up to the rest of her gang that was cruising along the street, looking for their next target. Pony Boy turned back to Widow Chou.

"Here, Lao Chou. Let's get you up," he said, holding out his hand. "Wren, help me get her inside. I'll come back out for her birds. They deserve a decent burial at the least."

Widow Chou began to wail again, the sound striking Pony Boy deep in his soul, stirring such sorrow for the woman that he could barely stand it. She was devastated and he couldn't imagine how she'd go on living without the very things she'd actually lived for.

An hour later Pony Boy stayed in the kitchen, but near enough to the bedroom door that he could help if needed. He could hear Wren and Widow Chou talking, and was impressed with the way Wren was handling her sudden role as a caretaker.

While Wren bathed Widow Chou's scrapes and bruises, and found new slippers to put on her feet, Pony Boy had collected the bodies of her birds. He put them in the back courtyard and after finding a small shovel in her out building, dug a line of holes. He hadn't buried them yet, though, as he knew that the widow would want to say a final goodbye to each of them. Some would think it silly, but he knew that to her they were like her children.

When he'd finished there, he'd quickly retrieved the scattered mail and pushed it back into his satchel, then took off and delivered it as fast as he could. When he'd come back, ragged and out of breath from running, he'd found Wren sitting on the bedside beside Widow Chou, holding her hand as she listened to her talk. He'd backed out, feeling that the woman wouldn't approve of him being in her sleeping room. He wasn't sure what they'd covered in his absence, but now they were talking about the widow's feet—a subject usually closed off to males.

He listened closely, intrigued at the tale she told.

"How old were you?" Wren asked.

"I was thirteen and my sister was just twelve. Some girls waited until they were fourteen to start, but my mother thought we had progressed faster than others."

"Did it hurt?" He heard Wren ask.

There was a long pause, then Widow Chou spoke. "It hurt very much. I tried not to show my pain because I was supposed to be a model for my younger sister. But each time my mother unwrapped my ach-ing feet, only to wash and then re-wrap them even tighter, I had to bite down on a rolled towel to muffle my screams. The pain was excruciating and worse than any I'd ever experienced back then or since that time."

Wren didn't reply and Pony Boy imagined that she was most likely horrified.

"The worst part for my sister was the stench," Widow Chou continued. "She had a delicate system and when the bandages were being changed, she vomited from the smell of rotting flesh. We even put flower water on towels to hold over our faces during the process, but the stink worked through and found its way into our noses. There it would stay, only dissipating a short time before it was time to do it all again. But my mother was strict—her goal was for her daughters to have the tiniest lotus feet in the village."

"And did you?" Wren asked.

"I did, yes. But my sister's process was a failure. The nails on our toes had to be continually trimmed to keep from cutting into our flesh. It was a task that was difficult, and one that if not done just right, would result in infection."

"And your sister, hers got infected? Then what happened, she had to start over?" Wren asked.

Pony Boy waited for the answer his gut felt coming.

"No, she couldn't start over. She died before her thirteenth birthday, succumbing to a fever that burned day and night for weeks. Toward the end she begged for my mother to simply cut off her feet, and then she begged for death. My mother couldn't do what she'd asked, so the gods granted her last request."

Then there was silence. Pony Boy chanced a peek around the corner and found Wren still holding Widow Chou's hand, but now the old woman's eyes were closed. He could see one lone tear that had squeezed out, making its way down the lines and crags in her face.

He sighed, wondering if she had any family left at all.

"This is a cruel, black world that has nothing good in it anymore. I don't have anything left. No reason to keep going," Widow Chou said from behind the arm she'd thrown over her face.

"Oh, don't feel that way, Lao Chou," Wren said. "There's still some good. I can attest to that, as I've had some luck recently."

Chou moved her arm and opened her eyes. "You have? What?"

"Well, I just met Pony Boy not too long ago and we're building a strong friendship. That's why I was with him today."

"Friendship? I think it might be more than that," Widow Chou said, her voice low and sly. "How did you meet?"

He listened, wondering how Wren would describe their meeting. His cheeks burned, remembering that it was outside a reeking street toilet. He wished so hard that it was on the banks of a beautiful rushing river, or the peak of a majestic mountain—anywhere other than where it really was.

When she answered, her voice was softer than usual, almost melodious. "Well, it was the most romantic thing you ever saw. One minute I'm on the street, feeling all alone in a huge crowd, then next thing you know, he's standing in front of me holding out a delicious-looking apple."

"An apple?" Widow Chou asked.

"*Dui*, an apple."

There was silence for a moment, then the question he knew was coming. "Was it a caramelized apple?"

He held his breath, hoping Widow Chou wouldn't be angry.

"Why, yes it was," said Wren. "How did you know?"

"I know because—" Widow Chou stopped talking and sat straight up in the bed, her eyes open wide. "I forgot about Mynah! I have to find him," Widow Chou said, swinging her legs over the side of the bed.

Pony Boy went into the room. "I—I'm sorry, but I didn't find Mynah's body." He'd found all the others, but so far the talking bird's corpse remained elusive. He would've thought he'd have found him first, as he was the biggest and most brightly colored. And the most cherished.

"You haven't found him because he's not dead," Widow Chou declared, then crossed the room and struggled into a fresh housecoat that hung by her door. "He pecked the boy that grabbed him and then flew out of the house. I told him to stay away until they all left. I have to find him, please—please help me."

Pony Boy felt a burst of hope and he prayed the bird hadn't flown too far. Widow Chou headed toward the back door, walking as unsteady as he'd ever seen her, as if just showing her feet to strangers had made them clumsier. He felt a burning rage rising in him toward the Red Guards who in the name of the revolution could bully someone as innocent as Widow Chou.

She threw open the door and stepped out. "Mynah . . . ?"

Pony Boy and Wren followed her out and looked around. "I don't see him, Lao Chou," Pony Boy said.

"Me, either." Wren walked around the back of the house, looking into the trees that surrounded the courtyard.

Widow Chou walked around the walled gate, alternately whistling then calling out the bird's name. She didn't look down at the line of dead birds that lay in the far corner.

Pony Boy said a prayer under his breath that the remaining live bird would hear his mistress and come back. Widow Chou needed it. How unfair it would be for someone else to find Mynah and raise it, keeping it captive while it was so loved by this woman.

Feeling a tiny bit ridiculous, but willing to look that way for Widow Chou, he called out, "Mynah!"

"Mynah," Wren called.

"Mynah, baby, come home," Widow Chou sang out, even louder this time.

Pony Bird heard a squawk and then a flutter of wings. He turned and saw Mynah gracefully swoop down from the rooftop and land on Widow Chou's shoulder. She reached up and held out her hand, letting the bird hop down on it.

"Oh, Mynah, you came back," she said, her voice full of emotion and her eyes filled with tears.

"It's so pretty," Wren whispered to him.

And at that moment, when Widow Chou was again in tears—of relief this time—and puckering her lips to give the bird a kiss on his black beak, Pony Boy would've sworn it was the most beautiful sight in the world.

"He sure is," Pony Boy said.

He and Wren walked inside, giving the widow some time alone with Mynah. They watched out the window as she took the bird to where the others lay in a row on the ground. She knelt, taking care to stroke each of them on their backs, straightening their feathers when needed, speaking soft words of sorrow to each of them as she said her good-byes.

"Come on, let's go be with her," Pony Boy said to Wren and they quickly walked out and joined her.

They both kneeled beside her on the ground.

"I'm so sorry, Lao Chou," Wren said. "It's a horrible way to lose them all at once. And what a morbid sight to have them laid out here by these holes. Pony Boy, couldn't you think of a better way to do this?"

Widow Chou reached over and patted Wren's hand. "It's fine. It has to be done and Pony Boy did a fine job. A real burial is perfect as my birds would want me to show them dignity and not just throw them in the garbage. And one of those horrid Red Guards wanted to take them home and eat them! Can you even imagine?"

"From what I saw of them, yes, I can imagine," Pony Boy said. "Do you want me to put your birds in and cover them up?"

"You can bury Pao Pao. She'd like that," Widow Chou said. "But I'll do the rest."

Pony Boy nodded, then gently moved the little bird into the hole and pushed the dirt over her until she was covered. Then he stood, swallowed hard, and looked back at Widow Chou. "Are you going to be fine here alone?"

She hugged Pony Boy first. "You be sure to tell your father about today—about all that those vicious Red Guards did and how you stepped up to help me. He'll be so proud of you," she whispered. Then she let him go and embraced Wren. "And you. You acted like a daughter and I can't tell you what that meant to me. This is the first time I've talked about my sister since the day we buried her and I think I needed that. It's strange how light my burden feels now, though most all I've loved is now gone."

She let go and Wren nodded at her. "See, first I get Pony Boy as a new friend, and then you get me. Things work out sometimes."

Widow Chou gave them a small smile. "Friends, huh? Well, you two *friends* go ahead and get out of here. And don't you worry, I'm not alone—I have Mynah. And no one is going to take him from me."

Chapter Sixteen

"You're leaving," Benfu's mother said.

She was in *his* room—the room she never came to because when he'd turned thirteen, he'd made it clear that it was his one and only sanctuary away from everyone, though especially her. But here she was—and she was packing a satchel. She looked calm for once, but the determination on her face made him wary.

"Where am I leaving to?" he asked. He was a few minutes late coming home from school, but he wasn't overly concerned, though he was irritated at her for invading his privacy. He assumed she was finally planning the trip to Nanjing to see Juan Hui's estate. It wasn't something he'd looked forward to so he'd refrained from reminding her. It wouldn't do to fight it, though. Propriety demanded he jump through whatever hoops she deemed important. She'd accept nothing but total obedience.

"A small commune where you'll be safe. You can stay there until things simmer down."

Her words took him off guard and Benfu felt nauseated. What was she talking about? He wasn't leaving Shanghai—his home, his music, his friends!

"Mother, what you're saying sounds unreasonable. I'm not going anywhere."

She sat down on his bed and patted the coverlet beside her. He saw she'd also pulled out his violin and laid it on his pillow. Benfu swallowed the resentment he felt that she'd touched his instrument, and he sat down.

She took a deep breath before speaking. "Schools are closing down all over China. The party has even abolished exams! There's no way to even gauge a student's ability to pass him on to the next grade! It's only a matter of time before this chaos comes to Shanghai. Children are being sent out to the country—most for their own good, but some as punishment for being born in the wrong class, to the wrong parents! Things are happening too fast and I want to keep you safe, Benfu. You're my only child and if something happens to you, I would die."

"We'll be fine," Benfu said, though he wasn't sure if he believed it. The rumor was that the Red Guards were being encouraged to find and expose anyone who showed signs of being unpatriotic. Everyone's background was being sifted through for possible links to unbecoming relatives or hidden secrets. But wouldn't their past be deemed acceptable? What worried him was who would be the judge of that. He felt the little bit of control he'd thought he had draining from his life. "Where's Ba?"

"In his library," Mother said.

Benfu wouldn't waste any more breath talking to his mother. He'd find Ba and they'd get everything ironed out. Together they'd do as they'd always done—they'd calm his mother back into a state of normalcy. But then he realized, this time his mother was calm. That was the most frightening part of the entire situation.

He stood and left his mother sitting on his bed.

In the hall he almost ran into Cook, who was leaning against the wall, obviously trying to eavesdrop. When she saw him she tried to slip away, but he grabbed her sleeve. She looked at him and her eyes were swimming with tears.

"I'm not leaving, Cook," he said.

She tried to look strong, but he was touched that his possible exile had affected her so much. Before he could say anything more, she turned and headed back to her kitchen.

Benfu found his father in the library with his nose deep in the newspaper.

"Ba?" Benfu said. "What's going on?"

The paper was lowered and Benfu saw resignation in his father's expression.

"Benfu, this is best for you. For us."

Benfu sat down on the stool his father had removed his feet from. "How can it be best to send me away like this? I need to be here—you know that Mother needs me. What if she goes into another episode and you aren't here?"

"Cook will have to deal with her. Old Butler will help."

"What about my lessons? Remember, you were going to talk to Mother about my application for music school?"

"That has to wait, Benfu. I don't want to hear anything else about it. This time your mother is not overreacting. It kills me to do this, but we have to keep you safe," he said, his voice shaking with the emotion he was trying to keep at bay.

Keep you safe. Both of them had spoken the words and Benfu could see that his father was not going to back down. There were few times in his life that he couldn't get his way, and obviously this was going to be one of them. It made him feel like a child again. No say in the decision, no arguments—just the command that he had to go. He looked behind him, a part of him hoping that his mother would be standing there waiting to say she'd changed her mind, or even Cook to possibly speak up for him just this once. He noticed Old Butler in the hall, but the man's head was bowed. He'd never interfere in family business.

It was hopeless.

"When do I have to leave?"

"In the morning," Ba said. He didn't look up, but Benfu could hear the sadness in his voice.

"Can I at least know where you're sending me?" He kept his voice low and respectful. He'd do their bidding, but he'd do it his own way. Like a man.

"I can tell you that it's a quiet, smaller commune outside of Wuxi, but that is to stay between us. We don't want anyone to know where you are. Just in case," Ba said. He then raised the paper back up, indicating that the discussion was over.

Just in case what? Benfu didn't ask, instead he looked around at the room, trying to imagine what the commune would be like. Would there be books? Newspapers? Any kind of comfort?

For a split second he almost asked permission to go see Pony Boy. But since he didn't want to take the chance he'd be told no, he simply stood and quietly left the room. After stopping in his room and packing a few things in his bag, he walked down the hall and out the front door. He wanted—and needed—to be the one to tell Pony Boy that the first edition of the newsletter might have to wait.

Benfu stared at Zu Wren like she'd grown horns. What she was describing couldn't have really happened. Could it? Was China truly becoming so out of control? Was this what had sent his mother over the edge of reasoning? Benfu hadn't even had a chance to tell them he was leaving. His words were still stuck in his throat, frozen there because Zu Wren had only waited seconds after he and Pony Boy arrived to tell them of what she'd learned from her father. From what he'd heard, a headmistress of an all-girls school in Peking had died from being beaten by the very girls she'd sworn to protect and educate.

"We can't put that in our first newsletter," Pony Boy said. He ran his fingers through his hair, a gesture Benfu had seen him do for years.

He understood his distress. Getting the first issue planned and executed wasn't as simple as they'd thought. Even after several meetings they were still debating over the best opening article, and Zu Wren was still waiting for the right moment to get the keys from her father so they could make copies to distribute.

"It would surely cause a lot of stir," Benfu said. He still hadn't told them about his leaving. But they'd been deep into discussion when he'd arrived, and so far, the right time hadn't come.

But he'd be gone tomorrow. He had to tell them. His heart pounded in his chest.

They were sitting around the kitchen table again. Zu Wren's house was becoming their haven as it was the only place empty on a regular basis. Her parents worked long hours, and most of the time when her brother wasn't in school, he was with Zu Wren's father at the office.

With all the chaos going on, their newsletter launch had fallen to the wayside for several weeks before Zu Wren had talked Pony Boy into reviving their plan. Now Benfu was going to spoil it for them. He felt sick to his stomach.

"Yes, we can use this, and we should," Zu Wren said. "You won't allow us to use Widow Chou's story, so this is the next best one."

"I don't want to cause her any more pain," Pony Boy said. "If our newsletter gets into the wrong hands, they'll know it is her and might return to her home. I won't take the chance."

Benfu agreed with Pony Boy. From the story they'd relayed to him, the old woman had suffered enough.

Zu Wren rapped her pencil on the table. "Well, then this is our story and it's even better. This woman didn't deserve to die and they're trying to push it under the rug. My father said it won't appear in any news because it'll besmirch the reputation of the Red Guards."

Benfu was speechless. Why was the Red Guards' reputation more important than this woman's death? If it was true, Mao's personal army was out of control.

"All these officials are encouraging their teenage children to sign up and then they're recruiting their friends. There's nothing formal about it. It was bound to get ugly," Pony Boy said.

"But torture?" Benfu said. "Aren't most of them teenagers?"

"Yes, they're teens! My father said the headmistress was beaten, kicked, and trampled. They broke chairs and used the legs to beat her, then when she finally fell unconscious, they poured boiling water over her. It's horrible. Pony Boy, she's a mother of four children!" Zu Wren said, her eyes filling with tears.

Pony Boy scooted closer to Zu Wren and put his arm around her. She only let him embrace her for a moment, then returned to scribbling her notes.

Benfu thought of his mother and how she'd react if and when she heard about the woman. Then he thought of the woman's husband and children, who no doubt had to claim her broken body and bury it.

Zu Wren composed herself and her voice gained strength. "That death should be on Mao's conscience. After all, he's the one who ordered the Red Guards to bombard the headquarters. The factions took it to mean they should start a rampage against their teachers and school officials. My father heard the madness hasn't completely hit the Shanghai schools yet, but there have been students spitting on professors and refusing to turn in any work."

Benfu wasn't surprised on that note. In his classes there was hardly ever any emphasis on studies anymore. He sighed. "Pony Boy, can I talk to you outside?"

Pony Boy looked up from the paper he was watching Zu Wren scribble notes on. "What's going on?"

Benfu pushed his chair back from the table and the screech of wood on wood made him cringe. "I—I'd just like to speak to you alone."

Pony Boy looked from Benfu to Wren. She nodded at him and he rose, following Benfu out the door. When it closed behind them, Benfu sat on the stoop.

"Zuo xia." He told Pony Boy to sit and patted the concrete beside him.

Pony Boy obeyed. "You're scaring me, comrade. Is something wrong? Is it your mother again?"

"My mother is fine. It's me that's in trouble," Benfu said.

"Trouble? You? What could you have done? You're the ultimate rule-follower," Pony Boy said, a disbelieving grin crossing his face. Then it disappeared and he looked worried again. "Wait—did you get caught with the negatives?"

Benfu shook his head. "No, not that. I'm leaving Shanghai, Pony Boy."

"Leaving? Where? Why? It's not a good time for you to go to Nanjing chasing after that girl, Benfu. She can wait. We need you."

"I'm not going to Nanjing. My parents are sending me away."

"Away where? And for what?" Pony Boy asked, his voice rising with indignation. "Did they find out about the newsletter?"

"No, they don't know about that. They think they need to send me away to keep me safe. Mother must have already caught wind of what happened in Peking. She's on a rampage—and she's determined and she's made Baba agree. I know this is terrible timing for the paper, but I can't help it."

"Ironic, isn't it?"

"What?"

"Since you were in split pants she's tried to drill into you the teaching of Chairman Mao, weaving in tales of his revolutionary conquests to prove to you how wonderful he is. Now it's supposed to be his most important time in history and she's so fearful she's sending you away," Pony Boy said.

It was true, Benfu thought. What was once a faithful sort of idolatry his mother had for Mao was quickly turning into a fearful submission—and now it was mixed with distrust.

"I'm all she has for the future. That's what she keeps telling me," Benfu said. "I don't agree with her choices, but I still have to obey."

"Where are you going?" Pony Boy asked softly.

"I'm not allowed to say."

Pony Boy dropped his head in his hands and mumbled something too muffled for Benfu to understand. Something about secrets.

"What'd you say?" Benfu said.

Pony Boy stared out over the courtyard. His voice started out low, but by the time he was finished, he was yelling. "I said that of all the years we've known each other, this is the one time I need you the most and you can't be here. Even worse, you don't even trust me enough to tell me where you'll be!"

Benfu felt lower than a cockroach. Pony Boy was right. Here his closest comrade was shouldering most of the responsibility for an entire family as well as embarking on something that could potentially be dangerous to him and those he loved. And Benfu was skipping out on him.

"I'm sorry, Pony Boy. I really am."

Zu Wren picked that moment to open the door to check on them.

"Is everything all right?" she asked. "We don't have a lot of time before my mother's due home. We need to get to work and then you two have to get out of here."

Pony Boy stood up quick as a firecracker. "No, it's not fine. Why don't you ask Benfu what's going on?"

Before Benfu could respond, Pony Boy was strutting out of the courtyard. He didn't look back, but Benfu knew that if he did, he'd see tears on his face. He knew that sound in his voice—Pony Boy had sounded the same at the hospital the night he'd thought his father might die.

"Wait!" Benfu called, but Pony Boy turned and slipped out of sight, leaving Benfu standing with Zu Wren, the air between them suddenly static and not a little awkward.

"What just happened?" Zu Wren asked quietly. "He looks upset."

Benfu turned to her. "It's a long story, and he can tell you when he returns. But can you give me a piece of paper so I can leave him a note?"

She hesitated a moment, and they stared silently at each other. Then she turned and went back to the house, holding the door open for him.

He was thankful she respected his silence. Benfu was sure that when Pony Boy returned, he'd tell her everything, but at least for now he didn't have to repeat it. His gut felt heavy, full of despair, and even a bit of anger. It wasn't his fault he had to leave. He thought he'd made that clear. Pony Boy usually gave him the benefit of the doubt but this time, he'd exploded without logic. He had to wonder if the new relationship with Wren was changing him in ways that weren't necessarily good.

At the table, Zu Wren handed him a piece of paper and a pen. Then she turned and walked out of the house.

He sat down and leaned over the paper. He didn't know what words would make everything better, but he had to try. He had to at least attempt to leave something behind to save his friendship. Embarrassed, he felt something wet slide out of his eye and roll down his cheek, landing on the very paper at which he stared.

Chapter Seventeen

Benfu checked his satchel one more time. At the last minute, his mother had switched it out for his father's larger one so that the violin and bow could be wrapped and added without their looking obvious. He'd asked for a few moments to be alone, and now he sat on the bed, looking around his bedroom at the many articles that were evidence of his childhood.

His desk held his own collection of books—gifts bought and displayed before he was even born, that he'd since devoured. He stood and went to them, running his hand across several spines, tracing the embossed characters that made up the titles. His hand stopped on a favorite.

Should he take a few of them with him?

He considered it for a moment, then turned away. It would be too risky. As much as the thought of a comforting book of poetry in his hands under a lonely moonlit sky might appeal to him, he'd not chance being caught acting like an intellectual.

Returning to the bed, he reached under his feather tick, pulling out the brown envelope. With his hand in midair, he paused to listen for a moment. The house was eerily quiet, making his decision seem even more reverential. He had to decide what to do with the negatives from Teng Bao. He should've handed them over to Pony Boy, but he hadn't thought of it earlier. Now, if he left them, he was taking the chance that his parents might find them, or worse, someone else. He wouldn't want anyone—but especially his parents—to be blamed for possessing anti-revolutionary items.

He should just burn them. He'd considered it time and again, but something made him hesitate. He wasn't sure why, but he felt it was important to keep the man's last request sacred. To burn them might offend his spirit, or something Benfu didn't know about, but he wasn't taking any chances. He tucked them into his journal, along with the folded sheet music for the composition he'd been trying to conquer, then slid the book into his bag and pushed it down to the bottom.

"Benfu," Cook called out softly.

He looked up and found her standing in the doorway, a paper bag in her hands and worries spread over her face. He noticed that she looked older, as if she'd aged a few years just overnight.

"I'll be fine."

She nodded, then came in and handed him the bag. "I was going to make you something fancy for your trip, but these will last longer and won't get you into trouble."

"What is it?"

"Marbled tea eggs and some balls of sticky rice. It's what we ate for months upon months back when our village didn't have much else."

Benfu held the bag to his nose before adding it to his satchel. "Mmmm. I'll go in smelling like tea and cinnamon and they'll all know I had someone at home coddling me."

She smiled.

They looked at each other, both knowing they were leaving a lot unsaid. He wished he could tell her how much he'd miss her. She was much more than a cook to him—more than a housekeeper or the nanny who had powdered his butt years ago. She'd been an ally in the house—a willing ear, always available when he needed to talk. She'd been a voice of reason when he'd felt belittled by his parents' attempt to treat him like a child. To him, she'd been what he'd always imagined a mother figure should be.

He would like to tell her all that, and more.

"Please take care of Mother," he said instead.

Cook nodded again. That was the other thing they had together— years of helping each other meet his mother's expectations when she was at her worst, and working to calm her when her nerves got the best of her.

"Don't trust anyone, Benfu," Cook said. "Never tell them where you came from."

"I won't." His parents had given him his fabricated identification papers. With the sudden bias against those considered intellects, they'd decided it was best not to admit to being the son of two scholars. He'd be allowed to keep his given name, but his family name would remain buried until he returned. The forgeries on his papers had cost them a small fortune, his mother had told him, but one that they felt was warranted.

"It's much different out in the country. You've only known city ways—I'm worried about you," Cook said, putting her finger to her lips as if she hesitated to tell him something.

"I'll be fine," he said again. He couldn't think of anything else to say to reassure her.

"Stay out of trouble and don't waste anything!" she said quickly. "A real farmer knows that even water used to boil rice will be utilized. Nothing goes unused and if you don't pay attention to the little details like that, they'll find you out."

Benfu could see that Cook was truly upset that she wouldn't be there to guide him and watch over him.

"It's time to go, Benfu," his mother called from the hallway.

Cook backed away and looked cautiously behind her, and then met him halfway. Benfu held her close, in their first embrace since he was a child. She felt tiny—her small stature a direct contradiction to the strong force she'd always been in his life. Her affection for him was evident in the small sniffles she made, and when they stepped apart he wondered why she'd never had a child of her own.

"I'll be home soon, Cook. You can sleep in here if you like."

She nodded and stepped aside. He picked up his satchel, then passed her and Benfu felt their arms brush against one another. He knew without a doubt, Cook would be a big part of what he'd miss about home.

He walked down the hall and paused at the mirror that hung on the wall, looking at his reflection. It didn't even look like him. His hand unconsciously went to his hair and he felt unrecognizable, and in that he guessed their efforts had not been wasted.

Cook had given him a peasant's haircut the night before—one more step in their plan to disguise him. He didn't think it looked so bad. A bit choppy, but much less formal than his usual style. Now all he had to do was wet, then ruffle it with his fingers.

When he reached the parlor, he peeked in and saw that his parents weren't there. He continued down the hall and out the door, finding them standing in the courtyard.

Old Butler was waiting at the curb in the pedicab. His parents stood together on the path, his mother wringing her hands and his father still and quiet.

"You're coming with me to the depot, aren't you?" Benfu asked.

His father shook his head. "Benfu, we can't. It's not safe to be seen with you, as those riding with you could report back to the officials."

"What he means is we can't possibly make ourselves look like peasants," his mother added, her tone a bit too superior for Benfu's taste. "Old Butler knows which bus you're to get on and he'll make sure you get a good start."

Old Butler didn't look up from his seat.

Benfu crossed the courtyard until he was standing before the two who had brought him into the world. The moment felt surreal—he'd never before embarked on a trip without them.

His mother attempted a smile. "It'll be fine, Benfu. Don't worry so much. Think of it as an adventure—your last solo event before you become a married man. And when you return, Juan Hui will be waiting, so be true."

He sighed. The last thing he wanted to talk about was Juan Hui. They'd wasted enough of his last night at home talking over the story his mother would relay to his fiancé, a far-fetched tale that he was taking a few months to study violin with a prominent teacher in Beijing. Benfu only wished it was true.

"Remember, we have a contract with her family and we are Zhengs, we keep our word," she added. "I'll send a letter to—"

"Enough, Feiyan." His baba held his hand up, stopping her in midsentence. "The boy is leaving the only home he's ever known. Can we just say good-bye? Everything else can be sorted later."

The silence stretched between them for a moment before Benfu broke it.

"Do I really have to go, Baba?" he asked, hating himself for sounding like a child.

He could see his baba struggle to swallow past the lump in his throat, then nod. "It's what we think is best, son. And I'm proud of you for being strong."

Benfu didn't have any more to say. What other words were needed? He was being exiled from his own home, his family, even the city that he loved. Were they doing the right thing by sending him away? He didn't know. He only knew it didn't feel right.

His baba stepped forward and wrapped Benfu in a rare embrace. Over his shoulder he saw his mother watch them for a second or two, and he hoped she'd join in and they could embrace as a family, but she turned and went to the pedicab. Benfu could hear her giving orders to

Old Butler—probably the same ones she'd already given a dozen times that day.

The old man simply nodded.

"Benfu, look at me," his baba said as he let go, his voice gruff.

When Benfu stepped back he could see tears in his baba's eyes.

"Take care of yourself and never share too much information. From here on out, remember that you are the fourth son of a couple from the country and they have loyally sent you to help bring in the crops. Other families are sending their boys, and you'll just slide in and be one of many."

Benfu nodded.

"Keep your head low and don't get too close to anyone. No one—and I mean no one—is to be trusted," Baba said. "Also do what you can to keep your violin safe. Don't play it. Just keep it hidden. It is safer with you than here in Shanghai. With these Red Guards on the loose, who knows what might happen to all of our things."

Benfu would be obedient and take this detour—for his parents—but he couldn't wait to get back to his life and pick it up where he was leaving it this day.

Together they walked to the curb and he climbed into the pedicab. He tucked his satchel in the seat beside him, then looked at his parents again, trying to memorize their faces.

"I'll miss you both."

His mother clicked her tongue and pointed at him. Her voice was sharp. "Enough of that, Benfu. Stop being so overly emotional."

"Be careful, son," Baba said, his voice somber and heavy with sentiment.

Benfu was grateful for that bit of emotion. He would be missed—his father's eyes told him that. There was nothing left to say and his mother gave the word to Old Butler. He began to pedal. Benfu waved until his parents were out of sight, then he settled back against the soft cushioning of the seat. They turned the corner and Old Butler came to a sudden stop.

Benfu sat up, looking around. "What's wrong?"

Old Butler climbed down and came around to him.

"Nothing's wrong. You're always squalling about wanting to drive me, and my bones are aching today. So get up there, lad." He waved his hand at Benfu, gesturing for him to climb out of the cab.

Benfu grinned. Finally, after all these years, Old Butler was letting him take charge. It felt like a monumental moment, but inside Benfu knew it was a small way for the old man to show his affection, so he climbed out of the back of the cab and obediently took the driver's seat.

Old Butler got into the cab and let out a long groan. "*Aiya*, this is so much softer than my seat. I think I could get used to this."

The pedals were at first slow under his feet but soon, Benfu had the hang of it. Another pedicab passed him on his right and for a moment, he almost ducked his head. Then he remembered that with his old clothes and newly chopped hair, he looked the part of the peasant work-horse. And one look over his shoulder told him that Old Butler was so slicked up with his hair parted and oiled, and his pants pressed neatly, that the two of them painted the perfect picture of a young boy earning money by taking around a rich customer.

The role reversal felt good to Benfu.

He leaned forward, using his upper body to add weight to the pedals. He felt himself getting out of breath, but the hard work it took to keep the pedicab going was just what he needed. With each turn of the wheels and the familiar smells of Shanghai blowing into his face, he felt his heaviness lifting.

Yes, he was embarking on a frightening new experience. But no, he wouldn't let it change who he was. He'd get through it and make it back to the city he loved. Then he'd study hard and be accepted to the Shanghai Conservatory of Music. He'd make a name for himself. And he wouldn't follow in his parents' footsteps and be a scholar. He told himself all this, repeating it in his mind so that he wouldn't forget to hold on to his dreams. For without dreams, what was a person to live for?

From behind him he heard Old Butler shift in his seat, then teasingly call out to hurry him along. "*Kuai yi dian,* Benfu. We don't want to be late for your date with destiny."

Benfu smiled at Old Butler's words, glad he could finally separate his mood from the doom that had plagued him all morning. He leaned in and pedaled harder. A simple task—yet one that would soon be a reminder of just how easy a life he'd led thus far.

PART THREE

Calamity Reigns

Chapter Eighteen

Pony Boy stood half-hidden behind a large tree as he watched from across the street, his heart pounding in his chest so loud he feared it might be heard over the din that was happening around the temple. Though it was past dusk, the courtyard was lit and packed full of people. It looked as if a festival was about to take place with red flags hung and draped around, and voices raised, singing revolutionary songs. But unlike any festivity he'd ever been a part of, this one was not intent on celebrating—instead the motive was to wreak havoc. To put it simply, a faction of the local Red Guards had taken it upon themselves to take down the temple. Out of everything he was seeing, the most significant was the line of monks kneeling together just inside the gates of the temple courtyard, their gowns pooling loosely on the filthy ground below them.

The monks didn't look up, but Pony Boy could swear he heard a collective murmur coming from them, obviously their attempt at prayer to save their beloved sanctuary. Though he knew that Buddhism was a peaceful religion with a focus on self-sacrifice to avoid harming others, something in him wished that together they'd stand and fight, at least make some sort of stand to save their refuge.

"—an unparalleled moment in history," a random voice called out from the ruckus. "Wipe it out, wipe it all out!"

The Red Guards were out of control. It was the latest in the attempt to remove every trace of China's cultural history, all in a quest to please Chairman Mao. He'd made it clear that to have a successful revolution the people were to attack the Four Olds. While he'd not specifically stated what those were, the consensus was that it was old customs, culture, habits, and ideas. And lately many of the Red Guard factions had decided to focus on the temples and churches throughout China.

Pony Boy wasn't particularly religious, but it was unsettling to see such a vicious attack on what was once a beautiful building that served so many. As he watched, four of the guards had climbed the steep roof of the temple and were methodically removing the glazed tiles and kicking them off the roof, where they shattered on the bricks below, some of them striking the monks as they fell. Every few minutes a different Red Guard came out to yell at the monks, kicking them as he hurled insults and accusations.

The monks didn't respond. Pony Boy couldn't imagine how devastated his mother and the other patrons of the temple were going to be when they saw what was being done to the building that housed so much history and reverence.

Earlier that day he had passed a wall plastered with new propaganda posters. One pictured a young man dressed in army fatigues with a red band around his arm. He held an anvil, ready to slam it down on a pile of textbooks, religious beads, and a statue of Buddha. The poster read, *"Destroy the old world; Forge the new world."* Pony Boy supposed it was posters like that which fueled the latest fervor. Then later, when he'd delivered mail to Widow Chou, she'd whispered across the gate about the rumored plans to attack the temple. Once she'd told him, she'd hurried back into her house, not bothering to even suggest that Pony Boy step in to visit Mynah, and leaving his question on his lips.

Once he'd delivered the last piece of mail, he'd hurried to the street where the temple stood, wishing to see for himself if Widow Chou's rumors were accurate.

Sadly, they were.

Coming down the street, he saw another small band of guards carrying piles of thick ropes. They made their way into the temple and a moment later he heard a crash. A girl dressed in the now-familiar green army uniform soon poked her head out of the huge double doors. "We're taking down the columns!" she called, then was rewarded with shouts of encouragement from those outside. She ducked back in just as another crash sounded. With this one, Pony Boy could've sworn he felt the earth tremble and he cringed, knowing the columns were a special part of the sanctuary. He'd seen them many times on visits with his mother, and they were covered with intricate paintings from famous artists, as well as verses of poetry from the classics.

He looked closer and saw a plume of smoke coming out of the temple.

It was on fire!

Pony Boy heard a gasp from those around him. Doing structural damage was one thing—but setting the temple on fire sent a strong message to the people.

The message was: *the Red Guards could do whatever they wanted.* He looked around and though there were many pedestrians like him, watching from afar, everyone's attention was on the temple. He picked two low-hanging branches, then used them to swing himself up into the tree. Once he'd balanced himself as well as possible, he waited for the perfect moment to take a few photos. Even if he couldn't get them developed right now, he still planned to get Wren to write the story for the newsletter and later, if needed, he'd have evidence to back up what he'd witnessed.

Soon a half dozen or so guards stormed out of the temple with their arms full of books and other papers. Some carried smaller statues of

Buddha, some held boxes of candles. One tall boy—probably the same age as Pony Boy, he thought—seemed to lead the others and pointed to a place on the walkway in front of the doors. He threw down his load and the others followed until the pile was several feet high. Then he bent and set a match to it. When the flame spread and smoke began to rise from the books, they all cheered.

An elderly woman close to the tree whispered and her words carried to Pony Boy. "*Aiya*, they're burning the scripture books. Some of those are relics from the Ming dynasty."

Pony Boy took another look around to make sure no one was paying him any attention, then he slipped his camera from his bag and quickly snapped a few photos, then slid it back into the bag. He climbed down from the tree and watched, waiting to see what else they'd do.

One monk took a chance to look up from where he knelt. The Red Guard standing over him pulled out his belt and began flogging the man, much to the horror of those watching from the street side.

Pony Boy started to step into the street, intent on stopping the beating, but a stranger held his arm out, blocking his way for a moment.

"You'll be jailed," he said softly. "Don't interfere."

Pony Boy fumed, but he stayed in place. If he got arrested, his family would suffer. He watched, sickened to his stomach as the Red Guard heaved blow after blow until the monk finally collapsed, falling to his side and lying still on the cobblestone path beneath him.

The boys from the roof came sliding down, and the guards inside filed out of the church, red-faced and coughing but still jubilant. The tall one raised his hand and yelled out, "Long live Chairman Mao!" The others chanted the same thing as he turned and led them away from the temple. The crowd shrank back, giving them plenty of room as they all left the courtyard and moved down the street, probably to their next destination of destruction. When they'd turned the corner, one brave old man ran toward the temple door.

"We can't save what they've destroyed, but we can put out the fire," he called, beckoning others to join him.

Only a few found the courage to chance going against the Red Guards, but those who did followed him to the curb. Others muttered their excuses as they slunk away. Pony Boy took note of the man's small posse, then secured his bag strap around his shoulder and began the walk across the street, straight to the temple.

He didn't know what he could do, but he'd find a way to help at least put out the fire. His decision was easy. It was simple; his father had taught him to always do the right thing.

As he entered the smoke-filled temple, he pulled a handkerchief from his pocket and tied it around his mouth and nose. The embroidered cloth carried his father's name, *Chop*, and was a constant reminder that he was stepping into someone else's shoes.

He hoped his Ba was proud of him. Or maybe would be, one day. His father couldn't know about the newsletter just yet, but when everything settled down he'd realize that Pony Boy had done more than just the right thing—he'd chronicled *the wrong things* for all to know.

With the excitement and horror of what he'd seen earlier still on his mind, the rest of the evening had moved at the pace of a snail, but now Pony Boy was finally turning the corner into his own *hutong*.

As he approached his house, he noticed that all the lights were on and he perked up. Usually everyone was asleep when he finished work, all but his mama who waited up to keep his dinner warm for him each night.

He hurried and when he got to the door, quickly slipped out of his shoes, leaving them on the porch. He'd have to take the water hose to them in the morning—give them a fresh start for his postal run and ready them for another trek through the Shanghai sewage shift that night. His mother had fretted that they couldn't afford to buy him an extra pair, but Pony Boy was just glad for the ones he had.

Opening the door he took care to be especially quiet.

His mother sat on the edge of his father's bed and his brother and sister nestled in on each side of Baba.

"What's going on?"

It wasn't unusual for Mei to be cuddled against their baba, but Pony Boy couldn't remember the last time he'd seen Lixin behaving like a child. His brother took his responsibilities seriously and usually acted much older.

"Baba's sick again," Lixin said.

His mother rose from the bed and came to stand in front of him. She looked at him, her eyes swimming with tears. "We received some bad news and your baba got shook up, but he's fine now."

"What? Has the post office found us out?" He felt the first alarm bell go off in his head.

She shook her head. "No, not that."

"Then what?" He couldn't imagine what could be worse than that.

From the bed, Lixin sat up. "I'm being sent up to the mountains. The letter was hand-delivered by a courier from the county seat."

"What? No, you're not. You aren't going anywhere," Pony Boy said. "Let me see that paper."

Lixin climbed off the bed and came to him, holding out a stiff letter. Pony Boy took it from him and read the perfectly drawn characters. As the words penetrated his brain, he felt his stomach sink. The letter said that as a second son, Lixin was being recruited as part of the *Up to the Mountains* movement—a directive that was sending youth to the countryside to learn from the hardworking and loyalty-driven peasants.

"This is nonsense," Pony Boy exploded. "He's not cut out for farm-work and he's as loyal as he needs to be. What's this going to accomplish except leaving us in a bind?"

"Mao wants to bridge the gap between the laborers and intellectuals," his father said. "This is one of the ways he thinks he can do it."

Pony Boy slung the piece of paper as if it were a rock, then felt more irritation when it floated gently to the floor, defying his show of bravado. "Baba, surely you know someone at the post office who can step in? Someone can do something, right?"

His mother reached out and patted his shoulder. "Calm down, son. We don't have a choice in this. It's mandated from much higher up than our meager contacts. I heard this afternoon that there're several boys from this street going, and even a few girls. A lot of families are affected. We just have to get through it."

Get through it? Isn't that what she'd said about his father's heart attack and recovery? Isn't that what she said the week before when they'd not had enough funds for fresh milk for Mei? Why were they the ones always having to *get through it?*

Pony Boy didn't know what to do. What could he do? Any refusal would launch an investigation into their family, probably exposing his father's inability to work, putting all of them in danger of starving to death and possibly even forced out into the streets. They couldn't survive a Shanghai winter without their home. He felt so frustrated. So helpless.

He thought of Benfu.

Though Benfu's exile was by his parents' choice, how ironic that both his best comrade and his little brother would spend time living in a world they knew nothing of—their days filled with farming and reeducation.

Lixin came and stood before him.

"I can do this, Pony Boy. I'll be fine," he said bravely but he couldn't hide his fear, not from his big brother that knew him so well.

Pony Boy didn't answer. He didn't trust his voice. Instead, he reached out and pulled his little brother to him, clutching him as tightly as he possibly could. They stayed that way for a moment, then he had an idea.

"We can leave." Pony Boy pushed Lixin out of his arms and turned to his parents.

"Leave where?" his mother asked. Her voice told him that she didn't have any confidence in his words.

"We can go to the country—just like they said. But we'll go together," Pony Boy said.

Baba sat up. "It won't work. We can't just run."

Pony Boy went to his father's bedside. "Baba, we can and we will. You're strong enough to walk now. We'll take a train and go stay with your sister for a few months until this all blows over. You know Auntie won't turn us away."

Lixin looked hopeful. "She might appreciate the extra help with her animals."

Pony Boy watched Baba turn to Mama and the silent questioning between them. He'd always admired how his parents could communicate without words, exchanging only a look to convey agreement or shut something down.

She shrugged.

Baba sighed, his breath heavy. He stared long and hard at Lixin for over a minute. Then he pulled the coverlet off and swung his legs over the side of the bed.

"If we're going to do this, we need to leave tonight."

Pony Boy grinned and Lixin gave a holler of joy.

"We can only pack one bag apiece," Mama said. "But we can all carry something for the household. So be prepared, boys—you'll carry two bags."

"Lixin and I will carry three," Pony Boy said. "Baba will only have to walk. We'll share his load between us."

Mama crossed the room and held out her arms. "Pony Boy, you are growing up so fast. What am I going to do with you?"

Pony Boy buried his head in her hair, inhaling the familiar smell of her. He pulled away when he heard his father begin to cough, and caught sight of him just as he bent over to catch his breath and fell flat on his face.

He ran to him and after rolling him over, felt relief wash over him when his father's eyes fluttered open. His mother knelt there, too, and when Pony Boy looked at her, she shook her head.

Words weren't needed.

They wouldn't be going anywhere tonight. His father was weaker than Pony Boy had thought, and that meant that soon—much too soon—their family would be separated. He locked eyes with his brother, who stood staring at them huddled on the floor. His face showed that he knew his life was now out of their hands. No matter what their wishes, he'd be leaving them. Pony Boy just hoped that Lixin was strong and could make it through until they could be together again.

"Come on, Baba," he said. "Let's get you back to bed. We'll talk about this in the morning."

Chapter Nineteen

The temperatures were hot and the unusual late September rain should have been soothing, but if it was anything, it was an unyielding reminder to Benfu of how far he had fallen. At home, he'd have watched the rain from the dry comfort of his bedroom window or even from the calming surroundings of his father's study as he played his violin, matching the somber weather chord by aching chord, using the elements to inspire new music from his hungry soul. But here, in this new life he'd been thrust into, nothing was the same. He'd awakened and began working at five o'clock that morning—the blaring of revolutionary music blasting over the commune speakers had sent him jumping from his bed in alarm yet again—and his limbs felt heavy with fatigue. He thought once more of his violin, wrapped securely in thick burlap and hidden in the depths of the unused well, and he hoped he'd lowered it deep enough that it would remain dry.

He looked at the sun in the sky—or at least what he could see of it behind the gray curtain of rain—and figured they still had at least another three hours in the field before they could return to the dining hall for a modest dinner.

After that, they'd go straight into what he silently deemed the *Hall of Hell.*

The Hall of Hell was only a courtyard with three walls and somewhat of an overhang to help keep out the bulk of the rain, but it was the center of the commune and where the struggle sessions were held. Then later the nightly entertainment of small plays, put on by some of the people, as well as a few rounds of revolutionary songs closed the evening before they were all dismissed to their bunks.

The first night after he'd arrived he'd been led to the hall along with others from the bus, and there had received a lecture about the commune and its goal to support the military units in and around Shanghai. The leader also remarked that they worked to grow enough crops to help poor city folk whose limbs refused to move enough for them to learn the basics of farming. He'd thought of his mother and father, spending their lives educating the youth of Shanghai—a choice that was now considered bourgeois and bordered on antirevolutionary. It all felt so wrong. But since he was posing as a farmer's son and not a child of intellects, he'd bitten his tongue to keep from defending the *poor city folk and their laziness.*

At least after that first night, the insults that he felt were aimed at his very heart had stopped and they'd returned to the mindless exaltation of Chairman Mao.

He prayed the rain would cease. Sitting through hours of the same routine every night was excruciating, but even more so with the wetness that had covered them and seeped deep into his bones for so many days and nights. And here he was still out in it picking worms from a late crop of corn. Tiny, tedious little creatures who held on like leeches even as he plucked them and tossed them in the small basket tied to his pants.

Two weeks in and they'd had rain for ten of those days. It wasn't a particularly heavy rain, but it was steady. Even his shoes—the boots his mother had scoured the secondhand shops to find for their hardiness and worn look—had stopped keeping out the moisture. He knew exactly what his toes looked like under the leather, as he'd spent the night before with them propped on a large piece of wood, trying to fan the wrinkles from the now-waterlogged blisters he'd earned.

Misery.

With that thought, he stepped into a huge mud hole that swallowed his left foot. He struggled to free himself, then felt the suction of the mud clinging to his shoe.

He couldn't lose his boots. If he did, he'd be forced to work barefoot as many around him did. He was lucky to have something on his feet, even if they weren't the most luxurious things he'd ever worn. Others had much worse than a few blisters—many of the barefoot villagers strapped wide pieces of corn husks to the bottoms of their feet to use as a sort of slipper. How they walked like that, he didn't know.

"Benfu, comrade. Need some help?"

He half turned, careful not to move enough to lose the last bit of hold he had on his boot. It was disappearing fast.

"Gong Ran."

He was glad to see the older boy, even more so than the day he'd stepped off the bus and Gong Ran had told him he'd be his new roommate and would be showing him around. Like a fish out of water, Benfu hadn't known what to do. He'd been lucky—other boys had been matched with men who didn't want a sidekick to slow them down as they worked for their rations. But Gong Ran hadn't seem perturbed and most importantly, hadn't asked a lot of questions.

"Looks like you're stuck," he said, laughing out loud.

Benfu didn't appreciate the laughter, but he needed his boot so he hid his irritation. "If you can just—"

Gong Ran covered the distance between them quickly. "Oh, I know what to do, but obviously you don't. One thing you never do in these muddy fields is stop moving. It's the rhythm of movement that keeps you from sinking and being swallowed whole." He reached out and grabbed Benfu under one arm.

"What do you want me to do?" Benfu said, already envisioning himself hobbling around with one boot.

"Just lean into me and lift only your heel. Once it starts to work free, the air pocket will release the front of your foot and when you feel that—only when you feel that—you jerk it free."

Benfu did as he was told, using all his strength to lift his heel just a tiny bit. He could feel the mud start to release, and when it felt like a bubble was forming under his foot, he yanked it free. Unfortunately, the motion of his movement sent him reeling backward until his back side was sitting in yet another puddle, the basket of worms spilling out around him.

Through the rain pouring down his face and into his eyes, he could see Gong Ran holding his stomach with laughter. "Hurry, grab the worms!" he called out.

Benfu carefully balanced himself until he could get into a standing position. Finally free from the cold, sucking mud, he sighed. He bent to pick through the mud, capturing what worms hadn't made a dash under the water in their quest for freedom. His hands shook. He was cold, exhausted, and famished.

"*Aiya*, your pants are a mess," Gong Ran said, pointing at the huge splashes of mud all over Benfu.

Benfu looked down. *"Keep your pants hung at night and you'll not have to wash them as much,"* Old Butler had said as they'd waited for the bus what seemed like ages ago now. Since then Benfu had learned to wash his laundry in the creek when he couldn't barter clean water.

He studied the soiled undershirt he wore, his thickened arms now browned dark from the sun. Old Butler had also said, *"Always wear layers, even in the hot temperatures. It will keep away most sicknesses if you don't expose your skin to the air."*

What he wouldn't do to see Old Butler right now. To hand him his wet pants and shirt and feel the shelter of his care. Benfu had taken so much for granted for so many years. He would sleep for days, only rousing when the sweet smell of one of Cook's recipes tantalized his senses.

"How are you doing?" Gong Ran asked, the smile disappearing, replaced with one of concern.

Benfu came out of his daydream and nodded. "I'm fine. Just wet."

"Well, we're all wet, comrade. Just be glad I got you taken off latrine duty or you'd be wet *and* covered in shit," he said, winking at Benfu through the wet strands of hair plastered over his forehead and falling into his eyes.

He was right on that. Benfu had spent the first few days working with a group of the newest arrivals, shoveling the deep recesses under the troughs that served as toilets, filling dozens upon dozens of buckets with the reeking waste. From there they carried it out to the fields, following whichever brigade leader they'd been appointed to that day, and shown to one plot or another where the feces-turned-fertilizer was to be spread. Through most of the chore, his mind had been on Pony Boy and his willingness to shovel the public toilets just to help add to his family's reserves.

He wished for just a moment of warmth, of privacy—and what he wouldn't give to put his hands on his violin again. He missed it more than anything. But so far he hadn't felt safe enough to bring it out of hiding. All in all, his misery was complete.

"Would a little comfort be too much to ask?" he mumbled under his breath.

Gong Ran heard him. "Sorry to tell you, but you aren't here for comfort. You're here to eat bitterness and learn from the peasants—just like me. Now let's finish this row. Then the next. And the next. Maybe we'll see a patch of blue in the skies if we work a bit harder."

Benfu was examining the newest wound on his hand, made when he'd spent a few hours that morning helping to clear a patch of briars where another plot of root crops was about to be planted, when Gong Ran turned to look at him. Benfu quickly dropped his arms to his side and moved to catch up. For his abrupt action, he was rewarded with a perplexed expression.

"I know one thing. For being a farmer's son, you sure need some toughening up," Gong Ran said, leaving Benfu speechless and horrified that someone had seen through his lie. Perhaps Gong Ran wasn't as friendly as he'd first thought. Benfu just hoped he could trust him not to go to the village leader with his suspicions. He thought of when he'd arrived and had stood in line, waiting for his identification check-in. His card had *farming* on the line beside family background. He'd passed then but he was going to have to start working a lot harder and smarter if he was going to fool everyone.

Finally the work detail was done, and Benfu was allowed to follow Gong Ran into the canteen to stand in line for his evening meal, a task that if he hadn't known it would soothe his belly, he would've been too exhausted to do. As he waited, he held his hand to his chest, a move that kept the throbbing to a minimum. As far as he could see, the briar was gone yet the pain had continued to get worse. Keeping it up only helped a little, but he was willing to do anything to get a bit of relief.

He'd had a bandage on his hand earlier in the day. A squat, elderly man—memorable in the fields because of the red wool hat he wore—had brought him a clean piece of what appeared to be a torn sheet. He'd seen Benfu cradling his hand at some point, even though he'd tried to be discreet, and he'd silently come and poured his ration of water over it before tying the cloth around it. After several hours of labor, the material had finally worked free and Benfu had lost it.

The loud chatter shocked his system and gave him a jolt of energy. All around him people sat on wooden benches at scarred tables, or even crouched against the wall cradling their dinner in front of their faces, chopsticks moving like a blur from bowl to mouths, talking between bites. The din was a welcome change from the constant quiet of being in the fields all day.

A communal kitchen was a new concept to him—one thought up by Chairman Mao almost a decade before during his Great Leap Forward Campaign, the race to put out as much steel in China as humanly possible. That was when the majority of communes were formed. It was out with individualism and gathering in private, and in with coming together for all things, including meals. Benfu also discovered that because there were separate sleeping quarters for men, women, and children in the commune, dinner was usually the only opportunity for men to be with their wives or children, and he could feel the excitement as families huddled together, sharing a quick word or embrace before they were once again separated and the children sent off to their quarters.

As he pulled a bowl from the stack at the first table, then stepped into line behind Gong Ran, he thought of the way his evenings used to be—a tasty meal prepared by Cook, followed by time in his father's library. He envisioned them sitting in their usual places and he swallowed past the lump in his throat. He missed them. Even his mother with her constant hovering and controlling ways, a trait she couldn't help but he knew was motivated out of love. This commune experience—it wasn't for him. He couldn't wait to get home.

The line moved forward a few feet, enough that the aroma of the steamed noodles reached him, causing his stomach to roll painfully. After he'd explained the point system to Benfu, Gong Ran disappeared in the sea of dark heads, those who weren't shy and pushed to the front of the line. Benfu couldn't do it. Others were just as hungry as or even more so than he. He noticed the red-hat man ahead of him, holding his bowl to his chest as his eyes never left the row of servers in front of their stations. Benfu marveled that no matter how hot or wet the weather, the man never took off the hat. As the large bowls of food quickly disappeared, threatening to be all but gone before they got to it, the man quietly shuffled forward without complaint.

Benfu would wait his turn. And he hoped the man didn't see that he'd lost the material, as that would look ungrateful. He willed the man not to turn around.

When he moved forward another step he looked out over the room, struggling to keep from looking everywhere at once. At first he hadn't understood why the people all seemed so hungry when they were living on a piece of land on which many crops were grown. It was bewildering, but soon after he'd arrived, the truth had begun to sink in. Most of what the people had harvested that season was sent to the cities. There was only a slim amount of food left behind for the kitchen staff to use for creating modest meals to feed too many people.

Now finally at the serving station, he handed over his ration coupon and a short and square-shaped old woman ladled the noodles and broth into his outstretched bowl. He thanked her and turned to find Gong Ran. He saw him at a table with other boys from their work group and walked over. As soon as he sat down, he picked up his bowl and went at it, ravenous with hunger, before he saw that the red-hat man was also seated at the table. Their eyes connected and the man looked at Benfu's hand, then nodded and returned his gaze to his bowl.

"Tomorrow we plant dragon beans, onions, and turnips," a boy said from the head of the table. "I heard that they're pulling at least a dozen of the strongest to build another Happy Home."

One of the boys pointed at Benfu from across the table. "You're bigger than most. You'll probably be chosen to go. Just be sure to pull your weight or they'll make you work both jobs."

He nodded. He'd pull his weight, no doubt about that. Being ordered out of the fields was a fine option to him, as long as he didn't get sewage duty. "What's a happy home?"

The boy finished slurping the last of his broth and used the back of his hand to wipe his mouth before speaking. "A hut. They use packed mud to build smaller huts for the elderly. Right now we've got five to six seniors in each place, so they need to build more to separate them out a bit."

Benfu mumbled a few words, then looked around to see if anyone had heard him. When no one reacted, he was thankful they hadn't heard his slip. The famous words of Lao Tzu had rolled off his tongue, meaningful words that had no place in the country. No one could know he'd memorized poetry, or they'd wonder if he was who he said he was.

The boy talked more about the hut and as Benfu ate, he wondered if it was any better than the small cabin he, Gong Ran, and two other men shared. Theirs was basically a dark, airless wooden cabin with only one real bed, a scarred table with one chair, and a small propane stove to heat water. They were supposed to take turns sleeping on the bed but so far the two others had not relinquished it, leaving Benfu and Gong Ran to sleep on scratchy bamboo mats on the floor, sometimes competing with beady-eyed rodents for the space.

Benfu looked down at his bowl, suddenly empty though his stomach told him it was still hungry. He turned to glance at the food line and saw there were still people waiting for their own supper. He'd never get by with going through it again.

"What's wrong, comrade?" Gong Ran asked. "Not enough for your strong farm-boy appetite? Was that just the appetizer and you're waiting for your main course now?"

Benfu's face reddened. "Why are the rations so small?"

Gong Ran laughed. "Small is better than nothing. Food's scarce. Don't you know the communes are feeding the men in the People's Liberation Army? We support one of the largest Shanghai factions."

Benfu also suspected the peasants were feeding the Red Guards as they worked their way around China wreaking havoc in their paths. Another boy took a break from raking the noodles into his mouth to point at Benfu. "You think this is scarce? We're eating double the size portions we were given from March to June."

Benfu tried to hide his shock, but the boys at the table saw it and laughed. "Why?" he asked. He couldn't imagine surviving on only half of what was currently sitting in his bowl.

Under the table the red-hat man gave him a slight kick. "Oh, he knows why," he said to the other boys, his voice low and gravely. "He's just making conversation."

Gong Ran nodded his head agreeably. "Yes, Benfu grew up on a farm and understands that from March to June not enough vegetables are in season to keep a big kitchen going. Right, Benfu?" He looked at Benfu, raising his eyebrows.

"*Dui*," Benfu said, thinking quickly, "but I thought since this is a commune that there would have been plenty of stores put up from past crops."

The red-hat man gave a slight nod and Benfu realized he'd have to be more careful not to show his city ignorance again. If they ferreted out that he wasn't familiar with farming, they'd know he'd lied about his background; an unforgiveable sin in the eyes of those forging a new China.

Chapter Twenty

Pony Boy nervously turned the corner to the next street and told himself that these mailboxes would be the ones to finally receive the first edition of the newsletter. Not for the first time, he considered that maybe he and Wren were like flies on an ox, using all their energy and taking a chance with their freedom for what—the opportunity to sway a few opinions?

But Wren had convinced him. She thought it was the right thing to do and Pony Boy knew that between them, she had the most insight and sense of right and wrong. And for her, he'd do anything.

Thankfully in the *hutongs*, most hung their mailboxes on their courtyard walls next to the gates, saving Pony Boy from getting too close to the houses. As he approached the first box, his fingers dangled inside his mailbag, touching the stack of papers that he'd slipped in beside the various envelopes and small packages, just behind his camera. His heart beat faster, a sign that he wasn't as brave as he'd indicated to Wren the night before. But he wanted her to know that she wasn't the only one taking a big chance.

It was just before midnight the night before when they'd met at their secret place, then kept to the backstreets and alleys until they'd reached her father's office. She'd swiped the key from her father's bag and escorted Pony Boy to the building, slipping inside to show him the way to the ancient—and much too loud—printing press. He'd been amazed at her ability to put it all together and create such a clean copy of the original mess. It was a dangerous mission to be sure, as the consequences of her father finding out could be tragic. So he'd agreed to deliver every single copy, promising to put them into the boxes of those he thought the most important on the streets he'd come to know so well.

But as they'd thought it through, he and Wren had determined that he would only deliver to boxes that weren't on his route, and only in the dark. The hope was that no one would see him, but if by chance he was spotted, he could duck his head and they'd only see a young man with an official mailbag. If their real mail carrier was questioned, he'd not know anything about it.

The first box was only steps away and Pony Boy felt a tremor start in his toes and work through his body. The first recipient would be Lao Cui, the leader of the neighborhood committee and a respected man from all accounts. If he was as noble as he claimed, then he'd have an open mind. If not, then he'd most likely start a posse to try to determine who was behind it.

Quickly, before he could lose his nerve, Pony Boy pulled one of the copies from his bag and slipped it into the box, then walked as fast as possible to get away. He looked around, seeing no one on the quiet street, before going to the next box and slipping a paper in there, too.

Other than a few passing by on bicycles, most of the street's inhabitants were having dinner or settling in for the night, the lights on in the kitchens and main rooms indicating that he had chosen the perfect time for his deliveries. With the first few delivered, Pony Boy felt a burst of exhilaration. When he finished that street, he walked over to the next one they'd chosen together.

This time he approached the first box faster. Just in case some of those from the last street already had the paper in their hands, he needed to keep moving.

They had, after many nights of discussion and a bit of debate, decided to print the story of the head of the girls' school in Beijing being beaten to death. Wren had made a good point when she'd said the first story needed to be a shocker. And hard as it was to believe, they were confident that the news of the woman was true and that officials were intent on covering it up. And if her demise was covered up, how many more cases just like hers were being hidden from the public?

He stuffed a few more boxes and darted in and out of the dark shrubs, keeping low as he went until he finished the street. As he approached another mailbox he spotted an old woman outside in her courtyard, throwing a pot of scraps to a dog. He hunkered down behind the thick trunk of a Yulan magnolia tree and waited for her to finish and go back inside. When she did, he stood and continued on.

He thought about their main headline, taken from a revolutionary poster that was hung all around Shanghai. It showed several Red Guards holding up Mao's book of quotations, with the popular slogan *"Hold high the great red banner of Mao Zedong Thought—Revolution is no crime, to rebel is justified!"* Underneath and just over the story of the headmistress's murder, Wren had written her own slogan—*"If revolution leads to murder, is that justified?"* It was a strong statement against the Red Guards and one they'd debated, but she insisted it was the only way to make a huge impact right out of the gate.

He felt the stack of papers in his bag, realizing he only had a few dozen left. He'd skipped more boxes than he'd planned to, and now would have to hit at least one more street. He couldn't return home with any in his bag—first because of his promise to Wren and second because his mother might find them.

He walked past a few more streets, skipping them for one reason or another: someone outside, too many lights, or sometimes just going on instinct. Finally, he came to another quiet lane and turned in. After pausing to look around one more time, he dug into his bag and pulled out the rest of the papers. As quickly as possible, he left them one by one in every box on the street, coincidentally running out just as he hit the last house. Without even a look behind him, he took off, anxious to put a lot of distance between him and the foreseeable chaos the paper was bound to bring the next morning.

Half an hour later, Pony Boy's legs were wearing out. He would've preferred to go straight home, but thinking about Benfu had made him feel guilty enough to swing by his street. But now that he was near, he was reconsidering his detour.

He took out the small note from his pocket and read it again as he walked. Benfu had asked him to keep an eye on his parents during his absence. How he was supposed to fulfill the request when Benfu's mother literally hated him, he didn't know. However, now that time had settled his resentment and allowed him to realize it wasn't Benfu's fault he'd had to go, Pony Boy knew he'd been immature and had almost ruined a lifelong friendship.

He'd been too harsh on Benfu. And even after Benfu had said he couldn't relay the information to anyone, he'd written in the note where he was being sent. Or at least he'd told him as much as he himself knew. Pony Boy didn't know his exact location, but he knew approximately where he could be found.

Pony Boy folded the note and pushed it back into his pocket. That his friend had trusted him enough to share his secret meant the world to Pony Boy and the only way he knew to show his gratitude was to at least try to fulfill Benfu's request.

He hurried his pace, hoping that Cook would still be up to act as a buffer, or mediator—or whatever might be needed. Mrs. Zheng probably didn't like him any more now than she did when her son was still under her own roof, but to tell the truth, he felt the same about her. He'd only barely stomached her disapproving looks and sharp retorts. He'd felt sorry for Benfu, having a mother who was so cold and unable to show affection.

As he turned the corner he sensed he was hearing and seeing something familiar. Just inside the gate he saw several stacks of carpets, rolled up as though they were being readied to move. Pony Boy remembered the times he'd felt envy when walking upon the luxurious floor coverings, knowing his own floors were either bare or covered in remnants. He began to run and arrived just as a young man ran out the front door and leapt off the porch, his hands full of books.

Oh no, not Lao Zheng's collection, Pony Boy thought, then let himself into the yard. He went around the group of Red Guards, ignoring their demands to know who he was, and he strode inside the door.

"Lao Zheng, Mrs. Zheng," he called out, feeling a rush of panic. Where were they? He thought of the headmistress in Beijing and of how her body must have looked so broken at the end. Like her, Mrs. Zheng was also a part of the educational world. Was that the reason the Red Guards were there? To do something as heinous to them as was done in Beijing? As much as Benfu's mother was a nuisance to Pony Boy, he still didn't wish that kind of outcome for her—or even his worst enemy.

He moved around an overturned antique chair and kept calling out to them. When no one answered he made his way down the hall toward the library, the noise emanating from there indicating it was the room getting the bulk of attention in the raid.

When he arrived at the doorway, one look told him that Benfu's parents were in trouble. His father sat in his usual chair, but this time it appeared he was there by force. Mrs. Zheng knelt on the floor beside him, clutching her husband's hand as a Red Guard towered over them, his face red with rage as he held up a book.

"This is bourgeois propaganda!" the apparent leader shouted, raising shouts of approval from the three other members of his team who were busy pulling other books from the study shelves. They stacked them in their arms, competing to carry the most in their frenzy to empty the room of the decadent material.

Lao Zheng calmly shook his head, his voice low and resigned. "It's not propaganda. It's a classic story of loyalty and justice, read and enjoyed by thousands of Chinese, including some of the top students I've taught over the years."

Wrong thing to say, Pony Boy thought, then stepped into the room. Surprisingly, his appearance went unnoticed, just one more body in the chaos of human activity in such a small enclosure.

"*The Water Margin* is about renegades fighting against those in control. Is that what you want to happen to our dear Chairman Mao?" the leader yelled, raising the book again for emphasis.

"No, you are wrong. *The Water Margin* is about the common people coming together to bring down corrupt officials. From what I know, Chairman Mao and his party officials are stellar in their reputation," Lao Zheng said.

"We love Chairman Mao," Mrs. Zheng cried out, her head bobbing in affirmation.

"That's not what we see here around us," the leader said. "Now you'll have a chance to prove it, starting with doing away with all your beloved classics—as you call them. Follow me."

He strode out of the room with the other members of his group behind him, struggling beneath their loads of books.

Pony Boy moved aside and let them go just as Lao Zheng and his wife stood.

"What are you doing here?" Benfu's mother said, still hanging on to her husband's arm.

Lao Zheng turned to him. "Pony Boy, I think you picked the wrong night to visit. As you can see, we're in a bit of trouble. One of our neighbors turned us in to the committee—and our house is tonight's seek-and-destroy mission for the Red Guards."

On that note, they heard a crash in another room.

"My paintings!" Mrs. Zheng cried out and her husband grabbed her arm as she attempted to go toward the source of the noise.

To Pony Boy, Benfu's father looked much older than he ever had before. His face had paled in shock. But his voice was strong and he held himself erect, keeping his pride intact.

"What can I do?" Pony Boy asked, desperate to help in some small way. He knew that Benfu would be devastated to see what was happening to his home—to his parents. That made him think of Cook and Old Butler and he wondered where they were.

"We have to get out there," Lao Zheng said. "If we don't, they'll try to say that we refused to follow their instructions. You go on home, Pony Boy. You have enough trouble in your own house without taking on ours."

He moved by Pony Boy, taking Mrs. Zheng with him, but when they passed she paused.

"Go ahead, see what they're doing out there," she told her husband. "I'll be right along. Let me talk to Pony Boy for a moment."

Lao Zheng gave her a curious look but another crash and yell from somewhere in the house caught his attention and he quickly moved out of the library and down the hall.

Mrs. Zheng turned to Pony Boy, then pushed something into his hands. "They're going to find everything. Please—please keep this safe until Benfu comes home. It's very valuable."

When he looked at the hard object she'd pushed into his hands, he saw it was a miniature water buffalo. He remembered seeing it when he and Benfu had sat in his father's library, but he didn't remember it being such a delicate and expensive-looking piece of jade.

"Mrs. Zheng, I can't," he said, trying to hand it back to her.

They heard a shuffle in the hall and she covered his hand with hers, making him close his fist over the piece. "For Benfu," she whispered, then stood back as another Red Guard entered.

"I found a musician's stand," she said. "Where are the instruments?"

Mrs. Zheng shook her head, then shrugged at the girl who stood glaring at them. "We don't have any."

"I seriously doubt that but since I can't find them, let's finish up outside," she said, turning her attention to Pony Boy. "And is this the spoiled son? I saw his bedroom—looked fit for an emperor. Maybe he knows where I can find the musical instruments in this house."

Pony Boy slyly slipped the buffalo into his pocket, then held his hands up. "I don't live here. I'm just a mail carrier stopping in to see what's going on."

Her face transformed and she stood aside, beckoning for him to pass. Pony Boy noticed the green military pants and jacket she wore were at least two sizes two big, but her bright red armband appeared to be brand new. "Mail carriers are of the people and a respectable job. I apologize for the insult," she said.

Pony Boy didn't reply. He looked at Benfu's mother just as she visibly flinched. Reputation and family name were everything to her and he knew the words the Red Guard spoke cut deep. To her credit though, she kept her mouth shut and followed the girl down the hall. They were led out the door to where others had gathered in the courtyard. At least seven of them stood around a huge pile of the Zhengs' books, laughing and full of excitement as if they were at a festive outing.

"My flowers," Mrs. Zheng cried out, covering her mouth with her hands as she looked around the dimly lit courtyard. Between all the heavy boots stomping back and forth and the huge pile of books, her cherished flower garden was ruined. Petals were scattered everywhere and bushes lay flat against the ground.

Lao Zheng stood in front of the books, staring down at them with pity as if they were wayward children waiting on him to reach down and pull them out of their predicament.

"Chairman Mao says that these books teach bourgeois values and must be obliterated," the faction leader called out, then grinned as the members of his gang whistled and cheered. "Only books that teach Mao Thought are allowed!"

"Down with the Four Olds!" another member called out.

"Burn the books, burn the books, burn the books," one began and others joined in as they chanted together.

Pony Boy felt helpless as he watched the Red Guards kick at the books and push them into a taller, tighter pile. On the other side of the courtyard, he heard a ruckus and turned to see a guard carrying out a box, with another guard following along trying to peek inside.

"Treasures to be turned in to help fight the cause," the one carrying the box said.

Beside him Benfu's mother began to cry. The two guards took the box out to their cart in the street and piled it atop a huge stack of silk linens.

"Oh no, they've found the collection," Mrs. Zheng whimpered, pulling on her husband's sleeve to get his attention.

Pony Boy thought of the jade buffalo in his pocket and knew it was the other jade miniatures that she spoke about—a collection that Lao Zheng had begun years ago and spent a lot of money and time building. However, her husband paid her little attention. His eyes were on his beloved books.

The Zhengs were scholars. Taking away their books was like ripping their hearts from their chests. Pony Boy knew that Benfu would've fought to the end to save them. He felt sadness well in him, and with it a new passion to record all that was happening. He slowly backed away until he was out of sight, then slipped his camera from his bag and took a shot, the first one with Benfu's parents in full view, their bent and broken profiles like ghosts in a mist.

As they watched, the team leader began picking up books and tearing pages from them, wadding the paper and throwing it back on the pile. When the team leader finished, he walked over to Lao Zheng and dug in his pocket, then extended his hand.

Pony Boy could see that the hand held a lighter and his breath caught in his throat.

"You, *Teacher* Zheng," he spat out, his voice full of self-righteous condescension. "If you are truly repentant for your decadent lifestyle, you will light the fire yourself," he said.

"Ju, don't do it," Mrs. Zheng hissed at him. "We can salvage some of this. Talk to them!"

Lao Zheng held his hand up to stop her talking. "Feiyan, they're right. To own such books is an affront to the New China. We must join in and do away with the Four Olds to come out stronger and more united."

Mrs. Zheng was struck speechless and looked confused, but Pony Boy knew what Lao Zheng was doing. He was trying to keep the raid as non-violent as possible. Complying was the only way to pacify the Red Guards. Pony Boy could only imagine how both of Benfu's parents felt, being attacked and ridiculed by students—the very demographic of people they'd spent their careers trying to mold into successful adults. Like rabid dogs, the students had turned on those they once respected. All in the name of Mao.

Benfu had been right all along.

For how could this be good for their country? How could students turning on teachers, neighbors on neighbors—even children on parents—end in anything but a senseless slaughter?

To Pony Boy's horror, Lao Zheng slowly took the lighter. He then bent and after a few false starts, he lit the first book. When the initial small flame took hold and more flames sprouted from other pages of books, Pony Boy could make out the glistening of silent tears running down the old man's face. He looked away, giving him at least that much dignity.

Feeling helpless, he left the courtyard. Mrs. Zheng's sobs rang in his ears and settled into his heart until he got far enough for them to fade away. When the chaos was behind him and he drew closer to home, he knew one other thing—tonight, for the first time, he was relieved that his family owned no prized possessions that could bring down the wrath of Mao's personal army.

He felt exhaustion seeping into the deepest part of his bones. After a full day of work, then the exhilaration of delivering their first edition of the newsletter, and finally witnessing the persecution of good people, he felt much older than his years. He needed to find Benfu. He needed to see him with his own eyes, confirm that he was still getting by, was perhaps even thriving in the clean, country air. The thoughts swirled through his mind, competing with remnants of what he'd just seen. Hanging his head, he slowly picked up his legs, one at a time in his yearning to get to the one place he felt safe.

Home.

Chapter Twenty-One

It was much too early as Benfu struggled to get his aching body up from the bamboo mat that served as his bed. A month in and not much had changed. It was time for another long, agonizing day of work followed by hours of mind-numbing meetings designated as education sessions, skimpy meals, and a wash in the muddy creek bed to try to retain some semblance of dignity.

No longer did he even dream of making music, attending theater, or even socializing with Juan Hui. And he'd tried to erase memories of poetry and music from his mind. Someone had indeed turned him in after hearing a few words they'd deemed inappropriate, and Benfu had experienced his first and so far only turn at a self-criticism. To get it over with and keep the ire of the commune down, he'd had to admit to bourgeois thoughts and swear to study Chairman Mao's works harder.

He needed to accept his new life and stop thinking of the past. But it wasn't easy when others gathered each afternoon, waiting to see what the postman brought—eagerly crying out when their names were called. The first time he'd seen the mail call, the man with his mailbag draped around his body, Benfu had thought of Pony Boy. He'd wondered if and when they'd ever see each other again. Thoughts of the newsletter and ideas for articles also swirled in his mind—ideas that would never see the light of day because he was stuck in this forsaken commune, being treated like a slave, missing his opportunity to educate the people about what was really happening in their country.

He realized that seeing the postman bothered him.

Not that he ever expected to receive a letter, he mused when Gong Ran's voice penetrated his concentration. He fought the heaviness of his body and, once standing, peered at Gong Ran who was saying something. Benfu only saw his lips moving on the blurry smudge that was supposed to be his face, the sound of his words drowned out by the blaring of the latest revolutionary song on the loudspeaker outside their room. Their other two roommates were already gone, most likely racing to be first in line at the kitchen.

The sun hadn't even come up as they prepared to go stand in line for what would most likely be a bowl of congee for breakfast, before making a beeline for the fields.

Another day.

More time to think about home and all he was missing. *Oh wait— I'm not supposed to think of it*, he told himself as he fumbled in the dark. He wouldn't go there again. He concentrated on visualizing his work order for the day. What was it again?

With his pants finally up, he reached for the drawstrings. They'd have to be pulled tight, as he'd lost a lot of weight since coming to the commune. Pony Boy wouldn't even recognize the thin person he'd become—no longer the thickest one in sight. Benfu was grateful that Cook had thought to sew the strings into his waistband, though she hadn't explained why.

He groped, realizing his right hand wasn't obeying his brain. Something had taken a turn for the worse over the last few hours. He'd tossed and turned most of the night, feeling feverish as his hand throbbed. In the dark, he couldn't see it. He walked to the table at the window. He reached for their lantern, turning the knob to make the flame bigger.

Holding his hand closer to the light it made, he blinked a few times, trying to clear his vision.

He couldn't be seeing what he thought he saw.

His hand was at least twice its regular size—red and puffy with a solid red stripe down the middle of his pale palm. He stared at it, his thoughts jumbled as he tried to think of what he could do to make it go away.

"What's going on, Benfu?" Gong Ran said. He sat on their only chair, pulling his boots on. "You kept me awake all night, moaning and moving around."

Benfu turned to him, thankful that Gong Ran's voice was sympathetic instead of accusing. "It's my hand. I think it's infected."

Gong Ran stood and crossed the room. He took Benfu's hand, holding it up and examining it in the dim light from the lantern.

"*Aiya*, this is bad. When did this happen?" he asked.

Benfu shrugged. "A few days ago. Maybe? I can't remember but I know I got a briar in it when we were clearing that area behind the dining hall."

"That was a week ago. You've let this go on that long? Why didn't you say something?" Gong Ran said.

"I didn't want to look weak."

"Would you rather look dead?" Gong Ran said. He held his hand to Benfu's head. With his stern voice and disapproving expression, he reminded Benfu of Old Butler and he felt a wave of homesickness for the man. Gong Ran sighed loudly. "You're burning with fever and your eyes are all jittery."

Benfu felt his stomach roll. He bent over, then headed for the door. He got there and opened it just in time for a wave of hot vomit to spew onto the dirt in front of their entrance. He dropped to his knees, his hands on the ground to support his weight. The effort of purging his stomach's meager contents left his head spinning and his limbs no longer working the way they were supposed to.

He heaved again, then felt Gong Ran come behind him and reach down to grab his arm.

"You can't work today," he said, helping him to his feet.

Benfu tried to struggle free. "I have to work. If I don't, they'll make me speak self-criticisms for not doing my part."

"How about this—you can choose to go back to bed or you choose to go out to the field and probably drop dead in an hour or two. Your hand is past infection, brother. It needs to be looked at. I'll go find the team leader and see if he can get you some help."

Benfu sighed. What choice did he have? To be honest, his body felt heavy and sluggish. His hand ached and he was nauseated and dizzy. What could he possibly do in the fields? Other than like Gong Ran said—just drop dead? He thought of their recent team leader and his strict lecture on showing up for work on time, every day. What would his punishment be? Would he receive any mercy at all? Still, he had no choice. He couldn't work. If possible, his shoulders slumped down further, acknowledging defeat.

Gong Ran took it for submission and gently led him back to his pallet and helped to lower him to the floor. "Don't worry. I'll be back soon. We'll get you fixed up."

Benfu didn't have the strength to argue any more. As his head hit the floor, he immediately passed out.

Benfu wasn't sure how long Gong Ran was gone, but when he returned it was still dark. Benfu struggled to roll over so that he could get to a sitting position, but he couldn't do it. Gong Ran puttered around the room, putting a pot of water on top of their small stove. Benfu wondered what he was doing and strained again to sit up, but then gave up and waited for his friend to come to him.

"Benfu, I'm sorry I was gone so long," he said. "They wouldn't let me come back. I had to work all day."

Benfu opened his eyes again, straining to see Gong Ran. Work? All day? What time was it? "But you just left, didn't you?"

Gong Ran reached down and put a cool rag against Benfu's forehead. It felt like heaven and he sighed his gratitude. He wished it could stay that way but already, in just seconds, the coolness was disappearing and the rag was getting warm.

"No. It's dinnertime now. You've been sleeping all day but they promised to send someone to tend to you after work hours. Come on, try to sit." He pulled on Benfu's arm, helping him to a sitting position that made his head spin.

"Where's Cook? She'll fix me up," Benfu muttered. "I have lessons in an hour, I can't be late."

"What lessons? What cook? The only cooks around here will slap you silly for wasting a day of work, no matter what ailment you have," Gong Ran said. "Come on, Benfu. Wake up."

Benfu shook his head, trying to clear the cobwebs. He could've sworn that he'd seen Old Butler in the doorway a second ago. He looked around, examining the bare room. It was sparse—void of furniture as well as any semblance of comfort.

Gong Ran was saying something else but Benfu couldn't concentrate. His lips moved so fast—it didn't look real.

The door opened and a man entered. A rectangular brown case with a red cross on the front of it hung from a sash around his body and he wore thin spectacles around his neck on a frayed piece of rope. As he came closer, Benfu realized that he didn't look much older than him, yet he held a stoic expression.

Gong Ran stood and moved back, allowing the young man to take his place beside Benfu.

"I'm Doctor Yu and I'm here to see about your hand. Please hold it out," the man said.

"You're a real doctor? You don't look old enough to be a doctor," Benfu mumbled, but held his hand out obediently.

"I'm as close as you're going to get here," the doctor said as he pushed around on Benfu's palm, peering closely at it.

Benfu remembered a conversation held between his parents, talk of the barefoot doctors being sent out into the country to see to the people. A directive handed down from Chairman Mao indicated that just about anyone could be a doctor—not only those with extended educations. He looked down at the man's feet and saw he wore no shoes.

He laughed, thinking how amazed his father would be to know that one of those very doctors was now tending to his son. He wondered for a moment just how much training the man had received, but in the next instant realized he didn't care. He just wanted to sleep.

"Can I lie back again?" he asked.

Doctor Yu shook his head, then held his stethoscope to Benfu's chest. He listened for a moment before answering. "You aren't going back to sleep until we tend to this hand. It's infected—obviously. If we do nothing, you'll either lose it or worse, the infection will spread through your body and we'll lose you." He dropped the stethoscope and pointed at Gong Ran. "You—take the water off the heat. I don't want it to boil."

"The gods know we need every able man in those fields," Benfu said, chuckling and realizing at the same time that he sounded quite drunk. Again, he didn't care. The man's cool hands crept around his hand and arm, making Benfu feel enough relief that a sudden burst of gratitude filled him, a thankfulness that Gong Ran had found someone to tend him. Then the doctor squeezed the area where the briar had gone in, sending pus squirting out and Benfu jerking upright before the doctor finally stopped his torture and went back to feeling the skin going up his arm.

Gong Ran noisily did as directed with the water, then cleared his throat. "I'm uh—uh—going to go ahead to the dining hall. If that's acceptable, doctor?"

Doctor Yu nodded, waving his hand in the air to dismiss Gong Ran. A gesture that also made Benfu's funny bone react. Why did everything seem so funny all of a sudden?

The doctor let Benfu's hand drop and he rose, going to the small table that served as their only piece of furniture in the room. His back was to Benfu but he could see him begin to remove things from his bag and set them on the table. He went to the stove and picked up the pot of water, holding a shirt around the handle to keep from burning his hand as he brought it to the table.

"When did you become a doctor?" Benfu asked, eager to break the eerie silence of the room.

"I was sent into the country only months ago," Doctor Yu said as he took out a few bags, then took something from each of them and put them in a small stone bowl. He poured some of the water in, then used what appeared to be some sort of tool to mash it.

"Did you have training?" Benfu asked. At least his brain was kicking in again, his curiosity overriding his pain.

The room filled with the scents of garlic, onion, and ginger—an aroma that once again reminded him of home and sitting in the kitchen with Cook as she chopped and peeled vegetables for their dinners.

"A bit." The doctor shrugged. "Perhaps about four months of study."

"Do you treat patients all day?" Benfu thought it must be wonderful to be able to steer clear of all the field work, no matter what he had to treat.

"I still work in the fields for half a day, but my evenings are spent seeing patients, unless there's an early morning emergency. Your ailment was deemed by the team leader as not life-threatening—though if he could see it, he might've changed his mind and let me come earlier," the doctor said, his disapproval evident in his tone.

"Am I going to die?" Benfu asked, half-jokingly.

The doctor looked up briefly, his face solemn. "I don't know."

Benfu was shocked. It was just his hand! How could it have gotten so serious? He realized that he didn't want to die. He had a lot to accomplish and he wanted to get out of the commune to finish his life. He looked at his hand, astonished that one tiny briar could threaten everything he had to look forward to.

The doctor must have sensed his fear. He reached out and patted Benfu on the shoulder. "We'll work through this. It'll be painful, but I think you'll survive."

Benfu felt a rush of relief so strong it kept him silent for the next half hour as the doctor finished his poultice, soaked a ripped piece of material in it, then pressed it onto Benfu's hand and tied another piece of material atop it to keep it tight against his palm.

"In fifteen minutes, we squeeze out more infection, then put on a new poultice," the doctor said as he rose with his tools and returned to the table.

Benfu sighed, glad to be free for a moment. "I can't wait, doc."

The doctor didn't bristle at his sarcastic reply. Instead he took a glass from the shelf above the table and poured some of the hot water into it, then mixed something else in. He brought it back to Benfu and held it to his lips. "Now you drink. Then you sleep. I'll watch over you," Doctor Yu said, the kindness traveling from his lips to his eyes as he held the bitter concoction and made Benfu drink.

"*Xie xie*, doctor," Benfu muttered. He was already feeling groggy only seconds after drinking the warm liquid and feeling it pool into a lake of comfort in his empty belly.

Sleep.

That's what he needed most of all and he let his eyes close as he lay back down on his pallet. He felt the doctor cover him with a blanket before he allowed the darkness to overtake him. His final thoughts were of a huge plate of crab legs, cooked with the savory blend of garlic and ginger, and the touch of affection that always accompanied a meal in his kitchen at home.

Chapter Twenty-Two

"Chairman Mao is the red sun that shines the brightest in our hearts. He is the greatest leader, teacher, and father of all, selected by the people of China to lead their revolutionary struggles. Declared the most brilliant mind to—" The commune leader droned on and on, almost putting Benfu to sleep because he'd heard it so often in the last few weeks.

He straightened, forcing himself to wake up. Anyone spotted sleeping would be ridiculed, or worse, and he didn't need that. With the others in the commune, he sat around in the Hall of Hell, waiting to see if their nightly reeducation would turn into a denunciation session. No one said it, but it was clear that all were on full alert to see if someone, and if so, who, would be led forward for some unforeseen transgression. Benfu looked at his bandaged hand, feeling relief that it was almost back to normal. In the week following the ministrations of Doctor Yu, the infection had all but disappeared and the strength was slowly returning to his fingers. His other hand was getting a workout, since his workload had not decreased just because of his injury. If anything, he was expected to do more to make up for the time he lost while being treated.

One good thing came of it though. With the many visits from the doctor, he and Benfu had built a friendship of sorts, and the gratitude he owed the man was immense. Benfu just hoped that one day he'd be able to repay him.

"Most of us will have to eat bitterness sometime or other," the commune leader said from his place at the tall upturned stump that served as his pulpit. He'd been talking for the last hour, reiterating passages from Chairman Mao's red book as he intermittently named off the list of quotas his team had made in regards to feeding Mao's troops.

Behind them, Benfu heard the sound of an engine. Along with others in the back rows, he turned to see a bus pulling through the large metal gates of the commune.

"New arrivals," someone murmured.

"Fresh meat," someone else said and others in the crowd snickered.

"Hear, hear," the team leader yelled. "We'll stand and welcome the new members of our commune. Let's give them a hand as they come off the bus."

Benfu looked down at his bandaged hand. They wouldn't want his if they knew what it had been through, but he was glad for a diversion to the mind-numbing lectures. For an hour, as the team leader had lectured, he'd daydreamed of going to the well and pulling out his violin, then returning to stand in front of the people in the hall to really give them something to think about.

Music.

And not the glut of new revolutionary songs that everyone but him seemed to know the words to and butchered with their off-tune screeching. He meant real music—sounds that could bring peace and comfort, and were actually pleasant to the ear. He missed it even more than food. The longer he went without it, the more he obsessed over it. The night before he'd even slipped the folded sheet of music out of his bag, squinting at it in the dim light just before he went off to sleep.

Mentally he played the notes, his heart accelerating in just the appropriate places, his mind thankful that he hadn't forgotten.

Breaking through his thoughts, a squad leader yelled, then stepped off the bus and waved the others down. One by one, they emerged, looking frightened. Benfu wondered if that was what he had looked like when he'd arrived. Most likely like he had, they were speculating what life in the commune would be like, and he knew one thing—it was worse than their imaginations had probably dreamed up. Perhaps some of the communes around China were great places to live and thrive, but this wasn't one of those. He felt pity for the newcomers.

The team leader started them off and soon everyone in the open-air hall was applauding the new arrivals as they were led in a line toward the crowd, then seated in a newly made back row. Benfu examined them, noting that a few boys looked as young as Lixin. Only two of the dozen or so people who stepped off the bus were girls, and they looked the most frightened of all. If they thought they'd only be doing women's work here, Benfu knew they'd get a surprise in the morning when they were ordered alongside the boys and men. Here women worked in the fields, gardens, and even helped build the small huts for the elderly. In Chairman Mao's vision, he claimed that women held up half the sky so were considered equal. That meant equal in everything, including using their strength to work, work, and work some more.

Finally all the new members had sat down and the bus driver pulled away. The team leader banged his tin cup on the top of the stump, gaining attention throughout the hall.

"Welcome, welcome," he said. "Let's all join together in a song of rejoice for the cause of the Cultural Revolution!"

Benfu quietly fumed as he moved his lips soundlessly to appear that he was joining in the singing of a song about the kindness of Chairman Mao. As Benfu looked around, he felt like sneering at the words. For, as far as he could see, there was no kindness sent their way. The men and women, young and old—mostly looked exhausted, hungry, and bordering on feeble. They worked hard and for what? Where was their reward? To be sweltering in the summer heat and freezing in the winters? To wade through wet fields during the long days and nights of rain? To feel such hunger that their stomachs were concave instead of healthily rounded like Mao's Red Guards' probably were?

Yet he wasn't so stupid that he would voice his thoughts aloud. His father's warnings rang in his ears, especially during those moments that his indignation was at its highest. His was that lone, calming voice Benfu focused on to keep him out of trouble.

The song ended and the people sat again, most squatting but a few finding comfort on a small rock or one of the few benches in the front of the hall. Benfu saw the top of a red hat and realized that he hadn't seen the red-hat man on any of the passing work teams lately. He hoped he'd not been unwell, but even if he had been, no one complained of fatigue. To complain was counterrevolutionary. Criticisms were of the enemy. *The people should be thankful that they were so well taken care of in one of Mao's best communes,* or at least that was what was repeated to them daily.

"Tomorrow, all you new arrivals will be assigned to your work duties and prospective brigade leaders," the team leader said. "Tonight we have an unfortunate incident to discuss."

Everyone immediately quieted. *Unfortunate incident* was a phrase only used when something serious was about to be exposed.

"As you all know, in a commune we are brought together as a collective," he continued. "And as a collective, we share everything."

Benfu looked around, trying to gauge the expressions of others. Someone had obviously been caught with more than their share of something.

"And everyone knows the rules—if you don't work, you don't eat." He looked out over the crowd, people shrinking lower in their seats under his gaze. "But someone here has been eating without working. Moreover, it has been reported by his neighbor that he has been growing his own small garden, a direct insubordinate action and evidence that he is not interested in working or sharing as a collective."

A buzz came over the crowd as people looked left and right, searching for the traitor. When a hush came over them again, Benfu gasped to see the red-hat man slowly rise to his feet, his head bowed.

Those who only seconds before had sat beside him as comrades now pushed him violently toward the front of the hall. Others joined in as he passed, until he was tripping over his feet in his effort not to fall to the ground. It shocked Benfu how the people turned on him, without even hearing his defense. He held back his urge to go to him.

"*Dui*, I'm pleased you came forward, Lao Kuan," the team leader said. He pointed to the empty wooden chair that stood beside his makeshift podium and the old man obediently climbed atop it. As he knew would be required, Kuan bent low at the waist, bowing to the crowd and the impending criticisms sure to come. Benfu hoped they wouldn't make the old man do the usual helicopter pose, as twisting his arms behind his back as he bowed would most likely be more than the man could physically handle. Benfu felt sick to his stomach. He only knew the red-hat man to be quiet and kind, staying to himself so much that he'd never even shared his name. Benfu had seen him work just as hard as the younger men, up until the last week or so when he hadn't been around. And who was the neighbor that had disclosed his secret? That person should be the one on display—tagged as an individual with no heart or honor, even a coward who preyed on the weak.

"What do you have to say for yourself, Lao Kuan?" the team leader asked. When Kuan didn't immediately answer, he gave the chair a kick, almost toppling the man and making him grasp the chair back for support.

Kuan looked up at the crowd, his face pale with fear. "I am deeply sorry but the team leader is right, I have not been working as I should. The pain in my body has flared up from the rain and—"

"We all have aches and pains!" someone shouted from the crowd, interrupting Kuan into silence again.

"Tell them about the crops you've kept hidden," the team leader urged, his voice rising to a yell. Others in the crowd seconded his demand, sounding like mocking birds to Benfu's ears.

"It's only a few heads of cabbage and some sprigs of ginger—not really even a garden," Kuan said, holding his hands up in a plea to the crowd. "I thought if I could grow my own cabbage, I wouldn't have to take food from the dining hall when I'm unable to work. The ginger is for tea to treat the ache in my bones."

"Save your excuses, old man, and bow your head! You know the rules. All tools, food, and shelter belong to the people as a collective. Any crops are to be turned in for counting and distribution."

Kuan immediately went back to a bowing position, his body trembling from the effort to keep his balance on the small seat of the chair.

"He's a snake in the grass," said a girl from the middle row of people.

"No, he's a dumb cow," someone added, making Benfu wonder how people could be so cruel. The man was old and obviously in pain. It was all he could do not to speak up in defense of the man. But he knew what that would get him. He'd be standing right beside him, balancing on another chair as he fielded insult after insult.

"Put him in the cowshed!" the crowd began to chant together.

This time Benfu didn't pretend to join in. It made him sick. He'd seen more than one person be held as prisoner in the cowshed and it was a cruel punishment of days on end with minimum water and only morsels of food to keep them alive. The man was too old to withstand such treatment.

Someone else leaped forward and pushed the chair, sending the man to the ground in a heap of flailing arms and legs. The team leader jerked him up by his arm, pulling him to his feet. "They are right, a dumb cow should be remanded to his shed," he said.

Benfu stood frozen in place as fear flooded Kuan's face. With a few more jerks, the team leader began leading him away from the hall and toward the back of the commune where the cowshed stood empty, awaiting its next prisoner. The crowd followed, leaving only a few stragglers behind.

When Benfu looked back to where the chair lay toppled, he saw the red hat. He went and picked it up, turning it over in his hands. Something white inside the brim caught his eye and he turned it inside out, straining to see the white piece of cloth sewed inside the top of it. He could barely make out something written there. It was just a few characters, but the words they made up brought a lump to Benfu's throat.

It read, *"Stay courageous, my love."*

Chapter Twenty-Three

The letter felt like it was burning a hole in his bag, but Pony Boy needed to finish his route. It was a different feeling than the one he experienced when he'd delivered the first edition of *The Palest Ink*. This time, what he carried had the potential to bring a smile to those he loved, but also a chance of tears instead. He tried not to think of it, and turned his attention to his route and his thoughts to their next project.

Thus far, he'd not heard any buzz on the streets about his delivery of the newsletter, but it was imperative that he keep all his actions as normal as possible. He turned the corner and picked up the pace. If he hurried, he'd still get to his second job on time.

Already he'd been by Widow Chou's house and though she was grieving, he had to give her credit, she was still going strong. She and her last bird, kept hidden in a back room but free from any cage, spent their days doing just as they'd done before. Of course, she wasn't able to take the bird to the park any longer, but at least she still had him to keep her company and she felt sure the Red Guards wouldn't be back. Pony Boy had spent some time during each route helping her to straighten up around her home, fixing a few broken pieces of furniture and hauling off what couldn't be salvaged, but mostly he'd just let her know that she wasn't alone.

After dropping a few letters as he went, he finally came to Wang Zi's house. The old man sat on the front stoop. When he saw Pony Boy come around the bend, he stood and met him at the gate.

"Pony Boy, I need to talk to you," he said, opening the gate and beckoning with his arm.

"I—I don't have a lot of time today, Lao Wang."

"Please, it's important." Wang put his hand on Pony Boy's shoulder, urging him in.

With the look on the old man's face, Pony Boy couldn't tell him no. He slid in, hoping they could keep it quick.

He'd never been in the man's house and when he entered, he looked around, surprised at how neat everything was. The main room was sparse, but nothing appeared out of place. A small rattan settee and a table with three chairs were the only furniture, so Pony Boy went to the table and pulled out a chair, then sat down.

"I'll be right back," Wang said, disappearing through a door that was most likely his bedroom.

Directly on the wall in front of Pony Boy hung a wrinkled poster of Chairman Mao, his mole bigger and brighter than ever. On the table were newspapers read and refolded, stacked high, but Mao's Little Red Book sat atop them, obviously the last thing read by the old man. Pony Boy once thought Chairman Mao's thoughts and inspirational quotes were enlightening, but now he pitied Wang if he believed everything their so-called beloved leader said.

Wang returned with a tall stack of letters in his hand, tied together with burlap string. He came over and set them on the table, then sat down across from Pony Boy.

"Your father is a noble man."

Pony Boy nodded. What did his father have to do with a stack of letters?

"Very trustworthy."

"Dui," Pony Boy agreed, resisting the urge to look at his watch. He needed to get back on his route.

"Well, a tiger does not have dogs for sons." Wang nervously tapped his long nails on the table, watching Pony Boy's face carefully.

"I—uh—that's true, Lao Wang," Pony Boy said, wondering where the man was going with his uttering of the proverb that meant a son usually followed in his father's footsteps.

"Then I can trust you as I would your father?"

Pony Boy nodded. *"Dui,* you can trust me, Lao Wang. You are a friend of my father and that means a friend of mine."

Wang jumped up, his nervous energy showing in his quicker-than-normal actions. He went to his cabinet, picked two cups from it and then used water from the teakettle to fill them. Bringing them back to the table, he paused once halfway there, then continued and set the cups down before taking his seat again.

Pony Boy took a sip of the lukewarm water, waiting for Wang to say what he wanted to say. He didn't want to rush the man, but he wished he'd hurry with it.

"I am not Shanghainese," Wang muttered, looking around as if others were in the room trying to eavesdrop on their conversation.

"You aren't? I didn't know that."

"Most people think I am from here because I'm one of the oldest on this street and others who were here before me have gone on to the afterworld."

Pony Boy eyed the stack of letters, wondering what they had to do with the man's story. He waited for him to say more.

Wang took a deep breath, then began again. "I am originally from a small village many, many miles from here."

When Pony Boy didn't respond to his words, he kept going.

"In 1950, after Mao declared the Land Reform law, I was one of the first to be affected. My land—the twenty acres that had been in my family for many generations—was to be taken from me. I fought it, taking my grievances all the way up the ladder in the hopes that the decision would be overturned."

He looked down at his hands, turning them over as he stared.

When he returned his gaze to Pony Boy, his eyes were glistening. "But they declined my efforts. I thought it unfair—I'd been good to all the people who worked for me. From the house *ayis* to the field workers, they were treated fairly and had better lives than most in the country. Unlike my neighbor, I gave my people three weeks off to celebrate every new year. I provided them with fresh milk for their children and gave them the freedom to grow their own gardens. Yet when they smelled a possibility for them to prosper from the new law, they turned on me. They told lies, made accusations that their pay wasn't fair and that I refused to provide upkeep on their small homes. Homes that I let them live in for free as they worked my land!"

His voice rose in anger, then he looked at the door and quieted again.

"It was chaos, much like is happening today. All around our county there were rumors that landlords were being stripped of their property, some even sent to prisons. A few beaten and more than a couple actually executed as they resisted. Holdings were being seized and distributed among the people. It was insanity! I tried to reason with them, offering them other incentives if they'd let me hold on to the land I'd worked with my own two hands, all my life. And my small home—not much bigger or better than what I provided for those who worked for me—suddenly I was about to lose it, too."

"That's really tragic," Pony Boy offered. Before now, he'd only heard bits and pieces of how the land reform had affected people, and he'd always thought that it was a good idea to distribute China's land among those other than the rich. From what he remembered, thousands if not millions had been impacted by the move. Now, Pony Boy wasn't so sure it was as fair as history lessons depicted.

Wang continued. "My land and home were my only way to give my family a better future, the only things that, as a man, I could leave my children when I was gone. When the officials threatened to take them away, something came over me—a rage like I'd never encountered before."

Pony Boy felt something big was coming, something he probably didn't want to know about. He wished the old man would stop talking—stop giving away his secrets to those who couldn't carry the burden for him. "Lao Wang, maybe you shouldn't—"

The old man held a hand up, silencing him. "Please. Hear me out. I sent my wife and children away before the officials came to deliver the order of the court. I didn't want them to see me break when the final word was handed down and I'd lost everything I'd worked my entire life for. So they went, and I made my wife promise not to come back until it was time for the next planting. I assured her that I'd fix everything and we wouldn't lose our home."

He paused again, his Adam's apple bobbing up and down as he tried to regain composure. "I'm thankful that I at least kissed each of my three young children, for I was not to know that it would be our last time together."

"Why? They didn't return?"

"Because when the officials came knocking, ready to evict me from my home, I was ready for them. The county office sent two to do their bidding, but none returned. For you see, Pony Boy, when a man is faced with total desolation, something rises within him to fight for what he believes is right." He thumped his chest with his fist.

"They didn't return? What does that mean?"

"It was an accident—at least somewhat. I only meant to scare them, get them to leave my land. But they both attacked me at once, claiming that I was to be taken to jail, then brought before a judge to answer for my crimes against the peasants. Crimes! I'd given them a fair wage and a roof over their heads and now I was accused of crimes!"

Pony Boy got up and retrieved the kettle from the stove. He put his hand to it, feeling if it was still warm, then brought it to the table and filled their cups again. It was a gesture not needed, but one that gave Wang time to think about his next words. Pony Boy hoped he'd stop before he said anything more.

But he didn't.

He continued. "I couldn't let them take me. I couldn't live in a metal cage, Pony Boy. I needed the countryside air and the sun on my face to even breathe. I couldn't imagine never again running the soil between my fingers, smelling the earth that my ancestors had helped to bring to such a deep, rich aroma. You see, the land and I—we'd always been connected. It was more than dirt to me—it was my lifeline. When they tried to take that from me, I snapped. Things escalated and it became a fight for my life—a situation of them or me."

He hung his head.

Pony Boy reached out and touched his hand. He couldn't imagine such a gentle man as Wang ever hurting anyone. "You killed them?"

Wang nodded, then spoke barely above a whisper. "I did. Then I ran."

"Why here?"

"I didn't come here at first. I hid out in the country, surviving off remnants of raw corn I nibbled on—sometimes soups I could make with herbs and the rare potato. I slept outside, battling the elements of the cold winds that were easing in for the winter. When I'd lost at least a third of my body weight and knew I was falling apart, I had to find refuge and this was the only place I knew to go. The real Wang Zi is my wife's brother. He allowed me to hide out here and when he got sick, I nursed him until his last breath. He never had his own family—there was no one to tend to him so I did it. He was full of gratitude and I swear to you, I did not steal his identity. He gave it to me as a gift to my wife, the little sister he'd loved and hadn't seen in decades. Keeping me safe was a way for him to show his familial loyalty. He made me give him my word that I would use his name and live in his home as long as I needed to. So I took it. I became Wang Zi and pretended to be a retired carpenter."

"I'm so sorry, Lao Wang," Pony Boy said, then immediately realized he was calling him by someone else's name. But what else to call him? He didn't even want to know the man's real name. He thought of the real Wang Zi and wondered how he'd been buried, if no one had even known he'd died. He wouldn't ask, but the question swirled in his mind.

"There's more," Wang replied. "My wife and children never returned to our home. They'd heard that I was wanted for murder and for their safety, they renounced me and embraced the peasant life."

"They turned on you?" Pony Boy could hardly say the words. He didn't understand how Wang's family—or whatever his name was—could just leave him high and dry.

Wang shook his head. "No, no, they didn't turn on me, they had to do what they could to stay together, even if that meant pretending to break ties with me. Eventually, through letters from her brother with some tricky wording, my wife understood I was hiding here. She traveled once to see me and we—her brother included—decided that she could send letters addressed to him but they'd really be to me."

Pony Boy looked at the tall stack of letters that Wang had set on the table. Now Pony Boy understood why Wang was so eager for each piece of mail. It was his only connection with the family he loved.

"But why are you telling me all this?"

Wang pushed the stack of letters toward him. "Because I need your help. With the announcement of the Cultural Revolution and the battle against the upper class, it's rumored that my case has been reopened. Last week I had a visit from the county registrar. He said he needed to validate my *hukou*—or Wang's *hukou*—to be sure I was indeed a Shanghai native. He took it with him."

"Perhaps they're doing that to everyone," Pony Boy offered. Indeed he did know that family records and residential permits were being scrutinized all over. It was common knowledge that the officials were coming down on people moving around the country without permission. To live in the city, you needed a city *hukou*. If you were from the country, you stayed in the country unless given special permission. Those were the rules.

Wang shook his head. "I don't think so but even if that is true, these letters might say more than I think they do. I'd never want to put my wife and now-grown children in jeopardy, but I can't bear to burn them. It's all I have of them and one day, I hope to be reunited. But if we aren't—the letters are my only memories. Please, Pony Boy, take them for me. I am so afraid of what the officials will do when they return with the *hukou*."

Pony Boy eyed the letters and weighed the possibility. The letters could be a trail that led to dire consequences—consequences for which Pony Boy didn't want to be responsible. This wasn't a case of a man just hiding; it was a case that involved murder. And what about the real Wang? Surely a hidden death and stolen identity were crimes punishable by execution? Wang appeared to be more focused on his letters being discovered than his crimes. He was more worried about his loved ones than himself.

"I can't, Lao Wang. I can't put my family in danger, and if the letters are found in my home, who's to say they won't investigate and interview your family? I can't take that chance that my keeping those would result in either hurting my family or hurting yours. Please, I beg you to just burn them."

Lao Wang sighed, then he met Pony Boy's eyes. "I can't." He held up the stack. "To you this is just paper, but to me, these letters represent my family. I've read each of them hundreds of times, trying to imagine the faces behind the words, pretending they are here with me as I read each line." He sorted through the stack, then pulled out a red envelope, shaking a photo from it. "Do you know what this one is? It's news of my first grandson. I'm a grandfather, Pony Boy!"

"Congratulations," Pony Boy said. He picked up the photo and looked at the child, searching for a resemblance to Wang.

The old man took the picture back and sighed loudly. "He's eight years old now. But these letters are all I have and I can't destroy them. But thank you. Thank you for listening to my story."

Pony Boy wished he knew what to do. Then he wished the man would've never shared anything, as he had enough burdens of his own. He didn't want—couldn't handle—anything more. As much pity as he felt for Lao Wang, he couldn't help him. He stood. "Lao Wang, I must go. But you have my word, your story will never leave my lips."

Wang nodded, but he didn't move to escort Pony Boy to the door.

Pony Boy hurried across the room and when he slipped out, he turned to take one last look at Wang. He saw the man with his eyes closed and one letter in his hand, holding it to his heart as if embracing the woman who'd written it.

Pony Boy saw his mama peeking out of the window as soon as he rounded the corner on his block. When he was close enough, their eyes met and he smiled. She shrieked and her face disappeared. He knew that she could read him with one look and know that he'd received a letter from Lixin. Hurrying up the path, he put his hand on the door and it opened before he could turn the knob. She stood there wiping her hands on the apron tied to her waist.

"You got a letter," she stated more than asked. These days he wasn't stopping at home between jobs, so seeing him had obviously alerted her that finally, a new letter had come. He'd practically run through his route before heading home, and he was proud that he'd kept from ripping open the envelope in his impatience to see how his little brother was faring. It had been far too long since the last letter had arrived, leaving all of them in an unspoken cycle of worry.

He nodded to her, then hung his mailbag on the hook beside the door.

He noticed Wren and smiled. He'd finally introduced her to his family and like he'd predicted, they loved her. Mei had really taken up with her and Wren enjoyed bringing her special bows for her hair and even castoff clothes that with some adjustments, Wren and his mother made into new things Mei could wear. He appreciated her visits, even if he wasn't there to enjoy her company as well.

After he and Wren locked eyes for a moment, his attention went to the bed where his father lay, and he struggled to keep his worry from showing. His father had been having a bad few days and the grayness in his face belied his attempt at a reassuring smile.

"Bring it in, Pony Boy. Read it," he said, waving his hand weakly for Pony Boy to come sit beside him.

His mother shut the door behind him and went to the small wok balanced on the propane cooker. She switched it off, moving the noodles from the heat. Mei looked up from her place on the floor where she sat watching Wren cutting shapes from thin sheets of red paper, her eyes full of worry.

He sighed, then hurried across the room, perching on the bed and taking care not to bump his father. He looked down at the man who'd always been so strong and fearless, but now was relegated to being cared for by everyone else. "How are you feeling, Baba?"

His baba waved his hand in the air again. "Doesn't matter. Open the letter."

"What does he have to say?" his mother asked, her voice impatient as she wrung a dishtowel in her hands. "Hurry up, will you?"

Pony Boy ripped the end from the envelope and pulled out the sheet of paper. With one glance at the familiar writing, he felt a lump rise in his throat. He swallowed once, then he began to read.

"*Dear family, I hope this letter finds you well and that Baba's health has continued to improve. As for me, after a period of unrest, I'm settling in, but I am still very homesick. I'm also worried about how you all are getting by with Mama's cooking.*" Pony Boy stopped reading for a second to look at his mother, but the small smile on her face told him she knew Lixin was kidding. Pony Boy wasn't so sure, but he continued.

"*I'm only doing field work in the mornings now as I finally convinced the leader of the work group that I'm a better cook than farmer. The reprieve came after I bartered for the supplies and stayed up late to make him a dish of my special stir-fried pork shreds. The old woman who gave me the chives thought I'd be punished for the sudden appearance of the outlawed herbs, but the leader overlooked my ignorance this once because when the aroma reached his nose he couldn't turn away the dish. After tasting it, he decided I was right about my culinary skills."*

"What is he talking about—outlawed?" Baba said. "And where is he getting pork?"

"I don't know about the pork," Mama answered, "but from what I understand, the chives are forbidden because of their likeness to capitalists."

"I don't understand," Pony Boy said. Any hint of going against the law these days brought a shiver of fear to them all, but he was especially disturbed knowing that someone had intentionally tried to trick his brother. He felt a ripple of anger and a wish to knock some heads together. "What's the big deal about chives?"

Mama shook her head, the disdain showing on her pursed lips. "Like cutting off the tail of capitalism, once chives are chopped down they quickly grow back."

"It's so ridiculous," Wren said. "Why does every simple little item or action have to have an ulterior meaning? It's getting so that people are afraid to breathe for being accused of being selfish for taking air from their fellow neighbors."

"Let me finish the letter," Pony Boy said, turning his attention back to the awkwardly drawn characters. He couldn't let his parents see the glimmer of tears in his eyes as he read the rest of the words. It was his fault Lixin was gone—exiled to some forsaken place in the mountains of China. If only he'd found a way to support the family as well as keep Lixin safe, even if it meant hiding him. The ever-present burden of guilt lay heavy on his shoulders, but then he felt his mother's touch.

"I know you miss him, Pony Boy. We all do," she said. "But we just have to do the best we can to keep this family together so that he has something to come home to."

Her words were kind and forgiving, and made him want to burst into tears. But even without looking up, he knew his baba was watching him. Pony Boy breathed deeply, then stood. From the floor, Mei watched them quietly. More than anyone, he knew she missed having Lixin at home with her. Now she stayed with a neighbor when he and his mother worked. And his father had to make do by himself, other than the few friends who stopped by to check on him occasionally.

Pony Boy wished he could talk to Benfu, share with him all the trials he was going through. But he couldn't even do that. He thrust the letter at his mother and went out the door. He didn't even have time to spend with Wren. He needed to get to the street bathrooms. He had work to do, money to make, and a family to support. He might have let Lixin down, but he'd be damned if he'd do the same to everyone else he loved.

Chapter Twenty-Four

Benfu waited in line, his empty bowl cradled in his hands as he moved one step forward at a time. His limbs were heavy—weary from a day in the field, but the spark of hope that he'd have something good for his last meal of the day spurred him forward. He didn't get too excited, though. He'd learned to keep his expectations low in order not to experience epic disappointment. Only the night before they'd had corncakes stuffed with wild greens—a flavorless, hard concoction served to them after the commune leader had made a speech about the food teaching them of past sufferings by the Chinese before Chairman Mao had rescued them from famine.

"The Peasant Family is Happy," Gong Ran whispered over his shoulder.

Benfu's heart fell. They'd already had that dish. Basically it meant just a few root vegetables and a bread roll would be thrown in his bowl. His stomach let out a long, low rumble of displeasure and Benfu pushed on it with his free hand, trying to force it into quiet submission.

Earlier that day, he'd been reprimanded when he'd grumbled about replanting some of the cornstalks that had been uprooted by the flooding in some of their fields. He'd thought they looked dead and that it was a waste of time, and unfortunately some of his doubts were overheard.

His brigade leader had stood over him, shouting about some girl his age named Guo Fenglian—nicknamed the Iron Maiden—who'd organized a team to replant their corn after a big flood a few years before. Made a legend by Chairman Mao's praise, others had begun iron maiden teams all over China. Benfu had never heard her name before but after the berating he'd taken, he'd never forget it.

Behind him he heard a groan, and it sounded female. He turned.

A girl of around eighteen or so was there and she also held one hand on her stomach. But unlike his, hers was round and looked quite out of place on her petite body. Her two long braids hung over her shoulders, a style that was fairly common in the country, but always reminded him of Mei, Pony Boy's little sister.

"Root vegetable only? Not again," the girl whispered. "This is getting to be too much."

He nodded. "You heard?"

"I just don't understand these names they give this terrible food," she said. "How can a peasant family be happy if this is the kind of thing they are expected to live on?"

The line moved up a pace.

"What's your name?" the girl asked, barely turning her head to the side to speak to him.

"Benfu." He didn't elaborate on family name because it still felt so weird and deceitful to use the borrowed name on his *hukou*.

"I'm Hsu Yu," she said, and turned her attention back to the line moving.

She was the first female to speak to him in a friendly manner in all his time at the commune, and Benfu thought it ironic that her name meant *happy rain*. More than any other discomfort he'd experienced in his exile from home, it was the rain that had plagued him the most in the beginning, when he was so homesick. Now that it was gone, he hoped it stayed away for some time, even if that meant dealing with the unseasonably hot temperatures.

He studied her profile and noted the girl looked more than tired. Exhausted, actually, and he knew from talks with Gong Ran that simply being pregnant did not give any pardons from the long workdays. He'd even told of one woman who had worked through her labor, screaming in pain as she continued to cut and sew leather to make her quota of shoes, loyally fulfilling her assignment to assist the People's Army.

Finally it was Gong Ran's turn in front of the server, then the girl's, and then Benfu's. He stared down at the gray lump of vegetables that were plunked down in his bowl. Before he could determine what exactly they were, a chunk of hard bread was thrown atop it.

He turned, heading to where Gong Ran had gone.

The girl—Hsu Yu—had already found a place to sit at a table filled with other women and Benfu walked past it, then hesitated and stepped back until he was standing behind her. He picked up his bread, then placed it on the table beside the girl's bowl. She saw his hand come down and looked up, a question in her eyes.

"I don't eat bread," Benfu lied, then continued on to the table where Gong Ran sat and which now looked empty without the quiet presence of the man who wore the red hat.

Benfu looked around, making sure no one was following him. He'd carried the red wool hat, clutching it with one hand as he kept his bag secured under his arm. He'd been walking for some time and he wanted to be alone.

He paused to take a breath, steadying himself against the trunk of a tree. He had quite a trek ahead of him, and was glad his hand had healed and his health had improved. He was still weak, but he was stable enough to work, and thankfully—especially this afternoon—to walk.

Looking out at the sun setting over the field he saw it casting its rays in golden lines that illuminated the tops of the wheat, and knew he'd picked the best time of day for his furtive trip. No one would miss him as they would be gathering and clamoring for the reeducation meeting, and probably hoping for some drama with a renunciation or two. Like a pack of wolves, when the crowd got together they seemed to lose their humanity and turned on each other with one random word or baseless accusation. Benfu could barely stomach it, though Gong Ran had warned him repeatedly to hide his compassion, lest they come after him.

Dinner was still on his mind and he cringed, thinking of the bland and mushy vegetables he'd forced down, but at least it wasn't more of the strange cakes or the watery soup they'd been eating. Though frustrated beyond belief, he'd kept his mouth shut and for the last few days had quietly gone to the cowshed and covertly slipped half of his black bread under the door, sharing what he could with Kuan as he finished out his punishment.

Unfortunately it had finished the old man first.

Benfu wasn't sure if it was the scorching temperatures inside the shed, or the shattered pride of the old man that had taken him, but he was sure that his death was uncalled for and unfair. Those chosen for the burial team had carried him out of the common area and put Kuan in the commune's makeshift graveyard, doing nothing to commemorate the life he'd led or the sweat and tears he'd given to the commune. Just a mound of dirt and a forgotten name—or at least one now considered a traitor for the few bits of food he'd tried to grow, and the scattered days he'd been in too much pain to work.

But Benfu wouldn't forget Kuan. He'd been the first to show him genuine kindness—the first to treat him as something more than just a number on a work crew, or as in Gong Ran's case, as a subject assigned to mentor. He and Kuan had talked more, too, in the days since he'd been put in the shed. Outside the door, just after dinner each night, he'd sit on the ground, leaning against the hidden side of the shed, just being there so the old man would know he wasn't alone. Between ragged breaths caused by the aching of his ribs where Kuan had been kicked by those who put him in the shed, he'd poured out his heart to Benfu. In him, without even seeing his face, Benfu had found common ground. In only a few days, the stories they shared were like salve to Benfu's soul as they'd discussed literature, politics, and finally, when the right amount of trust was built between them—music.

Excited that someone else in the commune appreciated the arts, Benfu had confessed to Kuan that he was an accomplished violinist. When the words were out there, he'd held his breath, waiting to hear condemnation. Instead, Kuan had congratulated him, whispering that he wished he could hear him play. He'd softly reminded him that his music couldn't be taken away from him, as it could always be heard in his soul.

He then shared his own secret. He'd admitted that he had a grandson in the commune—a boy who was suffering alongside him, but on other work teams and in a different barracks in this new directive for the urban dwellers to learn from the peasants. He'd also admitted that they'd decided to keep their family connection quiet, and now he was glad that he had, for he would have never forgiven himself if his actions had caused something to happen to his grandson.

With his voice hoarse from thirst and weak from hunger, Kuan talked of the boy as if he had the most noble and gifted grandson in the world. Through the wall, his emotion was palpable as he spoke of days past when they'd shared meals together as family, something frowned upon now by the commune leaders but at one time were moments cherished. The longing to talk to, or just see a glimpse of his grandson, was evident. Though Kuan wouldn't speak his name, Benfu had left that night dreaming of Kuan on the banks of a muddy river, sitting alongside a faceless boy as they reeled in carp and turtles, treats they'd later eat around the family table.

The next morning as Benfu had stood in line, his heart had jumped into his throat when an announcement was made that the old man Kuan had died in the night and his body would be buried that afternoon—with an addendum that no mourners were welcome as the man had died in defiance of the new, red China.

Benfu was devastated. Then he'd thought of the grandson. Benfu had asked around, but everyone claimed that Kuan had no family at the farm. The old man had been right when he'd said the boy would never come forward, that officials could and would use their relationship to hurt one another.

Now Benfu stepped between the graves, making his way to the freshest of them all. He looked around, hoping to see some evidence of the grandson—proof that someone who Kuan had cared for had been there, had grieved for him, too. When he saw no one, he kneeled and put the red wool hat on the highest peak of the mound.

"Kuan, you will be missed," he whispered, then quietly slid his violin and his bow from his bag, cradling them for a moment, feeling a sense of longing and sorrow that he'd neglected them for so long. He knew he was taking a chance by bringing them out of the well, of even holding them, even if he didn't play a single note. If he were caught with the banned instruments, it would mean a punishment far worse than a few days in a scorching cowshed. But still, if Kuan did still haunt this earth with his ghostly self, Benfu wanted him to know that he mattered. Maybe not to everyone, but to someone—he mattered.

For a moment, he considered throwing caution aside and playing with all his might until the people of the commune heard and came running, ready to throw accusations and persecutions. He'd go out in a flurry of music, yes he would!

Then he thought of his mother and his father. If found that they'd orchestrated such fraud in sending their pampered son to the country under a false identity, they'd be punished. They could end up like Kuan. He would not take that chance.

But he wanted to be brave.

Looking around once more to be sure no one had crept up on him, Benfu held the violin to his shoulder where it burrowed in like a long-lost child into a father's embrace. He brought the bow to it and slid it lightly across the strings, with just enough pressure for one long beautiful note to be born, then die off in the wind. With ease he was able to produce the note so that if someone heard it, they'd wonder for a moment what it was, then decide it was simply the breeze tickling their ears and playing tricks on their mind.

For a moment, he could've sworn he'd heard someone behind him. He held his breath, waiting to see if he'd been caught. When no one came forward, he relaxed again, sure his paranoia was creating sounds. He studied the mound of dirt, waiting for something, anything to show him his offer was received. If legends of unsettled spirits were true, he hoped the old man knew he was only there to show his respect.

"Did you hear that, Kuan? That was for you," he said, then lowered the violin. He bowed his head and offered up a prayer to the gods that they'd find the man and lead him to his afterlife so that he wouldn't wander alone and lost. Then he slipped the violin and bow back into his bag and stood. He would need to hurry to slip it back into the well before others came out of the dining hall.

With one final look at the ground, he turned and began walking away, back toward the commune that he loathed, back to a feeling of oppression such as he'd never known before.

"Good-bye, Kuan. You were a good man," he whispered, hoping that like his music, the sound of his voice would be carried away on the wings of the suddenly chilly gust that swirled around him, urging him to move along quickly and conceal the things that could bring him suffering.

Chapter Twenty-Five

A few weeks went by and with the loss of the first real friend he'd made at the commune, Benfu decided to work on his connection with Gong Ran and see if it could become more than a relationship built on responsibility, possibly even a real friendship like he'd had with Kuan. Under the sadness he carried, Benfu realized that to have a friend meant everything in the conditions under which they were living, if only for the moral support.

Gong Ran was a peculiar sort—the kind of man others flocked to and followed. Benfu knew they were opposites, as Benfu liked to blend into the background, avoiding squabbles and ruckus when possible. Having a friend like Gong Ran could be advantageous. Obviously though, he wouldn't be sharing any secrets with Gong Ran anytime soon, but he was making it a point to talk more and to let him know that he appreciated every bit of help given him. As someone who'd grown up tending fields and making ends meet in the country, Gong Ran's instruction was invaluable to Benfu, and slowly, he was learning how to live like a peasant. His strides amused his new friend, but also brought them closer as Benfu felt the older boy considered him somewhat of a project—a student to mold into whatever he deemed appropriate. But Benfu also had one more reason to attempt to get closer to Gong Ran.

He hadn't discovered it until the night before, but someone had been in his belongings.

The sheet of music that Benfu had hidden under his bedroll was gone. And his hidden money. And how could he report his money stolen when he wasn't supposed to even have any?

Luckily, the brown envelope containing Teng Bao's negatives was still there. But the question was, had someone seen them? While it could have been any of the three bunkmates who had been in his bag, Benfu had a feeling that he'd be the luckiest if it were Gong Ran. And if it weren't, and someone brought it up at a denunciation meeting, he hoped Gong Ran would defend him. Benfu was nervous about it, but he could always deny it was his and tell them to prove it. Unlike Kuan, he'd never admit his error and hope for mercy.

"Throw that crate up here," Gong Ran called out from his place on the bed of the truck.

Benfu obliged, throwing up the box and then another, and another. He and Benfu had been chosen to help load the trucks for the city. Mysteriously, on the day the trucks came, at least fifty crates of bok choy had emerged from the storerooms. It was disheartening to see, as that bok choy could've taken the place of the watery soups and black bread that they'd all been existing on. But he'd swallowed his bitterness and kept his head low, intent on not making waves. Their constant hunger was ironic—here they were on the outskirts of Wuxi, a town known for its abundance of fish and rice, yet he felt close to starvation.

"Mail call," someone yelled out from the other side of the truck.

Benfu didn't react. He knew he wouldn't have mail so instead, as others flocked to the front gates of the commune to see if their name was called, he spent the time rearranging the crates into a more stable order.

He worked fast, sliding the last one into place before jumping down from the truck, then he headed for the pump to fill his canteen before the rest of the loading crew returned.

There were a few others in line to get water, so Benfu kept walking. When it was mail call, it was an unspoken break if you were within the walls of the commune, and he wanted to stretch his legs and his back.

He neared the gate and saw the last few stragglers around the mail carrier, hoping for news from loved ones. Benfu shook his head, feeling sorry for those who'd walk away empty-handed. At least his disappointment was consistent—he knew coming in that there'd never be anything for him, so he didn't have to go through the agony of waiting each week.

Looking closer, he saw that from the back, the mail carrier resembled Pony Boy. The tall, thin man even wore his green pants a bit short at the ankles, just as Pony Boy was forced to because he wore his father's uniform and stood at least half a head taller than the man who begot him. Benfu looked at the hair, sticking out from the official government cap, noticing it was shaggy and unkempt, making him remember the many times he'd told Pony Boy he needed a trim.

He turned his canteen up, letting the last few drops of water drain into his mouth as he watched the crowd disperse and the mail carrier turn back toward the gate. The lock of hair that lay over the man's eyes caught his attention the most, but when he saw his face, he dropped his canteen.

Pony Boy.

Benfu froze, not knowing what to do. His accelerated heartbeat told him to move—to go to his best comrade, embrace him and thank the gods that he'd come. But his brain told him not to give anything away, that to acknowledge him with even a word could be deadly to the charade he played.

He began walking toward him, still unsure what to do or say, his heart keeping beat with his footsteps as he bridged the distance.

Pony Boy tucked a small stack of letters into his bag and then appeared to be looking for someone, checking every corner of the inside of the courtyard. When he'd turned almost completely around, he spotted Benfu. A smile began to emerge, but then Benfu saw him tuck it away and replace it with an empty look.

"Do you have anything for me?" Benfu said the only thing he could think of.

"Let me look," Pony Boy answered, then began digging in his bag. He finally found a soiled envelope and handed it to Benfu, his hand lingering just a second too long as they met each other's eyes and held gazes.

Benfu took the envelope, then unwillingly nodded his thanks and turned away. It was the hardest thing he'd ever done in his life. He wanted to embrace Pony Boy, laugh with him, ask him if he'd seen Benfu's parents. Ask him about his father.

But he did none of that.

He kept walking as he opened the envelope and pulled out the paper. He unfolded it and read.

Every commune has a dining hall. Bring the negatives and meet me behind yours.

Benfu smiled, then quickly hid it as he tucked the paper back into the envelope and put it into his pocket.

He still had to figure out how to get away from work duty. Suddenly, he bent over, holding his stomach, then groaned.

"Hao bu hao?" Gong Ran called out to ask him if he was fine.

Benfu looked up and saw his friend on the truck, already taking his place to grab the crates and stack them higher.

"I need to visit the toilet," Benfu said, making his words sound heavy with pain. Stomach cramps and worse issues were common because of the lack of nutrition and the many strange things used to make meals for the people. On any given day, Benfu's stomach could go from fine to agonizing within minutes. So far, he'd been allowed to run to one of the several outhouses when needed. Hopefully today would be no different.

Gong Ran waved him away. "Go."

Benfu made a show of turning toward the nearest outhouse, stumbling in pain with his hands holding his stomach. When he reached it, he looked to be sure no one was looking, then slipped behind it.

From there he could see the dining hall, but first he crossed to the row of small buildings and crept into his. He fumbled through his bag, found the negatives, and slipped them in his pocket. Then he went back outside. Quickly, he bridged the distance, not making eye contact with anyone. At the dining hall, he turned the corner and nonchalantly strolled until he was behind it.

He didn't see Pony Boy, so he went to the line of barrels by the back door and waited, standing close enough that he blended in, but out enough that he could see anyone coming.

When five minutes went by, he began to get a bit nervous. He hoped Gong Ran wouldn't go to the outhouse to check on him. Since he wouldn't know which one Benfu was going to, that might buy him a bit of time, but still, he needed to get back to the truck as soon as he could.

Suddenly, he saw Pony Boy come around the corner.

He couldn't help it. This time a smile broke free so wide he felt his face might crack. Pony Boy returned the sentiment, and they met a few paces from the building. First they slapped hands, then Benfu held his arms open and Pony Boy accepted. With one embrace, all the bitter words they'd had between them were forgotten.

Finally, Benfu pulled away and wiped the tear from his eyes. "How did you find me?"

Pony Boy laughed but his eyes glittered too. "Your note said outside of Wuxi so I had a clue. But I'll tell you this; yours is the third commune I've visited today. I was just about to give up and head home."

Home. Benfu felt an aching wave of want for what the word meant as he waved Pony Boy closer to the building. "I can't stay but a minute. Tell me, are you here because something's wrong?" Benfu asked, searching Pony Boy's face for news of his family.

"No, nothing is wrong. I just had to see you to make sure you were surviving out here in the country. I traded routes with one of my father's friends for this week, but I'll be glad to get back to Shanghai. I thought I had to do a lot of walking in the city—but this is too much."

Benfu laughed as he pictured Pony Boy walking up and down the country roads, going from one commune to another in his search.

"*Aiya,* you're so skinny! I could take you in a wrestling match now," Pony Boy said, socking Benfu in the arm. "You'll appreciate the gift from Mama. She sent you a sweet potato cake for your birthday."

Benfu had forgotten or just missed somehow that it was his birthday and was touched at not only the gift from Pony Boy's mother, but that he had come so far to recognize a day that had been forgotten. He was now officially seventeen years old—but felt at least a decade older. He looked down at himself, noting the belt and the new notch he'd made with a borrowed knife.

Pony Boy handed him the small cake from his bag, then popped him in the arm again.

Benfu accepted the food gratefully, already putting it to his mouth and savoring the first bite. All he'd had that day was one tightly packed ball of rice and now the mouthful tickled his taste buds, reminding him of home and the way food was supposed to be—tasty and filled with flavor. He looked at his watch, feeling even more nervous. "Please give my thanks to your mother. And my parents? Have you seen them?"

He noticed something off in Pony Boy's eyes, but then it was gone and he nodded. "Yes, I've seen them. They look the same, getting by and anxious about you. Your mother sent this."

Pony Boy dug in his satchel and pulled out something wrapped in newspaper. He handed it over to Benfu.

Benfu unwrapped it, smiling when he saw the familiar jade buffalo from his father's library. Then he tucked it into his pocket quickly. "Why would she send that? She knows I can't show it here."

Pony Boy shrugged. "You are right. She told me to keep it for you, but I thought you might want to have a little piece of home with you." His face took on a sadder look than Benfu had ever seen on him before. "Comrade, you need to make it back to them as soon as you can."

"I wish I could go today. I know now that I took home for granted, but never again. Just please tell them I'm fine," Benfu said, pushing back thoughts of the deadly infection he'd conquered, and the nights his stomach was so empty it ached painfully. He'd never want them to know how he suffered. "What about Cook? Or Old Butler? Did you see them?"

Pony Boy shook his head. "They weren't around when I was there."

Benfu finished the last of the cake, and licked his fingers. He started to ask if Pony Boy had seen or heard any news of Juan Hui, but stopped himself. Juan Hui could wait—he'd be back in Shanghai soon. For now, he wanted to talk about other things.

"What about Zu Wren? The paper?"

Pony Boy snapped his fingers, then spoke as he dug into his bag. "Oh, I almost forgot. I brought you a copy." He pulled out a folded piece of paper and handed it to Benfu. "I know it's too dangerous to discuss all that's going on, but at least this will catch you up on some of it."

Benfu stuffed it into his pocket along with the short note Pony Boy had slipped him. "I'll read it later. Have you had any feedback since it went out?"

Pony Boy shook his head. "Not a word. But then, I wouldn't hear anything because no one knows it came from me—I mean us. We've got another edition ready to be printed and distributed. We'll work on it this weekend and get it out there soon. It's going to be a good one. Wren's father heard through the tangled vines that Mao sent the former Emperor, Pu Yi, to a labor camp, claiming he is the ultimate symbol of Old China and needs to be remolded."

"Remolded how? It's not like we're ever going to have an emperor again."

Pony Boy shrugged. "I supposed it's more a show of Mao's power than anything. Pu's supposedly part of a work team that transports vegetables using a bicycle-propelled flatbed truck. Rumor is the first time he took off, the load was so heavy that he lost control and ended up in the ditch."

Benfu shook his head. Everything had gone crazy—a deposed emperor working at a labor camp? Teachers being detained and reeducated, even persecuted if they resisted? He felt a sense of relief that his parents were protected by his father's connections.

"And your family?" Benfu remembered to ask. He could tell by Pony Boy's voice that he was exhilarated by the newsletter, but talking about it aloud made Benfu way too nervous. After what he'd seen happen to Kuan, he knew being linked to anything that protested the rationality of the Cultural Revolution could be deadly for them all. He didn't want to dwell on that when their time was running out.

Pony Boy let out a long sigh, then told him Lixin had been corralled with other boys from the city and sent north in compliance with another new directive from Chairman Mao. An opportunity for him *to learn from the people*, Pony Boy said with a sneer.

"We got a letter from him. He's struggling but getting by, I guess," Pony Boy said, kicking at the dirt beneath his feet. "And Baba is still trying to recover. It's crazy—one day he'll seem so much better, then the next he has a setback. We need to get him to a new doctor, one that knows hearts. But there's no money for that."

Benfu wished he had time to tell Pony Boy about Doctor Yu and his technique of trial and error to treat the peasants. "You still working both jobs?" he asked instead. To him Pony Boy looked older, more weathered and definitely more mature.

Pony Boy gave a hollow laugh. "*Dui*, still delivering mail and shoveling shit. But it pays the bills and oh, the things I see on my route. I wish we had more time, I'd really entertain you with some real life stories."

Benfu wished they did, too. But he'd been gone too long already and didn't want to get caught. Even his budding friendship with Gong Ran might not be solid enough to make up for this sneaky behavior. He just didn't know if he could trust him that much. "I know, but I need to get back before someone comes looking for me. Pony Boy, I can't thank you enough for coming. It means a lot—just to see a familiar face. I've felt so alone here."

Pony Boy reached out and they grasped hands, their fingers immediately going through the motions of the secret handshake they'd created when they were just boys, an easy gesture that brought a lump to Benfu's throat.

"Best comrades."

"Best comrades," Benfu agreed, glad for the relief that rushed over him, a sign that they were back on good terms. "Please, tell my parents I'm fine and don't mention how skinny I am."

Pony Boy nodded. "I have to tell you that I'm sorry I ever doubted a word you said about Mao. You were right. I was wrong."

"I'll take it." Benfu didn't want to appear too self-congratulatory. He didn't like being right about Mao. He wished he were wrong.

"I know this isn't a new revelation, Benfu. But what really set it in stone for me—the thing that totally turned me against him—was meeting Wren. Mao Thought says that to love someone is a sentimental trap—a bourgeois feeling. But I know that what I feel for Wren cannot be wrong. And if Mao can condemn such a special thing as love, then how else could anything he speaks be true? I could have never remained a Maoist knowing what I know now."

"I'm not arguing with you, but can you tell me then, after all that you've seen and recorded, just why have so many Chinese pledged their loyalty to him?" Benfu said.

"Fear. Plain, outright fear, that's what it is. But I'm not going to let one man ruin my chances at a future with Wren. Together we'll keep our ears to the ground, collecting stories about what is really happening.

And with the newsletter, we'll tell the people just how honorable their leader really is. Maybe one day he won't be able to wash the blood from his hands so easily and he'll have to answer for all he's done."

Benfu had no reply. He'd never heard Pony Boy talk with such passion and conviction. The weight of his words was monumental.

"And also—I just never really liked the man," Pony Boy said, giving Benfu a wink that instantly made him look like the old Pony Boy that Benfu remembered. "He's much too arrogant, having his life-size portraits pasted anywhere and everywhere. I'm quite sick of looking at that hairy mole every time I turn around, to tell the truth."

Benfu laughed and they stood for a moment, just taking in the sight of each other before they heard someone holler from in front of the dining hall. Benfu looked around the corner, then back at Pony Boy. He pulled the brown envelope from his back pocket and handed it over. "Here're the negatives, Pony Boy, but really—I want you to be careful."

Pony Boy took them and put them in his mailbag. "I'll be careful, I promise. Look, I know you have to go," Pony Boy said. "I do, too. It's a long way back to Shanghai. I'll hitch a ride to the nearest train station, then I'll have a few hours from there. I've got Wren stepping in for my part-time job, but I'm sure she'd be thrilled if I get back in time to take over tonight's toilet cleaning."

Benfu cringed thinking of Zu Wren with a shovel and a cleaning rag, taking on one of the worst jobs in the city.

Pony Boy saluted him. "It was great seeing you, Benfu. Don't forget while you are here that you must sacrifice personal choice to the societal good."

His raised eyebrow was a familiar gesture that told Benfu he was kidding, his words making a mockery of one of Mao's most popular slogans.

"I hear you, comrade. But one last thing—" Benfu said, "are you still in love?"

His question was rewarded with a beaming smile and a suddenly flushed face from Pony Boy. "You'd better believe it. I can't foretell the future of this so-called revolution, but Wren and I are forever—that much I can promise. *Aiya*, I might even be married before you!" With those words he threw up his hand, waving good-bye as he walked away, grinning from ear to ear.

Benfu watched him go, longing to call him back. Pony Boy's visit was bittersweet. He was relieved to have news of his family, yet just seeing a face so connected to home made his heart heavy.

He waited until Pony Boy was out of sight, then emerged from behind the dining hall, jogging back to the trucks.

Gong Ran saw him coming and yelled out. "I was just about to send someone to rescue you from the trenches of human waste!"

Benfu hung his head in proper embarrassment and went back to work, the knowledge of the paper in his pocket, and the jade buffalo spurring him on to work faster and make the day disappear.

Benfu waited until everyone in the small house was asleep before he quietly crawled from his pallet and headed toward the door. He grabbed the small propane lamp and slipped out, then went around the side of the house and leaned against it. He still couldn't believe he'd actually seen Pony Boy earlier that day. If he weren't completely recovered from his infection, he'd have sworn it was another delusion. But no, the paper in his pocket proved it was real.

He'd tucked the jade buffalo into his bag when he'd first arrived to the cabin, but he'd not had a chance all afternoon or evening to be alone. He burned with curiosity to see what they'd published in the newsletter. He imagined Pony Boy moving through the back streets of Shanghai, covertly slipping the papers into the mailboxes of unsuspecting citizens, enlightening them with news that would probably never make it to the public media. It made him smile, but also made him nervous.

He turned the flame of the lamp up and set it on the ground. Looking about him one more time, he pulled the paper from his pocket and unfolded it. The first headline caught his eye.

"Dedicated Head Mistress Killed by her Students in a China Red Haze"

So they'd decided to use the headmistress story after all. Even though he'd already known about the death, the words were still shocking. There were no photos, but his mind was quick to create a scene in his head—one of bloodthirsty Red Guards and a woman's broken body.

He moved on to the next article, a criticism of the strict rationing going on in Shanghai and other cities. He'd known from Cook even before he'd left that, for some people, things were getting harder to come by, but somehow she'd always made do. Now he could only imagine it was even more difficult to please his mother with satisfactory meals when according to Wren's—or maybe Pony Boy's—sources, families were being cut down to only about five hundred grams of grains and even less cooking oil.

Finally, in the last piece, they'd covered the charade the Red Guards were conducting by emulating the heroic Long March made earlier in Mao's career—the six-thousand-mile trek that saved Mao and the communists from falling to the Kuomintang. But now, the Red Guards were coming from every corner of China, stalking across the huge country to meet in Beijing and pay homage to Chairman Mao. It reported that in their obsession to get there, Mao's private army of China's youth had taken over the entire transportation system of railways, buses, and even airplanes, causing havoc for everyone else. And word was that Mao had given his blessings for it! Benfu read on, amazed and startled at what was going on in the cities as he faded away in the countryside.

Quickly he read through everything once more and then held the edge of the paper to the flame from the lamp. When it caught fire, he let it burn for a moment, watching it curl into red embers, then black ashes, before dropping it to the ground. When it had faded to nothing, he dug a small hole and buried the ashes, then covered it with the overturned dirt.

He stood over it for a moment, contemplating what it all meant.

The Palest Ink—a tiny drop of truth in an enormous barrel of injustice. Could two lone voices possibly be heard over the clutter of revolutionary din? Probably not, but Benfu was proud of them both anyway.

Chapter Twenty-Six

It was nearing the afternoon hour when Pony Boy usually finished up his route and started on his way to the People's Square to work his second job. He looked at the sun in the sky and determined that if he didn't finish soon, he was going to be late and then he might lose his toilet-cleaning job to another hungry man trying to make a coin.

He glanced at the letter in his hand, again trying to decide which direction to try next. It was frustrating as hell, but since the revolution had begun, everything was being turned upside down and made senseless. He'd discussed it with his baba but even he had shaken his head, unable to come up with a solution to help Pony Boy in the confusion that now made delivering mail to many almost impossible.

The biggest problem was that in the fervor to erase all evidence of foreign imperialism from China, names were being changed to sound more patriotic. Just that morning he'd passed the department store he'd always known as Eternal Peace Department Store and saw the sign had been ripped from its place above the huge double doors. In its place someone had painted its new name, People's Department Store.

Obviously, anything that reeked of Chinese tradition was being attacked, and that included street names. Most of Pony's Boy's route was fairly easy, but the problem came when he got the odd letter to a Mr. Zhao or a Mrs. Hu on some street he'd never heard of before, or addressed to an old street name that didn't exist any longer. He'd spent way too much time trying to find the right Zhao or Hu, as there were literally hundreds within just a few city blocks. And trying to deliver mail to the tea shops and noodle stores, with their new non-bourgeois names, was near impossible. Suddenly every business was adopting names like Food Shop Number One and Food Shop Number Two. But who decided who was number one and so on and why didn't anyone tell him? Now he was confusing the new street names with the old, words and family names snaring together like tangled vines through his mind.

He stuffed the letter back in his bag and heaved a frustrated sigh. The postmark on it was two weeks old, and the recipient would likely want to give him a tongue-lashing, even if it wasn't his fault the postal system was in an upheaval. It would just have to wait until tomorrow and he hoped it wasn't found out that he'd not finished his delivery that day.

For now, he had to make up some lost time.

"Excuse me." He pushed through a crowd of people who were gathered on the sidewalk, exclaiming over a big poster that obviously named someone as a counterrevolutionary. He didn't pause long enough to read it and didn't care what it said. The big posters were getting to be such a nuisance around Shanghai and his mother had said the Red Guards had even entered her factory. They'd stopped production, organized a meeting, and handed out big sheets of paper and ink. His mother said the supervisors hadn't said a word; they'd simply stood back and allowed the disruption to happen.

He quickened his walk to a jog, hurrying toward the square. As he ran, he thought of his meeting with Wren the night before. She'd insisted she could return to her father's workplace alone this time, an offer made to help him since he was so strapped for time. Still, it made Pony Boy nervous to think of her there alone, without him to protect her if someone else happened upon her.

She was stubborn, he'd give her that. Yes, she'd claimed he was a fast learner when it came to using the fancy new typesetting machine, but she was the one pulling ahead with the best ideas of what to publish, as well as struggling through the wording of each article. In just minutes she'd come up with an interesting piece about the use of razors up the sides of women's pants in public, a humiliating attempt to bring back modesty by making them appear baggy. Scissors were even being wielded like weapons, Red Guards hacking off hair to lengths they deemed appropriate, to present a united front against decadence. No one with any sense of individualism was safe on the streets anymore. Wren had written the article in literally minutes, and it was brilliant.

But Pony Boy hoped he was somewhat of a help. After all, it'd been his idea to print an article that emphasized that while the country tried to rid China of the old ways, they were also purging every spiritual, physical, and emotional aspect of what China used to be. He pointed out that it was a disservice to future generations to strip China of the history that should be theirs to experience.

Wren had looked at him with a new respect, and in that moment, he felt she saw him as more than a simple delivery boy of the newsletter. They were partners—cohorts, she'd laughingly said, then included Benfu in the mix when they'd made the last-minute decision to publish the negatives.

He passed a government building and noticed that the bronze lions that were there just a week before were now gone, most likely another gesture to eliminate superstitions. He mused that many Shanghainese would be disappointed, as it was common for locals to stroke the lions as they passed in the hopes that their power and wealth would rub off on their own lives. Now they were gone and in their place, he saw a line of children, ranging from at least as young as nine years old and up to thirteen or so. In front of them, a Red Guard was going from one to the next, tying red scarves around their necks.

Initiation day, thought Pony Boy, as he kept moving. He knew the younger followers of Mao used to be called the Young Pioneers of China, an organization that had been around since before he was born. Now like everything else, the name was changed for the revolution and they were being called the Little Red Guards, a title given to remind them they were to do whatever their older counterparts required. One young boy caught his eye and Pony Boy nodded to him, then turned the corner and saw the line of toilet cubicles, with his boss standing alongside, his hands on his hips as he watched the street.

"*Ni hao,*" Pony Boy hollered out with his most friendly voice, hoping the man would be lenient. Now what? He'd lose his job over being half an hour late? *Please be happy today*, he chanted as he jogged faster.

His hopes were dashed when he approached close enough to see the scowl that waited for him.

"You're half an hour late," the boss said, then pointed at the bucket and a mop. His clothes were more soiled than normal, telling Pony Boy the man had made a rare attempt to clean one of his many toilets, probably the reason for his terrifying scowl. "Two trucks for tonight, make sure the first one doesn't get overloaded before you start on the second one."

Pony Boy felt a sudden rush of relief. He wasn't getting fired.

"Yes, *laoban,*" he agreed. Two trucks meant a lot more work, but Pony Boy didn't care as long as he still had his job. He needed every penny he could get, especially since his mother's hours had recently been cut. Also, with the new city regulations on rations, they were hurting and there was no way that Pony Boy could continue to pay the bills and feed the family on only one job.

He slipped into one of the toilet cubes and quickly changed out of his postman clothes and into the freshly washed trousers his mother had packed that morning. In record time, he had his day uniform folded and pushed into his bag, his shoes back on, and had returned to the street. He was relieved to see his boss had left, hopefully for the night, and he got to work.

Six hours later, Pony Boy leaned against a tree, taking a break as he watched a small drama unfolding on the street. Not unusual to see, a trio of Red Guards was causing discord as they ridiculed each and every person walking by. Ironically, Wren had just written the piece about the hair cutting and pants ripping, and now he was getting to see it with his own eyes. The guards—two boys and one girl—had stopped a young woman and were berating her over her choice of clothing, claiming the pants she wore were too tight.

"Our great leader, Chairman Mao, has given us the authority to do what we see fit in order to spread the flames of the Cultural Revolution," the female Red Guard said, answering someone in the crowd who dared to question their actions against the humiliated teenage girl. Pony Boy didn't think the slacks were tight at all, but what did he know about fashion or modesty? He also wasn't going to get into the middle of it. He had enough battles of his own and the Red Guards had already proven they could turn vicious in seconds. But suddenly, a few of those yelling at the young woman turned and he was almost sure that the one who stood there giving orders was Juan Hui, Benfu's betrothed.

Pony Boy listened closely, watching her dictate the next move with just a flick of her finger and a few words. She was tiny—just like Benfu had said, but she had a strong voice. And the mole—it was exactly where Juan Hui's was in the photo. If it wasn't her, the resemblance was uncanny. And if it was, then the coincidence of their paths intertwining was remarkable.

"Qing wen," he said loudly, getting her attention. He had to know.

"Yes, excuse you. Can't you see I was talking?" she answered, shooing him with a shake of her hand as if she were brushing off a pesky fly.

Pony Boy didn't see evidence of the well-mannered girl that Benfu had spoken of, yet he felt strongly that if it wasn't Juan Hui, it was indeed her twin. But if it was her, how could she be in a Red Guard uniform?

Like Benfu, her parents were scholars. It didn't make sense. "Sorry to bother you, but you wouldn't by chance be Juan Hui, would you?"

"Yes, I'm Juan Hui," she said, wrinkling her nose as if something putrid had made its way to her nose. "Who are you?"

The others around her quieted, waiting to see why a boy with smears of shit was bothering one of their own. The girl who'd been the target of their ridicule quietly backed away and practically ran down the walk as the attention of her aggressors was diverted.

Pony Boy looked down at his clothes, seeing that yes, he was a bit soiled. But that was to be expected. "I'm Pony Boy, your fiancé's closest comrade."

His statement was first met with dead silence from Juan Hui. One of the boys in her small group raised his eyebrows at her, then muttered something under his breath that Pony Boy couldn't catch. What he did understand was that the boy wasn't happy at the mention of a fiancé.

Finally, she spoke, "I don't know what you are talking about. I've sworn allegiance to the new order of proletarians, and there is no room here for marriage. We live to serve Chairman Mao's dream of a new China."

Pony Boy rolled his eyes. "Drop the lecture. Just tell me, do you know the name Benfu?" he asked, unsure for a moment, but taking a chance. When he spoke the name, he saw her eyes change. She knew exactly whom he was talking about.

"Maybe I do," she said, gesturing at the bucket that sat on the ground next to him—the bucket that was unforgivably half full. "But he didn't tell me that he cavorted with those who dealt in human waste."

A smattering of laughter came from the boys who listened intently. Pony Boy crossed his arms, then nodded at them. When he spoke, he knew his words could get him in trouble but his indignation pushed his common sense aside. "Well, he didn't tell me that his fiancé runs the streets with human waste."

"Hey—we can have you brought in for questioning for that little remark," one of the boys said, his voice losing all traces of amusement as he took a step toward Pony Boy.

Juan Hui held her hand out, stopping him from coming closer.

Within seconds, Pony Boy could see the fire that Benfu had talked about. It lit up her eyes like fireworks. When she finally got her thoughts together again, she put her hands on her hips and glared at him. "He's not worth it, just leave him be to keep shoveling his shit."

She turned and beckoned for the boys to follow her. Over her shoulder she called out one last retort. "And you can tell Benfu that the goose is dead," she said, then stomped off, her entourage trailing behind her.

Pony Boy wasn't sure what she meant by the goose being dead, but he did know that Benfu would be as shocked as he was to know his soon-to-be bride was wearing the garb of a Red Guard, sporting the official armband, and most shockingly, had cut off all of the magnificent hair he'd seen in her photo.

His thoughts were all over the place, avoiding the inevitable conclusion, that Benfu's girlfriend had now joined up with those who were walking that thin line and crossing into enemy territory. He wasn't sure how it had happened, but he was sure that even if he got a chance to see Benfu again, he'd never tell him. He'd just hope that when the chaos of the revolution had died down, things would get back to normal and just maybe Benfu would never need to know. As he watched Juan Hui walk away, he wondered if Benfu's mother knew about the transformation of her beloved future daughter-in-law.

"She looked at me like I was the bucket of shit instead of the one filling it up," Pony Boy said, then brought the glass to his lips and took a long draw on the warm water. He still hadn't gotten over being insulted by Juan Hui several nights ago. But until now, he'd not had the chance to share it with anyone and he had to admit, it felt better getting it out of his system.

"I'm sorry she made you feel that way, but she's wrong," Wren said. She blew him a kiss. "She just doesn't know how wrong."

He smiled at her. Now that they'd been meeting in a house he'd found empty on his route—the family gone away for an extended time—he and Wren had gotten much closer. Without a constant audience, they'd made time to really get to know one another.

They'd just finished finalizing a new edition of the newsletter and both of them were tired. Now they'd have to plan the next best evening to go to her father's building to get it printed and copied, as he'd decided he didn't want her going there alone anymore. Her father had mentioned within earshot of Wren that they'd recently had some ink and paper come up missing and the manager was suspicious of everyone.

"I just don't see how she could've been accepted into that faction with her parents being teachers," he said.

Wren looked up, her eyes glittery. "I know how. She renounced them. It's happening all over China, Pony Boy. That's what we should've put in this edition!"

"What do you mean?"

"I mean that now people are giving each other up. Wives are going against husbands, children against parents, you wouldn't believe how many relatives are renouncing each other, claiming to cut all ties in order not to be touched by the blemishes their family members might have. Pointing fingers and calling each other reactionaries. I don't know her, but it sounds like Juan Hui is caught up in the fervor."

Pony Boy grimaced. "That's horrible. What do you think is happening to her parents?"

"According to my father, not all counterrevolutionaries are being arrested. Some are willingly going off to hard labor camps in a good-faith effort at purification and reeducation." Wren shrugged and began gathering her notes, stuffing them in her bag. She'd been keeping all their material with her, as his mother was nosier than hers and would easily find it.

"I guess hard labor or renouncing them wouldn't be a hard decision for a girl. The labor camps are rumored to be not much more than hell on earth."

"Most likely, her parents made her renounce them in order to protect her future." Wren said it like it was nothing, but Pony Boy knew in his heart that nothing could ever make him go against his parents. Nothing.

"I wonder how this will affect her and Benfu's engagement."

She shrugged again. "If they did make her do it, that probably means when all this is over that they intend to keep to the plan. I'd be surprised if Benfu and his family ever caught wind of it, unless you tell them, of course."

He didn't answer.

"I've got a surprise for you," Wren said, digging into the bottom of her bag.

"What?" he asked, his voice low and teasing. He hoped her surprise had something to do with her lips upon his. Today she wore her hair in long braids, the most common hairstyle for the times and the one that satisfied her parents that she was conforming as expected. But Pony Boy knew the real Wren—and she was far from conforming.

She rolled her eyes at him. "Not that. Get your mind out of the gutter, Pony Boy."

He laughed just as she pulled out a red armband and twirled it in the air.

Holding his hands up, Pony Boy shook his head. "Oh no, I don't want any part of that."

"You don't even know what it is," she said. "It's a journalist armband. I got it from my father's bag. You can get closer to some events just by wearing it. You can even take photos without hiding behind trees. This gives you permission to do what I'd love to but can't. My parents would never let me disappear for a few days. You'll have to go in my place."

He took the armband that dangled from her fingers. He studied the characters, noting that they did indeed indicate the wearer was an official press reporter.

"Where would I wear it?" He couldn't imagine he would need it to observe anything around Shanghai. So far he hadn't had any troubles, though he was usually fairly discreet when he had his camera out; on that one she was right.

A knowing smile spread across her face. "I have just the idea. Do you know that early next year, Chairman Mao is going to be in Beijing to address the Red Guards?"

Pony Boy waited for her to say more, to get to why that should matter to him.

Wren reached out and put a hand on his chest. "I want you there—officially. No dumbing down and reporting facts as the party wants them reported. For this I want a true account."

"Beijing? How could I possibly get away from my jobs long enough to manage that?"

She came closer, and just before she melted her lips to his, in just the way he'd anticipated, she whispered to him, "You let me take care of the details. You just do what I tell you to do."

Pony Boy couldn't reply. All he knew was that with the touch of her mouth on his, every nerve ending in his body reacted and, of course, he'd do anything and everything that she told him to do.

PART FOUR
Changing Course

Chapter Twenty-Seven

Wuxi

Summer, 1967

Benfu tried to still his trembling as he listened to the chorus of crickets. He was relieved that evening was finally upon him. Carefully he paced the three feet of space with his hands tied behind his back, squinting in the dimness but knowing there was nothing new to see. Through his swollen eyes he saw the same murky shapes he'd seen since they'd dragged him there days before, though he was not sure of how many. He tried to take a deep breath but felt the crackling in his chest. He thought of poor Kuan when the ragged breaths he was forced to take told him his ribs were bruised, if not a few broken. He wished he could wipe the sheen of sweat from his brow, for it burned as it ran into the cuts on his face. It was a bit better since the sun had stopped beaming down on the tin shed, but it still felt like he was being baked. He reminded himself to remain calm, that the cooler night temperatures were coming, a welcome reprieve that would give him the energy to move again, as he tried to make sense of his sudden captivity.

By now he knew every step and each impression in the muck. He also knew from experience where the deep holes were that dropped to the pits of waste. He'd fallen into one that first night and had to be fished out of it like a flailing whale. He still reeked and his stomach rolled with nausea each time he thought of the squishy, putrid substance he had been covered in.

He was like a caged tiger, and though he was weak from lack of food and water, if someone else came through the door to beat him again, he'd fight just as hard as he had the last four days. He would not let them see him broken, and he'd never give up and renounce his parents like they wanted him to do. Mao might be in control of most of China, but Benfu would not let him take possession of his mind the way he had so many others'. His parents were teachers, not revolutionaries! They'd done nothing but spend their lives molding intelligent minds and strong character; he would not let someone tell him they were criminals.

He shook his head and tried to shake the stench from his nostrils. Outside he could hear the work groups coming in from the fields, some trying valiantly to lead the others in a weak rendition of *The East is Red*, a song to exalt their glorious leader, the only semblance of music allowed and a song that after more than an entire year of hearing it, made Benfu want to scream.

When the work group had left that morning their voices were stronger—ready to take on the challenge of meeting their ever-rising quota of gathering more vegetables, planting more rows, watering more crops. They'd had a tough winter—working in the frigid winds, doing backbreaking work to build small huts and dig new reservoirs, going as much as twenty-four to thirty-six hours with no sleep and barely anything of substance to keep them going. As thin as scarecrows, they'd labored in freezing waters to dredge the rich mud from pond bottoms to fertilize the crops, and in the spring they'd planted until they were bent with fatigue, fingers swollen and aching for a rest.

Just when they'd entered the coldest weeks of the year, they'd been visited by ten or so traveling Red Guards. The faction had brought extra Little Red Books and taught the commune quotes they'd never heard. Given the best kang beds in the commune, they'd reported each morning after a full night's rest, then plied the workers with questions about their work teams and asked if they were getting enough points for their hard work, all the while reinforcing Mao Thought while feeding them news of the astounding quotas that other communes were reporting. Of course, no one spoke up to offer insight into how it really was; instead, like eager children, they swore to do more, produce more, to make Chairman Mao proud.

The Red Guards had thrown a contest to see who could write the best big-character poster and those who could write had worked hard, some staying up all night to practice their best strokes in the hope of winning the side of pork as a prize. Benfu, and others who claimed to be illiterate, only stood back and watched, quiet as the posters were made and the winner chosen.

Then they'd competed to see who was the most red. As the Red Guards had told them, it was better to be red than expert. That meant that people from any background could be lifted to a higher level than any expert, as long as they could recite from memory more quotations from Mao's Little Red Book. The competition hadn't lasted long before it was clear that a young lady from the shoe-sewing circle was the most red. For her loyalty to Mao Thought, she'd been granted a week off from work duty and asked to lead study sessions and teach others her memorization techniques.

The Red Guards had also mandated that those who'd been sent down from the city and could read and write should all take interest in teaching the peasants who couldn't, that exchanging expertise was what Chairman Mao intended in mixing the classes. Then, suddenly, the faction was gone and Benfu and the people were back in the fields, freezing as they worked with hungry bellies. The lucky ones were grateful to pull basket duty, collecting twigs from trees and shrubs that lined the creeks, then returning to the commune to weave baskets to use or sell. But they'd all pulled together to dry, salt, and put away squash, cabbage, and turnips to store for future meals, though Benfu doubted they'd see even a portion of it, but at least he'd learned a new skill. He'd thought of Cook so many times, marveling at how astonished she'd be to see all that he'd come to know about preserving food.

Now the scorching summer days had come back around and still, they worked long and feverishly to meet impractical production goals set by those who knew nothing of farming—officials who lived in the cities and reaped the rewards made possible by the peasants.

He'd kept quiet about it as long as he could, but when he'd finally exploded with frustration, his sarcastic remarks had gotten him in trouble. He'd been called in to speak to the elders and he'd thought he'd settled them down enough. What he hadn't known at the time was his outburst had caused an investigation into his background, and they'd discovered he wasn't who he'd said he was. He'd immediately been accused of hiding the truth about his family line, and when he'd refused to give up his parents' names, things had taken a turn for the worse.

After a few days locked in a small, dark room off the dining hall, they'd moved him to the outhouse to try to break him. He had to admit, they'd come close when the sun was at its highest and the temperature in the metal privy had soared. As his head pounded and he sweat out the remaining moisture in his body, the flies and mosquitos never let up from their relentless attack. With his hands tied, Benfu was helpless to fend against them or the stench of human excrement that filled his nostrils and mouth. To keep his sanity, he recited his favorite poem over and over, allowing his mind to focus on the works of Li Shang Yin, rather than the squalor around him.

The east wind sighs, the fine rains come . . . He paced as the whisper of his words punctured the silence of the small enclosure. He thought of the girl, Hsu Yu, and wondered if she'd had her baby yet. Then he wished that fine rains really would come and the roof would open so he could lift his face to the sky, and take in mouthfuls of sweet water.

Twice already, earlier in the day, before and after beatings, the commune leader had come to the shed to ask Benfu if he was ready to cooperate. Simple, he'd said, just tell him his parents' names and address and Benfu could go back to work with the others. Benfu knew if he did, his mother and father would be persecuted. They'd sent him to what they thought was a safe place to hide from the Red Guards who were so vehemently against those with undesirable family backgrounds—black families, they called them—and he wouldn't put them in danger by revealing their identity.

Benfu backed up gingerly and sat on the makeshift shelf over one of the deep holes. It was ironic that he was in misery from holding his bowels but was imprisoned in an outhouse. Only twice had someone come to unfasten his belt and allow him to relieve himself that day, ignoring his shame as they stood over him and watched as his dehydrated body expelled nothing but black waste. Only once had they sent a frightened young woman in with a cup of warm water to ease his swollen throat and cracked lips. He'd begged her to help him, to give him more water or bring him a ball of rice, but the girl had scampered away like a scared rabbit, too afraid to jeopardize her own freedom.

The voices faded into the night and Benfu knew they were all now in the communal kitchen for dinner, competing in line with their coupons to get their rations before the food disappeared.

Benfu couldn't understand it; was the world going crazy around him? He once again wished for the calm assurance of his father and mother. But he'd never give up their names or tell the leaders where they were. He'd do all he could to keep them safe. Judging from the way the last few evenings had gone, Benfu knew he had about two hours before his next beating. It was usually after dinner and right before lights-out that they sent someone to do the deed.

He looked into the dark as he heard the metal chain outside the door being rattled. It was too early! He wasn't ready! Yet he stood, lifting his chin in defiance as the chain slid from handles and the door cracked open. Quickly a young man darted in and shut the door behind him, the flash of light from the receding sun too fast for Benfu to make out who it was.

"Benfu?" the boy called out.

Benfu stayed silent. He wouldn't make it easy for whomever they'd sent. Even though usually they left the door open, Benfu suspected there were probably two or more others waiting outside to assist with his evening beating.

"I'm here to help you," the boy whispered in the dark.

Benfu straightened up. Help? He couldn't believe it. He hoped whoever it was, he had brought food and water. Anything—he'd eat anything at all.

"What help? Who are you?" He tried to keep the pleading tone from entering his voice.

"It's me. Pei. I work on the other work team. You've seen me. I'm always at the end of the line."

Benfu struggled to remember who Pei was and suddenly his voice sounded familiar. If it was who he thought it was, the boy was several years younger than him and they rarely crossed paths due to the work teams being segregated by age and ability.

"Pei? What do you want? Are there more of your cadre out there?" Benfu didn't trust anyone at this point.

"No, just me. Come closer. I'm going to unbind you."

Benfu felt the young man's hands touch his shoulder. Then a sliver of light entered the shed again as the boy cracked the door enough to see Benfu better.

He examined Benfu from head to toe and inhaled deeply. "*Aiya,* it's much worse than I thought. You're covered in welts and bruises. Is anything broken?"

"Why are you untying me?" Benfu asked, his swollen eyes frantically trying to see through the slit in the door to what lay waiting outside. He could handle a beating from one, but he didn't know if he could take on three or more tyrants. His body hurt so much and though he'd try, he didn't know how long he could remain strong.

But surprisingly, the boy was gentle and had brought a small kitchen knife. He moved around Benfu and cut cleanly through the rope around his wrists. With the sudden release, Benfu's shoulders throbbed and he rubbed his hands together, trying to restart the blood flow.

"I asked you why are you untying me?" Benfu stared in the dark, trying to see the boy's face.

"Let's just say I found my good sense again." The boy began rustling in his pockets. He brought out four balls of rice and a chunk of bread. With his overflowing hands, he reached out to Benfu. "This is my share of rations from the last two days. I've been saving it for you."

Benfu took the food and his mouth watered right along with his eyes. Food. He'd been dreaming of it all day. But why? He swallowed past the sudden lump of gratitude that rose in his throat and he fought the urge to stuff it all in his mouth at once. He knew if he started, he'd look like a ravished animal and his pride couldn't take any more shame.

Then the boy unlatched the canteen hooked to his belt. He reached over and snapped it on Benfu's waistband. "And here's my water. I'll tell them I lost it in the fields."

Benfu looked at the canteen and shook his head in confusion. "You can't leave that here. They'll find it when they come back and your initials are carved on it."

"It won't be here when they return. Because *you* won't be here. I'm here to let you go, but you have to hurry before they are done with dinner."

The boy spoke in such a low voice that Benfu had to strain to make out his words. But Benfu could have sworn he said he was going to let him go. Now he knew he was finally losing it—there was no way he would have said that.

"Did you say let me go?" he asked, his voice just as low but shaking now with hope.

The boy went to the door and peeked out, then gestured his hand toward Benfu. "Yes, the coast is clear. Just run through the cornfield until you reach the other side. You're about ten miles from Wuxi, follow the lights. From there, you'll have to find a place to hide for a few days. Then you need to keep moving far, far away from here."

Benfu knew where they were; he'd watched carefully when they'd been bused in from the city. But he couldn't believe what he was hearing. Was the boy really offering him his freedom? He tried to clear the tornado of thoughts in his head—he wouldn't let his confusion stand in his way of possible freedom. He stuffed one rice ball into his mouth and the others into his pocket. He'd eat them on the way. The bread he first held under his nose and inhaled the sweet aroma. Then he put it in the other pocket.

"They'll start looking for you soon. So you can't stop. Don't even turn around until you hit Wuxi. I'm going out there to trample down the field leading in the other direction, then I'll double back. They'll think it was you and that might buy you some time, but be careful to not leave a trail."

Benfu's head was spinning. He still didn't understand why this boy whom he barely knew had come to help him. And he realized what would happen if the boy was caught. He sighed and his shoulders dropped. He spoke the hardest words he'd ever said.

"I can't go. I appreciate what you are trying to do for me, but if they find out it was you, there will be nothing that can save you. Thank you, but I can't have that on my conscience. You're just a boy!"

Pei began stubbornly pushing him toward the door, ignoring his whispered protests.

"You *will* go and don't worry about me. I'm older than I look and I'm fast and smart—they'll never know who it was. I need to do this for you, Benfu. I've heard them beating you and stood in the shadows like a coward. You've already repaid me in ways I cannot say. Just go. Please, I beg you to just go!" With that, he pushed Benfu harder than expected from such a small fellow and Benfu stumbled out of the shed. He looked around and seeing no one, bent over and ran toward the first cornfield. At the edge he turned to see the boy one last time but he was already gone. Benfu wished he had thanked him for such a selfless act, but now it was too late. He turned and ran.

Benfu watched from the safety of the cornstalks for a moment, then made a dash around the old shed and behind the kitchen building to the old well. The thing was dry and no one attempted to draw from it any longer, making it a great hiding place for the one thing in his possession that would have been confiscated if found.

Looking around to be sure he was alone, he leaned over the rounded bricks and began pulling on the frayed rope. He felt the weight on the end of it but didn't release his sigh of relief until his bag came into view. He quickly untied it and held it to his chest, then ran back to the field.

Pausing for a moment, he ate only a nibble from one more rice ball, scared he'd need to ration it for a while. He listened intently for voices, for he was sure there was probably a chase going on. But he didn't hear anything and once again he thanked the gods that perhaps Pei had successfully diverted them.

With one arm holding his ribs and the other clutching his bag, Benfu ran through the field until he thought his lungs would explode. As he ran, the stalks slapped his face and he could feel his cuts stinging, but he didn't let the sting deter him from his rush to freedom. Finally he stopped for only seconds to get his breath and take a sip from the most delicious water he'd ever tasted. He turned the canteen over and sure enough, there were the initials of the boy, reminding Benfu he'd have to be careful where he discarded it eventually. He sure didn't want the boy to face any repercussions.

He ran again until he reached the end of the row of cornstalks. There he stopped to rest and spread mud over the welts on his arms and neck. The mosquitos were still landing on him even in his sprint to safety, and the welts from the last few days burned like fire. Benfu quickly finished and took off again, by this time limping with each stride. He was halfway to town. He could do this, he told himself. *Don't stop, don't stop, don't stop,* the words becoming a mantra that kept him putting one foot in front of the other.

Finally he could run no more, so he staggered on toward the lights of town. He had plenty of time to think and marveled at how or why he had been given a reprieve. He bartered with the gods that if he could just make it through the night, he'd spend his life finding ways to be just as selfless as Pei had been with him. As he walked he stayed close to the ditches, ready to jump at any moment. He knew he looked a sight—beaten and staggering like a drunken man. He hoped the late hour would keep anyone from seeing him. He unscrewed the lid from the canteen and drank the rest of the water, unable to stop himself.

At least three hours later, much longer than it should have taken him, Benfu found himself on the outskirts of town. He took a break and dropped to his knees, using his hands to skim just a tiny bit of water from the top of the mud in a pothole. It tasted oily and salty, but it was gloriously wet. With that tiny reward, he felt he could keep moving a bit farther. As he stood, the rumbling and lights of a large truck came around the corner and Benfu stumbled to the high grass and hid as it went by. He figured it was the delivery truck coming from his commune, taking most of their day's crop intake on to Shanghai.

Still shaking from the close call, he stayed away from the main roads, choosing to skirt down the country roads until he came to one of the *hutongs*, the residential lanes that ran parallel to the major roads. He thought maybe he could find an old shed or barn to hide in while he rested. Just a few hours of sleep, then he would set off again.

As he staggered down one quiet lane, he saw a small home with the gate open. The house beckoned to him and since his gut instinct had not failed him yet, Benfu quietly slipped through the gate. He looked at the front window and only saw a faint light, and hoped the homeowners were asleep just as they should be at this time of night. First listening for noise from the inside and hearing nothing, he crept around the house toward the small utility shed. He wished it had windows as he could hardly make himself go back into such tight, airless quarters but alas, he had no choice if he wanted to remain hidden. He hoped he could find space in it to stretch out for a few hours.

Spotting an old rusty water pump on the side of the house, he stood there uncertain for a moment. He could take a chance and try to clean himself a bit and get some fresh drinking water to refill his canteen, or he could wait. He shifted from foot to foot. He didn't want to get caught, but he was so thirsty that his tongue felt swollen and rough, like fabric in his mouth. If he didn't get water, he felt he would just die. He was dizzy and weak, and so thirsty that if he succumbed to his painful hunger and ate one of his last remaining rice balls, he might even choke on it. What a cruel fate to finally have food in his pocket, but know his throat was too parched to get it down.

With precious moments wasting before daylight came upon him, Benfu made a choice. He had to drink. He only prayed the old pump would not moan and carry on, waking the family inside. With his ribs now in such intense pain he could barely walk, Benfu struggled over to the pump. He slowly and carefully lifted the handle and flinched when the old pipes began to rumble. Carefully he dropped to his knees. He'd be quick, just one drink. Turning his head to the side to catch the stream in his mouth, he heard someone behind him.

The quick movement to see who had caught him made his head spin and a wave of dizziness completely overtook him. As everything went black around him, he focused on the face of a girl about his own age. His last thoughts before he hit the ground were of how pretty and clean she looked as she stood there with her hands on her hips, a scolding frown making its way across her heart-shaped mouth.

Then all was dark and Benfu welcomed the curtain that fell across his vision and smothered the smell of his fear.

Chapter Twenty-Eight

Benfu slowly opened his eyes but didn't move as he looked around. Where was he? Directly overhead, in the corner of a wooden rafter, he watched a dark spider weaving its web, its front two legs moving gracefully as it glided in and out of the shimmering threads already made. From his view, he thought it a small room, almost not long enough for him to stretch out in, and if he'd been facing the other direction he'd have had to pull his legs in. On the opposite wall from him he spotted a counter that held a sink and a huge wok and some other smaller pots that hung from hooks.

Closer to him was a rusty old stove that a large, well-used kettle set atop.

It was an outside kitchen.

Suddenly he remembered the girl.

The thickness of his tongue reminded him that he had been trying to get water and had fallen. Maybe even fainted?

Then everything came rushing back and he felt a heavy fear surround him. Were they looking for him? Had the commune leader sent out a search party? Maybe they'd tracked him and were just outside. Panic threatened to overwhelm him and he tried to sit up. A flash of pain made him give up and relax against the blanket, and he realized his muscles were acting as though they belonged to a newborn baby.

His bag! His violin—where was it?

He felt around, a sense of relief filling him when his fingers found the familiar material of the bag and felt the shape of his beloved violin. He inhaled. He could smell the earth and knew that only the thin material he lay on separated him from the rich dirt. Yet he'd slept.

Then he realized he didn't know how she'd gotten him into the shed. *She'd given him a blanket.* What did that mean? That meant she hadn't called the local authorities on him, right?

He heard a rattle at the door and held his breath, waiting for what, he wasn't sure. Would he be carted away to jail? Or worse, back to the commune? He couldn't go back there. Just the thought of his imprisonment in the shed made him want to run. He'd rather die than go back—he would.

"Are you awake?"

The voice was soft and feminine. Even sympathetic. It had been a long time since anyone had spoken to him so kindly and this time he sat up completely. "I'm awake," he said.

She entered and the sun shone behind her, bathing her head in a glorious golden light so bright that he couldn't see the features of her face. She closed the door, shutting them into a dim light again. Still, he struggled to see, but her features remained blurry.

"Here," she said, bending to hand him a bowl. Her moves were graceful, like a dancer, and he noticed it immediately. He took the bowl, still unsure of just what her gesture meant.

"Am I in trouble?" he asked. The smell of the noodles taunted him, the aroma wrapping itself around his head, teasing his senses with the spiciness they promised.

"Well, I don't know. Are you a criminal?" she asked, sitting back against the wall and pulling her knees up in front of her.

Her words shocked him, taking him back to just days before when he'd been accused of some unknown crime, urged to confess, and then beaten for refusing.

"No!" he said, a bit too loud, then he lowered his voice. "I am not a criminal. I can explain."

She was quiet for a moment, then spoke softly. "I didn't think so. Please, eat. You look hungry."

He looked down at the bowl and realized that yes, he was very hungry, but that was nothing unusual. Hunger was no longer his enemy—he'd become so used to it that now it was just a part of his very being. More important than his hunger was his thirst.

"Could I beg of you some water?" he asked, searching for her eyes in the dim light.

She gestured to the place on the ground next to where his head had lain. He looked and saw Pei's water canteen.

"I brought you water last night. Your canteen is full."

He saw Pei's canteen then and went to move toward it, his mind reeling that it had been so close yet in his daze, he'd not known it.

"No, let me," she said, moving to pick it up.

She took the lid off and then brought it to him.

"I'll hold it, you just don't let those noodles spill," she said, then held it to his lips, her other hand cradling the back of his head gently.

He drank, pulling long and greedily on the cool, clean water until there were but a few drops left.

"That's probably enough for now," she said. "You may be dehydrated and we need to bring you back slowly, or you'll vomit everything up. Now, please eat. We can talk more when you're done."

Relieved he was safe for the moment, he cradled the bowl of noodles in his hands, grateful for the warmth he knew it would bring to his belly. He carefully scooted back until he was against the wall. Then, as she watched, he ate slowly, relishing every delicious bite in his mouth before swallowing.

"I have tea," she said. "I'll give you a few minutes to finish that and then I'll go fetch it."

Tea? Could she really have said tea? Hope flooded him and he realized that it had been months since he'd had a good cup of tea. In the commune, usually by the time he'd gone through the line and gotten to the kettles, the tea was nothing more than weak leaves and water. He remembered that Doctor Yu had served him good tea to help his recovery, but even that memory was so long ago it had all but faded from his mind.

"Tea would be ideal," he said between slurps.

The sound of her voice reminded him that the first look he'd had of her the night before told him she was a girl of about his age, maybe a bit younger, or maybe a bit older. As he took the last few sips of the broth in the bowl, he looked down at himself and was glad the light was dim so that she couldn't see his face flush with embarrassment.

He was so filthy that he could smell himself. The mud he'd used to ease the sting of the insect bites had turned rough and scaly, making his skin feel heavy. He knew he must look like a grave digger, or worse.

"I—I'm sorry," he said, shame filling his face.

"For what?" She came to him and took the bowl, standing over him as she waited for his response. "What did you do?"

"I didn't do anything. I'm just sorry that I'm so dirty," he rambled, remembering that his fall into the sewer of the outhouse had left dried remnants of waste on his clothes—probably even in his hair. His hand went up and touched his head, his fingers exploring the spiky strands.

She laughed. "*Aiya*, you do need a bath. You scared me at first last night, I couldn't see who or what was beneath all that dirt."

He nodded. A bath. He'd give anything and everything for a bath. But he'd promised her an explanation.

"I know what you're thinking but first, let's do this," she said. "We've gotten you fed and now we need to get you cleaned up. Everyone thinks better when they feel better. First, we'll get some hot water going, and while you're bathing, I'll wash your clothes. After that, we'll talk. *Hao le?*"

He nodded in agreement. If he ended up being sent back to the commune, he'd go with honor, clean and smelling like a human—not covered in filth like a common pig. More gratitude flooded through him and he thanked the gods for the reprieve.

A bath.

He was getting a bath and it wouldn't be in an ice-cold creek.

She came over to his side of the shed, passing him to go to the kettle. She picked it up and went back to the door.

"This is going to be quite a task, but I'll start bringing water in. You get that tub from off the wall and set it up. I'll put cold water in the tub, then heat you a few kettles of hot to pour in."

He sat there, unsure what to do. Everything felt surreal, as if it couldn't be happening to him. He stared at her, wondering if he was in a dream and she was a figment of what his heart was begging for—a touch of kindness.

"Hurry up," she said firmly, snapping him awake.

He scrambled to his feet, turning to the wall she'd pointed at, seeing a huge wooden tub. Thankfully his muscles cooperated, finally fortified by the soup and the water, and he was able to pull the tub from the wall and set it on the ground by his blanket. When he turned to see if she approved, he saw that she'd disappeared, the door shut behind her.

Then he heard the creaking of the pump and it made him smile.

With the blanket wrapped around his waist, Benfu waited for her to return. He looked around, taking in the shape of their outdoor kitchen. In his staggering shape the night before, he must've picked the oldest *hutong* in the city, as most families—like Pony Boy's—had moved their kitchens indoors, yet this one still appeared to be used frequently. On a shelf above the counter, he spotted a half-full bag of rice, a basket of vegetables, and a bottle of oil that only had a few inches left. They obviously weren't rich, but they weren't starving either. She'd said that she lived in the house with her parents, their only caretaker as both of them were suffering from some illness. He wondered how much she had told them about their unexpected visitor.

He'd had his bath—an almost heavenly event that had made him wish for home and the pleasant soap flakes his mother had always insisted he use on his body and head, though even without that luxury he was beginning to feel like himself again. Not the self who'd spent almost a year learning to work in the country, but the self who'd left Shanghai what now seemed like years ago. He no longer felt like just a boy. Commune life had brought the man out in him and the boy had disappeared forever, but he did find his old creative and inquisitive thoughts returning. He hadn't realized that in the last half a year he'd been mentally beaten down and learned not to question things, at least not until the moment he'd exploded at the commune and gotten himself into trouble.

But now, looking back from a new and safer perspective, he could see that through all of his resistance, some of the brainwashing had begun to slip in, making him wonder if he and his family weren't *bad elements* after all, just for living a privileged life. In his exhausted and oppressed state, he'd begun to think that perhaps Chairman Mao was correct, that anything to do with education or wealth was to be feared. For the last few months he'd been led to believe he deserved to be punished—that the long toiling and the absence of comforts was justified. But now, away from the collective that he'd miraculously escaped, words he'd memorized long ago flooded his mind. Snippets of poems and stories came alive in his thoughts—adventures that allowed people of every level to enjoy and imagine something more. He thought of his violin and the humble music that he himself made, occasionally even bringing happiness to his parents' friends. How the famous musicians

Kay Bratt

had brought the taste of culture to people all over China, but now were either being reeducated on labor farms or even sent away, exiled from their home countries, the beautiful pieces they'd created deemed *poisonous weeds* and banned from society.

And he knew that it couldn't be right.

Books, poems, and music—they were gifts from another world, something to be shared and celebrated. How could they be banned? Benfu would not let one man make him think that enjoying them was bad. He pledged to himself that never again would he let someone into his head, allow them to steal his sense of right and wrong. For the first time in a long time, he felt victorious—even triumphant that he'd made a decision on his own and would stick to it, come what may.

The door opened and this time the sun was higher in the sky, making the light just right.

With a rush of hot air from outside she stepped in and Benfu could see every feature on her face, and what he saw was so lovely that his breath was stolen from him.

"Ready to get dressed?" she said, her voice settling around him like a gentle breeze.

A sudden heat rushed into his face and he clutched the blanket tighter around him. Did she mean to come in while he dressed?

"I suppose," he answered, unable to disguise the uncertainty in his voice.

She laughed. "Don't worry, you're safe. I don't plan to help you. And your pants were quite a job because your pockets had dried rice in them." She tossed his clothes onto the floor and stepped out, then quietly shut the door.

Benfu quickly dropped the blanket and picked up his pile of clothes. He held them to his nose, inhaling the clean, sweet smell of lye soap. Hearing a noise, he realized she was waiting outside the door and he scrambled into the underclothing, then his pants, thinking of the

262

rice and the one who'd given it to him. Pei. Just a boy to many, but to him—more like his savior.

He looked for his belt and didn't see it.

With both arms going into his shirt, he almost lost his pants. Without his belt, the pants that had fit him so snugly upon his arrival at the commune now practically swallowed him up. He reached down and held them, cinching the baggy material in his fingers.

"I'm dressed . . ."

She came in and covered a smile with her hand. Then she pointed at the corner behind him. "Sorry, I should've told you, your belt is over there."

Benfu turned, saw the belt, and bent to retrieve it. Quickly he looped it through his pants and fastened it. While his hands moved nimbly, he wished she could've seen him before, when his body was strong—not the waiflike figure he was now. When he looked up, he realized something else.

"I'm sorry, I didn't get your name. I'm Benfu."

She held her hand out and he grasped it with his.

"I'm Calla Lily, but you can just call me Calli," she said. "And now that I can stand in the same room with you without cringing, I think we have some talking to do."

Benfu sat down on the dirt floor, feeling deflated. Would she now turn him over to someone official? Or would she hear him out and help him come up with a plan to get home? He wavered, trying to decide which story to use. He wasn't sure what she'd do, but he could only trust his instincts, and that meant pouring out everything to her—every last detail of the months he'd suffered in the name of staying safely out of Shanghai.

No more lies.

Before this day was over she would know exactly who he was and what he stood for. Then, and only then, would he accept her verdict.

Simply put, she'd either send him away or become his friend. He took a big breath, then began talking. "So, Calli, have you ever heard anyone play the violin?"

When he showed her the instrument and the bow, she seemed to believe him that he could play, but both of them were too nervous for him to do it, fearing the notes would make their way into the ears of a neighbor and cause questions. Instead, they talked for hours, with mostly him spilling the truth of his history.

It turned out that she was the best listener he'd ever known and Benfu couldn't seem to stop. Calli had brought another blanket with her and she rolled it up, using it to lounge against as they exchanged information. First they talked about his music and the dream he carried to attend music school in Shanghai—how his tutor and others had told him that he'd easily be able to gain admittance because of his gift at playing the violin.

Then they'd ventured into the subject of Maoism and how it appeared that many were sucked into it, longing to be part of the fervor that was raging across China. But he was relieved that she seemed to be her own person, seeing things through her own eyes and not the curtain of mind control that so many had adopted. Discovering that allowed him to speak freely, and as he told about the hardships of the commune—the backbreaking work and hunger he carried daily—she listened. From her place against the opposite wall, she only interrupted occasionally to ask him to repeat something he'd said so quietly it had dissolved before making it across the space to her ears. He described to her the plowing, seeding, and what would be a part of his duties come next spring. He hoped she understood that it wasn't simply farmer's work that he couldn't handle—some of that he had appreciated. It was the way the brigade leaders pushed them past what normal people should be able to do, driving them to work harder and longer, all with only minimal sustenance. It was when he personally had been forced to work longer than the others, tilling the corners of fields that the wide plows couldn't get to, working late into the dark nights as others reported for dinner or reeducation sessions.

Finally, he got to the worst part of his story. He took a deep breath and told her of the day he'd felt something was off—the day that his work duty leader had begun treating him as though he'd done something wrong. Then when the workday was over, how they'd called him in for questioning.

As he spoke about the ensuing interrogation, he felt his shoulders draw in, as if he needed to be smaller. He told her of his oath to protect the identity of his parents, of taking the cane across his shoulders repeatedly to keep them safe. She'd cringed when he described the open cuts, made by the lashes of the cane, and the bleeding that later brought hordes of insects to devour his skin. That led him to telling her of being imprisoned, the soaring daytime temperatures and the nighttime solid dark. He didn't tell her of wading in the feces, of his humiliation as he was pulled from the depths of human waste. She surely had figured that out when she'd scrubbed his clothes and he couldn't bring himself to admit it aloud. He stopped, swallowing hard as he tried to rein in his swirling thoughts.

"I can't imagine how dreadful it was for you. Are you sure you want to tell me more?" Calli asked, her question encouraging him to continue, encouraging him to purge the memories that lay heavy in his mind, brewing like a bitter stew and poisoning his thoughts.

"Yes, I'll tell you more."

"But you can stop if you want to," Calli said softly.

He didn't want to stop. He had to get it all out there. When he spoke, he felt the beginnings of relief, a burden being lifted from him as he shared his experience with her.

"They called me a criminal, though I've done nothing wrong," he said. He closed his eyes, drawing the depiction from deep inside himself, pulling on his memory to make her understand why he'd run, why he had not stayed and taken his punishment like a man. Why he didn't stay and face his accusers, convince them of his innocence.

"Being isolated was more than a lonely experience. The vast nothingness I faced daily wreaked havoc not only on me physically, but it also affected my mental health. I soon found it hard to finish a thought before it dangled aimlessly, lethargically dissolving like a raindrop on the tongue, leaving me wondering what it was that was so important but now lost." He paused, taking another deep breath.

When he looked up, Calli was watching him intently.

He began again. "My mind jumped between the unbelievable and tortuous present to reliving the past. Many times I found myself back in the only home I'd ever known, wrapped in comforting memories. *Thank you, Cook*, I'd mumble as she brought me a phantom bowl of my favorite noodles. My hands even went through the motions of bringing the smooth porcelain to my lips, while my stomach longed for it to be reality. Then I'd have a thought that my actions were that of a crazy man and I'd shake off the visions, and I'd take back up reciting the poetry my parents had so adamantly demanded I learn—the poetry that had most likely placed me under suspicion."

He looked up to see if he'd put her to sleep with his rambling yet. She watched him intently.

"Finally, I could feel gratitude for the endless tutoring of my youth, for only with lines of poetry and remembered passages of books could I prevent myself from becoming the blithering and begging idiot that my conditions demanded." He stopped, aware that his face was wet. Embarrassed, he used his sleeve to wipe at it, his eyes meeting Calli's across the dim room.

Her face was also wet.

She stood. "That's enough for now, Benfu. I think you need to lie down and rest. I'll return at midday with some ginger soup. It'll help heal your stomach."

Benfu didn't argue with her. He felt a wave of exhaustion and the sudden need to lay his head down, to sleep and hopefully dream of nothing. He turned and lay on his side, curling into himself.

She hadn't uttered the words that he'd hoped she would. He'd imagined her saying it through the whole time they'd talked, even once or twice sure she was about to do it.

'You've come to the right place,' was the reply he'd longed to hear. But he hadn't heard that.

He'd said too much, of that he was sure. Perhaps Calli was retreating softly so that she could get away from him—flee from the madman she must think him to be. But Benfu was tired—so very tired. He didn't care any longer. He just wanted to sleep, and then, if he awoke to officials standing over him, ready to take him in, he would accept his fate and be grateful for the respite from insanity that Calli had given him.

Drifting off to sleep, he felt something tickle against his shoulder. A blanket, he realized, and it was being put over him by the girl who'd rescued him, if only for a moment in time. But he'd take her offering and moment of peace. He'd figure out the rest later. He gave in to his fatigue; then, he felt nothing.

Chapter Twenty-Nine

The next morning Benfu was awakened from his deep slumber when Calli opened the door and dragged in a stuffed mattress with one hand and a broom with the other. He sat up, rubbing his eyes, then blinked against the light that poured in around her. She hurried in, shutting the door behind her.

"Get up, Benfu. Let's make this place presentable."

He stared, unsure what she was talking about.

"Come on," she said, "if you're going to stay here for a while, we need to make you comfortable. You can't keep sleeping with only a blanket to separate you from the hard dirt."

His mind caught only a few words, but he knew she'd said *if you're going to stay.*

She wasn't turning him in! He felt a rush of adrenaline, fused by hope.

He stood, using his hands he tried to rub out the wrinkles on his trousers.

"I can stay for a while?" he asked, moving out of her way as she bent to pick up his blanket.

"Well you can't go back to that hellhole and you need to wait to try to return to Shanghai, at least give them a few weeks in case they have somehow traced you back to your parents."

She was right. Going back now might put his parents in danger. Hopefully if someone had determined he was from Shanghai, his father would claim him to be a runaway. But if anything, he knew his mother would be the one to quickly come up with a story. He could see his father crumbling under the news that his son was being called a criminal, but his mother, she was the more resourceful—and sly—of the two and would do what it took to save herself.

"What about your parents?" he asked.

"I've told them I've hired you to do some of the heavy work around here and we'll pay you with meals. They never go outside so don't worry, they won't know you're staying in their own backyard."

"I'll do any work you tell me to."

She laughed. "Oh, I know you will. I was serious about that, though I've nothing to pay you other than a roof over your head and food to fill your belly. If that's enough, you can stay here until you feel you're ready to make the trip to Shanghai safely."

Benfu felt immense gratitude, so much so that it left him speechless.

"First things first," Calli said, then handed him the broom. "You sweep and I'll push some of this clutter to the other wall. We'll make you your own space in here so you feel more comfortable."

He picked up his bag, stifling his urge to bring out his violin and instead, carefully placed it on the counter by the deep sink. Then he took the broom and began sweeping at the dirt, pushing it out the door while Calli worked to set up the stuffed mattress. He wondered where she had gotten it and noticed it looked pieced together with many different colors and textures of materials. It couldn't even compare to the luxurious mattress that topped his own bed at home, but it was fit for a king compared to the scratchy bamboo mat he'd slept on in the commune. Calli didn't know it, but he would've gladly slept on the packed dirt forever, that was how happy he was that he could stay.

They continued working together and he began to whistle, something that he'd almost forgotten he could do. When they stopped for a break, he had his own space and everything looked perfect to him. Calli folded his blanket and put it at the end of the mattress, then sat down. She patted the space beside her and Benfu obliged.

"Do you have any brothers or sisters?" Calli asked.

"No, my mother was too interested in pursuing her career ladder at the university," he said. "What about you?"

"I'm the only one. But my mother wanted more children. She lost a few pregnancies before me, and several after. I was the only one to make it to term."

They were both silent for a moment.

"I'm sorry, Calli. That must be hard for your parents, and for you."

"Mama only talked to me of it once, but she said that I was a single flower in what was supposed to be a full garden of children," she whispered even lower. "But she never let that get her down and she's been a wonderful mother—the kind of mother I hope to be someday."

They'd only known each other for a short time, but Benfu could already sense that she'd be a good mother. "You will, Calli. I can see it now—you'll make a compassionate and loving mother for many children. I just know you'll get your wish."

She playfully swatted at his shoulder, then stood.

"We've got a lot to do. Me in the house and you back here in the yard. Then I've got to make it to the neighborhood struggle session."

"You have those, too? Ours was nightly in the commune."

"Ours are weekly but this one was scheduled at the last minute by the neighborhood Party Committee. One of my neighbors, a woman named Lao Cheng, lost her mind and in a fit of rage over their family's rations being cut, she tore Chairman Mao's picture from her wall and cussed him."

"But how did the neighborhood committee know about it if it happened in her own home?"

She looked away for a moment before answering. "Her son turned her in. He drew a line and denounced her. Now she's been ordered to make a series of self-criticisms, and who knows—she might still be sent away."

Benfu was stunned at the thought of a son turning in his own mother and he couldn't think of anything to say.

"So I need to hurry and get my chores done so I'm not late," Calli said. "We'll begin with cutting wood. I know it's summertime but if you up and leave, at least I'll have a start in preparing for winter. Maybe this year I'll get by without so many calluses and blisters."

He stood, too, and stared at her hands, unable to imagine them doing the work of a man. She was such a gentle person—soft in all the right ways. At least from what his eyes could see.

"You do know how to chop wood, don't you?" she asked, raising an eyebrow.

A year before, he would've had to tell her no, that his hands had never known a day of labor but instead had earned every callus from the instrument they played so well. Yet today, after all he'd been through and all he'd learned about living the rougher side of life, he was proud to just nod and ask her where the axe was.

"Follow me," she said, then led him outside where he got his first breath of fresh air since he'd stumbled into her courtyard. He looked up at the blue sky and felt a tremor of excitement. Things had turned around for him and his life had changed course. So far, it appeared to be a good thing, but only time would tell if he'd made the right decision when he'd picked this particular courtyard in this specific *hutong*. And only time would tell if he'd live to embrace that decision, or regret it dearly.

Chapter Thirty

And you're sure that you'll be fine traveling alone?" Pony Boy asked Widow Chou. He stood on his toes and pulled the bamboo birdcage from the ceiling hook, then set it on the floor. It was another scorching hot day and he looked forward to getting back outside where at least he might catch a breeze. Thankfully, his deliveries were easy that morning, allowing him to accept Widow Chou's plea for assistance. Working as quickly as he possibly could, he'd already helped her pull her suitcase from a high shelf as she flurried around him, preparing clothes to pack; he followed the orders she pelted at him and did all the other tasks that a short, delicate woman couldn't take care of. He smiled at her show of irritation, for it was just that—a show. After over a year of knowing her and seeing her daily, she felt almost like a grandmother to him and he worried for her safety.

"I'm sure," Widow Chou said. As she moved around the small house, Mynah perched on her shoulder, looking pleased as he clutched at the material of the widow's shirt with curled claws. "Shanghai is getting to be too much for me. Now there're some renegades who are even printing up papers, detailing stories of all kinds of mayhem happening around China. Who knows if it's true—all I know is that those Red

Guards are frightening and I want to get out to the country and as far away as I can."

Pony Boy cringed, regretting slipping a copy of the newsletter into her box the week before. He'd thought she should know what else, in addition to killing innocent birds, the factions were up to. Now from what he'd heard, the countryside was also in turmoil. Despite the massive crops the government collected, there was a food shortage and those left the hungriest were those doing the harvesting. He thought of Benfu, now out there for almost a year and he wondered how he was faring and if the chaos had found its way to his commune.

He knew the Red Guard factions were everywhere now, not just the city. But if Widow Chou wanted to leave and head to somewhere that she felt safer, he was all for it. He hoped she'd gotten her *hukou* in line and had obtained the proper permissions to leave the city.

"You'll need warm clothes," Pony Boy said. "I know it's summer now but before you know it, fall will set in and then winter. Take your biggest coat and your best boots."

"Oh, I will. I'll need you to seal off the water pump outside, too," Widow Chou said, handing Pony Boy a rusty wrench. "And if I get any mail, you hold it for me, *hao le*? I'll write to your mother when I know where I'll be and she can forward it."

"The usual protocol is to take it back to the post office for forwarding," Pony Boy said.

Widow Chou rolled her eyes at him. "Listen to you, trying to be all official and the like. Just do as I tell you, Pony Boy."

He laughed, then nodded. Of course he'd do as she wanted.

"Your family should also find a place to go," she'd said as soon as she'd told him her plans to leave. "Here it is over a year after this so-called revolution and things are in such upheaval that people have lost their lust for life."

"I'm still excited about living," Pony Boy had told her. Of course, Wren's face had come to mind, though he kept that to himself. The truth was, he was optimistic about what the future would bring, now that he'd found the woman he wanted to spend it with. Sure, times were chaotic, but just like other upheavals in history, it would pass and eventually he and Wren could get on with the rest of their lives.

Widow Chou had pointed her finger at him. "I hope that with all the respectable upbringing you've had that you'll keep your morals."

He held his hand up, a silent oath to remain noble and become a Red Guard.

"I mean it." She shot a look of chastisement at his attempt to make light of the moment. "I'm aghast at what parents are expected to teach their children now. No longer does losing face matter—it's all about loyalty to country, which would be fine if our generations weren't expected to forget all they've been taught otherwise!"

He'd listened patiently while she ranted on.

"It's all about what we can do for our country. The institution of family means nothing now. You watch—soon I'll be gone and I won't even be able to depend on my ancestors to sweep my grave, or even care for my familial tablet. *Aiya*, we're not even allowed to pray to our gods anymore, or even worship anything but—"

She'd stopped there, refusing to utter the name of the man whom she felt wronged by and who others exalted in public and most likely in the privacy of their own homes. Pony Boy looked at the huge poster of Chairman Mao that hung in her living room, and wondered how many times she'd passed it and wished to rip it down and burn it.

Now he moved toward the door, aware that he needed to get back on his route.

"Widow Chou, I'll watch out for your house and care for your mail."

She stopped her scurrying to and fro and crossed the room to him.

"Pony Boy, I'll miss you," she said, embracing him and holding him close for a second before turning away from him and lifting her hand in the air, beckoning for him to go.

Respectful of her wish to hide her emotions, he grabbed his bag and ducked out of the door. He took the path and let himself out of her gate, then sorted in his bag for the next piece of mail.

Wang Zi.

He groaned.

From the histrionics of Widow Chou, now probably on to the pleadings from Wang Zi, as he felt doubtful that the old man would refrain from taking the opportunity to once again ask him to keep his letters safe, as he'd done periodically over the last months. House raids by the Red Guards had become commonplace, inspiring Wang's paranoia to greater heights because of his secret, but also reminding Pony Boy that even his own house could be searched. He was already hiding the envelope of negatives, and when he was home, his camera. That was enough. So once again, to protect his own family, he'd have to decline Wang's plea.

He thought of the newsletter and felt a second of shame. His involvement with it might also be jeopardizing his family, but it was something he couldn't stop now if he tried. And many things were causing his parents stress—his father's health, making the monthly bills, and even their worries about Lixin. Only the night before his mother had cried, and that had torn something deep inside of Pony Boy. It was another letter from Lixin describing his newly appointed job working the rice fields. As he'd read to her about Lixin's ten-hour days full of constant slapping at his legs to rid himself of the leeches that found him in the dirty water, his mother had hidden her face, her knowledge at what her youngest son was going through causing her unspeakable pain. The sounds of her muffled, grief-filled sobs had stayed with him all day, and he tried to shake them again.

He looked down at the handwriting on Wang's letter, a definite female grace to it telling him that, once again, correspondence from the man's wife had arrived. Now that Pony Boy knew Wang's story, the contents of the letters made him even more curious. How a man could stay away from the love of his life for decades, not watching but only reading about how his children had grown up, had to be excruciating. Wang Zi was a strong man, Pony Boy knew that much. He'd never want to be separated from Wren, and they weren't even married!

Yet.

He thought the word and it made him pause at the next mailbox. His mind had said *yet*. Did that mean he really wanted to marry Wren and make it official? He thought she felt the same about him, but what did a man truly know of a woman's mind? What if he was totally wrong and he was just a passing fancy for her?

He felt a lump in his throat, then told himself to stop being ridiculous and he moved on to the next box. Wren cared for him deeply— she'd told him that time and again. Usually at the same time that she bemoaned the fact that she still couldn't introduce him to her family. Her father, he'd not approve, she'd said.

"How's your father?" A woman called out from her porch when Pony Boy stopped at her box. He opened the gate, hurrying to hand her the letter.

"He's getting by."

"You tell him I said hello," she said, taking the envelope from his hand and studying it intently.

"I will," Pony Boy said, then moved on, his thoughts returning to Wren and their relationship, thoughts that plagued him day and night, about a girl he could not stop thinking of. He would've thought over time he would lose the attraction, but alas, if anything, he was now even more infatuated.

But she might be angry with him later today.

He'd asked her to meet him at the toilets later so that they could talk. A sad place to come together, but unfortunately, the gap between cleanings was the only time he had free for at least a few days. He was already set to meet Wren on Sunday, the only day he didn't have to deliver mail, but this couldn't wait.

He had to tell her. He'd missed the first opportunity to see Mao in Beijing, and now it had come up again. But there was still no way he could possibly go—Red Guard armband or not. It was simple; he just couldn't leave his family for that long. Or his jobs. Yes, his father was doing better, but what kind of son would he be if he just abandoned them? And his job at the toilets—most nights he wished he would get fired, he was so sick of dealing with the waste of others. Then he'd come home late and his mother would be waiting, a warm bowl of something to ease his hungry belly and a full dose of affection to ease his heart. She was so thankful. They both were. Even little Mei seemed to look up to him more since he'd taken on the role of the main provider

He just couldn't let them down.

Turning the corner to the last street, he hoped that Wang Zi wouldn't be waiting outside. He breathed a sigh of relief when it appeared he'd caught a break. The man was nowhere in sight.

Quickly he pulled out the last stack, a pile of about six pieces of mail. Then he saw the one for Wang Zi. He held the letter, ready to plop it in Wang's mailbox and hurry on.

Just as he approached the gate that held the box, he noticed that Wang's front door stood ajar just a few inches. An uneasy feeling came over him.

However, to leave the door open wasn't all that unusual; maybe the old man had gone next door to borrow something and had forgotten to close it behind him. *There could be a million reasons why it was open,* Pony Boy told himself. He looked down at the sudden goose bumps on his arm. Every nerve ending in his body told him to go look—just one peek to be completely sure that all was well.

He opened the gate, cringing at the creak it made. Wang needed to get some oil on the old thing, and he'd tell him just that.

"Lao Wang," he called out, stepping onto the stoop.

The house was silent and Pony Boy waited for a moment before rapping on the old wood of the doorframe.

No one answered.

He pushed the door open, peeking into the living area.

The scene that greeted him made him jump backward and he dropped the stack of letters he held. Telling himself he was being ridiculous, that his eyes were playing tricks on him, he bent down and picked the letters up, pushing them back into his bag before once again peeking around the open door.

It wasn't his imagination.

Wang Zi sat against the wall, a plastic sack over his head, tied at his neck. His face was visible through the bag and his bulging eyes and eerily white skin made it evident that Pony Boy was too late to help him, but he ran to him anyway, attempting to untie the string but failing. The action made Wang fall over to the side, his head making a loud thump on the hardwood floor. Quickly Pony Boy dropped to his knees and tore at the bag, ripping it open anyway, hoping for some sign of life.

But there was none.

Pony Boy was horrified that such a kind human being was just gone, in one irreversible moment. But most of all the heaping pile of ashes beside the man told him that Wang hadn't been overreacting when he'd said he couldn't live without his letters. He'd burnt them—probably to continue protecting his family.

And then he'd stopped living.

Pony Boy stood and felt hot tears running down his face. He was ashamed that he hadn't heeded the man's request and taken his letters, just hidden them. Would it have changed the outcome? Was Wang dead because of him? He choked back a sob and straightened his shoulders.

No. Wang Zi was dead because of a country that had gone mad, and he deserved justice. Pony Boy pulled out his camera, took a few shots, then stuffed it back in the bag.

He reached over and closed Wang's eyes.

In the moments since he'd entered the courtyard and intruded on the death scene, his plans had changed. No matter what, the next time

Chairman Mao was scheduled to be in Beijing, Pony Boy would go and he'd find a way to get to show him what was really happening to the people in the face of all his new directives. To witness for himself the path of death and destruction that he was blazing.

Pony Boy backed away, then just before he slid out of the house, he gave Wang one more look, a lasting, pleading gaze, and then looked around the room, half believing he'd see a phantom shadow lingering behind.

"Forgive me, Lao Wang," he said, then closed the door.

Chapter Thirty-One

Benfu drifted in and out, dreaming of children—of shoddily dressed girls and boys trudging through dark halls, shivering from the cold and crying out that they were hungry. It felt like only moments ago that Calli had left him, closing her book after she'd read aloud the last chapter of a story called *Jane Eyre*, the words hand-copied into a notebook and kept hidden like her other treasured but banned books. He'd been more than pleased when she'd hesitantly told him about her secret stash, then offered to share with him. Their friendship had truly blossomed in the last months since he'd literally dropped at her feet.

"What is it about this story that leaves you so sad, yet you call it your favorite?" he'd asked her when she had stopped to compose herself more than once.

Calli had laughed at herself, embarrassed at the tears that ran down her face. "Jane was just a child—it wasn't her fault her parents died and left her an orphan. But she was treated so badly, first by her aunt and then by the children at the orphanage. It's just so unfair that because no one wanted her, she had to live in such a place as that. The cold, dark rooms and horrible food—can you imagine how frightened she was?"

Benfu hadn't laughed at the deep emotion she'd shown toward the story of a girl thrust into a life of hardship—flung away from any blood relatives and branded an orphan. Their exchange about orphans and life in general had left him exhausted and when she'd left, he'd fallen off to sleep quickly.

But was he sleeping now? He couldn't quite be sure—

"Benfu! Wake up," he heard, then bolted upright.

Calli burst in; a candle held in her hand illuminated her face.

"What's the matter?" he said, grabbing at his shoes that lay next to the mattress.

"I need your help," she said, throwing him his pants and then turning around to give him privacy to put them on.

"With what?" Benfu scrambled off the mattress and quickly put his legs into the trousers, pulled them up and fastened his belt.

"One of my parents' old friends has knocked on my door and told me that she heard a raid might be happening at her house tonight. She is desperate to hide some of her family's most prized possessions. Will you come?"

Benfu looked around, his eyes stopping on every corner of the small shed.

"But where? Under the mattress? What if they come here? You'll be in danger." They'd already dug a hole out of the sod siding inside the shed and hidden his violin and bow. But to add more to her property was playing with fire.

Calli threw him his shirt. "No, not here. If you can help, I'll tell you where to go and what to do with her things."

He pulled his shirt over his head. "Are you sure you trust this woman, Calli? What if it's a trap, intended to show your disloyalty?"

"No way—" she said vehemently. "Lao Yun is my godmother and has been a dear friend of my parents for more than three decades. She's been in my life since the day I was born and I won't believe that she'd ever turn against me."

Benfu felt the first creeping of distrust, not for Calli, but for the faceless woman who was asking her to do something so clearly against the Communist Party's rules. He slid his sockless feet into his shoes and turned to her, ready to go.

She put her finger to her lip. "*Anjing*. We'll have to move through the alleys very quietly so we don't draw attention to where we're going," Calli said.

They left the shed, and instead of going around the house to the front courtyard, they moved through the back and into the alley that ran between two rows of houses. Benfu wanted to ask her more questions, but she'd said to stay quiet, so he followed obediently. Only once did he wonder if he'd misjudged her and considered that she might be leading him to authorities, then his face flushed with heat and he felt ashamed of his thoughts.

Calli led him through the dark alleys of the *hutong* and into the back garden of a small home. She pointed at a few large woven baskets, the kind with handles to make carrying easier, and Benfu picked up one with each hand.

They crept through the gate, then into the door that had been left ajar.

"Shh." She put a finger to her lips, then beckoned him to stay close.

The room they entered was the kitchen and living area, with a door on the opposite wall that obviously led to the bedroom.

"She's probably in there," Calli said, pointing at the closed door. "Let me go first."

Benfu moved around Calli and pushed the door open. An old woman sat on the floor, her lap covered with piles of old photographs from an emptied box beside her. She looked up, her face wet with tears.

"Calli—you came," she said, relief evident in her voice.

Benfu watched as Calli ran to her and dropped to her knees, embracing the old woman. "Of course I came. Mama and Papa wouldn't have it any other way. They send their regards."

"I can always depend on Ro." A smile appeared briefly on the woman's face, then it disappeared to be replaced with fear again. "It's happening, Calli. They're really coming. I've heard it from several sources now," the woman said.

"Then let's get you packed up. Have you decided what you want to save?" Calli asked.

Benfu stood silently, surveying the room. On the old kang bed a stack of long dresses and men's smoking jackets were piled high. Next to them was a small silk jewelry box, opened with several strands of pearls visible. The woman looked overwhelmed, if not a bit confused.

"Let's just see how much we can get in these baskets," Benfu said, hoping to take some of the agony of the decision from her. He was sure all the clothing wouldn't be able to fit, but they could at least pile some of it atop the photographs, once in the basket. Then, if they turned it inside out and bunched it up, maybe it would look like discarded rags.

Calli picked up a pile of the photos and brought them to Benfu, then he set them in the bottom of the first basket. One fascinating photograph on the top of the stack caught his eye and he picked it up, looking closer. In it two Chinese women perched somberly on a very old wheelbarrow while a much darker man supported their weight by holding the handles. The man's short pants, baggy shirt, and bare feet indicated he was a laborer while the two young women wore long but simple gowns that matched the formal, swept-back hairstyles they sported. Their slippered feet showed sticking out of the clothes, yet another indication that they knew at least some small bit of wealth.

"It's my mother and auntie on their trek into Shanghai. They were at the front of the procession and other coolies were behind them with their trousseaus of clothing and furnishings," Lao Yun said.

Benfu dropped the photo like it was hot to the touch. He was surprised to hear the old woman use the racial slur *coolie* that had all but faded out of use.

"Dui bu qi," he apologized for his nosiness.

"It's fine." Lao Yun waved her hand in the air. "I know they look privileged, and I guess from the perspective of the coolie that toted them around, they were. Yet my mother's family was by no means considered wealthy."

"But Lao Yun, it's just those types of photos that the Red Guards would use against you," Calli said. "If we want to be totally safe, you need to destroy all family records that can point back to anything to cause them to dig into your past."

The old woman shook her head vigorously. "I can't. I just can't burn or destroy them, Calli. It's all I have left of who I am—my own history."

"Lao Yun, I'm not going to be the one to destroy these, you have my word. But my mother also said to remind you of your promise to follow my instructions if she were to send me. You'll have to trust me," Calli said.

"And they'll be safe?"

Calli nodded. Benfu looked away as the old woman hesitated, looking like a small girl in her reluctance, before she held out another pile of snapshots.

"I don't want to be called the daughter of a dog landlord," Lao Yun mumbled, along with a few other things that Benfu couldn't catch.

They worked fast, concentrating on the photographs and then the woman's wedding dress and a few other old gowns. They turned them inside out and bunched them out until it appeared the baskets were full of rumpled rags. Then Benfu set the baskets by the door.

"How much time do we have?" he asked.

"Not much," Calli said, looking with doubt at the pile of extravagant old gowns left on the bed. "We need to be leaving soon."

"Take them," Lao Yun said, finally firm in her decisions, or just ready to get on with it, Benfu wasn't sure which it was.

While she was agreeable, Calli moved fast and disappeared outside the room, then returned with a few burlap bags. "Hurry, Benfu.

Pile them in these and I'll stack them in the alley under the trash as we leave."

Lao Yun slowly rose from her place on the floor. She went to the bed and patted it, beckoning for Calli to join her.

While they talked, Benfu worked quickly to stuff the clothing into the bags. When he finished and the room was cleared of all things that could be considered bourgeois, he waited by the door. He felt a wave of impatience, knowing they had to hurry out of there before the Red Guards came knocking.

"You do know that when they asked me to be your godmother, they also allowed me to choose your name," Lao Yun said to Calli.

"Yes, I did know that," Calli replied.

The old woman placed both her hands on either side of Calli's face, pulling her close as she spoke. "The lily symbolizes virtue, sweetness, and humility. I gave you the name Calla Lily because I knew the moment I saw your face that you would bring color to your mother's life. But you haven't yet grown into your name—you still have years to go."

Calli looked at Benfu, then back at the woman, shushing her. "Shh, Lao Yun, save your energy. You will need it later when they arrive. And we must go."

The woman nodded. "I know, I'm not supposed to be telling of the things I see, but let me finish. One day you will face tragedy at a seemingly unbearable level. Stay strong because later your home will be filled with love and laughter."

Benfu listened, trying to understand the hidden meaning behind the old woman's words. Before he could put too much thought into it, though, Calli was saying good-bye and rushing him out the door.

They had some hiding to do.

Once again Benfu followed Calli through the dark alleyways of the *hutong*, trusting that she knew where she was going and hoping they ran into no one on the way. The last image of Lao Yun standing in the doorway, waving her good-byes, stayed in his mind. He prayed the old woman would be safe and that the Red Guards would find nothing to use against her.

"How far are we going?"

She didn't answer, but motioned for him to keep following as she led them through hedges, around random outbuildings, and down shortcuts around several courtyards. He moved faster, covering the few feet between them. Finally, they rounded another corner and Benfu was surprised to see they were once again at the back of Calli's courtyard. She turned to him and in the light of the moon, he saw an impish grin on her face.

"Here?"

She nodded. "I took the long way around just in case someone was following us. Hurry, Mama and Papa are waiting."

With those words Benfu felt sweat pop out on his head. In the months he'd been there, he'd never actually met Calli's parents. She'd said that they knew he was sleeping in their outbuilding, but thus far he'd not been invited inside the house. He didn't mind. He actually respected that they didn't let just anyone inside their home.

"But—"

Calli led him to the back door and opened it, holding it wide. "But what? Are you coming in or not? If not, hand over those baskets to me."

The baskets were loaded down, their weight bowing the pole they were attached to, gouging him in the top of his shoulders and across the bottom of his neck. Calli couldn't possibly carry them. He turned sideways and slipped through the door, careful not to lose anything as he moved past her.

His first look at the inside of the house instantly reminded him of Pony Boy's home. It was simple—just one huge room with one side taken up by a makeshift kitchen counter and table, and the living area composed mostly of a few chairs, two armoires, and a huge kang bed. The bed took up almost an entire wall and looked comfortable with all the bedding and pillows piled high on it.

He also saw Calli's parents waiting quietly, both perched at the table. Her father was a small man, lean and wiry with a shiny, bald head and round, wired spectacles. Calli's mother had pulled her chair close to her husband and sat with one hand on his back and the other on a spoon. Like Calli, she was pretty, her long hair wound into a loose bun at the back of her head. When she turned to them, Benfu could see that also like her daughter, she had deep, kind eyes. She turned back to her husband, coaxing him with the spoon.

She'd been feeding him.

Benfu looked at Calli, his eyebrows raised.

"I told you, he's sick," she whispered, then turned to her parents. "Mama, Papa, this is Benfu. He's the fellow who's been helping me around here, the one I told you about."

Her father turned to look closely at Benfu, his face wrinkling in confusion.

"*Ni hao,*" Benfu said, unsure exactly what to say to the people who'd given him shelter.

Calli's mother lifted her free hand in a greeting. "I'm Guirong, but you can call me Lao Ro." She turned her attention to her daughter. "Calli, did she try to predict your future?"

Calli shrugged. "Not really—just a few words of wisdom. She was too frightened and upset to do much predicting."

"Poor thing. I hope she'll be fine, but we should hurry. I'll need to get your Papa back to bed soon," Calli's mother said.

Her words jump-started Calli, and Benfu watched as she went to the kang bed and stripped the quilts from it. She looked up and waved him over.

"Come on, you can help me," she said. "Now that you're here, Mama can have a break from the heavy lifting."

Benfu set the baskets down and went to help her.

So the bed was the hiding place, he guessed when Calli got down to the thin mattress and tossed it aside. He'd never seen one close up, but the kang beds were common in most households, especially in the *hutongs*. They were built with a chamber beneath where a fire could be kept, heating the entire bed and keeping a family warm through the tough winters of China. Benfu remembered his mother saying once that a kang bed was a sure sign of an impoverished family who couldn't afford to heat their house. He never believed that, as the concept of heating a bed always sounded quiet ingenious to him.

Some kang beds Benfu had seen were made of clay or concrete, but this one was contrived of bricks around the exterior, supporting a flat panel of wood. He got his first clue that it wasn't a working kang when she lifted the panel and he saw the pipe going from the large coal stove into the side of the bed wasn't actually connected.

"Help me move this," Calli said, struggling to hold the panel.

Benfu grabbed the other side and they lifted it up, then set it a few paces to the side, dropping it atop the mattress. Under the panel was a layer of bricks, which is what anyone doing a search of the kang bed would be expecting to find. But if they dug deeper, they'd be surprised because as Calli bent over it again, she quickly picked the bricks up and began stacking them on the floor, revealing another wood panel beneath. Benfu stripped his side too, and then looked at her.

She reached up to wipe the sweat from her brow. Her cheeks were flushed and strands of hair had worked loose from the elastic, falling into her face in a most becoming way.

Carefully they lifted the second panel. Normally there would've been a fireplace of sorts under the bricks but as they lifted it, Benfu was surprised to see a deep hole packed with parcels and other miscellaneous items.

Calli let out a deep breath, then looked at Benfu. "My parents and

I are big believers that one day, this so-called Cultural Revolution will be one of regret. When most everyone has demolished or lost most of their family history, at least for some of us, it can be regained."

From the table, her father took the spoon and banged the table with it, nodding his head in agreement. His wife laughed quietly, then shushed him. The first thing that came to Benfu's mind was that the elderly couple was giving up their best way to warm their bed, all for their friends and neighbors.

He couldn't believe of all the people in the world, or even this one small city and *hutong*, he'd ventured into the lives of those who felt the same as he. His gratitude and respect for Calli and her parents, and what they were jeopardizing their own lives to do, left him speechless.

Calli's mother came over with a long rope and several large pieces of material she'd pulled from somewhere. Benfu watched as Calli worked fast to take Lao Yun's things and bundle them into the pieces of material, then tie them and lower them into the pit of treasures, jostling the rope until each parcel fell out onto the others beneath it.

When he realized he was just standing there, letting her do all the work, Benfu went into action. Together they worked to get all of Yun's belongings into the pit, then rebuild the kang to where it needed to be. When they had the last pillow propped atop it, he helped Calli walk her father over to it and assisted him onto the bed. As the old man pulled his legs up to get comfortable, he met Benfu's eyes. In them, Benfu thought he saw a silent challenge—or maybe a reproach. A look that told him he'd better tread carefully around the man's daughter.

Benfu nodded, a silent reply to the man's questioning gaze. Though no words were said, a promise was made, though from his perspective, it wasn't even needed, for he'd never hurt Calli.

And he'd never let anyone else do so, either.

When everything was back in place, Benfu picked up the baskets and went to the door. It was late and he was exhausted.

Calli's mother went to the table, picked up something and brought it to Benfu. She held it out and he saw it was a steamed bun, the first he'd seen in ages. He took it, grateful for the treat.

"Xie xie," he thanked her, then turned to Calli, putting a hand up to say good-bye.

"Benfu, thank you," Calli said.

She also looked exhausted. But in the tired lines of her face, Benfu could still see the beauty and the compassion that she held for others. She'd risked her life tonight, all in the name of saving someone else's treasures. Who did that sort of thing? Especially now, when all it took was one misstep or one betrayal to lose your life to the madness that was infecting the people of China?

Simple.

He knew just who did that.

Someone remarkable.

"Good night, Calla Lily," he said, then went out the door.

Chapter Thirty-Two

Time passed quickly in his new safe haven, almost skipping over autumn in a rush to set winter upon them. Benfu shivered once, then adjusted the weight and kept going. The baskets were loaded even heavier than usual, putting weight on his shoulders that, looking back on his time in the commune, he knew wasn't all that significant. More than tired, he was excited that with the scavenging he'd taken up in his free moments, he'd finally found a way to contribute to Calli's household. He'd been with them for several months now and while he couldn't help their pantry with ration coupons, at least now with his meager income, he planned to help alleviate the upcoming tax bill for the house.

Passing a row of pedicabs with the drivers all propped in the passenger seats waiting for customers, he saluted and kept walking. It was strange how a small community once so unfamiliar to him now felt like his own.

He adjusted the pole across his shoulders and thought back to the first evening he'd been asked to help hide family treasures and heirlooms. It was on a cool night with a gentle breeze tickling his neck as he and Calli had traversed the back alleys. They'd carried what some would call contraband but even he had recognized they were simply items symbolizing a life led. Now the weather was bitterly cold and since then, they'd made another half dozen adventures in the night, gathering and storing items before each rumored Red Guard raid. During the days, when he wasn't doing some task that Calli needed help with, he walked the back streets of Wuxi and gathered discarded old clothes and ragged quilts from alleyways. At first, he wasn't sure what to do with them, but after some investigating, he'd found a center for army preparations and after some talking back and forth, had earned a few coins for his load. Finally Chairman Mao was doing something that showed some benefit, as he'd recently released his frugality directive and people were all competing to find new ways to save money.

At the center the first time, he'd approached tentatively, unsure if they'd ask to see his *hukou*. When they hadn't, he'd watched as the foreman added the old cloth to the bins that were lined up behind rows of sewing machines. With a few questions, he'd learned that after washing, then dying, the old material would be just one more step in the new recycling program that contributed to the thousands of new army uniforms needed each month. When the foreman had paid him and told him to come back if he found more, Benfu knew he was in business.

Cast-off clothing and bedding was just the beginning, too. Once he'd discovered he could earn a few coins for other things found in the trash bins or discarded around town, he'd made it his mission to rise earlier and stay up later than anyone else, to always be the first one to collect the castoffs and the first to figure out how to turn the trash into treasure. And who cared if a one-time violinist bound for a successful future was now making his way as a scavenger? For the first time in his life, he felt somewhat at peace, but he knew it wouldn't last because sooner or later he'd need to go home.

"*Ni hao,*" Benfu called out to the grocer on the sidewalk as he passed.

The man tossed him an apple and Benfu caught it in midair, then replied with a thank-you. He'd already been by once that morning and dropped off an old crate for the grocer to put to use, knowing it would buy him at least a few more pieces of fruit and even some heads of cabbage to add to Calli's pantry.

"Stop dawdling around and move a bit faster. What do you think, you're old like me?" the grocer teased, winking as he turned back to his work.

The friendly banter was another perk he'd enjoyed since he'd begun his new quieter life in Wuxi. Their *hutong* and others around it were different than those in Shanghai. While he'd heard that all over China, neighbors and even family members were turning against any and all to save their own hides—in Calli's *hutong* there was more of a protective feeling toward each other. Her neighbors were more likely to defend one another than turn their backs, and he knew that was unusual.

When the weather had first begun to turn, Calli had brought him a small heater and more blankets to make his room cozier. She fretted about him constantly, even making him wear some of her father's long underwear and sweaters. In the evenings when she brought his dinner, she read to him. He was surprised at the number of classics she owned until she explained to him that throughout her life, for every birthday or holiday, she'd been given a book from her parents. Her mother had told her that they may be poor, but reading was a way to explore the world. Luckily Calli had accepted their gifts and embraced reading. And she kept her books hidden well but easily retrievable. She'd showed him her hiding place under the sink—a few planks pried up revealed a cache of banned books.

She was a brave one, that Calla Lily. Looking at her, one would think she was a quiet, humble, law-abiding citizen, but Benfu knew differently. And that made him proud to be her friend.

He wasn't yet ready to leave her. It amazed him how, in such a short time, he'd become almost entranced by her and her soft ways. She needed him—that much she'd shown. Not with words, but more with the way she talked to him, even the way she lit up when she saw his face. And he wouldn't even think of the way his heart jumped each time she entered the shed. All he knew was that no one had ever made him feel so appreciated before, but soon he'd need to go because his first responsibility was to his parents.

He also tried not to think of Juan Hui. He hadn't told Calli of his engagement. He felt like a coward for keeping the secret from her, but he just couldn't make himself speak the words. He and Calli weren't romantically involved, but they had a connection and he feared she might be troubled that he'd failed to tell her about that part of his life.

Benfu walked faster as his thoughts returned to the planned events of the evening. After all she'd been through, the old woman Yun wanted to move out to the countryside to live with her daughter. Unfortunately, her possessions couldn't be sold without risk to herself, so she didn't have the money to travel.

When Calli had told Benfu of the problem, he'd come up with the idea of having an auction in the *hutong*. People could bring something for a large kettle of stew, as well as one item big or small to donate and be sold to send Lao Yun home to her daughter.

At first Calli had been skeptical. Money and food were tight—so scarce that she found it hard to believe that anyone would participate. But Benfu convinced her that they had nothing to lose and everything to gain. He thought it might just work because the people of the *hutong* were likely sick of their evenings being filled with education sessions and self-criticisms, and would probably like to take part in something different.

He just hoped that no one turned them in to the neighborhood committee.

As he turned the corner and saw the Army Preparations Center, he picked up the pace, eager to finish his day of work and get back to the neighborhood.

It was half past seven and so far, no one had shown up for the auction. He and Calli sat outside, bundled against the cold air, waiting for others to arrive as Lao Yun and Calli's parents chatted inside the house. Benfu had built a fire in the corner of the courtyard, and they'd set up a few poles and a huge pot of water hung from them.

"I know for sure that old man Shu is coming. He owns the neighborhood herb store and told me he's bringing some of his aged tangerine peels," Calli said.

Benfu looked at her expectantly. Surely she wouldn't just leave that strange statement hanging.

She didn't disappoint. "Aging tangerine peels have been around for centuries and they're valuable. People use them for homeopathic teas, as well as to flavor soups. I think he's got some that are more than seven years old that he's donating for the auction, but I hope he adds at least one to the pot. That's just what our stew needs to start building taste."

"What do they taste like?"

"Well, they definitely don't taste like a tangerine. Once it dries the peeling can make a soup tasty, but if used in tea it's bitter. Lao Shu is old-fashioned when it comes to his concoction—he soaks it in snake bile before he puts it up to dry." She wrinkled her nose, creating a face that made Benfu laugh.

He wasn't so sure if he wanted to eat a soup with ingredients that had been soaked in snake bile. Calli had flavored the water with a selection of herbs and mushrooms she grew behind the house. A few onions and a sprig or two of ginger, and already the smell tantalized Benfu's stomach, though it was nothing more than scented water at this point. She called the soup *Chicken Stew with Black Fungus*, though thus far they didn't know if they'd have chicken or not. He hoped there'd be other offerings for the stew, at least for Calli's sake. She'd finally gotten excited about the event and he didn't want her to be disappointed. He was amused at her and how once she put her mind to something, she embraced it full force. She'd spent the day before knocking on just about every door in the *hutong* to remind them of the auction dinner and to bring something to contribute, though only a few neighbors had promised to attend.

That's another thing he liked about Calli. She was so optimistic. Not only in the way she lived each day, but also in every aspect of her being. Her personality was completely opposite of the only female he'd ever lived with—his mother. Even Cook, who had made life easier for him, was nothing like Calli.

With each new story or horror the revolution revealed, after a few words of sympathy for those involved, she always found a way to look ahead to a brighter future. Benfu had noticed that her parents absolutely doted on her, and though her father was sick and sometimes didn't even recognize his own daughter, he still lit up when she entered the room. She was that kind of person, the kind who made you feel good just because they were in your life.

He would miss her, for he'd decided just an hour before that this would also be his going-away party. Calli just didn't know it yet. He wanted the night to be memorable, not sad, so he planned to wait until the end to tell her.

Benfu looked up as Calli's mother came out of the door, carrying a tray covered with a towel. She took it to the makeshift table that Benfu had constructed out of some planks and a few barrels, and she set it down.

"What's that, Mama?"

"Marbled eggs," she answered.

"Mmm . . ." Calli winked at Benfu. "I love Mama's eggs steeped in tea."

They all knew the eggs were a luxury, and the gift to Lao Yun wouldn't go unnoticed.

"She's been saving tea leaves for months," Calli whispered to Benfu. "They were going to be used for the Spring festival."

"*Aiya*, shush that talk, Calla Lily," her mother said.

It didn't sound like a chastisement to him, but Benfu waited to see how Calli would respond. She was saved by a procession of neighbors, all making their way down the lane to the courtyard. Calli's mother clapped her hands together with excitement as people came through the gate and into her yard.

"Look—they're coming from the other direction too," Calli said, pointing at the other side of the lane.

They watched quietly as people entered, filing past the simmering pot and dropping things into it. Some didn't have much—just a carrot or a random potato—but it was the thought of them looking through their sparse pantry and finding anything to contribute that touched Benfu. When two teenage girls came through, their elbows locked in a sisterly way, Calli ribbed him in the side.

"There you go—some pretty girls for you to ogle tonight," she said.

Benfu shrugged. "I'm not interested." And the truth was, he wasn't. He had no urge to talk to anyone except Calli. They both waved, but Benfu could see that Calli had no clue she was in a totally different league than the giggly girls.

One old woman carried a dish in one arm and with her other, held a limp plucked chicken by its feet. She winked at Calli and dropped the chicken in the pot, then took the dish to the table.

"That's Niyan, another one of Lao Yun's closest friends," Calli leaned over and said to Benfu. "They went to high school together but I can't believe she donated one of her beloved hens. And I'll bet she made her famous steamed egg custard for the auction."

Calli pointed out Shu, and Benfu watched the stooped, wrinkled man as he pulled a shriveled black peeling from a paper bag and dropped it in the stew, then set the rest of the bag on the table. A few more old men came doddering through the gate, and one emptied a tin pan of corn kernels into the pot as the other set up a crate and game board he'd been carrying. It appeared that they were there for more than a meal and an auction.

"It might be a long night," Calli said, a grin on her face. "But we needed this. I can't remember the last time we got together and oh, how I've missed it."

Benfu imagined that they did need it. Just because the people of the *hutong* weren't laboring in the fields and creeks as he'd done didn't mean they hadn't seen their own hardships from the revolution. He knew it was a tense time for everyone. Not only with food and supplies being rationed, but just the paranoia and risk of being blacklisted that settled around every neighborhood and home—the constant public denunciations and mandatory self-criticisms happening around them every day. The fear of being accused of something from their past, or even a distant family member's past.

The new way of life was enough to exhaust anyone.

As the courtyard filled, the stew began to bubble and take on an almost heavenly aroma, causing Benfu's stomach to beg for a taste. One old widowed man brought a pork bone, void of any meat but plenty good for flavoring, he declared loudly to everyone. As for items to be auctioned off for a coin or two, besides the many food treats, Benfu saw things like special stamps, old postcards, and even a tiny porcelain doll placed on the table.

More than a few times, he saw dishes contrived with some sort of eggs added to the table, even one that reminded him of home—scrambled eggs and tomatoes, a dish served to him often by Cook. When he pointed out all the egg dishes to Calli, she reminded him that many in the *hutong* kept a small batch of laying hens to supplement their food rations, as well as to share with their neighbors. Everyone had become quite efficient in devising many different and creative ways to use eggs.

"Mama, is Papa going to be able to make it out here?"

"No, not tonight. He's had a rough day, but I'll take him a bowl of stew when it's done. He should be hungry by then."

Her mother moved over to talk to a group of ladies her own age and Benfu and Calli were left alone again. As they talked, he saw several familiar faces, neighbors whose homes he and Calli had visited when packing away treasures. With a slight nod or a wink, they acknowledged him and he knew these were people he could trust. It amazed him how easily he seemed to fit in and feel natural within the circle of friends and families who'd grown up with each other. Benfu didn't know what made it so, but he felt he belonged.

With that thought on his heart, he scooted over a few inches and put his arm around Calli. It was a cold night and he wanted to make sure she was warm, that was all. At least that's what he told himself as she snuggled closer and he felt a surge of protectiveness.

"What did you bring for the auction?" Calli asked, her voice so soft that in the noise of those chattering around him, he had to strain to hear.

Benfu felt at a loss and despite the cold, a flush heated his face. He hadn't brought anything—he didn't have anything except his violin and the jade buffalo. Both of those were family heirlooms, things he couldn't part with.

And really, he just hadn't considered that he should contribute, too.

Calli must've felt his discomfort because she turned to him and smiled gently. "Maybe you could offer a dance in the moonlight. I'm sure some of the neighborhood girls would give a bid or two."

He laughed to himself, thinking of the many dancing and etiquette lessons his mother had put him through over the years. Calli would be shocked—but dancing was something he could actually do, though he'd never done it willingly. Then he wondered if she had found any coins with which to contribute to the auction items. When he saw a small smile creep across her face, he had another thought.

Maybe he wouldn't go home to Shanghai just yet after all.

Chapter Thirty-Three

On a cold December day, Pony Boy stood on the platform, waiting to board the last train of the day bound for Beijing. It had taken quite a bit of cajoling for him to get a ticket, as the girl in the office had insisted that only Red Guards were allowed on the direct routes to Beijing. Finally, when Wren had stepped up and pulled at the girl's sympathies by feeding her a story that Pony Boy's mother was on her deathbed, holding on just until he arrived, the girl had relented and sold him a ticket. He was already exhausted—physically and mentally—and his trip hadn't even begun yet. He patted his bag, feeling paranoid that someone could see through it and read the stack of newsletters it held.

"No one will know they are there," Wren said, her voice a whisper that somehow found its way to his ears over the din of chaos around them.

He nodded. She was right. He was being overly paranoid when in reality, no one was paying him any attention. All around them were Red Guards, saying their good-byes to family and friends, jubilant to be a part of the latest trek to Beijing to prepare for Mao's next appearance. He wasn't wearing a uniform, but he was sporting the red journalist band on his arm, allowing him to carry his camera around his neck, instead of hidden in his bag. Wren had packed him a bag of food, too, her last-minute gesture of gratitude that he'd relented and was now going.

"Pony Boy." She pulled on his sleeve, urging him to duck his head down so that she could speak into his ear. When he did, her words surprised him. "I've changed my mind. I don't want you to go."

He raised up, meeting her eyes. There he saw for the first time, a chip in her usually brave armor. She looked frightened.

Here was his chance. He could walk away and she wouldn't hold it against him, for it would be at her urging. The line of monks he'd photographed came to mind, their bent heads and broken spirits, their church in shambles. Benfu's parents' faces swam in front of him—especially Lao Zheng's tears as he was forced to light his own beloved books afire. Then he thought of Wang Zi, remembered the way he'd spoken of missing his family, and the way he'd looked with the bag over his head, his face frozen in a death grimace. So much destruction, for what?

"No, I've got to do this. So far, we've heard almost nothing about the newsletters and that tells me it's not working on a local level. People are too frightened to question anything. So someone has to take a stand."

"You don't," she said. "We'll keep working from here. We'll make more copies of the next issues and we'll pass them out farther."

He shook his head. "Wren, you said yourself that the best way for us to be heard is to get these into the hands of those in Beijing—maybe even into Chairman Mao's hands. What if he isn't the demon we think he is? What if this is all being done against his wishes or he has no idea of the rampage spreading across China?"

"But it's too dangerous."

He knew her words were true. Just the night before, when they'd lain in each other's arms in their secret hideaway, she'd told him that her father had arrived home, livid after discovering that someone had been taking ink and paper from his office. Their inventory counts were way off and he suspected a traitor.

Pony Boy wasn't going to tell her until he returned from Beijing, but he wasn't going to let her continue with the newsletter. It was much too risky for her and she was right, everything they were doing was wrought with peril. For the first time since it had all begun, he truly understood the repercussions if found out, and he wasn't willing to expose Wren to them.

"I know it is, but every endeavor worth following carries danger," he answered, reaching down and covertly grabbing her hand. They stood there, surrounded by strangers, wanting to be locked in each other's arms but knowing it would make them targets to those around them. Instead they used their eyes to speak the words of love that couldn't be said aloud.

He'd do anything for her. He'd said it before and he'd say it again. No deed was too big or too dangerous to make her happy, and he knew her well enough to know that despite her words of a last-minute reprieve, she wanted him to take this trek.

It had taken some maneuvering and planning, but finally his father was well enough to start delivering mail again. He'd convinced his parents that this was his one and only chance to be a part of history—to join the millions who trekked to Beijing. They weren't happy about him leaving, but they'd left the decision to him. Then he only had his second job to worry about and Wren had insisted that she could take over for him while he was gone. He couldn't imagine her, in all her beauty, dealing with inconsiderate customers and heaping buckets of human waste, but she'd proven to him in a test run that she could do it. For an entire shift she'd worked alongside him, cleaning toilet stalls and carrying overloaded buckets, heaving them into the back of the farmer's trucks. He smiled when he thought about it and the fact that she'd never complained even once.

The whistle blew and the loud clanging of an engine told him that their time was up, the train was pulling in. He felt uneasy, but it was too late to show doubt now. He smiled down at Wren.

"It's time for me to go," he said.

"Can I embrace you? Please," she asked, her voice pleading.

Pony Boy looked around and seeing a large concrete column some yards behind them, he pulled her to it, slipping behind it and out of sight from the others on the platform.

Quickly he opened his arms and she melted into them, molding her body against his in a silent good-bye. He bowed his face in her hair, taking in the sweet smell of her, savoring it. When the whistle blew again, signaling the last chance to board, he pulled away.

"Stay back here until I'm gone," he said. Her face was red with emotion, tears streaming as if a leak had sprung in her eyes. He didn't want her showing her feelings in public because of the trouble it could bring her.

She nodded, then whispered, "I'm afraid."

He walked backward, gravitating toward the train even as his eyes refused to part from her face. She made him feel so brave. "Don't be."

"Come back to me, Pony Boy."

He mustered a smile, trying to leave her on a good note.

"Meet you on the mountain."

The train chugged along as Pony Boy counted down the hours until its arrival. He'd already spent at least four of the twelve watching those around him, taking in the euphoric spirit of the Red Guard faction in his cabin as they sang and exchanged stories of valor. Many of them made remarks that they'd never been to Beijing—while some claimed to have already seen Mao at one of his previous appearances. Pony Boy had his doubts, feeling strongly that there was a lot of posturing going on as they fought to tell the biggest and most envied stories. And he was glad to get away from Shanghai if only for a few days. He'd grown tired of the nightshift, watching as the denounced circled the city blocks like sleepwalkers, placards hung around their neck while they served their punishments.

Hopefully Beijing would be too focused on Chairman Mao's visit to do much in the way of criticizing and denouncements.

His seat partner had ended up being a girl, but so far she hadn't talked much. When she finally said something, he at first didn't realize she was talking to him.

"Have you been to Beijing and seen Chairman Mao before?"

He shook his head. "This will be my first time. You?"

"This is my third."

"What's it like?" He couldn't help it. Even if he didn't approve of the man, Mao had become a legend and millions descended on Beijing whenever he was about to make an appearance.

"It's the most remarkable thing I've ever witnessed."

"What makes it so extraordinary?" He noticed she wore a real army uniform, baggy and unkempt, but real all the same. The girl also wore the red armband, the characters reading *Hong Weibing*—to mark her as an official Red Guard.

She smiled. "It's just wonderful what he's done for all of us. For the first time we have a voice. We can do what we want—where we want. And for him to make the journey to address us in Beijing, that shows how much he cares for us. Chairman Mao is China's hero and just wait, when you see him for yourself and you experience the emotion of the crowd he stands before, you'll see. There will be singing and crying—even fainting by some who become overwhelmed with his presence. It *is* quite remarkable."

Pony Boy didn't really want to get into the politics of Mao Thought. "Where do you stay? Do you just sleep on the streets?" He couldn't imagine any family letting their daughter travel alone to Beijing—even one who looked as self-sufficient as the girl next to him.

She shrugged. "Each time is different. Last time I was able to stay in one of the university dorm rooms with six other girls. There aren't any classes any longer; they've opened the entire campus to Red Guards. Most of the boys sleep on desks pushed together to make tables, so if you get there early enough, stake out your spot. But even if you can't get a place there, there'll be depots set up to receive us all around Beijing—complete with blankets and food. This time I plan to camp out on the square in front of Tiananmen Gate. I don't want to miss a thing."

"You're going to sleep there?"

"*Dui*, if I can get a foot of space, I'm staying there until Mao shows up. But if you don't want to stay on the square, don't worry, you'll still get a space somewhere, especially since you have that armband," she said, looking down at his red journalist band. "You sure don't know a lot about it considering you are with a news team. Didn't they brief you?"

Pony Boy had forgotten about it until she'd mentioned it. "Oh, they told me so much I've forgotten half of it, but you're right. I'm sure I'll be allowed close enough to get a photo. I just hope I can hear what our great Chairman Mao has to say."

He didn't mention that he also hoped he was close enough to give him one of the newsletters before disappearing back into the crowd. From what Wren had learned from her father, since the revolution had started, many leaflets and newspapers were handed out in Beijing on a daily basis, but especially when Mao was present, and that he liked to read them to see if his country-wide directives and announcements were being reported accurately. If by some miracle they could land one of their newsletters into his hands, it might be their chance to see if once confronted with the truth, Chairman Mao would do anything to stop the violence.

"Oh, they'll have loudspeakers set up. But I want to be as close as possible because this time I'd like to at least touch his sleeve."

Their conversation was interrupted from behind.

"*Ni hao*, want to take my photo?"

Pony Boy and his seatmate whipped around to see who was talking and found a boy about his age sitting in the seat behind him. He looked down at his armband, remembering he was supposed to be there on official business. He'd hoped to remain on the outside of attention and felt the sweat bead upon his brow, nervousness making his hands shake as he lifted his camera, adjusted it, and took a photo. He didn't want to waste the small amount of film he had, but he also needed to stay in character.

"Be sure to put me in the paper," the boy said, then settled back down and out of sight when the flash went off. Pony Boy had noticed the top of his red book of Mao quotes poking out of his pocket. Wren had poked a copy of the book down in his own pocket and reminded him to keep it close in case he was questioned. The uniform the boy wore was obviously his own clothes, dyed a sickly army-green. Others in the train car wore clothes like his—stained green in their attempt to fit in with the lucky ones who wore real army uniforms, most likely ancient clothes dug from attics and passed down to them from fathers or grandfathers.

"How did you get that position, being as young as you are?" The boy behind him leaned forward again.

Pony Boy remembered all that he and Wren had rehearsed and was grateful for her foresight. They'd even come up with a fictitious name to help his cover. "Haven't you heard of the Red Journalists Youth League?"

The boy shook his head.

"Each of us was chosen specifically to represent our provinces and gather news to turn in to our supervisors," he said, smiling proudly. "And I was chosen to travel to see our great leader, the awesome Chairman Mao. If I can get a photo, I'll be promoted into the Senior League."

The boy raised his hand and Pony Boy clasped it.

"Good luck, comrade," the boy said, settling back in his seat.

Yes, he would definitely need it, thought Pony Boy as he turned his attention to the blurry landscape speeding by outside his window. He thought about the newsletter in his bag—sixty copies, meaning sixty more stolen pieces of valuable paper. But it wasn't the paper that concerned him. It was the story they'd decided to run.

Finally, they'd figured out what Teng Bao's negatives represented and had used the photos developed from some of them. Until recently, they'd only guessed at what the pictures portrayed but now that they knew for sure—the details were particularly condemning. Once again, the information had come from the hushed rumors that Wren's father had whispered to his wife. But Wren had learned to listen well, and the story he told was shocking.

A case of Mao's directive to persecute taken too far.

In his photos, Teng Bao had captured the moment that the Red Guards had invaded a quiet afternoon at the Beijing Writers Association headquarters and stepped over the line. This time, they'd taken things too far in their goal to round up class enemies.

After gathering together more than two dozen of China's leading writers, they'd beaten them, then trucked them to an old temple that was in shambles from the latest rampage. Herded into another group of waiting victims including opera singers and other artists, they were then made to huddle on their knees around a huge bonfire of historic costumes, well-known books, and other objects that represented old culture. Wren had overheard her father whispering to her mother that the selection of victims was so precise that it had to have come from top officials. The question was, did Chairman Mao know of it?

Pony Boy thought of the night in Shanghai outside their neighborhood temple and knew the facts they were reporting were even more brutal than the similar event he'd witnessed. In this one, it wasn't only the monks who'd suffered, but also artists of every trade—even renowned writers who'd for years been lauded as gifts to China for their wisdom in words. He didn't understand how wreaking such havoc could help a country move toward a better way of life. And now he understood why Teng Bao had been taken in for questioning—obviously someone was trying to bury the story and any possible proof.

The fact that Benfu had been in the park that day and received the negatives from the old man was fate—at least that's what Wren said.

And it was their responsibility to tell the world. When he'd done that, he'd hurry back to Shanghai as fast as he could, back to his family, and most of all, back to Wren. He closed his eyes, letting her face emerge in his mind. He was grateful they'd found a discreet place to embrace on the platform, and glad that their last night together was the most special of all they'd had yet, because those two memories were going to be what he depended on to get him through the next few days.

PART FIVE

A Loyal Farewell

Chapter Thirty-Four

Pony Boy lifted his head from the cold concrete when the rolling metal cart jolted him awake. He watched as the man pushing it stopped at their cell, then pushed three bowls through the open slot. Three! Not just two like he'd been doing occasionally, leaving Pony Boy to watch the others eat as his own stomach rumbled painfully, but three. Still, he waited. It had only taken him a day or so to realize that in a place such as this, you did nothing without permission from those who'd earned seniority. And still after now over a month in this hellhole, he knew he ranked at the bottom of the pole.

"*Guo lai*, Dog Fart," the boss man of the cell beckoned to him to come forward.

Pony Boy scrambled up and went to the man, then bowed at the waist respectfully. He waited silently, not even minding the fact that he was no longer called by name. Officially he was Prisoner 6789, but he'd answer to Dog Fart or whatever else they thought of if they just allowed him to eat.

The man plucked the steamed cornbread from the bowl, then handed Pony Boy the container.

Pony Boy expected to see a solitary salted vegetable, as the others had been getting for breakfast the last few mornings, but this time it was something different.

He squatted right where he was and began eating. It didn't matter that he had nothing to eat with but his fingers, and it didn't matter that the congee was cold and lumpy. It was sustenance and Pony Boy ate it like a wild animal, finding himself at the bottom of the cold porcelain much too soon. When he looked up, the other two men were watching him, amused smirks on their faces as they nibbled at the bread. Pony Boy eyed the bread that was meant to be his, then looked away. He used his hand to wipe the excess food from his face, before licking his fingers clean.

He thought of his mother then. He'd rather die than allow her to see him in such squalor, being treated like an animal. It would kill her—that much he believed to be true. The consequences of his actions weren't something he'd considered that day he'd boarded the train. Now that he'd had time to think on it, he didn't know how he'd expected the newsletter would get to the top, a place he and Wren thought it needed to be. He also now felt maybe in their rush to make a difference—to give the common people a voice—that they'd acted recklessly. He wasn't sorry they'd created *The Palest Ink*, but they should've continued to keep it under the radar instead of attempting to go bigger.

Even so, he hadn't expected it to be snatched from his bag as he slept on the way to Beijing, then turned in to the Red Guard leader in his train car. One minute he'd been sleeping soundly, dreaming of Wren, and the next he'd been rudely jerked out of his chair and put into the livestock car, tied to a railing with pigs rooting around him as one of the Red Guards slapped him with the now-rolled copies of the newsletter, waved his camera around, and screamed accusations at him.

They'd never told him exactly what he was being arrested for, though he could offer a guess. He'd simply been held against his will all the way to Beijing and then taken into custody. After a day in the local jail, in which he'd been roughed up more than he cared to admit, he'd been transferred to prison.

"Clean up," the second-in-charge man ordered, and Pony Boy went to his place on the floor and picked up the lone blanket he'd been given. The days had moved slowly, turning into weeks, and now shockingly, it was January. The thin material was scant protection against the bitter winds that roared through the open windows, rushing between the iron bars to find him in the coldest hours of the nights, but it was at least something and he was grateful for it. He folded it, then put it in his corner. Next, he did the same with the other blankets his cellmates used. It was his job to keep their cell tidy, at least that's what they'd told him the day he'd been pushed through their door. He'd nodded his agreement, thankful to simply be in the company of other human beings and out of the dark isolation room he'd spent his first three weeks in.

He looked at the long plank affixed to the wall. Oh, how he hated that board and all it represented. Whenever the guards were ready to take a break, eat a snack, or get a few winks of sleep, they order all prisoners on their block to the board. At first Pony Boy had been confused, but he'd followed suit when his cellmates had heard the order, then retreated to the sturdy piece of plywood and climbed atop it. There, their feet dangled, not touching the floor as they waited obediently to be allowed off. Some, with better balance than he, squatted upon the board, their slippers kicked off so that their bare toes could grasp the edge of the wood like some sort of monkey, a way to keep their legs from falling asleep.

Pony Boy despised the board.

Today was Sunday, and the only day of the week they weren't roused at three o'clock in the morning to be taken to their work detail, and also the only day they wouldn't have to participate in evening self-criticisms and reciting passages from Mao's quotations.

As for missing work, Pony Boy was relieved for a day of rest and to get out of the wind, even if some of it would most likely be spent sitting on the board. Only a few weeks before, they'd been forced to work days on end in three-feet drifts of snow, digging into frozen ground to erect a wire fence that stretched for miles outside of some new government facility. One prisoner had complained, then been tied to a tree and had cold water poured over him.

Pony Boy had worked feverishly and quietly, not daring to look at the people inside the building, their warm, pale faces pressed against the windows to stare at them. Instead he'd counted the minutes until the truck had returned to transport them back to the prison where, though it wasn't warm, it was at least out of the elements. It was during those horrendous outside work duties that Pony Boy could barely believe where he was and how he was now spending his life.

Thus far, no one had questioned him extensively or even told him what exactly he was being charged with. In isolation, he'd been given paper and pens and told to write his confession. He hated to admit it, but in a moment of cowardice, he'd claimed that someone else had slipped him the stack of newsletters and paid him to get them to Beijing. So far though, he didn't think they were buying it. In addition to sticking to his story, each day he'd turned in whatever drivel he could think of—mostly just quotations of Mao's that he'd twisted to fit his and Wren's mission—and each evening the guard read it, then balled it up and threw it on the floor. Then he'd start over. It went that way for weeks until one day, the guard had unexpectedly accepted it and took the papers away with him. Then Pony Boy had waited, half hopeful and half terrified, for his interview or arraignment, whichever came first.

When he'd first been transported to the huge block building encircled with high fences of barbed wire, he'd tried not to think of Wren and how she was probably coming to the train station every day to wait for him. Even as they came close to drowning him while delousing him of the lice he didn't even have, he attempted to push her out of his mind—for the thought of her out there waiting for him as he rotted in prison was too painful. But now, as predicted, memories of their last night together and their embrace on the platform were keeping him on the safe side of sanity.

He still had hope that he'd get out and return to her, and the memory of her smile and her beautiful doe eyes reminded him to keep his head down and avoid trouble. When he looked down at his pasty white arms, he could almost see Wren's arms, delicate yet full of strength. When he licked his chapped lips and waited for his sparse allowance of water, he thought of her soft lips. And then—only then—did he let himself go back to the night they'd spent together. Having another chance to hold her in his arms was what he lived for now. What he dreamed of and focused on daily.

That was the only way to make it out alive.

Pony Boy had never even been near a prison but now knew that violence was commonplace, as he'd already witnessed several outbursts. An attack could start over a simple scrap of bread or a look that someone felt was too intrusive. It was best to stay quiet and not provoke anyone, as the whole place was nothing more than a frustrated kettle that threatened to boil over at any time. He picked up the three enamel drinking mugs and took them to the sink, washing them out before turning them upside down to drain on the ledge. The mug was the only thing, other than a plastic set of utensils, that he'd been given when he was checked in. They'd taken his bag, his clothes, and everything he owned, and when he'd been escorted to the isolation room, he'd looked and felt unrecognizable in his baggy black prison uniform and unwashed hair.

After his isolation period was over and the guard had come for him, he'd joked to Pony Boy that he was lucky, having been remanded over to the new building. However, it didn't look all that new to him—and even the toilet they all shared in the middle of the room was a hole they squatted over and water had to be carried from the sink over to it to flush it. Unfortunately, as the lowest man in the room, everyone used Pony Boy's mug, then laughed about it.

Next, Pony Boy got on his hands and knees and went from one

corner of the cell to the other, searching for and eradicating any dirt or crumbs. Keeping the floor clean was also his job and one that at least kept him busy. If he was found lacking in his duties they would make life worse for him. How much worse, he wasn't sure. Already he wasn't permitted more than one bath a week—from a cold bucket of water, no less—and he wasn't even allowed outdoor exercise yet, not until he'd learned what they called *prison regulations*, though no one ever told him how or what he was supposed to learn. Of everything, breathing outside air was something he missed dearly.

Pony Boy heard boots clumping down the corridor.

"Prisoner six-seven-eight-nine, ready yourself for escort," the voice said.

Still on his hands and knees, he looked from the shiny black boots up the legs and into the face of a man he'd never seen.

"It's the warden," one of his cellmates whispered. "I hope your confession passed muster, Dog Fart, or you're really in for it this time."

Pony Boy jumped to his feet, pulling his pants up and straightening his shirt. He hadn't confessed. At least not to being responsible for the newsletter. He'd also never met the warden, but maybe this was his chance to explain that he hadn't meant to commit a crime. He didn't even remember now what words he'd written last on his confession, but he hoped they were good enough to get him out of prison.

Next to the warden the jailor pulled the keys from the hook at his belt and unlocked the iron door, then worked to unlock the wooden one. As he waited, Pony Boy took the opportunity to look at the warden.

It wasn't a good first impression.

The man's face was void of any evidence of compassion. Pony Boy's cellmates had told him a story about one of Chairman Mao's officials condemned to this prison and breaking a bone in his foot during work duty. They said that when the man had been sent to the hospital, the warden had given the approval for both the man's legs to be amputated, a punishment for the man's refusal to admit to the crimes attached to his name. Pony Boy hadn't believed a word of it, but now, seeing the warden with his own eyes, he thought it could be true.

He met Pony Boy's eyes, sweeping his glance from his bare feet on up to his face, and the only expression he gave was one of ruthlessness.

The door opened and the jailor stepped inside, shutting it behind him. The warden waited in the corridor, his face stern and his hands behind his back.

"Turn around," the man said and Pony Boy complied. "Put your arms behind your back."

When he did, he felt a strip of plastic being tied tightly to keep his hands together.

"Where are you taking me?" Pony Boy asked, then got a solid slap across his head for speaking without permission. The slap made his eyes water and he saw stars, but he didn't cry out. To cry out would mean relentless ridicule from his cellmates later. Being named Dog Fart was bad enough and he didn't want to give them any more ammunition for further taunting, so Pony Boy bit his lip to keep from crying out if he was hit again.

The jailor finished bundling his wrists, then turned him around and opened the doors and led him out. He stopped him in front of the warden, putting them face-to-face.

"It's time for your interrogation, Prisoner six-seven-eight-nine," the warden said.

Pony Boy felt a shiver start in his toes and work its way up. He thought of Wren and swallowed hard.

Loyalty. As they walked, he repeated the word to himself silently as a reminder. They could hang him upside down and pull his fingernails out with pliers and he'd never give them her name as an accomplice. But he grimaced when his thoughts brought the ugly visual to his mind, and he hoped it didn't come to that.

Four hours later, Pony Boy wished they'd just let him go back to his cell. Even if he had to scrub every cellmate's feet and then the toilet, he'd rather be there. He was tired and he was hungry—and his forehead was sore from being slammed against the table so many times. The throbbing headache threatened to consume him and he wondered if somewhere in there his brain was bleeding. He'd begged them to believe him, but still they wouldn't accept his story that he had only been the delivery boy for the newsletter.

"Your quest for personal fame and gain is considered antirevolutionary in the new, redder China," the man yelled directly in his ear. "So tell me where you got the photos."

The park. Benfu. The white-haired man. His name is Teng Bao, I think.

Pony Boy answered all the man's questions, but only in his head. Aloud, he'd given the same statement repeatedly and no matter how many times they asked it, he would not change his answer. He would not bring pain or shame to his family and danger to Wren. So why wouldn't they just stop? He tried to think good thoughts, to just remove his mental state from his physical. However, the more the man yelled in his ear and slammed his head down, the more Pony Boy couldn't think at all. Everything blurred together and his thoughts jumbled. If the man kept it up, who knew what might slip out of his mouth?

"*The Palest Ink.* As if you think we are too ignorant to know what that means," the man hissed into his ear. "The only written history needed in this country is the one scribed and approved by Chairman Mao. Too bad for you that you chose such a provoking name—or your little paper might have been overlooked."

A vision of Benfu sitting at Wren's kitchen table came to mind, and the proud smile he'd worn when they'd liked his choice of a name for their paper.

"It's not my paper and will you please at least untie my hands?" he asked, attempting again to roll the soreness out of his aching shoulders. Having his arms tied behind his back for hours was excruciating, especially when some of his wrong answers resulted in the interrogator grabbing them and pulling upward.

"I suppose it's not your camera with the antirevolutionary photos in it, either?"

Pony Boy shrugged, keeping his mouth shut.

"Will you admit to creating this paper, being a reactionary, and divulge the names of your team members? Will you rewrite a new confession? One with details?" the interrogator replied.

He sighed. The warden stood outside the door, completely visible as he paced the floor, pausing now and then when Pony Boy was punished. The interrogation had begun innocently enough; Pony Boy had been led into a room and made to sit on a stool at a small desk, facing a semi-circular platform. On the platform sat three people at a table, microphones and writing tablets at their fingertips. His audience consisted of two grim-faced men in uniform and one woman. They'd began the session by taking turns reciting some of Mao's most famous quotes about toeing the party line and loyalty to country, pointing out the posters of the quotes around the room, interspersed with posters of Chairman Mao, of course. Then they'd moved on to politely questioning him, but when he'd been deemed unreasonable for not answering most of their questions, the interrogator who had come for him in his cell took over.

That's when it had gotten ugly.

"I've already told you—I did not create, write, or print that newsletter. Someone found me on the street and offered to pay me to bring them to Beijing and hand them out at the next Chairman Mao appearance."

He felt the man's hand grab the back of his head and braced himself. Bam.

His eyes watered again, but proudly, he didn't shed a tear.

"Where were you going on the train? Did you plan to try to get near our great Chairman Mao?" the man bellowed, yanking a handful of his hair and pulling his head backward.

That's exactly what my plan was, you Shit-For-Brains, he said to himself.

He prayed for courage. And for the assault to end.

"Where did you print the papers? Tell me . . ." The man's voice got less loud, actually began to fade. Then he thought of his mother and imagined her soft hands on the back of his neck, rubbing out the pain from the vicious fingers that had gripped it repeatedly.

It was working!

Pony Boy didn't care if he was acting and thinking like a boy—his mother's voice was taking over and the pain was diminishing, bit by bit. *Be strong, Pony Boy*, she said as her fingers massaged his temples, easing the throbbing inside his head. *Pull from your roots of courage and they cannot hurt you.*

He sighed, letting his head drop all the way to the table. His shoulders finally relaxed, losing the last few hours of tightness, relieving him of the struggle.

"He's done," he faintly heard the woman from the panel say, her voice so low it was almost a whisper. "He's not going to give us any more today."

They could all go to hell, Pony Boy thought.

They hadn't broken him and he was done. They couldn't hurt him any more today. *Done, done, done* . . . he chanted silently as he let his mother's hands finally cradle his head. Then all went black and deathly quiet.

Chapter Thirty-Five

Pony Boy wasn't sure how long he'd sat in the dark and had no idea
if it was now morning, noon, or night. He knew he'd slept, but
for how long he wasn't sure. And he was back in isolation, but this
time it was a different cell in an entirely different block than the one
he'd known before. This time he'd been led to the hole, as he'd heard it
called. It wasn't in the ground, but it might as well be, for after descend-
ing more than one set of metal stairs, the two officers had dragged him
down a long tunnel and thrown him into a dark and damp cell, then
locked the door and snapped the window closed before walking away.
As their voices faded, he'd heard them talk about their after-work plans
and some sort of celebration one was having.

Life.

They were talking about life outside of the walls—something he no
longer had.

His interrogation had ended, but he'd been sadly mistaken when he
thought they'd take him back to his regular cell. As bad as it was in there,
he hadn't known how much worse it was about to get. Feeling a crawl-
ing sensation run down his arm he jumped up from the floor, frantically
brushing the large insect away. Roaches—another highlight he'd been

warned about regarding the hole, and he knew that most likely he might meet a rat or two before it was over with. He shivered with revulsion and used both hands to make sure his skin was clear, slapping away at nothing until he was satisfied he wasn't harboring any crawly creatures.

He heard a rumble.

Despite the assault from the guard's boots, his stomach still growled and reminded him that he'd missed more than a couple meals. He tried to console himself with the thought that his cellmates were probably getting mushy turnips and rice, a combination he'd come to loathe, but it didn't work. His hunger was getting stronger and more vocal. More than that, though, was how thirsty he'd become. After searching the entire room on his hands and knees to keep from stumbling, he'd confirmed his fears; there was no water to be found. Now his lips felt cracked and his throat parched, yet when he'd banged on the door to ask for a drink, no one had answered.

He was completely alone.

The minutes crept by like sorghum, teasing Pony Boy with the promise of more endless dark and dead silence.

"Pssst—"

His head jerked upright. What was that?

Listening intently, he only heard distant buzzers from another block and realized he was hearing things.

"Pssst—"

There it was again, and this time, Pony Boy knew he wasn't imagining it. He put his head to the cold concrete wall, feeling along with his hand until his fingers came to some sort of metal grate. He paused, not knowing what to do. What if it were some sort of trick—a guise to get him to break the rules that had been screamed into his face on the long walk down? The guards had been firm that no contact, physical or spoken, was to be allowed in the hole.

He slowly sunk down to sit back on the floor under the grate. He was embarrassed that he was frightened. Where was the brave man who'd come barreling into Beijing, full of ideas, wanting to make a difference? He was glad no one he knew could see him now.

"*Ni hao,*" the voice whispered. "I know someone is in there. Please—please. You're my first neighbor since I got in here. I beg you to answer me."

It was the voice that did it. Only in his own mind had he heard such loneliness and desperation. Pony Boy felt something that had been seriously lacking thus far within the prison walls.

Compassion.

He rose until his head was against the grate again. He only hesitated one more time, albeit briefly before he spoke.

"I'm here," he said, keeping his voice as low and quiet as possible.

"Are you in the dark?"

"*Shi de*, and you?" Pony Boy thought that was a silly question.

"No, I'm being punished."

"But I'm in the dark, and I haven't been given food or water. Isn't that the punishment?"

The voice let out a low, hollow laugh. "You'll wish for the dark when it's your turn for this. I'd give five years of my life for a dark room and an hour of sleep."

"Can you explain?" Pony Boy said, though he wasn't sure if he wanted to know or not.

"They have spotlights shining down on me, so bright you can barely keep your eyes open. But if I close my eyes and try to sleep, I'll be doused with a bucket of ice water."

"You're not allowed to sleep?"

"No. I haven't slept for at least three days, maybe more. It's called sleep deprivation," he said. "Courtesy of Stalin's techniques."

Pony Boy could hear the heavy fatigue in his voice. "Can't you die from that?"

"I doubt it, but it doesn't matter. They don't care if you live or die down here," the voice said. "I've heard them drag bodies out of other cells and then try to guess how many days the prisoner's been dead."

Pony Boy didn't answer. The thought was so horrifying he didn't know what to say. A door slammed down the hall and he dropped to the floor, his heart pounding in terror at being caught communicating.

The voice lowered to almost a hiss, coming to Pony Boy's ear like a snake moving through the grass. "I know the routine. They'll give me two weeks of blinding sleep deprivation, an interrogation, then two weeks of dark isolation, then more interrogation sessions. In between I'll be beaten, starved, and only get enough water to barely live until I confess to something I didn't do."

As the sound of boots came closer, he tried to quiet his breathing and hoped the man in the next cell wouldn't speak again. The thought that maybe he'd been planted there to trick Pony Boy into breaking the rules came to him again, and he broke into a clammy sweat. The heavy boots stopped in the hall, then the small peeking window was slid open and a beam of light flooded into his cell.

Pony Boy squinted, trying to make out the face peering through it. "Prisoner six-seven-eight-nine," a voice boomed. "Step up."

Pony Boy scrambled to his feet, dizzy with fear. He went to the window. Beneath it was another much wider window. It was slid open and a tin cup appeared. Beside it a hand placed a green molded hunk of bread. Pony Boy took them both and the windows slid closed. He was back in the dark and he slid down onto the floor.

There was only about an inch of water in the small cup but he didn't care. He was careful, though. He didn't drink it all at once. First he used his finger to smear a bit of it on his cracked lips, then he took a small sip. The water tasted warm and rusty. But good.

His first bite of the moldy bread was bad—he had to admit it even to himself. But he also knew he needed something in his body. Using his hand to measure what he couldn't see, he broke half of the bread off and set it on his lap to save for later. He would have to keep it close to be sure a rodent didn't take off with it. He picked at the other half, eating small bites until it was gone. His stomach, once introduced to food again, became even more vocal, demanding more. But Pony Boy didn't know how long it would be until he was offered sustenance again, so he maintained his discipline.

The water, however, was another story. It was gone in less than a few minutes. His thirst was so great that nothing he could tell himself would make it possible to save some for later. He said a prayer that the guard would be back, and would bring more water. Soon.

He remembered the voice. He scrambled over to where he thought the grate was and felt along the wall until he found it.

"I'm back," he whispered.

"Good. I was afraid they'd taken you away and I'd be alone again."

Pony Boy wished that was exactly what they'd do, but he felt pity for the man, anyway. "Did they bring you bread and water, too?"

There was not a reply right away, then a long sigh.

"The only water he had for me was in a bucket, ready to be thrown on me if I was found sleeping. He left none of it for me to drink."

"I'm so sorry. How long since you've had any?"

"Not too long—maybe a day. Maybe two. I can't remember, but my swollen tongue tells me at least thirty hours or so."

"How long have you been down here?"

"Three months."

"What did you do?" Pony Boy asked, then immediately wished he could take the words back. He'd forgotten that behind bars, it was an unspoken rule that you never asked why someone was there.

"Just how old are you?" the voice said, sounding even wearier.

"Old enough to be here, I'd say," Pony Boy said, trying to keep the indignation from his tone.

"*Hao le*. You have a point there. My job," the man said, after a long pause. "I am here for nothing more than doing my job. My house was ransacked and my collection of English medical journals and essays was found. Because of that, they've accused me of being a spy."

"A spy? Were you writing them?"

"No, no. It was simply research. China hasn't quite embraced mental illness like some countries, so their case studies help me with the few patients I'd taken on."

"You can read English?" Pony Boy asked, impressed. He'd never known anyone who could read more than a few words of English.

"*Shi de*, I can," the doctor—as Pony Boy now thought of him—said. "Many doctors can, but I had no idea it could be cause for alarm. I didn't hide anything in my office. My colleagues warned me, they urged me to do away with any connection to other countries as they had, but I thought it ridiculous. Now my openness has led to my being here and, for all I know, I may end up being just like the mental patients I wanted to help."

"Chairman Mao doesn't believe in mental illness, does he?" Pony Boy wasn't sure where he'd heard that, but he had.

"It's not that he doesn't believe in it—I don't know his personal thoughts on it, but I've heard him declare that mental illness is simply the person being too weak to control his own mind."

"What do you think about it, after all your research?" Pony Boy asked.

"From my experiences, and from what I've read, I've found two main types of mental illness among patients. The first type can be temporary, and is usually brought on by extreme stress or life circumstances."

"And the other?"

The doctor paused, then spoke so quietly that Pony Boy had to press his ear against the grate harder.

"The second is a more permanent illness that causes a person to be dangerous. He or she acts rashly without control and suffers no guilt for their actions."

"You've met some like that?"

"Only a couple. But I've seen a few of those here in this prison—though I have to say they were wearing uniforms."

They talked for hours, discussing random subjects, even dissecting the case of the university teacher in Fudan who was beaten beyond recognition for teaching from the works of William Shakespeare.

"Before they took me in, I went through sixteen struggle sessions," the doctor said. "They even shaved half my hair, calling it the Yin Yang head. I looked like a fool and they ridiculed me for days on end. It's grown out now, though somewhat unevenly."

It was therapeutic, touching on so many subjects, many of them based on the very reasons that Pony Boy and Wren had created the newsletter—the reasons he now had dozens of negatives hidden under his floorboards at home—negatives that could be potentially damaging to many officials if not to Chairman Mao himself.

They also talked about family, the wife and children the doctor had left behind, forced to denounce him to avoid sharing his punishment. He said his wife had cried, begging him not to make her betray their marriage. But he'd done it for them, he said. The doctor telling of his sacrifice made Pony Boy think of Wren, and how he'd have done the same, just to keep her safe.

As for Pony Boy, he talked, too, ranting about Lixin being sent to the country, about his family close to starving from the unfair food rationing, and many other subjects close to his heart. After weeks of feeling so alone, he couldn't stop himself.

They talked about most everything, yet the doctor hadn't asked about his crime. Pony Boy wondered why, yet was thankful to have someone near. His own story wasn't important at the moment. It was enough that he'd found companionship—a voice in the dark to let him know he was not alone, that he continued to breathe, was even still human and not some trapped and desperate animal.

Chapter Thirty-Six

It hadn't happened overnight, but Benfu could finally acknowledge that he was no longer the same person he was when he'd left Shanghai. Gone were his constant thoughts of making music and getting into the Shanghai school of his dreams, and in place of those thoughts he now strategized ways to make a living, or on some days, just to help Calli's family get by. He barely thought of his old life, other than to push aside occasional feelings of guilt that his parents still knew nothing of his whereabouts. Most of all, he dreaded them knowing that as a son, he'd failed them. He'd been branded a criminal, then ran away like a coward. If found out, who knows what damage to the family name it would cause. Knowing his mother, a mark on their name would be worse than death. He'd have to try to make that right somehow—as soon as it was a better time to leave Calli. But for now, she needed him.

He thought back to the night of the *hutong* auction and how after everyone had fully accepted him into their circle, his resolve to leave the next day had dissolved. Days turned into weeks, then weeks into months, until finally the sense of responsibility to his parents began to fade and he embraced his life in Wuxi.

These days his mornings began even earlier than before. He needed to help Calli get everyone settled before he set off on his rounds to look for discarded items he could flip into rewards.

He knocked quietly on their door to alert them he was entering, then softly made his way in and without speaking, emptied the ashes from the old stove. Her parents were still curled upon the kang bed, her mother pressed into the curve of the old man's body. After a few of his visits into the house, he'd discovered that the stuffed mattress Calli had given him was her own, and though he'd tried to get her to take it back, she'd assured him that she fit fine on the kang bed with her parents. Now that he knew it was hers, he found himself sinking his face into the soft cloth more and more as he drifted off to sleep, straining for just a small taste of her flowery scent.

Now Calli stood at the counter, stirring a pot, and turned and gave him a smile.

Breakfast.

She'd taken over cooking all the meals because her mother was ill with a nasty chest infection. Doctor Shu let them borrow some elixir, and he'd come and made poultices of cooling herbs to place over Lao Ro's lungs, his attempt to lure the heat from them. He'd also used his needles in a technique performed to loosen the phlegm.

So far, though, Lao Ro had only gotten worse. Calli fretted that they'd waited too long to seek help, a situation caused by their lack of funds to pay anyone. Now the responsibility of the household was on her shoulders, and Benfu only wanted to help carry the load. He opened the creaking door on the stove front and added a small chunk of coal—a luxury made possible because of the huge pile of scrap metal he'd found and sold the week before.

He went to the stacked pile of clothes on the floor and picked up the first pair of pants and a shirt, taking them to the piece of wire he'd suspended over the old stove. He looped the clothes over the wire, letting them heat.

Lao Ro stirred, then slowly sat up, rubbing her eyes.

Benfu could see her in the corner of his vision, but he kept his gaze averted, allowing her privacy. He could've predicted it and been right, for as soon as she took her first breath sitting up, she began to cough.

Benfu quickly crossed the room and slipped out the door. That was his cue to give her five minutes of privacy.

He waited on the front stoop, shivering in the cold air.

Calli's father, who she'd described as always being kind and loving, had slipped so far into his dementia that when he arose and his confusion set in, he often became so frightened that he was combative.

Calli poked her head out. "She's dressed and Papa's ready."

He went in and walked to the bed where Calli's father sat, his legs dangling over the side, his arms hanging listlessly.

"*Zao*, Fei. Ready for your clothes? It's going to be a chilly day," Benfu greeted him first, then eased him into what would happen next. He took the pants from the wire hanger over the stove and brought them to the bed.

"Am I going to help you feed the pigs?" the man asked, his eyebrows raised high. "Baba said I could help you today."

Benfu nodded. "We'll see. Let's work on getting dressed and eating breakfast first."

They worked their way into the warm pants and Benfu slipped the man's shoes on and tied them before helping him to stand. When he finally pulled him up, the older man thought they were headed out the door.

"Wait, we have to get your shirt on," Benfu said, keeping his voice low and soothing. From across the room Lao Ro watched as she ate her congee. She'd been the most receptive to Benfu helping out with the morning routine.

He met Calli's eyes. It was complicated and getting through each day took on new challenges, but so far he was impressed at how both Calli and her mother stayed focused and patient, guiding the confused old man through the shadows in his mind toward some sort of peace and light.

Only after her parents were asleep and Calli came to him for their evening time together did she let her guard down and cry for the man who was once her strong and dependable father. And Benfu's heart broke for her because with the lack of medical care, her father's mind was straying farther and farther. He doubted they'd ever bring him back to stay, though there were some fleeting moments interspersed with the difficult ones where Da Fei suddenly recognized his wife, or even Calli.

No matter what they were doing or what they were in the middle of, when he became lucid, they both dropped everything and took advantage of those moments granted. It was touching to see them gather together in a mini reunion of laughter and tears, seizing the sparse gifts when they could, but then the letdown as he faded away again was tragic to witness.

Finally dressed now, Da Fei let his wife lead him to the sink to brush his teeth and wash his face. She tended to him with gentle movements, her own body bent and weak from a night of coughing. Many times over the last weeks, he'd been struck with the realization that they were exactly what a couple should be—committed to each other, despite the hardships. He thought of his own parents and the distance between them, even in the same room, and wondered if Lao Ro knew what a shining example she was for others.

"Benfu, I've got your breakfast ready," Calli called out.

He looked at Calli and noticed that she had not yet braided her hair and it lay long and slightly damp over her shoulders.

She saw him looking at it—at her—and her cheeks flushed pink. He tore his eyes away and went to the table and sat down. She'd placed his bowl where her father used to sit, a symbolic gesture that they now depended on him more and more. He wasn't surprised to see the watered-down congee—that was the usual fare for mornings in their home and somehow, Calli always found a way to make it tasty. But he was surprised to see the link of pork that lay across it. A luxury that he knew she couldn't afford.

He looked up at Calli. "Where did you get this?"

She smiled and shrugged her shoulders. When she spoke, her words didn't match the softness of her voice. "You don't have to know everything. Just eat and then get out of my kitchen. And Benfu, I've been thinking. Tomorrow you must go seek your parents. It's not right that they do not know if their son is dead or alive. We'll be fine here."

He dropped his head and sighed. She was right and he knew it. His parents might know that he'd left the commune and was missing. They might think him a criminal. Or they could be ignorant of the happenings of the last months. Either way, he owed it to them to go and see them, to explain where he was and why.

He felt a touch on his shoulder and looked up to see Calli staring down at him.

"I can't tell you how thankful I am for all you've done, but it's not fair of me to keep you here when they probably need you, too."

He didn't want to leave, but his long-ingrained sense of duty overrode his reluctance. Still, he was glad that Calli had seen through it and been the one to force his hand. Even without telling her, she knew what his heart needed.

And that was to be forgiven.

Chapter Thirty-Seven

Benfu walked up the lane, noting that though everything had changed for him, the neighborhood looked all but untouched. Looping over him, the beautiful plane trees still lined the street, casting shadows of shade and bringing a wave of homesickness to his heart. Then he approached the house and was somewhat surprised to see the once pristine green courtyard that his mother had taken such pride in was now barely more than a brown patch of dirt. Finally, he thought, she'd decided to follow the directive of pulling up grass and flowers. Just a small thing but it gave him some relief that his mother wasn't rebelling against the new ways.

Saying good-bye to Calli had been one of the hardest things he'd ever done. He'd broken down and told her about Juan Hui and their arranged engagement. Calli had looked hurt for an instant, then composed herself and wished him a happy future. She'd assured him that they would be fine without him and insisted he take all his things, telling him it was unlikely that his parents would approve of him returning to Wuxi. Her intuition was probably right, but still, walking away from her hurt him deep in his gut. Despite the impoverished life she and her family lived, their home was heavy with something that was hard to come by—unconditional love and loyalty. There, in their midst, Benfu had felt needed. And as much as he tried, he couldn't think of another time in his life that he'd felt that way.

Leaving just didn't feel right.

The train ride to Shanghai had been tense—even though Calli had borrowed identification papers from a friend for him to use, Benfu felt paranoid that everyone he locked eyes with was watching him suspiciously. Between the moments of unease, he'd had plenty of time to think about how he was going to tell his parents about Calla Lily and the relationship they were forging. It was going to be difficult and he didn't yet have the words in his mind that he would need to convince them he was his own man. He'd also thought a lot of Pony Boy and Zu Wren, especially when he'd overheard a conversation between two businessmen on the train, talking of what was apparently a huge purge against the media in China. It started the year before but was only now coming to light. They talked of editors having lost their fancy homes and cars, and being subjected to relentless criticism sessions, of newspaper offices being shut down with only pre-approved stories wired to the Xinhua News Agency getting published.

Benfu didn't know how Pony Boy and Zu Wren were faring with the newsletter, but he was sure they were determined enough to find some way to get it out there.

Seeing Pony Boy was his second priority after checking in at home.

He entered the gate, then went around the back of the house. He didn't see Old Butler so he entered into the kitchen. It was cold—much colder than he ever remembered it being. He wondered why they were not using the heat. Another government rationing rule?

Cook looked up, smiling from ear to ear.

"Benfu! What are you doing here?"

It was so good to see her and Benfu dropped his bag and opened his arms, inviting her in for an embrace. He was relieved when she complied.

When she finally stood back, he couldn't keep the question from his voice.

"How is Mother? Have her and Baba been affected by—" The words fading on his lips because his mother walked in, her head down as she shuffled through. "Mother," he called out softly.

She froze, her hand in midair, as she was about to use it to straighten her unusually unkempt hair. She looked up, confused.

"It's me. Benfu." That much should've been obvious but she looked like she was seeing a ghost, so the words slipped out.

When she heard his voice, she dropped to her knees, attempted to stand, then once again fell to her knees. Benfu rushed forward and helped her up.

"There you go, Mother," he said, keeping his hands on her shoulders to hold her stable. He was surprised at how fragile the once-imposing woman now appeared to him. But he'd been through a lot and was no longer a boy.

"Benfu, is it really you?" She searched his face, as though looking for her son through the disguise of a stranger.

"It's me, Mother."

She fell forward, into his arms and he supported her weight, keeping her from falling to the ground as she sobbed. He stroked her hair and realized another thing—he'd never seen his mother cry. Behind him, Cook rushed to get a dish towel and brought it over.

"Mother, don't cry. I'm fine. Really, I'm just fine."

He slowly guided her to the kitchen table, lowering her into a chair and then taking the one across from her.

"But—but—how?" his mother finally got out. She ignored the towel, instead using the back of her hands to wipe at the tears that ran down her face, moving fast to keep up with the torrent of emotion.

"Didn't they come here?"

"They who?"

"The commune officials—or the authorities—I don't know, whoever comes searching for people. I left the commune months ago, Mother. I was afraid that maybe they'd have found a way to connect me to you and Ba. That's why it took me so long to come home."

"You left the commune? Why? And where have you been?"

"That's what I want to talk to you and Baba about. You may be upset at me, but I'd like to tell you what happened. I want to ask you to forgive me if I've disappointed you. Is Ba here?" Benfu looked around, noticing for the first time that the kitchen was somewhat bare. He could see down the hallway leading to the parlor and saw that the Persian rugs that usually lined the floor were also gone.

"Where are all our things? The rugs?" he asked. "I've never seen the floors bare like this."

Cook stepped up and put a hand on Mother's shoulder. "We packed it all away and hid it high in the attic rafters. The Red Guards have been looting and we wanted to keep it safe."

Benfu nodded. He'd seen many houses in Wuxi wiped clean from the Red Guards, all their most prized belongings confiscated or demolished. He was glad his mother had gotten ahead of them and that after the revolution, there would still be furnishings to help them get back to normal.

"Son, I'm thrilled to see you, but tell me, why are you here?" Mother asked again.

Benfu looked at her, wondering if he looked as different as she did. His mother had aged dramatically, her once shiny black hair now gray at the temples.

"As I said, Mother, I had to leave the commune. I've been hiding out in Wuxi."

"Hiding out? But why? You were safe there," she said, her eyes filled with confusion. "We spent so much to arrange your papers, to find a place for you—to keep you out of the fray, out of danger. To keep you safe."

Safe. There was that word again. Benfu shook his head. How to even tell her how far from safe he'd been? Would she, or could she, even understand? He looked from her to Cook, then over their heads at the door again. He needed an ally before he began the story that they'd probably not even believe.

"I'd rather wait for Ba before I get into the details. I'll tell you what. I'll go see Pony Boy and his family, and I'll be back in time for dinner when Baba will be here."

"No, Benfu, I don't want you running around town," Mother said. She slowly came out of her chair to stand beside the table, looking down at him.

Benfu stood too. He put a hand out, touching his mother on the shoulder.

"Mother, who do you see before you? I'm a man now, and I still respect you, but I'm not asking you for permission. I'll be back within a few hours. I promise," he said. Then he leaned over and kissed her on the cheek.

She put a hand to her face, covering the skin where he'd kissed. She still looked puzzled, though he could see why. He never kissed his mother—not since he was a little boy, anyway.

She didn't speak as he headed toward the door. Cook lifted a hand, waving him away. "I'll have dinner ready by six," she said.

"Good," Benfu answered, opening the door. "I'll be on time."

He slipped out, anxious to see Pony Boy, to see the shock and then watch his familiar surprised smile stretch across his face. Of everyone, Benfu thought he'd missed his best friend the most of all, and it wasn't yet a homecoming if he hadn't seen him.

He made the walk to Pony Boy's street in record time, barely taking notice of the cold, his surroundings, or the way the people in the neighborhood who used to be so friendly now barely looked up as he passed them. It was afternoon, and if he were lucky he'd catch Pony Boy between jobs—that is if he decided to run by his house for a quick meal.

He approached the house and saw no one outside, so he entered the courtyard and went to the door, then knocked.

Mrs. Wei opened the door. "Benfu, so good of you to come."

She stood aside, allowing him to move past her into the house. Her face was pinched with worry, even more so than usual. He looked around and her husband wasn't on the bed. His stomach dropped—had the man died?

"Mrs. Wei—" He looked at the empty bed, his condolences on his tongue.

He was interrupted by Zu Wren, who'd been on the floor braiding Mei's hair. She jumped up, coming to him and throwing her arms around him. "Thank the gods, you came. Please—have you seen him?" she asked, pulling back to search his face.

"Seen who? Where is Mr. Wei?"

"He's still at work," Mrs. Wei said. "He went back but he's only doing half his route until he's completely recovered."

Benfu was flooded with relief that Pony Boy's father was well enough to be back working. He felt a weight released from his shoulders, then looked down when Mei came over and wrapped her arms around his legs, giving him an embrace. He smiled down at her, shocked to see how she'd grown. She no longer looked like a toddler—now she was a little girl. But something more was going on. He could feel it.

He looked from Zu Wren to Mrs. Wei.

Finally Mrs. Wei spoke. "It's Pony Boy. He's missing."

"Missing? What do you mean, missing? He came to see me at the commune and he was fine."

"No, he was here after that," Zu Wren said. "But then he left again and he hasn't returned!"

"Returned from where?" Benfu asked.

"From Beijing. He traveled there by train seven or eight weeks ago. He went to be a part of history—he wanted to witness Mao's next address to the people." Zu Wren spoke to him, but kept glancing at Mrs. Wei as the words left her mouth.

Benfu could tell she was holding back and he wanted to hear what she knew.

"Zu Wren, can you walk with me outside?" he asked, going to the door and opening it wide.

She looked at Mrs. Wei and waited on a nod, but then joined him. Benfu shut the door behind them, leading her out of the courtyard and away from where anyone could overhear them.

"Now," he said. "Tell me exactly what's going on. Why did he go to Beijing and don't leave anything out."

Zu Wren looked terrified and that in itself was shocking. Benfu had only ever seen her confident and brave. She glanced once behind her at the house, then took a deep breath. "He was going to hand deliver the latest newsletter either to Mao, or whichever official he could get closest to. We agreed he'd return the next week but he never showed up."

Benfu felt his stomach drop and recognized the first stirrings of frustration. Traveling to Beijing was exactly something Pony Boy would do in a quest to make a name for himself—or to be the hero. Benfu doubted he'd really thought through the consequences of what could happen if anyone connected the newsletter to him.

Zu Wren took a deep breath. "What do you think happened to him?"

"I don't know. How would I know, Zu Wren? Maybe he's sick. Or hurt. Or—or—what if he got arrested? This was a really bad idea."

Zu Wren shook her head, silently denying the last option.

"Why didn't you go there with him?" Benfu asked, trying unsuccessfully to keep the accusation out of his voice. "You let him go alone?"

Her eyes filled with tears. "I couldn't go. It would've been too risky. My father was already suspicious. He questioned me about the boxes of paper he's missing, even asked if I'd seen the armband, Benfu! I think he knows."

Benfu's knees felt shaky and he lowered himself onto the step. "What armband?"

She sat down beside him and put her head in her hands. "I gave Pony Boy a red official armband—one my father had to give out to their journalists. It was an instant credentialing tool. My father knows it's gone."

"And he's allowing you to come over here? Doesn't that put Pony Boy on his radar as a suspect?"

She shook her head. "He doesn't know Pony Boy or that this family even exists. I've been careful about that. He thinks I was accepted into the Shanghai People's street dancing team. At this moment I'm supposed to be learning revolutionary songs and dance routines for a tour around the country this summer."

"But you weren't careful about everything." Benfu couldn't believe what he was hearing. He didn't understand how they could've been so careless and naïve as to think Pony Boy could go to Beijing and basically hand over his identity, give them a reason to persecute him. What were they thinking? Had the revolution burned out all of their common sense?

He paced back and forth in the alley between two rows of houses, his head bent as he thought through scenarios. He lifted his eyes to Zu Wren briefly, then discounted her as she stood there, expecting him to produce some kind of miracle.

"How could you let this happen?" he finally exploded, throwing his hands in the air.

Zu Wren winced. "I'm sorry. I really am."

"Sorry isn't going to bring him back." Benfu pointed a finger in her face, then felt ashamed. He'd never before talked to a woman in such a way. He turned, stomping away from her.

"I wish we could take it all back," Zu Wren said, her voice pleading. "I'd never speak of the newsletter again if I could just take it back—just get him back."

Benfu heard the anguish in her voice. When he turned to look at her, she lifted her face and he saw she was crying, all her bravado gone. Too late, but she'd finally realized the danger in the game they'd played.

He sighed. "Come here."

She came to him and he held his arms out, letting her fall in as he embraced her. She loved Pony Boy, this he could see. It was real, the heaving of her crying told him that.

He let her go and she stepped back.

"I have a strong feeling he's been apprehended—probably arrested," Benfu said.

"What do we do?" Zu Wren looked even more frightened, if that was possible.

Benfu looked at the sky, watched as a dark blue cloud floated overhead, a silent reproach from Mother Nature, telling him they shouldn't have ever tried to mess with Chairman Mao.

"I'll go to my father and ask him to borrow some money, then I'll leave for Beijing at first light tomorrow. You can help by praying that I can find Pony Boy—and that if I do, I'm able to pay his way out of there."

She nodded, and visibly swallowed. They both knew it was a long shot. Beijing was a huge city and who was to say Pony Boy hadn't gotten lost on the way there or even on the return? It was all a gamble, but one Benfu was willing to take. After all, Pony Boy had come looking for him and given Benfu the encouragement he needed before one of his darkest times ever.

It was time to pay the favor back.

Chapter Thirty-Eight

ony Boy tried to rub warmth into his arms as he paced the floor, automatically stopping when he'd gone seven paces, then turning around and doing seven more paces the other way. At first he'd gotten more than a few bumps and bruises but now, a few weeks into his isolation, he'd memorized the cell and could easily navigate it in the solid black. Though with his success came the feeling that he'd been reduced to nothing more than some sort of nocturnal rat, but at least now instead of scrambling along the walls in confusion, he knew exactly where he was at any moment.

And that felt like a victory.

While imprisoned, he made it his new purpose to keep the doctor awake and free from more punishment. The challenge kept his brain busy and far from the despair that had threatened to envelop him before. They actually had let the man sleep, though only one hour at a time, just a taste to show him what he'd get if he admitted to being a spy, prepping him for each of his interrogation sessions.

Now, they'd taken the doc away again and thoughts of what they were doing to his new friend plagued his mind and he prayed to the gods that this session of interrogation wouldn't kill him. He could just imagine the angry shouts in the man's ears, the slamming of his head against the table, or the worst possibility, that he was being beaten.

He also worried that they'd move him, and then Pony Boy would be all alone again. He felt shame that he thought about his own plight more than the doctor's, but he assured himself that both were connected so were hard to separate.

Then he realized he was doing a lot of rationalizing to himself that some—if heard aloud—might call rambling. Was he losing it? Was he destined to become one of the mental patients the doctor strived to treat, whose minds were broken from too much stress? Using his hands, he brushed them against his clothes. He hadn't been allowed to change or wash since he'd been in the hole. He stank, that much was clear. His hair was getting longer and shaggier than even he liked to wear it. He was so thirsty, that he could honestly say he'd sell his soul for a drink.

Yes, it was true—he was becoming a madman.

Pony Boy felt himself reeling from despair to anger to paranoia. He even recognized that he was doing it, yet he couldn't stop. The dark was getting to him, and the fear of being alone again was terrifying. He stopped, realizing he'd lost count of his paces and would need to start over. Again. Then he felt a moment of hope when he realized that the doctor might get to see a clock on the wall—maybe even a calendar! He longed to know how long he'd been away from Wren, as though it might tell him if she was still waiting for him or maybe had even come to Beijing to find him.

He hoped she didn't.

But he hoped she did.

No, he told himself, *for her to come would be much too dangerous.* But oh, how he longed to see her, if only through a piece of glass or through the metal bars. He scolded himself for his weakness. Wren needed to stay away, to break anything and everything that could tie her to him. He hadn't even attempted to write to her, afraid of who might intercept the mail. He hoped she'd been smart enough to burn all her editorial notes, anything that could be connected to the newsletter.

He began to pace again. He thought of the armband and wondered what the officials had done with it. Put it with the rest of the damning evidence against him, he supposed. And now that he'd had so much time to think about it, he realized that believing he'd get close to Mao had been insane. All he'd done was set himself up to look suspicious, causing the girl next to him on the train to report him to the Red Guards. And to think, she'd looked so impressed when he'd shown her his armband that gave him permission to take photos and make official reports.

He froze, fear clutching at his throat. His thoughts returned to the armband.

With enough luck—or bad luck, on his part—it possibly could be traced back to Wren's father's office. Then to her father—and then possibly to Wren! His procession of thoughts caused him to start shaking again, a now common reaction his betraying body had adopted when afraid. He couldn't believe he hadn't thought of it before, but now he knew that if he continued to deny that he was responsible for the newsletter, Wren could be in danger. What should he do? Confess the truth? Keep denying?

His mental spiral out of control was interrupted by a commotion from outside. Two sets of boots and the sounds he'd come to know as someone being dragged came closer, stopping near his cell.

The doctor was back.

After a few door slams and some cursing, the boots faded away again and Pony Boy rushed over to the wall, putting his ear to the grate.

He heard nothing.

"Doc, are you there?" he whispered.

Now he heard labored breathing. Was he hurt?

"Doc?"

"I'm here," he finally heard.

Pony Boy felt relief come over him. "Are you hurt?"

"Physically, I'm a bit bruised. But they haven't yet broken me."

"Broken you? What more do they want? They still think you're a spy?"

He could hear Doc's heavy breathing from the grate. Pony Boy would already swear they were wrong about the man, even though he hadn't yet seen his face.

Finally, he answered, "I'm almost beyond caring. I feel so sick. Even if I convince them of my innocence, I have no one waiting for me out there. They've taken away everything—my family, my work, my patients," he said, his voice dragging out slower and slower with each word. "I don't think I can stay awake and they're going to find me sleeping. As they were bringing me back, I heard someone mention your prisoner number. They may be coming back any time," Doc said. "I wanted to warn you."

Pony Boy was ashamed at how the doc's words made him cringe. Yes, he was afraid.

"You still there?"

"I'm here," Pony Boy whispered. He didn't want to go. He wanted more time to think about his revelation, that he was putting Wren at risk by not taking responsibility for the newsletter. He knew he wasn't thinking clearly, but so far the doc seemed to be completely in his right mind. He needed advice. Yet, could he trust the man? He had to make a decision before they came.

"I can help keep you awake."

"How?" Doc said.

"I'll share my story with you. Then, I want you to advise me if I should confess or not." He took a deep breath. He was going to need it. And when he was through, he hoped the doctor would tell him the best route to take to protect Wren, no matter the outcome.

The interrogator—a different one this time—screamed in his ear while Pony Boy tried to remember exactly what it was that he and Doc had decided on. He'd been beaten once already, the man's belt buckle falling across his back and even across his cheek, splitting open the skin enough that he now tasted blood. At first he'd spit the metallic taste out, but now he let it dribble in, pretending it was water.

His thoughts were scattered. If he could just have a minute of peace to think things through. He thought of Doc back in his cell, wondered if he'd succumbed to sleep as soon as Pony Boy had been taken away.

The man grabbed at his hair, using it as a handle to pull his head upright.

"I'll be back," he said, then as though a prayer had been answered, he left the room.

There were no others with him this time. It was simply Pony Boy and one man. One man determined to break him.

But hadn't he and Doc decided this time that he'd allow them that break?

That's what he appreciated most about his new friendship. The doctor had listened, all calm and logical, occasionally asking a question to help Pony Boy explore every option. And even when he'd determined the best way to keep Wren safe was to fall on his sword, the doctor had reluctantly agreed with him instead of trying to talk him out of it.

Then they'd discussed possible punishments and from what the doctor had seen over the last months behind bars, he was sure that based on his young age, they'd send Pony Boy to a reeducation camp. He'd do a few years, prove himself to be changed, and then he could get back to his life—back to Wren.

He wiped at the blood on his cheek, reminding himself it was not water and was going to make him sick if he kept swallowing it. Looking at the door, he saw through the foggy window another man had arrived and was talking to the interrogator. Pony Boy couldn't see what, but it appeared that the man held something in his hands.

The hairs stood up on his arms.

He and the doctor had also talked about possible interrogation methods. The prison guards had been known to use electric shock to get compliance, as well as to treat those who were deemed mentally unstable. Was he about to be shocked?

He tried to focus.

Take responsibility or deny. Protect Wren or face more investigations.

The door opened and the man entered. Pony Boy breathed a sigh of relief to see that instead of holding some type of shock equipment, the man carried a tray. On it was a plate of fruit, a glass, and a tall pitcher of water.

So that was their next tactic—make him suffer by watching them eat and drink.

The man brought the tray to the table and set it down. Immediately the aroma of the freshly sliced melon and ripe apples rose to Pony Boy's nose, and his stomach clenched even as he wondered where they'd gotten fresh fruit out of season. He eyed the water, so much clearer than the tepid water he'd so far seen at the prison. With some effort, he tore his eyes from the tray and looked at the man, ready for whatever would come next.

"How are you?" the man asked.

His question stumped Pony Boy. It wasn't even just the question—it was the look he gave him, one that appeared to be genuinely interested in the answer.

"I—I'm fine," Pony Boy stuttered. Couldn't the man see what bad shape he was in? He knew he stank—and his face felt bloody and swollen.

"You look thirsty," the man said.

Pony Boy looked at his badge. It only gave a number and like the others, no name. He'd never seen this particular man before and didn't know if he was an interrogator, a guard, or what. And he wouldn't dare ask.

The man picked up the pitcher and filled the glass with water. He slid it over to Pony Boy. "Drink."

Pony Boy felt his heart accelerate. Slowly, he raised his arm from under the table and reached for the glass. He knew at any second, the man's fist would either come down and break his wrist, or would snatch the water away. He could feel it, yet he couldn't stop himself from at least trying.

His hand was near the glass and he extended his fingers, letting them slowly wrap around the bottom, feeling the coolness against his palm.

He paused, looking up at the man.

The man nodded.

Pony Boy lifted the glass to his lips, then drank greedily, gulping the water so fast it went down like rocks instead of the cool river he was expecting. Some dribbled out of his mouth, running down his chin, but he didn't care. He drank until it was gone.

He set the glass down and looked up, unable to erase the guilt from his face. But it was wonderful—the best water he'd ever drank. He didn't regret his choice.

"What's going to happen now?"

The man wrinkled his brow. "What do you mean?"

"What are you going to do to me for drinking the water?"

"Nothing," he said softly, then refilled the glass. "I offered it to you."

He pointed at the tray.

Pony Boy shook his head. He couldn't possibly be telling him to eat the fruit. Could he?

"Eat. It's all yours."

The fruit looked so fresh it could've been a painting, yet Pony Boy couldn't make his hand move toward it. He looked at the window, trying to see where the interrogator had gone. The hall appeared to be empty. Still, the fruit felt like a trap.

"Who are you?" Pony Boy asked. He took another swig of water, this time letting it slide down easy, relishing the feel of it on his swollen throat.

The man shrugged, then nodded slightly toward the hall. "I'm not like him, if that's what you want to know. Now, if you want that fruit, I'm offering it to you. Just like the water."

Pony Boy picked up a rind of deep red watermelon. He brought it to his nose, inhaling the sweet smell.

He sighed, then took a bite.

Yes, it tasted as sweet as it smelled.

He swallowed, then took another bite. He paced himself this time. He would not let his circumstances turn him into some sort of animal.

When he took a bite of the slice of apple, he thought of Wren and the first night they'd met. He blinked back the emotion, realizing for the first time that it might be years before they'd be together again. Even so, he took another bite. As he was chewing it, allowing the taste to fill his mouth, the man spoke again. Softly. Ever so softly.

"Tell me where you got the photo of the writer's association. The one taken in front of the temple."

And between bites, Pony Boy did tell him. Or at least he told him the story that he and Doc had worked on together.

The story began with him, and not Benfu, running into the white-haired man at the park. It ended with him—and only him—writing, publishing, and distributing the newsletters around Shanghai. Nowhere in the story did he implicate Benfu, and especially nowhere did he mention Wren.

"But where did you get access to a printer?" the man asked, his voice still gentle as though he were a friend, discussing the weather or an afternoon outing.

Pony Boy looked up. "I broke into a newspaper office at night, found an extra key and used that as my secret headquarters. I was careful not to leave tracks so I could return each time to make the new issues. It took me weeks to learn how to set type, but no one ever knew I'd been there."

Some of it was true, making it easier for him to tell it while looking as honest as possible. Between words, the man pushed the fruit, allowing him access to every last piece of it.

"And the armband?"

Pony Boy bowed his head, looking ashamed. "My mother works in a sewing plant and brings home snippets of material. She taught us all to sew. I took some of her red scraps and made the armband—copied it from others I'd seen."

The man crossed his arms. "It looks authentic."

"*Xie xie,*" Pony Boy thanked him, showing just the right amount of pride.

"Can you tell me why you felt the need to publicize these stories?"

Pony Boy nodded. He swallowed the bite in his mouth and used his sleeve to wipe the juice from his face. "Because I felt the people should know the real ramifications that this revolution is causing. I wanted to show the hardships some are suffering—the persecution of the innocent. I hoped that Chairman Mao might be able to stop this, once he saw what was really going on around China."

"And Teng Bao, he didn't help you at all?"

"How could he?" Pony Boy asked. "He'd been taken off to jail."

When the words were out, he realized what he'd done. He'd all but admitted he knew Teng Bao, even though he didn't. He looked up from the last rind of melon, and saw a smirk spread across the man's face.

"And do you know what became of him?"

Pony Boy shook his head.

The man held his hand up, mimicking a gun as he put it to his head and pulled the trigger. "Pow."

Then he lowered the hand, beckoning for Pony Boy to give him his. Pony Boy complied and they shook, but the man held on, his grip getting tighter with each second.

"How nice to finally meet the collaborator to the famous, yet dead, Teng Bao," he said, then let go and stood.

The humanity his face had held throughout the meeting evaporated, leaving behind a satisfied grimace.

Pony Boy looked away. For the first time in weeks, his belly was full and his thirst quenched, yet he'd never felt sicker. The door opened and the bully interrogator walked in, a smile pasted on his face, too.

"So—you finally folded," he said. He came to stand over Pony Boy, looking down at him as if examining a floundering cockroach. "I have pity for you, I really do. It's a shame. You were just a boy—a man-child struggling to become a legend—but failing."

The other man looked at the interrogator and they both laughed.

"I knew you were responsible for the newsletter, but your confession of collaborating with that vermin, Teng Bao, was an additional and unexpected gift," the bully said. "The warden will be ecstatic."

"I didn't collaborate with him. I didn't actually—" Pony Boy began, but was stopped when the other one held a hand up.

The sympathy from his voice was now completely void and replaced with disdain. "I hope you are not too proud of your so-called newsletter. For all your trouble, it has done nothing to help the cause but has done everything to alienate you from the people and the party. Your empty written confessions have proven that you are not able to be rehabilitated, and as it stands, you are an embarrassment to our country."

Gone was every trace of kindness.

Now Pony Boy only saw vindication radiating from the man's face.

"Take him back to his cell," he said, slamming his fist on the table for emphasis.

The bully interrogator yanked Pony Boy out of the seat and pulled his arms behind his back again. After tying them much too tight, he shoved him toward the door.

"Back to the hole," he said. "And guess whose name is going on the list for transport to the ghost yard? Along with that of Doctor Betrayal?"

Pony Boy struggled to keep his feet under him, but he did. As he was pushed down the hall, he ignored the reference to the ghost yard— the nickname given to the execution grounds. He wouldn't embrace it, or let the terror in. The only thought he let his mind focus on was the one in which he felt relief that they'd bought his story that he'd acted alone. But as the doors slammed behind him, he remembered what the guard had said about him and the doctor, and he had to wonder, how many more days did they have left?

Chapter Thirty-Nine

Benfu stared out the window of the taxi, tired beyond description yet optimistic that this time, someone might actually know where he could find Pony Boy. If this ended up a dead end, he would head back to Shanghai on the midnight train, and hope that he and his best comrade had crossed paths and that Pony Boy was safely at home, laughing over all the trouble he'd caused.

Going home wouldn't be easy, not after the way he'd left. He thought of Calli and the simple little house she lived in—so modest yet so full of love. Funny how when he thought of home, she came to mind.

He sighed, feeling a heavy sense of responsibility for his unwanted yet stubborn travel partner. On the far side of the seat, Zu Wren leaned her head against the window, sleeping soundly through the bumps and swerves as they navigated the streets. She was probably talked out—having expunged to him everything about her and Pony Boy's time together and their plans for the future. She'd talked non-stop almost the entire train ride and Benfu had been painfully aware that she was doing it out of nervousness.

They'd been in Beijing for three days and thus far had found nothing except a smoldering hot pot of Mao fanatics. He'd seen more waving of the Little Red Book, and more marching of Red Guards there than in any other place at one time. Even his journey on the train was nothing more than a tribute to Mao Thought—mostly mind-numbing hours filled with lectures, singing, and competitions to see who could recite the most Mao quotations. He'd been more than ready to disembark when they'd pulled into the station and was probably one of the first off the train.

Neither had ever been to Beijing and it was a bit overwhelming at first, but luckily, he'd been able to find a room to rent for cheap. Thus far they'd spent hours of every day and evening combing the streets, looking for any sign that Pony Boy had even been there. They'd looked at poles around Tiananmen Square, checked trash bins, scoured gutters to see if any copies of the newsletter had been hung or discarded.

Each day until well past dark, they'd braved the cold and searched, looking for any evidence he'd been there before grabbing a cheap bowl of noodles and closing themselves off in the room for the night. Benfu had given Zu Wren the bed, but the fatigue he carried allowed him to sleep soundly on the carpet. Despite their commitment, so far, they'd found nothing, save for hundreds if not thousands of Mao posters, most depicting cartoon caricatures of plump peasants in various poses of unbridled happiness while working the fields.

But Benfu knew better.

He'd even checked with as many local precincts as he could, taking the chance of coming face-to-face with officials and being questioned himself, to nervously inquire if his friend had been somehow mistakenly arrested. That he hadn't been was so far good news. However, a chance meeting of a policeman in a noodle shop had led him to hope that this prison—this one that was so secret not many knew of—was where he'd find his friend. As the scenery flashed by, Benfu thought of his father and felt a burst of frustration again.

The happy reunion that Benfu had envisioned was not to be.

He'd left Zu Wren and made his way home that afternoon, only to find that once he'd told his parents of Pony Boy's disappearance, neither had offered to help. All they wanted to know was about the commune and what he'd been doing since he'd left it. When he'd finally gotten to the part about Calli and her family, his mother had gone a bit mad— threatening him that if he'd done anything to ruin his engagement to Juan Hui, he'd be sorry for it. She'd almost made him lose his own temper when she'd suggested Calli was a money-hungry village girl only after his family name. It had taken some deep breaths and discipline, but he'd let it go, telling himself not to let his mother provoke him into words he'd regret later.

Benfu had tried to get the subject back to Pony Boy and the urgent need to find him, but his mother had refused to budge. She wanted him to confirm his plans to marry Juan Hui and Benfu couldn't bring himself to speak the words or even nod his head. She'd admitted that she hadn't heard a word from either Juan Hui or her mother since the chaos had begun in Shanghai. Who even knew if they were still on board with a future wedding? Couldn't his parents see that marriage plans were the last thing he wanted to talk about?

Finally, Benfu had talked his father into a private conversation. Despite his mother's protests, Ba waved her away and they'd gone to his library—a room shockingly devoid of anything familiar since they'd hidden everything—and there he'd asked his father for a loan.

"Where's the money you left here with?" his father asked.

"Someone in the commune stole it." *Right after I almost died from an infection*, he'd wanted to add but had kept to himself.

"But you have the violin?"

He'd nodded. "Of course I have the violin. I worked hard to keep it safe."

His father had looked relieved but even after Benfu explained to him about the living conditions and his illness, at how people in the commune scrambled for a way up, his father was still disappointed that Benfu had lost the small bundle of money. He'd then declined to loan him the funds needed to get to Beijing and possibly to bribe anyone who could be holding Pony Boy.

"I just don't have it, son," he'd said.

Benfu knew better than that. His father had been saving money his entire life and there had to be plenty of it left. It was easy to figure out that he didn't think Pony Boy worth the risk.

The car came to a stop and the driver turned back to him. "This is as far as I go. Just keep walking east and you'll see the ghost yards, then another mile and you'll get to the prison. You owe me four yuan."

He paid him and then nudged Zu Wren awake.

They got out. As they got farther from the city limits, they passed fewer and fewer people until finally, it was only them and the occasional car or truck. He'd been told the prison was far out of town, but hadn't understood just how far. His only choice was to continue moving and see where the road led. The driver had mentioned a ghost yard and Benfu assumed that meant the graveyard where prisoners were buried. Or shot. Or perhaps both. He felt a shiver run up his spine, thinking of it, then shook it off.

He needed to focus. And fortunately, he did have some money. But not thanks to his parents.

After the unsuccessful discussion with his father, he'd left his family home as he'd arrived, with just the bag over his shoulder. He'd let the door slam behind him, for once visibly showing his defiance. He'd gotten halfway out of the neighborhood before Old Butler had ridden up behind him and plugged the horn.

"Benfu," he'd called out.

Benfu had stopped, despite the embarrassing tears on his face. He hadn't had to explain, though. Old Butler told him that he'd been in the hall, listening to everything. Then he'd stepped off the bike and embraced Benfu.

"I'm proud of the man you've become," he said.

The memory of those words—words he'd have given anything for his own father to utter—still brought a lump to Benfu's throat.

After they'd embraced, Old Butler had pulled a small cotton sack from his belt and handed it over. "Take this," he said. "It's from me and Cook. If you need to use it to get your comrade home, then do it. We can always earn more."

Benfu hadn't wanted to take it. He knew that both Old Butler and Cook worked hard for their money and saved even harder. But the old man had pressed it into his hands, then got back on the bike to ride away. "Remember all I've taught you," he called out. "Loyalty and courage go hand in hand."

And he'd gone, disappearing into the crowded street as Benfu stared after him, longing for the time when Old Butler would step in and take care of everything.

But this time he wasn't a boy anymore.

He'd squared his shoulders, ready to take the trip alone, and had been shocked when he'd arrived at the train station and found Zu Wren waiting for him. Frightened for what her parents would do when she didn't come home, she'd still been determined to help him find Pony Boy.

Now here they were—two travelers on a long lonely highway, not even sure where they were going. But hopefully, about to discover where and what Pony Boy had wandered into.

After what felt like hours later, but was actually only one, they walked around the bend and saw an enormous gray building come into view. Visually, the place was depressing; its purpose evident by the high fence topped with barbwire that encircled it. Now he was glad they were far enough away that they hadn't yet caught the attention of the three guards that stood at the gate. Of small stature, considering they were security, the men wore all black and their body stances looked formidable. One took another glance around, then stepped into the small guardhouse, leaving his two comrades behind to keep a lookout.

Benfu pulled Zu Wren off the side of the road and into the trees.

"Just wait here long enough to let me talk to them."

"No, I'm not staying behind," Zu Wren said, crossing her arms over her chest. They stood in a gathering of trees, and though it was still chilly, the small grove at least shielded them from some of the wind. It would be a good place for her to wait.

"Listen to me." Benfu grabbed at her shoulders with both hands, making her look him in the eyes. "He's probably not even here. But if he is, and they've found something in his bag to connect you two, they'll detain you as well."

Her stubborn expression remained unmoved.

"How can I bribe him out of there if I have to worry about you? Can't you see what a fix we'd be in? Just let me check it out—please, Zu Wren."

She let out a long deep breath, then backed up until she was sitting on an overturned log, her action telling him as much as her words would've. Benfu could see that to concede had taken a lot from her. He didn't know if he'd ever met such a pigheaded person as her but he was relieved she relented.

"You keep my bag," he said, taking the fraudulent identification papers from it before dropping it at her feet. "I don't want to take any money in until I know he's there, and I get a feel for how corrupt they are. For all I know, they'll take my money and tell me nothing."

She nodded.

He pulled his gloves from his hands, thankful he'd grabbed them from the hall stand on his quick retreat out of his house. Now he dropped them into Zu Wren's lap.

"Use these at least until I get back."

She didn't respond but he felt sure she'd pull them on once he turned away.

He left her there and headed back to the road, hoping that she'd not let him get halfway and then run to catch up. If anything, she was unpredictable, though deep down he honestly thought her a good person who was genuinely in love with his friend.

Picking up his pace, he refused to look back. If the guards were watching him, he didn't want to tip them off that he wasn't alone. He had to admit, he was a bit frightened. Since the revolution had begun, the entire legal system had been dismantled and people were being arrested for any small thing, regardless whether it was a crime or not. Zu Wren had shared with him several stories her father had brought home. The one event that stood out the most to Benfu was the account of a group of poor and middle-class peasants in a far-flung county that had come together to form their own Supreme Court, then executed dozens of individuals who they deemed class enemies, barely giving them a chance to plead their cases.

Theirs wasn't an isolated case. It was happening all over China.

People were dying if they had even a scent of impropriety against the party. Many weren't given the chance to plead their innocence. One day they were living a normal if not paranoid existence, the next they were denounced as enemies.

He prayed that Pony Boy hadn't fallen into anyone's grasp.

"*Tíngzhǐ,*" the guard on the left yelled for him to halt as Benfu came into his view.

Benfu complied, holding his hands in the air as he'd seen criminals do in the movies.

The guard pointed his gun straight at him as the other guard approached.

"Papers?" he demanded, the long gun at his side pointed at the ground.

Benfu pulled his forged identification papers out of his back pocket and handed them over. Despite the chilly temperature, he felt beads of sweat over his eyebrows and hoped the men weren't that observant.

The guard examined the papers, looking at Benfu to match the photo. When he'd done it two or three times, he handed it back. "What are you doing here?"

"I—I—" Benfu and Zu Wren had discussed a new approach and he hesitated to use it. It had been her idea, and he wasn't sure it would work, but the guard asked him again, prompting Benfu to make a decision.

"I'm here to visit my cousin." In all other circumstances, asking if Pony Boy was detained in the facility had led to dead ends. This time, Zu Wren had suggested acting confident that he knew Pony Boy was there, and Benfu was simply there for a visit.

"Name?" the guard asked.

Benfu told him the name and waited as the other guard listened, then went into the guard shack. After some papers rustling and some conversation back and forth, he came out.

First he gave a small laugh, but one that sounded eerily menacing. "You're almost too late. But come back tomorrow. Visiting hours are only on weekends."

The news should've been somewhat welcome—the guard's words confirmed that they'd found Pony Boy. But all Benfu felt was a deep sense of worry. This wasn't jail and it wasn't some cowshed in a random commune. This was serious. Pony Boy was behind those dismal gray walls, sitting in a cell somewhere. In prison.

Alone.

Benfu turned and headed back down the highway. He tried not to look so dejected, as he knew he was being watched, but he felt as though he had the weight of the world on his shoulders. A direct contradiction to his slow pace, his thoughts moved erratically. He had only minutes to determine how he'd tell Zu Wren, and if he'd tell her about the confusing statement the guard had made—that he was almost too late.

Chapter Forty

The next day Benfu approached what appeared to be the same two guards, and once again went through the terror of having a gun pointed at his head by one man, while the other questioned him. The identification papers were handed over, and he'd waited nervously while they were scrutinized. He repeated he was there to visit his cousin, and again one guard went into the shack to verify his request, then came out holding a clipboard stacked high with curled yellowed paper. He looked down at it, tracing a line with his finger.

"Visits are allowed for inmates once per month, yet your cousin hasn't had a single one since he's been here," he said, looking up at Benfu as if asking for an explanation.

"We just got word back home that he was being held. What has he been arrested for?"

The guard stared at him for a moment. "You don't know?"

Benfu shook his head, sticking to the story he and Zu Wren had worked on the night before, hopefully the story that would keep him in the clear and not accused of being an accessory to whatever it was they were holding Pony Boy for. "Last we heard, he'd come to the city looking for work. His parents both work in a shoe factory in Yanqing County, yet they couldn't get him a position. I came to Beijing to see him and after he wasn't at the boarding house he was supposed to check into, I was advised by the local precinct that he was here."

He took a long breath. His story sounded long and concocted, even to him. Yet he waited, hoping it would pass muster. Factory workers were for the most part deemed completely revolutionary according to their hard work ethics.

"Then they'll be ashamed to know their son has become a class enemy. He and others like him will only be here for a few more days." The guard gave a menacing smile.

"Then where will he be transferred?" Benfu asked, hoping to get as much information as possible. This visit was important and a lot hinged on how he was accepted into the prison. It was frightening, but he hoped he'd come away with at least some sort of good news. With any luck, he'd even be able to spring Pony Boy and bring him to the grove of trees where Zu Wren waited.

It would be torture to watch the two lovebirds reuniting.

But it would be worth it.

The guard shrugged and gestured for him to turn around. Benfu did and felt the man's hands run up his pants legs, then inside and outside his arms. After checking the inside of his jacket, he threw a hand up to the other guard.

"Clear."

The guard inside the shack hit something and the gate began to open slowly. On the other side, another guard waited. When Benfu stepped through, he turned and bellowed out to follow him. After walking through more than a few small halls, Benfu was ushered into a small room and told to take a seat.

Within minutes, another guard came in and told him to stand. He did, and was searched yet one more time. The guard led him out of the small room and down a long, dim hall. Benfu knew they were getting closer to the prison population because he could hear the sound of men, becoming louder as they walked.

They came to another set of double doors and the guard went through, then stood to the side. Yet another guard took up the escort, and Benfu followed. Another hall, a few more sets of doors, and then they were in a huge warehouse area divided by cells on either side. Benfu stopped, startled, suddenly the target of hundreds of sets of eyes.

"Don't speak to them. Don't answer their calls. Keep your attention on me," the guard advised, then led him down the middle.

It was terrifying and Benfu resisted the urge to cross his arms protectively over himself. As he was escorted through, some of the men pleaded for help as others shouted obscenities. Benfu had been to the Shanghai Zoo before and that memory emerged as they passed compartments with two to three men inside each, their gaunt and bent bodies poised on wooden boards secured into the back of their cells.

Benfu didn't turn his head, but his eyes moved back and forth, unable to look away from the prisoners. His stomach rolled at the thought of Pony Boy being amongst the hard-looking bunch.

"Is he in this hall?" Benfu asked, then felt embarrassed at the tremor in his voice.

The guard shook his head. "He's been in isolation for three weeks."

Relief flooded Benfu, just knowing that Pony Boy was segregated from these men. He couldn't imagine his kind-hearted, gregarious friend anywhere near men like those he was seeing.

Finally, they reached the end of the large room of cells and went out through another set of doors, then down several flights of stairs into what Benfu could only surmise was the basement. When they reached the lowest floor, he was handed off yet again to another waiting guard, then escorted to a large room set up with one long table and dozens of chairs.

"Sit there," the guard said, pointing to a chair on the end. "No touching allowed. You will be watched, your conversation noted."

He turned around and went to stand by the door, his posture erect and his eyes focused on something Benfu couldn't see.

It took almost forty-five minutes but finally a door opened on the other side of the tables and first one guard entered, then Pony Boy behind him, then another guard brought up the rear. Benfu's first thought was that the way they handled him like he was some sort of vicious murderer, then his second thought was just . . . no.

No, no, no, no.

Pony Boy met his eyes and Benfu felt a lump rise in his throat and tears burst to the surface. They brought him to the other side of the table and one guard pushed him roughly into the chair.

"You have fifteen minutes. Say what you gotta say because you'll have no more visitations here," he said, then turned and went to stand beside the door that they'd come through. His partner took the other side.

Now they were guarded by three uniformed men and Benfu couldn't even make himself speak. Finally, Pony Boy did.

"How did you find me?"

"A lot of searching and a stroke of luck." Benfu studied the soiled baggy shirt and pants that Pony Boy wore, clothes several sizes too big. A cut on his cheek was sealed by dry and crusty blood, and patches of his hair appeared to be missing. He was barefoot, not even sporting the flimsy plastic slippers Benfu had seen on other prisoners' feet. "You've lost weight."

Pony Boy smiled slightly and Benfu saw a glimpse of his best friend—how he used to be. "It's not like Mama's food in here, I can tell you that."

The silence settled, making the air between them heavy. The situation was so surreal, so shocking, that Benfu could barely think of what to say. "Pony Boy, what the hell are you doing here?" he finally asked.

"I don't know. It all happened so fast." Pony Boy started to shrug, then winced. "One second, I was on the train and the next I was here."

"Your family is worried. They have no idea."

"Have you seen her?" Pony Boy asked, the desperation in his voice telling Benfu exactly which *her* he referred to.

"She's here."

He looked startled. "What do you mean—here?"

Benfu looked around at the guards. None of them watched, but they were only feet away. "She's in Beijing with me. She insisted on coming, but I wouldn't allow her to accompany me in here."

"Good call, comrade. Please, whatever you do, don't let her come here. I don't want her name linked to mine. Anyone who visits could later be investigated, or worse—detained. Don't let her come. Swear to me."

Benfu held up a hand. "I swear. One of the guards mentioned that you might only be here a few more days. Are they transferring you? Or maybe releasing you? Please tell me they're letting you go free."

Pony Boy closed his eyes for a second, taking a long, deep breath. "No, Benfu. They aren't transferring me and I'm not being released."

"Then what?"

"I'm scheduled for execution the day after tomorrow."

Benfu gasped, his breath stopping in his chest. The words didn't quite sink in, not until he looked closer at Pony Boy and saw the resignation in his eyes.

Execution.

He'd said he was being executed.

Benfu stared at him. He couldn't wrap his head around the words, no matter how much he turned them around in his head. He wouldn't accept it. He *couldn't* accept it. Finally, he spoke, but his voice sounded foreign with the weight of emotion.

"No, Pony Boy. You haven't committed murder. You aren't a real criminal. What—why—I don't understand."

Pony Boy gave him a slight smile. "I'm labeled worse than a murderer. In the eyes of the people, I'm a counterrevolutionary. Remember the white-haired man? He's already buried."

A feeling of hysteria threatened to bubble up in Benfu, making him feel a bit out of control. "I'll talk to them. I have some money. We can hire a litigator. What—what can we do? Just tell me what to do."

"There's nothing you can do," Pony Boy said softly. "It's done and I've made my peace with it. I don't want you to even try because they'll jail you, too, and then they might try to accuse others."

And Benfu knew exactly who he meant by others.

"But listen, we only have a few minutes. I have to ask you to do something for me."

He couldn't speak. He'd never felt so helpless in his entire life. He rubbed at the tears that threatened to spill.

"Benfu, are you listening?"

He nodded.

"I want you to look out for her. If she needs anything—anything at all—promise me that you'll help her. Swear to me that for the rest of her life or yours, if she needs you, that you'll be there for her," Pony Boy said.

"I swear, but this isn't needed. You'll come home."

Pony Boy lowered his voice. "And about that project we started."

Benfu instantly knew he was talking about the newsletter. He nodded, letting him know he understood. Just mentioning it made his burden of guilt heavier. After all, the newsletter was originally his idea.

Pony Boy continued. "Tell her to stop it. Tell her to do something else with her life. I want her to be happy but to remember me. That's all I want, is for her to be at peace, whatever she chooses to do. But I want her to choose something safe."

"Stop telling me this stuff, Pony Boy. This isn't going to happen. I'm going to—to—I don't know, but I'm going to do something."

For their whole lives, Benfu had always been the logical one, the part of their partnership to lend the voice of reason to whatever they did. Pony Boy had been the exciting, spur-of-the-moment half, always finding ways for them to experience adventure. Now, the tables were turned and his best friend was the one sounding calm and reasonable, and so much older than his years.

"And Benfu, I have something to say to you as well. You've always done what's right. You've been the good son—obeying and striving to meet the impossible responsibilities set by your parents. You can't keep doing that for the rest of your life. It's time for you to be your own man."

Benfu nodded, unable to speak past the sob that sat waiting in his throat.

"And I'll tell you another thing. You don't love Juan Hui and I don't think you ever did."

He was right about that. So far, he'd avoided even thinking about her and what to do about their future. Benfu wished they had more time. He'd tell him all about Calla Lily and his life in Wuxi. But time was running out. Fast.

"Do one thing for me," Pony Boy said, his voice pleading. "Don't marry her. I've tasted love and I can tell you, it's sweeter than anything else that'll ever touch your lips in your entire life. I want you to have that—to taste that. It's out there, Benfu. You just have to find it. But you have to stop living for others and just follow your heart. That's the only way you'll be led to where you're meant to be."

They locked eyes. Benfu had never before heard him give such a touching and insightful lecture. It didn't even sound like his old best friend. This person—he wasn't a boy any longer. He nodded once, letting Pony Boy know he was taking in every word. That was the least he could do, though to turn his back on his parents and their plan for his life—that would be extreme and he didn't know if he'd ever have that sort of courage.

"When you find it—find that one who sets your passions on fire—I want you to do whatever it takes to keep her," Pony Boy said, his voice barely more than a whisper.

"Time's up," one of the guards said. "Two minutes."

"Can I have a sheet of paper? A pen?" Pony Boy asked him.

The guard hesitated, then looked at the other one beside him. That one shrugged. The first one walked to the table and took out a pad, pulling a sheet of paper from it, then dropping it and a pencil on the table.

"My one act of kindness," the guard said with a sneer, then went back to his station by the door.

Pony Boy bent over it, sketching furiously. When he was done, he handed it to over.

"Give it to *her*," he said.

Benfu looked at it. It was a stem with berries, encircled by a heart.

The guard stated the time was now officially up.

Benfu couldn't believe their time was up already. The sadness that enveloped him was heavy. So heavy that he didn't think he'd even have the strength to stand.

"Tell my family I will see them again. Tell Baba I was brave and tell Mama I'm sorry," he rambled now, the words falling out in fragments as he tried to get everything in before the guard approached him. "When Lixin returns home, tell him I said he's to take care of our parents. Give Mei a last hug for me and tell my girl I would've married her—that in my heart, we've already wed!"

The guard reached him and Pony Boy stood obediently. Benfu stood, too, wishing he could embrace him before they took him away. Then his hand snaked out of the guard's reach and Benfu took it, quickly going through their handshake one last time as tears finally refused to be held back.

"Best comrades," Pony Boy said, his voice hoarse with emotion.

"Best comrades," Benfu answered gruffly, then added something new. *"Forever."*

The guard slapped at their hands and they let go, then he led Pony Boy to the door. Benfu watched and just before they were out of sight, Pony Boy turned and gave him a final look, then disappeared.

With him now out of sight, the other guard came to Benfu and grabbed his arm.

"Let's go," he said, leading him toward the door on the opposite wall. Benfu followed, then just before the door he paused, noting a poster that he hadn't seen on his way into the room. He held his hand up, silently asking the guard for a second to read what it said.

'THIRTEEN CLASS ENEMIES TO BE EXECUTED ON FEBRUARY 23,

HEREBY SENTENCED TO DEATH BY EXECUTION,

WITH ALL POLITICAL RIGHTS DEPRIVED.

FOR EDUCATIONAL PURPOSES, IT IS MANDATORY FOR ALL

PRE-APPROVED WORK UNITS TO ATTEND.'

The writing was covered by an enormous red check mark, an indication of its validation by authorities. It was official.

"Let's go." The guard jerked his arm, propelling him through the door and into the hall.

Benfu felt hope slipping away. There was going to be an execution and obviously, the only friend he'd ever trusted was on the list.

He thought of Zu Wren.

How he was going to get her through the next few days was beyond him, but they weren't leaving until they'd exercised every chance to free Pony Boy. They needed to think it through, and he hoped that she'd have some ideas. As for now, he needed to hurry. She was probably half frozen, waiting in the woods to hear some good news from him. Unfortunately, he was about to break her heart.

Chapter Forty-One

Benfu rolled his extra shirt tightly and pushed it down into his bag. His fingers brushed against the bow to his violin and he hesitated, then brought it out. Pulling out the violin after it, he put them together under his chin and began to play.

His bow moved slowly. It was a sad song—one full of deep sorrow and regret. It was the piece he'd been striving to conquer when he'd first left Shanghai.

The Butterfly Lovers Concerto.

He felt it fitting, considering, though now banned, it had been adapted from a tragic love story—a legend from long ago.

He closed his eyes, letting the music fill him as it floated gently through the room, endeavoring to soothe Zu Wren's pain, if not his own. For the first time since ever attempting it, the notes sounded pure and he felt wonder that he'd finally given it justice. His violin teacher would be proud. However, he realized that it was probably life circumstances that had given him the inspiration to play it well. He also realized that it would most likely be the last time he ever played the violin, his tribute and sacrifice to his best friend.

Two days were gone and it was the morning of the execution. At noon a final denunciation would be held, followed directly by the death of the latest counterrevolutionary criminals deemed impossible to rehabilitate.

On the last note he opened his eyes and looked across the room. Zu Wren stood there, the blanket from the bed wrapped around her shoulders as she gazed outside, her face averted from his. She stared intently, her shoulders squared.

When he'd gone to her in the grove of trees after seeing Pony Boy, he'd given it to her straight. He thought she deserved at least that. He told her all that was about to happen, and then he'd given her the messages and drawing from Pony Boy. He'd even told her that he'd said in his heart, they were already wed.

He'd have expected her to become hysterical—to cry, scream, even pull at her hair like women did in the old days when they mourned. But she'd surprised him. She'd remained stoic, taking the news silently, then uttering four words.

"This is my fault." She'd dropped to her knees, her head bowed. She held the drawing to her chest, barely moving.

He left her alone for a few moments, thinking she was possibly praying. A long time later when she'd not moved to rise up, even as the sun was going down and the temperatures were quickly dropping, he'd gone to her and gently helped her to stand. Her face was soaked with tears but she'd not made a sound. He'd thought her in shock, and quietly led her to the highway, then back toward town.

They'd thankfully caught a passing truck that'd offered them a ride for a fee of a few yuan. She'd climbed in the back, then huddled to the side until Benfu put his arms around her. She'd not said another word on the way to their room, or even when they'd arrived. She'd lifted the covers and climbed in, fully clothed as she turned over and shut her eyes.

It was unsettling then and even more so now, a day and a half later, that her energy and usual brave personality seemed to have been wiped out completely.

"Zu Wren?"

She showed just a tiny bit of movement, but enough that he knew she heard.

"Perhaps we should not go," he said. His main concern now was her, and he'd promised Pony Boy he'd take care of her. Would seeing the love of her life shot and left for dead really be what was best for her? Was that fulfilling his promise to be there for her?

"I'm going. With or without you, I'll be there. He will not die alone," she said, softly, but firm.

He nodded, though she didn't turn to see it.

He'd figured she'd refuse his suggestion. She was stronger than he'd first given her credit for. Also, her guilt lay heavy on her mind. As they'd discussed ideas of what they could possibly do to get him free, she'd confessed that most of the articles printed in the newsletter had come from her, directly from the lips of her father. She bemoaned ever repeating anything—regretting every single article they'd published. She said she'd take it all back in a second if she could do it all over again, that none of it was worth sacrificing Pony Boy for.

Benfu had reminded her that Pony Boy held the same passion to educate the people about the innocent casualties of Mao's revolution. That she hadn't twisted his arm.

"So he's a martyr is what you're saying," she'd said, then bowed her head.

Call it what you will, he thought. What was done was done and he didn't think that her believing it was all for naught would be good for her future mental well-being. Pony Boy would not want her to take any blame. He'd said he wanted her to live, to find peace. Benfu wanted to do what he could to help her.

But first they had to say good-bye.

He felt a wave of nausea and wished not for the first time that morning that he'd wake and realize it was all a bad dream. A nightmare. He thought of Pony Boy's mother, of his father who had been so proud of his son for stepping up to take care of the family while he recovered. Would they be any less proud of him when Benfu returned and had to tell them of his death? Would they have to renounce their own son? If given the choice, what would they choose?

Tucking the violin and bow back into his bag, he went to the night table and switched off the light. Zu Wren had already packed her things, refusing breakfast, just as she'd refused dinner the night before.

"Zu Wren? It's time to go."

She sighed. Then she pulled the blanket from her shoulders and draped it back over the bed. The room was warm, but since she'd heard of Pony Boy's fate, he'd noticed that she'd not been able to shake the cold.

"Here, wear my extra shirt," he said, pulling it from the bag and taking it to her.

She took it silently and pulled it over her head, then put her jacket on over it. She slowly buttoned up, then wrapped the new white scarf around her neck. She'd asked Benfu to buy it as well as some candles when they passed a street vendor the evening before, and now the crisp clean color stood out vividly against her dark hair and coat. He watched her, noting that she moved with the slow actions of an old woman, of someone weighted down by an unbearable burden.

The night before, she'd considered trying to make it home to beg her father to intervene. Benfu had convinced her that first, her father would never put his own fate at risk, and second, there was no time to get there and back. If there had been, he would've returned to his own father and gone to his knees to beg for him to find a way to save his best friend. She'd heeded his words, then agreed. She wouldn't take the chance that she'd not return in time. It was important to her that she be there, even if Pony Boy would never know it. Every other idea they'd had was quickly dashed.

The truth was, they were too late. There was nothing they could do.

If he'd only have left Wuxi sooner so that he would've found out that Pony Boy was missing. There were a lot of ifs—if Pony Boy's father hadn't had a heart attack, if the position of cleaning street toilets hadn't been available, if Zu Wren hadn't walked into one, if they hadn't come up with an idea to start a newsletter.

If Chairman Mao hadn't started the Cultural Revolution.

The chain of what-ifs was long and unfortunately, unbreakable.

He went to the door and held it open.

Zu Wren first lit the candles, setting them in the window. Then she picked up her bag and together they left the room for the last time.

Evident from the festivities surrounding the event, the people of Beijing obviously found execution day to be one of the most exciting of all. Because of the posters advertising the afternoon's events hanging everywhere, there wasn't a taxi to be found until they'd gotten almost to the outskirts of town. When one finally stopped, he'd claimed it'd be a double fare. Benfu had agreed and the man took them all the way to the ghost yard.

Grateful they'd begun early, Benfu now kept up a steady pace with Zu Wren as she weaved in and out of the people, determined to claim a place at the front of the crowd.

For such a morbid event on a bitterly cold day, many were jubilant. Benfu noted those who brought blankets to sit on, and he even saw a little girl running in and around the crowd, selling hard-boiled eggs. Her face was rosy with excitement, or maybe the cold, Benfu didn't know which but her presence there felt so wrong. He thought of Mei and how horrified she would be that her big brother was one of the criminals to be denounced and later, his life extinguished. Watching the little girl with the eggs reminded Benfu that Mei would never see that brother again.

He followed Zu Wren until they were at the head of the pack and she leaned against a tree. He moved closer to her, wanting to be ready in case she couldn't remain standing. So far she'd been the same as she was all morning, quiet and stoic, but things were about to get worse and how strong could she remain?

In front of the wooden stage, close enough to touch, someone had erected a life-size portrait of Chairman Mao. Benfu lost count of those who went to him and saluted, or kneeled in front of him as though he were a god. He wondered where common sense was. Why didn't they think for themselves instead of falling into a hysteria of hype?

They waited another half hour, silently watching the crowd as they sang one revolutionary song after another, interspersed with a few shouted slogans. Finally, the first speaker came out and climbed atop the platform.

He introduced himself as an official from the local Beijing government office, then he read from a sheaf of papers, calling out the names of the accused and listing their crimes.

When he got to Pony Boy, Benfu could barely see Zu Wren's profile around the edge of the white scarf, but he felt her flinch as though she'd been struck.

"Condemned for the crime of disloyalty to Chairman Mao," he charged. He added two other names under the treason charge and Benfu heard a murmur throughout the crowd when next a doctor was accused of being a spy. The renunciation went on for more than two hours and a long list of people took the stand, giving their own personal criticisms against those named as counterrevolutionaries. Benfu only half listened, his anxiety rising with each passing minute as he wondered how many of the condemned prisoners were falsely charged.

His thoughts were chaotic, and he discarded ideas one by one, shooting down solutions to help his friend, none of them viable. He bit back words of anger—rage at his father for not giving him more money, for sending him away from home, away from Pony Boy. He silently blamed Zu Wren a few times, then felt badly when he saw her stark, pale face. She looked like she was barely holding on, about to drop at any second. She'd claimed blame for Pony Boy being there and the admission showed in the way she held herself, but truthfully, the blame was Benfu's.

It was he who had led them to the idea of a newsletter. Honestly, when the words had slipped from his mouth in a time that seemed so long ago, he hadn't thought it through or even believed for one moment that it could be done. But it had been done, and now, before the day was over, the ground would be darkened with his best friend's blood.

In his mind he begged forgiveness. His pleas couldn't be heard, but he couldn't stop them, all the same. He knew it should be him about to step up there and accept punishment. It should've been him starving and being beaten behind the walls of that dark prison.

A small faction of Red Guards joined the crowd and Benfu felt revulsion as another round of revolutionary songs started up around them. Their words about smashing the old ways and following the red sun—their inspiring Chairman Mao—made his head pound. He watched young teens, most likely hoping to be the next Red Guards, scribbling down the words into tiny notebooks, or in the backs of their Mao red books.

"Will they ever stop?" Zu Wren said, speaking for the first time since they'd arrived.

Benfu looked around, making sure no one had heard her.

Another official took the stand and waved at the crowd to part down the middle. He gestured to the highway behind the crowd and Benfu saw a blue truck barreling toward them. The people parted, and the truck pulled to the side of the road.

At least a dozen prison guards and others dressed in police uniforms jumped off the back of the truck, then waited as one by one, the prisoners were unceremoniously kicked or dragged off.

Benfu spotted Pony Boy immediately, and judging by Zu Wren's sharp intake of breath, she did, too. He slipped his arm around her, not asking this time if she needed it or not. Like him, he knew she must've felt as though she'd received a blow to the gut seeing Pony Boy standing there, deemed a hardened criminal. He looked forlorn and lost, and they only knew him to be a kind, gentle person.

This cruel twist of fate didn't match up to the life he'd led.

As they watched, Pony Boy kept his eyes trained on the prisoner in front of him. They stumbled—or were pushed—in single file to line up in front of the stage. Most of the prisoners flinched at the sudden roar from the crowds, yet not a one looked up. Benfu didn't see any sign of bandages around throats, or any other indicator that jaws had been broken or vocal cords cut to keep the prisoners from speaking out, as rumored was happening at other executions around China.

Once they were all lined up, a woman wearing an official-looking uniform carried up a box and working quickly, removed placards from it, hanging one around each prisoner's neck. The signs were haphazardly made, just cardboard fixed on ratty ropes, but the characters written on them coincided with the numbers the prisoners wore. Each man's name was recorded, along with his prisoner number and his crime. To see Pony Boy's family name so prominent for all to witness his shame cut Benfu to the quick.

He wished for him to look up, to see them standing there. The last thing Benfu wanted—and he knew Zu Wren felt the same—was for Pony Boy to think he stood alone, hated by every person surrounding him. Benfu urged him silently, *look up, look up!* But Pony Boy kept his eyes fixed on the ground.

Beside him, Zu Wren began to tremble under Benfu's arm. It began as a small tremor and soon was a full quaking throughout her body. Finally, just as he wondered how much more she could take without falling from exhaustion, or how much more the prisoners could take without screaming their innocence, another official took the stand.

He announced it was time for the criminals to pay their dues. Shockingly, he said that the Beijing municipal government would not be responsible for unpaid burials, that if there were families of the condemned who'd not made arrangements with a grave digger, then those bodies would be pushed into a group pit and covered.

There would be no preparing the non-claimed dead for the entrance into the afterworld.

Again, Benfu wished that he could've talked Zu Wren into staying at the rented room. She didn't need to be hearing about such atrocities. Benfu said another prayer, asking for courage to fulfill his promise to Pony Boy. He'd sworn not to jeopardize Zu Wren's freedom by fighting the execution, but he realized now that it was going to be the hardest oath he'd ever taken. Every fiber of his being wanted to run out there and grab him, urge him to flee as they had when they were boys and had snuck an orange or two from a street vendor. But they were no longer boys and this was no petty crime he was being convicted of—and, Benfu had given his word.

The official invited all to walk the half acre over to the shooting grounds and stepped off the stage. Amidst the roar of the crowd, the guards and policemen began herding the prisoners to their next—and final—destination.

"Come, Zu Wren." Benfu took her arm and guided her to fall in behind the others. He didn't want to do it, but he knew they had to see it through.

Chapter Forty-Two

As they marched, Pony Boy tried to keep his eyes on the ground, as ordered by the guards. It was hard—he ached to know if Benfu had come, if his last minutes on earth would be shared with someone who cared for him or was he simply surrounded by despair and hatred. The denunciation was torturous. As he stood listening to the many statements of loathing, the ridicule of his life and those of the others, it was as though he were playing the wrong part in a movie. He felt like crying, or simply curling into a ball on the ground and making them kill him where he fell.

But something told him that Wren wouldn't have agreed to stay behind, that she was out there somewhere in the crowd. If that was so, he wanted to go out with courage, standing tall like a man.

And he knew he was naive, but he still felt that fate might intervene. They had half a mile to walk, one last time to stretch his legs before they were to arrive at the ghost yard.

Dui, he had hope. They could order him not to look up, not to speak, not to fight his punishment, but they couldn't take that away. At least that is what the doctor had told him the evening before when they'd talked through the grate for the last time. He'd also finally admitted that he was on the death list as well, something he'd kept from Pony Boy because he'd not known until then—after the taunting of the guard who'd brought their last meal—that they would share the same punishment.

Now Doc was somewhere in front of him, marching with the others. Pushed by the guards, they worked their way through the crowd, ignoring their taunts and the few things they threw. He thought he smelled a boiled egg after something soft hit his head but he didn't look up. He didn't want to be struck by the guards, just in case Wren was out there. He stumbled over a bump and looked up for an instant, and met Doc's eyes just as the man turned his head to look behind him. His expression flashed reassurance and they both looked back at their feet.

It was ironic—Doc was his first and only comrade in prison, and they'd be taking their last breaths together. It felt symbolic of the friendship they'd built, the camaraderie they'd shared to keep one another strong through the punishments meted out to them. A few hours earlier, they'd both been ordered to step out of their cells and that was when they'd seen each other for the first time.

"You are so young," Doc had joked, a smile emerging on his haggard face for only an instant before the guard had slapped it off.

"And you are an old man," Pony Boy had replied. He wanted to add that he didn't feel young—that at only eighteen, his life was about to be over and didn't that make him a man? But he kept his words to himself, not wanting to spoil their first meeting.

They were reprimanded for speaking out of turn, but at least they'd gotten a few words out, both of them surprised at what the other looked like. As they'd marched down the halls, up the stairs, and out of the prison, their arms had touched once or twice, a feeling that made Pony Boy long for his father and the quiet air of assurance he'd always carried. The doc reminded him of Baba, and just having him there, walking the same final walk, could have well been the one thing that made it possible for him to keep going.

They arrived.

It didn't look like much—just a wooden stage overlooking a long field. He saw a ravine, a gaping hole in the earth, waiting for him to take his last breath, and he felt his stomach roll.

He was right. The guards led them to stand just before the drop-off; then they were told to kneel and not move, that nothing would begin until the crowds had caught up. For the most part, the prisoners obeyed. It was quiet except for the occasional clanging of the placards they wore banging against their bony bodies, some making just barely enough noise to cover the sniffling and occasional sob or moan by one of the doomed.

As for him, he was silent. It still didn't feel quite real. After weeks and weeks in isolation, being outside in the crisp air was almost like a reward. He knew, however, what he was there for. But his brain avoided embracing the harsh truth. Shivering once, he felt the cold penetrate his bones but because that meant he was still alive, he didn't mind.

The minutes moved slowly and he took a chance and looked up, searching the crowd, scanning up and down, in and out and over all the faces.

Then he saw her.

Wren.

She met his eyes and in them, he saw the deepest sorrow he'd ever seen in his life. It broke his heart and he longed to break free of his captors, to go to her one last time and hold her, speak softly into her ear and promise it would all work out. He took in the beauty she embodied, holding it close, recording every inch of her to memory. With the white scarf pulled over her head and framing her face, she created a striking contrast of color against the backdrop of blue and black Mao-style clothes everyone else wore. But then, she always stood out wherever she was.

Before the guard behind him whacked him on the head to direct his eyes back to the ground, he saw Benfu there, too. He had his arm around Wren, supporting her weight with his body, but Pony Boy didn't mind. There was no one that he trusted more.

Knowing that Benfu had arrived to watch his exit from the world told Pony Boy that, as he'd believed for years, they shared an invisible red thread. And Benfu was doing exactly as he'd asked; he was helping Wren through what would come next. Pony Boy felt nothing but gratitude toward him for it.

The crowd moved as close as allowed and the guards ordered the prisoners all to stand. He'd have thought he would be made to turn away, to present his back to the rifles. But he wasn't.

On the wooden platform, one uniformed policeman to each prisoner climbed up and got into place. The rifles were drawn, waiting for the signal. Pony Boy looked into the eyes of the man who'd been directed to be his executioner. He searched for some semblance of humanity, but found nothing but a cold, black void. After a split second, Pony Boy looked away, not wanting to end his life looking into evil. He returned his gaze to Wren, and he hoped she heard the words he spoke to her in his head. Her face was ravaged with sadness, her eyes so desperate that he had to look away again.

The last official to speak on their behalf was the warden and he gave a short speech, the words nothing but a slight buzz in Pony Boy's ears. He was well past understanding what was being said. Instead, he looked to the side and a few men down, he found the doc. He was already looking his way, waiting for Pony Boy to turn.

He nodded solemnly, once more reminding Pony Boy of his father.

A defiant sob began to rise, but Pony Boy pushed it down and nodded back.

"Ready!" the warden called and the jumble of the guns moving into place made a harsh racket. Pony Boy flinched. "Aim!"

He looked up again, finding Wren at the front of the crowd. They locked eyes and once more he felt he'd burst with grief at the wetness that ran down her face, streaking imperfections into what he knew to be flawless flesh. Her chest visibly heaved with sobs he was too far away to hear.

He'd miss her.

So very much.

And he knew she'd miss him.

With no time to spare, he mouthed one final message to her, hoping beyond hope that she understood what his lips said. *Meet me on the mountain.*

"Fire!"

Pony Boy saw a flash of light, then nothing more.

Chapter Forty-Three

Benfu set the empty bag down and stretched his arms to the sky, working out the tension in his shoulders. He was just about ready. It was hard to concentrate when he knew that just on the other side of a few walls, Calli unknowingly waited. In another half hour or so, he'd see her face again and he just hoped she was happy to see his. He sighed, trying to expel the troubled breath and shake off the dark cloud that had followed him for weeks. To let go of his sorrow was difficult, but he knew it was what Pony Boy would've wanted him to do.

Looking around Calli's courtyard, he realized that for what he'd had to work with, the setting was coming together just fine.

Even more quietly now, Benfu bent back over the bag and took out the gnarly branches that he'd collected from the banks of the Wuxi canal. Spring was sneaking in yet had not quite arrived, so the plum trees gave out the only flowers around and some of them already bloomed with small pink-and-white buds. They weren't lilies as he'd have preferred, but they were still pretty. He worked them into the tin cans, twisting until the stems were supported firmly by the packed dirt. As he set them out around the courtyard wall, he thought of Pony Boy.

While in Beijing, he'd been strong for Zu Wren, remaining stoic even as he alone had dressed Pony Boy's body in the clean, white clothes they'd purchased. He'd never before faced such difficulty but he'd not made a single whimper while the grave diggers did their jobs. Zu Wren had finally released her silence, wailing her sorrow when they'd put Pony Boy's beaten body into the box, closed it up, and lowered it into the cold, hard ground. She'd leaned on Benfu as she'd said good-bye. Then together, they'd huddled under a Beijing red sky and burned the soiled clothes he'd worn, before solemnly returning to Shanghai.

While Zu Wren went back to her family, he'd returned to Pony Boy's house to break the news.

The shock he'd witnessed upon the faces of those who loved Pony Boy the most was something he'd never forget. His father turned pale, then bowed his head. When he'd recovered enough to speak, he'd made it clear to Benfu and the rest of the family that their son had not died in shame—that he would be remembered as a young man who'd died for what he believed in. After a private memorial, they'd offered Benfu a place to stay while he figured out what he wanted to do. That had been a blessing, though sleeping in Pony Boy's bed had felt surreal.

But it had given him time to think.

At first, he wasn't sure how he felt about the possibility of seeing his parents again. When he thought it over, he realized that they hadn't wanted to help him free Pony Boy. And they weren't interested in learning more about Calla Lily. Knowing both of those facts and how they'd reacted to the two people in the world who meant the most to him, returning home wasn't an option. But Pony Boy's mother had assured him he was welcome to stay and he'd taken them up on their offer, spending a few weeks there mourning as he tried to pull himself together again.

Then, he'd made his decision.

He'd be going home, but that no longer meant to the house he'd grown up in. His parents had betrayed him and he couldn't bear to look upon them, or even give them the news that he was moving on. It made his walk to the train station difficult, but despite the regret at breaking ties with his family, he was confident he'd made the right choice.

When he arrived back in Wuxi, he spent a day collecting items, then waited until he was sure Calli and her parents were settled in for the night. Under the cover of dark falling around him, he'd worked his way into the neighborhood and finally, their yard.

Now he moved around in the dim light from the moon, filled with anticipation, and maybe a bit of fear. What if she rejected his efforts? Or what if she didn't answer the door? And most of all—what if she wouldn't allow him to stay?

He told himself to breathe, and just focus on one thing at a time. Calli would be awake, he realized as he remembered her tendency to read before she turned in to sleep. He thought of Pony Boy again, of his plea for Benfu to follow his heart.

I hope this is what you meant, comrade.

He pushed the image of Pony Boy's crumpled body from his mind, and replaced it with one of them together, skipping rocks across the surface of the park ponds. He imagined the crooked grin his best comrade always wore, the sparkle of his eyes, and the constant joy in his voice.

He thought of Zu Wren and wished her well, hoping that when she was ready, she'd follow his advice and leave Shanghai for good. When he'd last seen her, she was still devastatingly sad, and had referred to herself as a widow. He hoped that in time, she'd be able to move on and embrace life again. They pledged to be friends forever, and in his hometown, she was the only one who would know where to find him.

With the branches of flowers now in place, he worked on tying the small fragments of glass onto the branches, hanging them just right to allow the moonlight to bounce from shard to shard. His days as a scavenger had done him well, and when he'd thought of how to make the stark garden beautiful for a night, he'd known just where to find the shattered glass. It was sad—many of the snuff bottles had once been painted with intricately laid scenes, but in the rush to rid their homes of anything deemed bourgeois, people now tossed them out with the trash, shattering the pieces of art even as their own lives had been shattered by the collateral effects of a revolution gone mad.

Benfu had gathered those he could find, not sure how he'd use them but confident some of their previous splendor could be salvaged. Then he'd come up with a technique to put a hole in each piece so that he could thread the twine through them. As he worked, many of the petals from the branches came loose, falling to the ground in an array of gentle color. He thought of Chairman Mao and his ban on grass and flowers, such a small thing to some but to others, who lived for a glimpse of nature's beauty, a reminder of the condition the country had fallen to.

He paused for a moment, then smiled. There was a gentle wind blowing and now that he was listening, the glass he had tied so far was making a pleasant tinkling sound—almost like soft tunes of music. Obviously the crickets approved, too, as they lent their own melancholy chirping to add to the ambiance. The blend of light, sound, and nature came pleasingly together, creating a much better scene than Benfu could have imagined.

Take that, Chairman Mao. You can refuse us many things that used to bring joy, but you can't take on Mother Nature.

Finally the last piece of glass was tied and Benfu stood back, surveying his work. The final thing to do was to light the small bonfire. He did that, then went to the door. He felt the lump of the wrapped jade buffalo in his pocket, a gift so insignificant for such a moment, but the only thing of value he had left. He hoped she would accept it as the unspoken promise he meant it to be.

Well, this is it, Pony Boy. I hope you're out there somewhere, watching this, since it was your idea. I need you now, friend.

He paused, trying to calm the pounding of his heart, then knocked using the signal they'd once planned of two short knocks then one long.

A moment later he heard the soft pattering of her slippers against the floor, then the door opened.

It took his breath but there she stood, her hair falling loose down her back and her face as lovely as he remembered. While he'd been away, he'd thought perhaps the memory of her was exaggerated in his imagination, but now he saw that it was true—her simple beauty and quiet ways made her the most striking girl he'd ever known.

"Benfu," she said, her voice breathless with surprise. She reached for her housecoat from a nail beside the door and wiggled into it, pulling it tight against the chill of the outside air. It was long, sweeping just over her toes and as she tied the sash, he thought of how appropriate it was for what he would ask next.

When she turned back to him, he threw his arm out wide in a gallant sweep behind him, then smiled at her. He put out his hand. "I believe you owe me a dance," he said.

She hesitated and Benfu realized that the rest of his life hinged on this moment, on this one response. He no longer needed an international career in music, fine things, or a lavish future surrounded by esteemed people. It was true—he didn't need much. But he wanted everything.

And now *everything* simply meant Calla Lily.

He longed to beg, to plead and tell her that if she only chose him, he'd spend his life honoring her and trying to make the world a better place around her. He thought of Pei and the commune, a boy he didn't know, and his one gesture of kindness that had led him to this moment. Would the boy's courage in freeing him be wasted? Finally, Pony Boy's face came to mind, along with his oath and the ultimate sacrifice he'd given to protect both Zu Wren and Benfu.

Could he possibly live up to the gifts he'd been given?

He knew only this—without Calli beside him, he was not sure of anything.

But it had to be her choice.

He waited, his heart in his throat.

Calli stepped out onto the stoop, quietly closing the door behind her. She turned, her hand over her mouth as she took in everything around her. Her eyes wandered over the branches, the delicate fallen petals, and lingered on the many swaying pieces of crystal, their once sharp edges now taking on an artistic curve of graceful movements.

"It's—it's so—" She didn't finish, but her eyes sparkled like that of a small girl, telling him that his efforts had not been in vain. The combination of the moonlight and the glow from the fire made the reflections leap from glass to glass, a musical dance of light that felt almost magical with the soft tinkling it made. Even the stars in the sky and the crickets—thank the gods for the crickets—they didn't dare to let him down, either.

Calli turned back to him and there were tears on her face. Gently—because every word and every action she ever did was nothing if not tender—she clasped the hand he offered, sending her familiar warmth rushing through him. "Of course, Benfu. I thought you'd never ask."

If you enjoyed *The Palest Ink* and would like to read more about the fate that awaits Benfu and Calla Lily, you can find the bestselling books that make up my series featuring the same characters on Amazon.

The Tales of the Scavenger's Daughters

The Scavenger's Daughters

Tangled Vines

Bitter Winds

Red Skies

Author's Note

This book was born after the publishing of my series, The Tales of the Scavenger's Daughters, a story set in modern day China that began with a prologue of Benfu as a young man. In the short piece, he is escaping a cowshed where he was imprisoned at a commune during the Cultural Revolution. Just one small peek into his past to give the readers a clue about why he is the kind of man he is—but enough to push many to say they wish they knew more of his early story. Therefore, the idea for *The Palest Ink* was conceived. With this book, I strive to pay tribute to the staggering number of victims—some believe in the millions—who lost their lives during the ten years of China's so-called Cultural Revolution. The truth is that too many innocent people succumbed to death by execution, beatings, and sometimes suicide to evade the torture inflicted by Mao's cadre or by his band of wrathful Red Guards.

Many details depicted in this book were inspired by actual events I read about in books, articles, and viewed through documentaries. I consider these gifts that come some forty years after the revolution ended, because it is only recently that survivors and their families have overcome their fear of retaliation from the government to come forward with the courage to tell their stories.

For decades the rest of the world did not understand the scope of what the people of China were going through during the ten years of the revolution. Such an oversight seems like a huge blemish on the face of humanity. Through much of my research I've also learned something more about the majority of the Chinese people—that they are resilient and they long for what we all long for—to live a peaceful life of family bonds, loyalty, and the ability to create a decent future for those they love. Unfortunately for many of them, it took self-sacrifice to bring that last wish to fulfillment.

I hope you will read the rest of the books in The Tales of the Scavenger's Daughters to see what sort of man Benfu's experiences molded him to be, and how those around him fared in the aftermath of the Cultural Revolution.

Acknowledgments

A t Lake Union, I want to thank my editor, Terry Goodman, and give a final farewell. Your guidance over the years has been invaluable to me and I wish you a wonderful and fulfilling retirement. To Danielle Marshall, the acquisitions editor who stepped in and immediately saw the worth of this book, thank you for embracing my enthusiasm and matching it with your own. To Gabriella Van den Heuvel, Megan Beatie, Dennelle Catlett, Elise, and the rest of the Amazon publishing and marketing team, thank you for making *The Palest Ink* a success. Also, Holly Lorincz and Hannah Beuhler did a phenomenal job with their eagle eye copy-editing skills. To Charlotte Herscher, I usually thank you for giving the final polish but it's more than that and can be compared to a bit of magic.

I must mention two astounding books and those who brought them forward. Li Zhensheng, the photo-journalist who captured and hid visual records of the Cultural Revolution, then decades later published them in the book, *Red-Color News Soldier: A Chinese Photographer's Odyssey through the Cultural Revolution*. Li Zhensheng's works allowed me to immerse myself in and really see instead of only imagine the hardships and persecution. I'm also grateful to Sasha Gong and Scott D. Seligman, for their book, *The Cultural Revolution Cookbook: Simple, Healthy Recipes from China's Countryside*. Both of these books, among many others listed on my reference page, were instrumental as I researched articles, photographs, and recipes to accurately portray the time period of the Cultural Revolution.

An ocean of gratitude to my husband, Ben, who cannot be acknowledged enough for standing by me as I first begin the research process of writing a book and am bubbling over with intriguing (to me) facts and ideas, then as I navigate the unpredictable ebb and flow of the creation process. After twenty years together, you are still my biggest supporter. And Amanda, I can't tell you how much the way you show pride for your mother's work means to me—celebrating milestones, handing out books, and slipping bookmarks into the hands of your college mates. I know one day the roles will be reversed and I'll be the one shouting your name to all who'll listen.

Lastly, thank you to my readers; it's your support and enthusiasm that inspires me to continue my attempts to bring my love of China and its people alive within the covers of my books. I hope if you've enjoyed *The Palest Ink*, you'll post a review on GoodReads or Amazon to help the story gain wider recognition. Thank you in advance. ~ Kay Bratt

Glossary

Aiya (I-yah)	Expresses surprise or other sudden emotion
Ayi (I yee)	Translates to auntie. Also used as title for household help
Anjing (Ann-jing)	Be quiet
Bu (Boo)	No
Congee (con-jee)	rice porridge
Kang (Cong)	A heated sleeping platform
Dàzìbào (Dah-zee-b-oww)	Big poster or announcement
Dui (Dway)	Correct
Dui bu qi (Dway-boo-chee)	An apology
Hao le (How-luh)	Okay or Yes
Hao bu hao (How-boo-how)	Okay or not okay?
Hukou (Who-ko)	Chinese identification
Hutong (Who-tong)	Lane or residential neighborhood
Kuai yi dian (K-why-ee-dee-an)	Faster
Laoren (Loww-run)	Form of title used for senior citizen
Laoban (Loww-bon)	Form of title used for a boss/supervisor
Ni hao (Knee-how)	Hello
Qing wen (Ching-one)	Excuse me
Shào nián (Sh-ow nee ann)	Lad

Tíngzhǐ (Ting-jer)	To stop
Xiawu hao (Sha-woo-how)	Good afternoon
Xiao Jie (Sh-oww-gee-uh)	Title for a young girl or woman
Xie xie (Shay-shay)	Thank you
Yangmei (Yong-may)	A type of berry
Zao (Zow)	Good morning
Zaijian (Zie-jee-ann)	Good-bye
Zuo xia (Zwoh-sha)	Sit down

References

Anonymous, *Rent Collection Courtyard - Sculptures of Oppression and Revolt*. Beijing: Foreign Languages Press, Peking, 1968.

Bernstein, Thomas P., *Up to the Mountains and Down to the Villages: The Transfer of Youth from Urban to Rural China*. New Haven,: Yale University Press, 1977.

Borton, James, "Book Review: Forbidden images of the Cultural Revolution, Red-Color News Soldier - A Chinese Photographer's Odyssey Through the Cultural Revolution." *Asia Times Online*. (2004): http://www.atimes.com/atimes/China/FB14Ad01.html.

"Butterfly Lovers." *Wikipedia, The Free Encyclopedia*. (Accessed October 16, 2014). http://en.wikipedia.org/w/index. php?title=Butterfly_Lovers&oldid=629472417

Chairman Mao Documentary: The Cultural Revolution - Destruction Of China. YouTube Video. Directed by NorthernControversy. (April 10, 2014)

Chang, Jung and Jon Halliday, *Mao, the Unknown Story*. London: Jonathon Cape 2003.

Chang, Jung, *Wild Swans: Three Daughters of China*. London: Harper Perennial UK, 2006.

"Cultural Revolution." Article. The History Channel Online. http://www.history.com/topics/cultural-revolution

Gittings, John, "Book Review: In Case You Missed It: Fractured Rebellion." *The China Beat*. (March 31, 2010): http://www.thechinabeat.org/?p=1792.

Gong, Sasha and Scott D. Seligman, *The Cultural Revolution Cookbook: Simple, Healthy Recipes from China's Countryside*. Hong Kong: Earnshaw Books, 2011.

"Hai Rui Dismissed from Office." *Wikipedia, The Free Encyclopedia*. (Accessed October 16, 2014).http://en.wikipedia.org/w/index.php?title=Hai_Rui_Dismissed_from_Office&oldid=588395161.

Hartono, Paulino, "In Modern Chinese Humanities, Reading Between the Lines, Understanding Fractures within the Production Processes of *Great Wall of the South China Sea*, 1964-1976." Presentation at Berkeley-Stanford Graduate Student Conference. (2014).

Pacific Affairs 58, no. 1 (1985): 5-27.

Red-Color News Soldier: A Chinese Photographer's Odyssey through the Cultural Revolution. London, New York: Phaedon, 2003.

"Jane Eyre." *Wikipedia, The Free Encyclopedia*. (Accessed October 16, 2014). http://en.wikipedia.org/w/index.php?title=Jane_Eyre&oldid=628772532.

"Mao Zedong." *Wikipedia, The Free Encyclopedia*. (Accessed October 16, 2014). http://en.wikipedia.org/w/index.php?title=Mao_Zedong&oldid=629764743.

"Myrica rubra." *Wikipedia, The Free Encyclopedia*. (Accessed October 16, 2014). http://en.wikipedia.org/w/index.php?title=Myrica_rubra&oldid=618551977.

Shang Yin, Li, *The East Wind Sighs*. Poem from the ninth century CE.

Sharpe, M.E., *China's Cultural Revolution, 1966-1969: Not a Dinner Party*. Edited by Michael Schoenhals. London: Routledge, 2015.

Short, Phillip. *Documentary: Mao's Bloody Revolution.* Directed by Adrian Maben. Revealed Videos.

"Tang Wei: Chairman Mao's Relationships." *The Telegraph.* (May 2011): http://www.telegraph.co.uk/news/worldnews/asia/china/8512567/Tang-Wei-Chairman-Maos-relationships.html.

"The Red Guards: Hong Wei Bing: In 1966, Millions Of Youth Stormed The Heavens During China's Cultural Revolution," *Revolutionary Worker Online,* no. 966. (July 1998): http://revcom.us/a/v20/960-69/966/redgrd.htm.

Thurston, Anne F., "Victims of China's Cultural Revolution. The Invisible Wounds: Part II."

"Two Stage Sisters." *Wikipedia, The Free Encyclopedia.* (Accessed October 16, 2014). http://en.wikipedia.org/w/index.php?title=Two_Stage_Sisters&oldid=620741620.

"The Water Margin." *Wikipedia, The Free Encyclopedia.* (Accessed October 16, 2014). http://en.wikipedia.org/w/index.php?title=Water_Margin&oldid=628542054.

Yiwu, Liao, *The Corpse Walker: Real Life Stories: China from the Bottom Up.* New York. Anchor, 2009.

Yongyi, Song, "Chronology of Mass Killings during the Chinese Cultural Revolution (1966-1976)." Chronological Index. *Online Encyclopedia of Mass Violence.* (August 2011): http://www.massviolence.org/Chronology-of-Mass-Killings-during-the-Chinese-Cultural.

READING GROUP GUIDE

The Palest Ink

The motives for Chairman Mao's decision to launch the Cultural Revolution are widely debated. Some claim it was a way to pursue vengeance over his political rivals. Yet others claim Mao was sincerely passionate in his support for the working class and distrust of the educated and elite. What do you think contributed the most to Mao's desire to launch the Cultural Revolution?

As is customary in China, Benfu was raised to give complete deference to his parents, to the point that even as he entered into manhood, he questioned the rationality of his own dreams and considered setting them aside. Do you feel China is the same today, or have current generations changed in regards to strict obedience to their parents' wishes?

After the Cultural Revolution began, class curriculums were replaced with the study of works by Chairman Mao, as well as discussing his past endeavors and current directives. What issues could arise from students only learning the ideas of Mao?

In *The Palest Ink*, the author draws attention to Mao's manipulation of the press. With stories of what happened during the Cultural Revolution finally coming to light, do you think it will affect China's future relationship between the government and its people?

As of this publication, China still has a ban on Facebook and many specific Internet searches and websites. Do you feel China's government will ever relax these regulations and allow their people total freedom? And what are the pros and cons of such a strict control?

Pony Boy declined to tell Benfu about the persecution he'd seen his parents go through, as well as the knowledge of Juan Hui becoming a Red Guard. How do you think the storyline would've changed had Pony Boy told Benfu of these things?

Females have long been held in lower regard than males in many countries around the world. Do you feel that Zu Wren's passion for the newsletter was fueled more by what was happening around the country, or by the indifference shown to her by her father because she was a girl?

There are many reasons some think the youth were so committed to Mao and embraced their roles as Red Guards—including their longing to be a part of something grand, their idealism of Mao, or possibly their frustration at the favoritism shown to students from elite or political families. If Mao had not had the Red Guards to do his bidding, do you think the Cultural Revolution would've lasted ten years and/or been as monumental?

As seen with Benfu's family, Lao Wang, and even Zu Wren in her disloyalty to her father, familial ties and loyalties were frequently broken during the Cultural Revolution. Do you think this was a goal set by Chairman Mao and his cadres, or an unintended consequence?

Zu Wren experienced a lifetime of sorrow in only a few months of her young life. Do you think she continued to carry guilt for her part in the decisions that resulted in Pony Boy's death?

Foot binding was first outlawed in China in 1912, but some families continued the practice. Widow Chou felt shame when Red Guards exposed her deformed feet. Why do you think she kept this secret and how do you think her life was affected by her feet being bound?

Chairman Mao was the first to announce equality for Chinese women in his Half the Sky Campaign, however later he implemented the one child policy which resulted in a devastating setback in regards to gender equality. Even today, political empowerment by women comes only after great struggle and personal sacrifice. Do you see the patriarchal culture women are born into in China ever changing?

The Cultural Revolution lasted ten years. Interestingly, when Chairman Mao died, his closest political cadre was arrested and the universities were immediately re-opened. Why do you think things began to turn around so quickly after his death?

Many Chinese historians and writers were exiled for daring to criticize the Cultural Revolution, and at this time, most of their work is still banned in China. Now that truths are being unearthed, do you feel the same exiled individuals should be publicly pardoned? Should their published works be allowed to be translated and distributed in China?

In the National Museum of China there is a photo of Mao Zedong with a faction of Red Guards. The caption under it reads, *"A Catastrophe Mistakenly Launched by the Leaders."* In direct conflict of that statement, China still has many supporters of the late Chairman Mao and his Cultural Revolution. Can you think of anything positive that came out of the ten years of the revolution?